FOREIGN AFFAIRS

Breathtaking beauty...

Tantalizing temptation...

The world's most eligible men!

Dreaming of a foreign affair? Then look no further! We've brought together the best and sexiest men the world has to offer, the most exciting, exotic locations and the most powerful, passionate stories.

This month, in *Italian Weddings*, we bring back two best-selling novels by Jacqueline Baird and Rebecca Winters in which two gorgeous Italian bachelors become bridegrooms. And from now on, each month in **Foreign Affairs** you can be swept away to a new location — and indulge in a little passion in the sun!

Visit the fiery heart of Australia next month in
OUTBACK HUSBANDS
by
Margaret Way and Marion Lennox

JACQUELINE BAIRD

Jacqueline Baird began writing as a hobby when her family objected to the smell of her oil painting, and immediately became hooked on the romantic genre. She loves travelling and worked her way around the world from Europe to the Americas and Australia, returning to marry her teenage sweetheart. She lives in Ponteland, Northumbria, the county of her birth, and has two teenage sons. She enjoys playing badminton, and spends most weekends with husband Jim, sailing their Gp.14 around Derwent Reservoir.

Look out for *The Italian's Runaway Bride* by Jacqueline Baird on sale this month in Modern Romance™!

REBECCA WINTERS

Rebecca Winters, a mother of four, is excited about the new millennium because it means another new beginning. Having said goodbye to the classroom where she taught French and Spanish, she is now free to spend more time with her family, to travel and to write the Mills & Boon novels she loves so dearly.

Look out for *The Bridegroom's Vow* by Rebecca Winters on sale in February 2002 in Tender Romance™!

italian
weddings

JACQUELINE BAIRD & REBECCA WINTERS

A TASTE OF ITALIAN PASSION!

MILLS & BOON®

*MILLS & BOON and MILLS & BOON with the Rose Device
are registered trademarks of the publisher.*
Harlequin Mills & Boon Limited,
Eton House, 18-24 Paradise Road, Richmond, Surrey, TW9 1SR

Italian Weddings © Harlequin Enterprises II B.V., 2001

Giordanni's Proposal and *Second-Best Wife*
were first published in Great Britain by
Harlequin Mills & Boon Limited in separate single volumes.

Giordanni's Proposal © Jacqueline Baird 1998
Second-Best Wife © Rebecca Winters 1996

ISBN 0 263 83182 5

126-1201

*Printed and bound in Spain
by Litografia Rosés S.A., Barcelona*

italian weddings

GIORDANNI'S PROPOSAL

JACQUELINE BAIRD

CHAPTER ONE

'No, NO, *nein, nada, non.* Is that clear enough for you, Mike? Or do I have to spell it out? N-O.'

'Don't be so negative, Beth, darling,' Mike drawled, his blue eyes dancing with amusement. 'You know you'll have fun, you always do with me.'

Beth stared down at her stepbrother in exasperation, but a hint of a smile pulled at the corners of her wide mouth. He really was the limit. Sprawled in her one and only comfortable chair, with one long leg draped over the arm, negligently swinging an expensively shod foot, he was the epitome of casual male elegance. The price of his shoes would have kept her for a month, she thought wryly. But that was Mike: handmade shoes, Savile Row suits, nothing but the best would do. Image was everything, according to Mike.

'Much as I love you, Mike, I am not going to dress up as a French tart to your *matelot* and let you throw me around the boardroom of Brice Wine Merchants, even if, according to you, the firm is celebrating its centenary and the chairman's birthday, and whatever else you care to tag on. The answer is still *no.*'

'But, Beth, I have a two-hundred-pound bet with my boss, the marketing director. He said I wouldn't dare liven up the chairman's party with an impromptu cabaret. Of course, I said I would, and I can't afford to lose.' He glanced up at her, his blue eyes narrowing assessingly on her lovely face. 'Unless, of course, you lend me the two hundred quid.'

5

'Oh, no! No way! Lending money to you is the equivalent of throwing it down the drain. You made the bet; you get out of it. Or, better still, why not ask one of your numerous girlfriends?'

'Ah, well, there's the rub... For the past six months I've concentrated exclusively on one particular, lovely girl.' His handsome face took on the expression of a love-sick puppy dog, much to Beth's astonishment. 'Elizabeth is the perfect woman for me. She is beautiful, intelligent and wealthy, and I fully intend to marry her one day. But unfortunately, when I suggested the wheeze to her, she told me to grow up and act responsibly, hence my throwing myself on your mercy.'

Mike in love... That Mike was contemplating marriage was mind-boggling. 'You really want to marry the girl?' Beth asked incredulously.

'Yes, more than anything else in the world.'

There was no doubting his sincerity; it was in his eyes, the unusual seriousness of his tone, the way he straightened up in the chair, before continuing, 'Which is why I daren't take the chance of asking another girl. If Elizabeth found out it would be curtains for me. She's very strong on fidelity. But as you're my stepsister, even if the joke does get out, she might be mad for a while, but at least she'll know I wasn't unfaithful.'

Then Beth did smile. This was typical of Mike's convoluted logic: it never occurred to him for a moment to forget the whole stupid idea. She remembered the first time she had met him. Home for Beth and her mother had been a small cottage in the village of Compton, not far from Torquay in Devon. Her late father had been an artist who'd never quite made it big before he died tragically young of a cerebral haemorrhage. Her mother also considered herself an artist, but in truth was a run-of-the-mill singer, who, between marrying men, craved fame. The summer Beth had met Mike, her mother had been performing in the summer season cabaret at a local theatre in Torquay. It was at the theatre that Leanora had met Ted, Mike's father. He'd been a widower and the agent of the star of the show.

After a whirlwind romance her mother and Ted had decided to marry. Beth, at eight, had been dressed up as a flowergirl in satin and lace, while Mike, at twelve, was supposed to be an usher. After a civil ceremony performed by a registrar they had, along with about a hundred guests, all descended on Torquay's largest hotel for the wedding breakfast.

During the reception Mike had crept under the top table unseen, except by Beth, and had tied the groom and the best man's shoelaces together. When the best man stood up to speak, the groom had been tipped backwards off his chair, and, as his arm was around his new bride at the time, Leanora had gone flying as well.

Thinking about it now could still bring a smile to Beth's face, and the four years that their parents had been a couple had probably been the happiest of Beth's childhood. They'd divorced when she was twelve, and Beth had spent the rest of her formative years at a convent boarding school, but Mike had always kept in touch; his letters and the few holidays they'd shared had been some of the brightest spots in her otherwise pretty miserable teenage years.

Which was why, she thought wryly three days later, as she stepped into the elevator of the Brice building at six o'clock on a Friday evening, she was about to make a fool of herself for the umpteenth time. Because of Mike...

'It is not too late to change your mind, Mike.' She cast an imploring glance at the man standing beside her. He was dressed in a long trenchcoat, as Beth was herself, perfectly suitable attire for an overcast October day in London. But the black beret perched at a flamboyant angle on his fair head looked decidedly odd.

'Stop worrying. It'll be fine. I've arranged with Miss Hardcombe, the Chairman's secretary, to start the music as we walk in the door. We throw off our coats and go into a one-minute routine, the same one we did for the school concert, and hey, presto, it's over! I am two hundred pounds better off, plus I score Brownie points with my boss for imaginative thinking.'

'But it's ten years since we last danced together at that school concert! We were just children, and still young and stupid enough to think we were going to be showbiz stars, for heaven's sake! We should have at least practised. I am bigger, slower and terrified,' Beth cried as the elevator door slid back.

It went fine at first. There were a few raised eyebrows as they entered the boardroom, but as bottles of wine and glasses littered the large table it was obvious a celebration was in progress, and Beth felt slightly reassured. A few grins made by the dozen men present, when Mike wished the chairman a happy birthday, did not bother her, and then the music started.

But when they slid off their coats the grins changed to chuckles, and Beth realised straight away she was at a distinct disadvantage. Whereas Mike looked reasonably decent, in tight black flared-bottom trousers and a navy and white striped sailor's jumper, she as the only woman present, looked outrageous, in a tiny black Spandex skirt, a red, scoop-neck clinging knit sweater and red stiletto-heeled shoes.

Worse was to follow, as Mike curved an arm around her waist and swung her round and away from him. She was supposed to let her feet slide along the floor, but unfortunately they had not counted on a thick-pile carpet, and her heel stuck. The chuckles turned to outright laughter. Then, when Mike picked her up and spun her around his head, to enthusiastic shouts of 'Bravo!', he got carried away and spun her around and around, until when he finally let go she was so dizzy she fell smack on her behind, her legs waving in the air.

Dazedly she looked up at the circle of sombre-suited men laughing down at her. Except that one of the men wasn't laughing. He stood slightly back from the rest, and, from her position on the floor he looked enormous. She tilted back her head and her green eyes clashed with a pair of icy grey.

He was the most compellingly attractive man in the room. How had she not noticed him before? Mesmerised, she stared up at him as he slowly shook his head, a stray curl of black hair flopping over his broad forehead. He arched one dark brow in a look that managed to be both entrancing and insulting before, making no effort to hide his boredom and contempt, he deliberately turned his back on her.

Arrogant devil, she thought furiously. But still her eyes lingered on his wide back, and his long, long legs, and she had the oddest feeling she had met him before. Impossible—he was not the kind of man any woman with a red corpuscle left in her body would ever forget. The word 'macho' could have been invented for this man. Also 'tough', 'uncompromising'... Beth's lips twitched. And with a gorgeous tight bum, she noted on a more basic note.

Suddenly, instead of looking at his back, she was star-

ing once more at his front, at a rather indelicate level.
She swallowed hard and jerked her head back, lifting
her eyes to his face, and she had to swallow again at the
transformation in his expression.

His hard mouth was curved in a wickedly sexy smile.
'Allow me,' he said in a deep velvet voice, and held out
a very large hand.

Blushing to the roots of her hair, Beth grabbed the
hand he offered and scrambled to her feet. She barely
heard the numerous congratulations from the rest of the
guests, or Mike's moment of triumph. Her whole attention was on the man before her.

Flushed and dishevelled, she had no idea how gorgeous she looked. She wasn't a conventionally beautiful
woman, like her statuesque, elegant mother—for a start,
Beth was only five feet two—but there was quite a lot
else about her that was memorable. She had big eyes of
a deep jade-green, a generously curved mouth and thick,
naturally curly auburn hair, which had now sprung from
the band holding it in check to riot around her small face
in a rosy cloud. Unfortunately she also had a rather large
bust that was in imminent danger of popping out of her
top.

'Thank you,' she muttered, finally finding her voice,
stumbling a little, scarlet with embarrassment. With her
free hand she hastily adjusted her top, while her other
hand stayed clasped in his much larger one. She looked
up into his grey eyes and wondered how she had ever
thought they were icy—now they were luminous, almost
silver, and glittering with obvious appreciation. And his
flashing smile was enough to make her want to collapse
at his feet again.

'My pleasure. It isn't every day I get to rescue such
a beautiful damsel in distress.'

He had said she was beautiful, and her own eyes widened in wonder as she drank in the sight of him. 'Tall, dark and handsome' did not do him justice. He was lethally attractive; he radiated a raw, primitive power that was unmistakable. Even in her bemused state she noted everyone had stepped back and given him space, as if it was his due.

'You all right, Beth?' She vaguely registered Mike's belated query.

'The lady is fine. I will take care of her,' the deep slightly accented voice responded curtly. But his gaze never left Beth's small figure, and, stooping slightly, he added, 'If that is all right with you, Beth. I may call you Beth?'

He could call her anything he liked, she thought stupidly, as long as he kept holding her hand and smiling down at her as if he had just discovered the crown jewels. 'Yes, yes, of course,' she murmured, enthralled by the wayward black curl that fell over his broad brow.

He squeezed her hand and slipped his other arm around her tiny waist. 'You look none too steady in those very dangerous shoes,' he said, justifying his familiarity as his silver gaze slid over her small face and lower, to her breasts, and on down to her feet, still encased in the ridiculously high-heeled shoes, and then back up to her face.

Beth was suddenly flushed with a totally different kind of heat. The warmth of his arm around her waist and the obvious admiration in his lazy gaze did weird things to her pulse-rate. What was happening to her? She had never reacted so instantly to a man in her life before. She had an overpowering urge to put her small hand on his broad chest, to run her fingers up the lapel of his immaculately tailored dove-grey suit, and to curl her fingers in the silky black curls that caressed the nape of his tanned neck. She lifted her hand, and gasped; she had almost done it...!

'I need a drink,' she blurted, and forced herself to step back. 'It's all right; I'm steady now,' she added, breaking free from his hold.

'You might be, but I don't think I will ever be again,' he husked, his silver eyes capturing hers. 'Don't move and I'll get you a drink.'

She couldn't have moved if she'd wanted to, her gaze following him as he turned and walked to the table, filled a fluted glass with amber liquid and turned back to offer it to her. She took it from him, the light brush of his fingers against hers sending a tremor up her arm that made her almost drop it. She took a hasty gulp of champagne, anything to hide her ridiculous reaction to him, but she had an uncanny feeling she would be unable to hide anything from this man, and yet she didn't even know his name.

'Who are you?' she asked, and was instantly horrified at her own bluntness.

'My friends call me Dex, my enemies, the bastard Giordanni. My mother christened me Dexter Giordanni. Dexter meaning, ''on the right hand''—possibly to compensate for my being born, on the ''left-hand side of the blanket.'' So take your pick.' He laughed at the look of shock on her lovely face.

'You're very blunt, Dex,' she said, stunned at his intimate revelation about his birth, but she could not help grinning back.

'So we are friends. Yes?'

'Yes.'

'In that case, can I take you out to dinner tomorrow night?'

'Tomorrow night,' she repeated, completely bowled over by his charm and obvious desire to see her again.

'Unfortunately this evening I have to dine with the chairman and his wife.' He gestured with his hand to where the head of the firm stood talking to Mike and a few others. Then, taking a card from his inside pocket, he said, 'Give me your address and phone number, and I will pick you up tomorrow night at seven-thirty. Okay?'

She hesitated, torn between the desire to say yes and her more cautious self, which reminded her that this man was a stranger who could be dangerous to her state of mind. He had already dented her ability to think straight simply by his presence. She looked at him with puzzled green eyes, and felt the tension simmer in the air between them.

He straightened up, squaring his wide shoulders. 'Unless, of course, your dancing partner has a prior claim to your time,' he added, in a voice that was suddenly hard.

'Mike?' she chuckled. 'You've got to be joking! He's my stepbrother. You don't really imagine I would make a fool of myself before a room full of strangers except with a member of the family? And, even so, I'm going to strangle the man when I get the chance.'

Dex's responding chuckle relieved the inexplicable tension between them. 'Good. So how about that address, please,' he pleaded huskily. 'I can see Brice heading this way.'

Beth looked around, and sure enough the chairman was walking towards them. 'All right.' In moments she had rattled off her address and telephone number.

Dex put the card back in his breast pocket just as the chairman arrived at his side.

Beth glanced at the man; not as tall as Dex, and quite a lot older, with a shock of white hair, he was still a very impressive figure.

'Thank you, young lady. You and Mike certainly enlivened the proceedings. That boy will go far.'

Beth blushed again, and mumbled her thanks, but the man had already turned to Dex. 'Sorry, Dexter, old chap, but I must drag you away from this very attractive young lady. My wife is expecting us at seven-thirty, and it is quite a drive.'

'Yes, of course, Brice,' Dex responded smoothly. And, as another man caught the chairman's attention for a moment, he leaned towards Beth and, in a quick aside, added, 'You've made quite an impression on Brice. Like older men, do you?' he asked with a smile, but the edge of cynicism in his tone was unmistakable.

She looked uncertainly into his grey eyes. Was he teasing or what? But before she could answer Brice cut in.

'Come on, Dex. I daren't keep my wife waiting.'

'Certainly, Brice.' Dex straightened to his full height and, slanting Beth a quick glance, confirmed, 'Seven-thirty, don't forget. But in case you do, I will ring tomorrow to remind you,' before turning on his heel and walking away with the chairman.

Beth followed him with her eyes; his dark head was bent towards the older man and he was seemingly deep in conversation with him as they exited the room. She let out her breath on a long sigh. She doubted if she really would see Dex again, and common-sense told her she would probably be better off without him.

Glancing around the room, she spotted her coat; someone had kindly placed it over a chair for her. The party seemed to be turning into some kind of stag night, with little appreciation of the fine wines on offer; it was more a case of who could down the most. There was nothing for her here. Crossing the room, she picked up her coat and pulled it on, wrapping it firmly around her.

Finally she spotted Mike near the door, and on her way out she collared him and hissed in his ear, 'I'm leaving you to your booze-up! But don't think I've forgotten. You owe me, and you owe me big for this, buster.'

'Hey, you should be thanking me. You've only pulled one of the wealthiest bachelors around. I heard him ask you out.'

The one trouble with auburn hair, she thought wryly, was the inevitable tendency for blushes to form on the pale complexion that went with it. 'Mr Giordanni? You know him?' She hesitated, torn between the desire to escape and the desire to hear more about Dex.

'Know him, sis? Not exactly, but I've heard of him. Everyone has. In the past ten years he has built up a huge business empire—he dabbles in everything, though there are some funny rumours as to how he got started. I know he owns a shipping line, and a string of hotels all over the globe—a couple of them here in London. Brice is hoping to get the contract to supply his hotels with liquor. Apparently, Giordanni has also just bought the Seymour Club in London—his reason for being here, I expect. His main home is somewhere in Italy, I believe.'

The more Mike talked, the more despondent Beth became. Dexter Giordanni was right out of her league, and she would be a fool to think otherwise.

'Okay Mike, forget it.' She tried to smile. 'I'm off. Enjoy your night.' And she left.

For a brief moment in time she had thought she had

met the man of her dreams. Who was she kidding? Love at first sight was a myth, and in any case things like that never happened to Beth—except in her fantasies!

Once more in the safety of her own apartment, Beth vowed for the hundredth time that never again would she get involved in Mike's hare-brained schemes. As for Mr Giordanni, obviously he had simply been flirting with the only woman around at the time, and would never give her a second thought. Beth dismissed him from her mind. She would never see him again.

She showered and changed into a soft towelling robe, then curled up in the solitary armchair and sighed with pure contentment. Alone at last. Funny, as a child she had longed to be a part of a large family. Her own father had died when she was two and she had no memory of him. Her first stepfather had not lasted past her sixth birthday, when her mother, Leanora, had divorced him, and Beth had very little memory of him either.

Then had come Mike and his father, the lovely house on the English Riviera, overlooking the bay in Torquay and for a few years Beth had felt part of a family. Until her mother had decided a young actor suited her better and had divorced Mike's dad to marry her toy-boy. Then she'd stuck Beth in a boarding school and taken off on tour.

For once, her mother had been the one to suffer when, a year later, the young man had divorced her. But nothing stopped her mother for long, though, Beth thought dryly, stirring in her seat. Three years ago, Leanora had married an Australian cattle rancher. The poor man had been visiting Devon to trace his ancestors when Leanora had convinced him he needed a wife. Beth had never even met Leanora's fifth husband—technically her step-father.

After the fiasco this afternoon, she had reached the conclusion that there was a great deal to be said for being an orphan. Without family to get her into trouble, life was a joy…

But later a little imp of mischief whispered in her head as she curled up in her cosy bed and tried to sleep. An even greater joy might be hers if the outrageously attractive Italian Dexter Giordanni actually turned up tomorrow night to take her out to dinner. With his handsome face clear in her mind's eye, she fell asleep, the eroticism of her dreams a testament to the earth-shattering effect he had had upon her.

CHAPTER TWO

BETH eyed the pile of laundry with a wry grimace. Saturday was her day for washing, cleaning the apartment and shopping—always in that order. Usually she enjoyed having the weekend to herself, but today she felt oddly restless. With a sigh, she picked up the garments and shoved them in the washing machine. Turning it on to the correct setting, she decided to break with habit and do her shopping immediately—not for a second admitting she wanted to get out and back quickly just in case Dexter Giordanni telephoned.

By late afternoon, her apartment spotless, her clothes dried and ironed, she was beginning to regret turning down her friend Mary's offer to go to the cinema with her. She had a sinking feeling her Saturday night was going to be spent alone in front of the television, and it was her own stupid fault. A man like Dexter Giordanni was not going to call the likes of her in a million years...

Still, she might as well shower and wash her hair; she had nothing else to do. And with that thought in mind she stripped off her jeans and shirt in the bedroom and padded to the bathroom. The ringing of the telephone had her sprinting back to the kitchen like an Olympic runner.

She snatched the receiver off the wall. 'Yes?' she said breathlessly.

'I hope I did not disturb you,' the deep, dark voice echoed down the line.

If only he knew, Beth thought, grinning to herself. Just

the sound of his voice disturbed her more than any other man she had ever known... 'No, no, not at all. I was just about to step in the shower,' she told him truthfully.

'Ah, the image is *incantevole*, but I must not delay you. I simply called to confirm our dinner date: seven-thirty, yes?'

'What does *incant*...whatever mean?' Beth asked, diverted by his lapse into his native language.

'Enchanting... *Ciao*.' And he replaced his receiver.

Beth stood holding the telephone for a long moment. Dex thought she was enchanting. Taking a deep, contented breath, she replaced her receiver and dreamily made her way back to the bathroom.

An hour later, wearing only a towel, Beth stood in front of her open wardrobe and viewed its contents with a jaundiced eye. Her date would be here in twenty minutes and she had nothing to wear. Apart from a couple of tailored suits she wore for work, the rest of her clothes were all casual. She was very much a jeans and sweater sort of girl, and somehow the red wool shirt-dress she kept for special occasions looked far too plain. Why, oh, why hadn't she spent the afternoon shopping for an elegant, sophisticated dress to match the sophisticated Dex, instead of lolling around her apartment?

She glanced across the room to the window. The weather hadn't changed; it was still a grey, cold, overcast autumn evening, and with a resigned sigh she took her only sophisticated dress out of the wardrobe. She had bought it in July for her graduation ball. A simple black satin slip dress, it had a delicate gold thread shimmering though it, tiny shoestring straps, a scooped neck and back and an A-line skirt that ended a few inches above her knee. She dropped it on the bed and turned back to the wardrobe. The frock was fine, but she would be freezing in today's weather.

Unlike some young woman of her age, who quite happily went out in all weathers with arms and legs bare, Beth was thoroughly sensible, and not prepared to get pneumonia for the sake of fashion. So reluctantly she dragged from the top shelf of a wardrobe a plain black wool shawl, a purchase from one of the high street chains, and threw it on the bed.

She crossed the room, opened the chest of drawers and withdrew a pair of delicate black lace panties and matching garter belt. Dropping the towel to the floor, she quickly pulled on her underwear, then, lifting the dress from the bed, slid it over her head. Cut on the bias, it was too low at the back to allow the wearing of a bra. But, eyeing her reflection in the mirror, she thought, not bad!

Sitting down at the dressing table, she quickly applied a moisturiser to her fine skin. She took a little longer than usual over her eye make-up, accentuating her large eyes with the merest hint of pale aquamarine eyeshadow at the corners and a fine line of brown kohl around the top lid, finishing off with brown-black mascara to enhance her long thick lashes. A gloss of natural pink for her lips, and she was almost ready.

She picked up her hairbrush and brushed her auburn curls vigorously. Then, with a deft twist, she piled her hair on the top of her head, securing it with a discreetly coloured band, and finished off by pushing a few strategic curls firmly in place.

Satisfied with the result, she stood up, and from the dressing table drawer removed a pair of fine black nylon stockings. Carefully pulling them on one by one, she clipped the small black suspenders in place and, straightening, smoothed her skirt down over her thighs. She turned to look over her shoulder at her image: no bumps or brief line! Good.

She slipped her feet into classic black patent leather pumps with two-and-a-half-inch heels. She needed the height, she reminded herself, before taking a small black patent clutch purse from the dressing table and quickly transferring a few essentials from her everyday shoulder bag.

The doorbell rang, disturbing the silence and panicking Beth. She grabbed the black shawl from the bed and slung it around her shoulders before dashing out of the bedroom to the front door. She pressed the button for the intercom and heard that familiar rich voice.

'Giordanni, here.'

'I'll be right down,' she responded. For some reason she was not quite ready to ask him into her home.

The elevator deposited her in the foyer, and when she saw him leaning indolently against the porter's desk, dressed in an immaculately fitting black dinner suit with a white silk shirt and perfectly knotted black velvet bow tie, her heart skipped a beat. Suddenly she had a vivid image of herself untying the bow tie and running her fingers over the broad expanse of chest, and she wished she had asked him up to her apartment. She caught her breath at the uncharacteristic erotic thought.

Consequently she blushed fire-engine red when, straightening to his full height, he strolled across and quite naturally took her arm, and looked down at her.

'I was right, you look enchanting. Shall we go?'

Her, 'Hello, Dex,' was greeted with the briefest of slanting smiles before he was ushering her out of the door and into a chauffeur-driven limousine.

'I don't keep a car in London. I am not here that often,

and when I am I use a rental service. So I hope you don't object to a driver this evening, Beth. Plus, I thought we might celebrate our meeting with a few glasses of champagne, and I never drink and drive.'

'A very laudable resolution,' she managed to say calmly. She cast him a sidelong glance, almost furtively. He was as devastatingly attractive as she remembered, and, sitting next to him in the close confines of the back seat of the car, with the pressure of his thigh lightly pressing against her own and the soft elusive scent of his aftershave teasing her nostrils—or maybe it was simply the scent of the man himself—she was completely overwhelmed by Dex, the car—everything.

A large hand closed over her small hands, which were clenched in her lap. 'Beth, really. "A laudable resolution"? My knowledge of your language is excellent, but what does that mean?' he asked with a chuckle, and lifted her hands to his lips so she was forced to look at him, his silver eyes glinting down into hers. 'Beth, I like you for your openness, your honesty. Don't go all stuffy on me now.'

The touch of his lips on her hand and the humour in his gaze excited her, but also calmed her nerves. If he wanted honesty he could have it, she thought, secretly pleased. 'You're right, Dex, "laudable" was a bit much. But you make me rather nervous. I've never been out with a man quite like you before, or sat in a chauffeur-driven limousine. It's quite awesome.'

He lowered her hands to her lap and gave them a gentle squeeze before letting go. 'You are not frightened of me, Beth, are you?' he asked softly, but before she could respond he added, 'You have no need to be. I have only your best interests at heart, and I am sure you will very soon get used to my great wealth and everything else; women usually do.'

Beth looked up, not all sure she liked his last comment, and thought she caught a flash of something very like cynicism in his eyes. But, realising she was watching him, Dex turned the full force of his megawatt smile on her small face and dropped a brief, swift kiss on her forehead.

'Don't look so worried, little one. Tonight we are going to have fun, I promise.'

The brief kiss banished all her doubts, and half an hour later, seated opposite Dex in the most exclusive restaurant in London, she wondered why she had worried. He was the perfect companion. Articulate, charming, Dex ordered the meal with an efficiency and knowledge of fine food Beth marvelled at. But he was not above making her laugh with his description of the waiter.

Very quickly he made her feel completely at ease, though every so often he very gently flirted with her, making her aware by a touch, a glance, of his purely masculine interest in her as a woman. Or maybe not so pure... Beth did not know, and she had not the experience to make a judgement.

They had exchanged snippets of information about themselves. Dex was thirty-three to her twenty-one. He knew she was a graphic artist, and she knew he was extremely wealthy, as he told her in great detail how many companies he owned. In fact, his wealth struck the one discordant note in her otherwise rapt fascination with the man.

'You're not one of those bleeding-heart radical types who object to a man being disgustingly rich, are you?' he asked jokingly.

For a second she felt his humour did not ring true. But, dismissing the uneasy thought with a toss of her head, she aimed for a sophisticated response.

'Not at all. Someone once said that no woman can be too rich or too thin, or something like that, and I'm inclined to agree.' She wasn't sure she meant what she had said, but it seemed to please Dex.

'Good girl! I knew the moment I saw you you were my type of woman,' he drawled, watching her with a gleam of satisfaction in his grey eyes.

Beth felt the colour rise in her cheeks. She was delighted he thought she was his type, but not absolutely sure if she had been complimented or insulted.

By the time the main course arrived Beth had just about got her chaotic emotions under control, and was actually beginning to feel as if she had known the man for years.

'Honestly, Dex, I don't think I'll be able to eat all this.' She eyed her duck and cranberry sauce. It looked delicious, but they had started with roasted asparagus salad, followed by a fish course—A trio of smoked fish with beetroot—and now, with the main course before her, she wondered if she would ever get through it all.

'Eat what you like and leave the rest. For myself, I am a big man with a big appetite. I intend to enjoy...' His silver eyes gleamed with blatant desire as they caught and held hers, then deliberately dropped to the soft valley of her breasts, delicately exposed by the neckline of her dress. 'Everything...' he husked, his gaze lifting to her face. 'It is the only way to live.'

Beth was not stupid, she knew what he meant, and she could feel the colour rising in her cheeks yet again, as her stomach clenched. She knew it had nothing to do with the food but everything to do with the potent appeal of the man opposite.

'Eat. I did not mean to embarrass you,' Dex offered quietly. 'But you have the most amazing effect on me. I look at you and I want you in my bed.'

Beth gasped out loud, and his eyes narrowed with piercing intensity on her flushed face.

'You know this is true, and you feel the same; don't try to deny it,' he commanded arrogantly, but then in a softer tone he added, 'But perhaps now is not the time to talk of such matters.'

She wanted to deny it. His supreme confidence was somehow insulting. But she knew what he said was true, so instead she contented herself with fiddling with her fork and asking, 'Are you always so blunt on a first date?'

'No,' he said, and, reaching across the table, he covered the hand holding her fork, 'Only with you, Beth.' Suddenly grinning, he added, 'So, tell me more about yourself. Your friends, parents, whatever. Talk to me, so I can take my mind off your luscious body and get back to my meal, hmm?'

He was impossible, but Beth found herself grinning back and doing exactly as he had said. 'Family—I don't have much. I don't remember my father; he died when I was a baby. I've spent most of my life in Devon with my mother. She had aspirations to be a famous singer, but unfortunately also a tendency to get married a lot. She is on her fifth husband now and lives in Australia. I haven't seen her for three years, though we do write occasionally.' Beth broke off, raised her glass to her mouth and took a gulp of champagne. She didn't really like talking about Leanora, and sometimes it still upset her, though she never liked to admit it.

'That explains a lot,' Dex murmured.

'Sorry, what did you say?' Lost in her own thoughts for a moment, she had missed his comment.

'That must have hurt a lot,' Dex repeated softly.

'No, not really,' she quickly assured him, comforted by the sympathy in his tone. 'I got used to it, and on the plus side I acquired a stepbrother—Mike. If it hadn't been for Mike I wouldn't have met you.' She stopped. The champagne was going to her head and she was revealing more than she meant to.

Dex, a smile curving his firm mouth, lifted his glass. 'A toast to a much-married mum and Mike, without whom you and I would never have met.'

Embarrassed, but oddly pleased, Beth lifted her glass and returned the toast. Replacing her glass on the table, she said, 'No more champagne; I think I've had quite enough.' And, pushing her almost empty plate slightly forward, she continued, 'No more food, either. It was delicious, but I really can't eat any more.'

'I don't have that problem,' Dex drawled, clearing his plate and placing the cutlery on it. 'In fact, I think I'll have a dessert; I love sweet things.' And, catching her green eyes with his, he continued throatily, 'You are the sweetest thing I have met in a long time. Can I have you, Beth?' Then, tossing his head back, he laughed out loud at her look of confusion.

She wanted to be offended but his laughter was infectious, so she smiled, then laughed as well. 'You know, I've discovered something about you, Dexter Giordanni,' she finally managed to say pertly. 'You are an incorrigible flirt.'

'Only with you, Beth, only ever with you.'

If only she could believe him, she thought, gazing at him as he paid the bill, adding a very generous tip. She had been out with plenty of men—well, not plenty, more like half a dozen. Her last date had been with a young man from the office. She had spent an enjoyable evening in a local wine bar with Dave, but they had both decided without a word being spoken they were destined to be workmates and nothing more. Now, watching Dex, she knew this was different. She could very easily fall in love with him, and it frightened her even as it excited her.

He turned his head and caught her staring, and one dark brow arched enquiringly. 'Have I got a smudge on my nose?' he asked, perfectly aware she had been studying him.

'No, you have a very nice nose,' she shot back. 'I was simply thinking what a lovely evening it has been.' That was not exactly a lie, she told herself, rather proud of her ability to appear cool and collected in his sophisticated presence, when inside her heart was beating like a drum.

'Has been? But it is not over yet; the night has hardly begun.' Getting to his feet, he took the shawl the waiter handed to him. 'Come on, you look the sort of girl who likes to take chances. I will show you my new casino.'

Beth stood up and smoothed her skirt down over her slender hips, intensely aware of Dex's blatantly sensual gaze following the movement of her hands as his own large hands carefully slipped her wrap around her shoulders,

'You look beautiful,' he murmured, his hands lingering for a moment on her shoulders. His dark head bent and his lips brushed the top of her head. 'Let's get out of here before I make a fool of myself.' Slipping his hand down to the small of her back, he guided her out of the restaurant and into the waiting limousine.

Inside, seemingly casually, Dex curved his long arm around her shoulders and pulled her swiftly close to him. All Beth's hard-won poise deserted her in an instant, and, looking up at him through the thick brush of her lashes, she quivered at the glimpse of fire that blazed in his eyes.

'You're safe with me, Beth,' he murmured softly.

'I know.' Beguiled by his many compliments and real desire for her, she believed him, and snuggled into his side with a deep sigh of contentment. The rest of the trip was accomplished in a companionable silence until the car stopped.

Sitting up, Beth glanced out of the window. 'Is this it?' she said feeling rather disappointed. There were no neon lights or flashing signs, simply an elegant black and gold door in the centre of what looked like a typical Georgian terraced house.

'Discretion is the name of the game,' Dex offered, helping her out of the car. Taking her hand in his, he led her across the pavement and through the black door into another world.

As soon as they walked into the entrance foyer a young woman dashed to take her wrap. Then a hard-faced man appeared and Dex introduced her—the casino manager, a Mr Black, a name Beth found very appropriate; he was swarthy, stocky, and looked dangerous while his voice oozed charm.

She had never been in a casino before, but when Dex ushered her into a huge room with a graceful curved staircase leading to the upper floor it didn't take her long to realise it was a very serious business. Glittering crystal chandeliers illuminated a dozen or more tables surrounded by smartly dressed people. The walls were lined with slot machines, like an army of alien, robotic guards, with yet more people seated in front of them. But it was the avid expressions on the customers' faces that Beth found somehow chilling.

'You look a little stunned,' Dex opined, with a dry smile. 'Surely you have been in a casino before?'

'No, I haven't, and I can't believe so many people are prepared to waste money this way,' she said bluntly. Her answer seemed to surprise him, but not for long.

'Then you ain't seen nothing yet, babe,' he drawled in a mock-American accent. His grey gaze swept down over the soft curve of her breasts and back to her face, and with a seductive look, he added, 'Stick with me, babe, and I'll show you a good time.' And, putting an arm around her waist, he chuckled at her look of outrage.

'Fool,' Beth laughed, realising he was teasing, and gave him a sharp dig in the ribs with her elbow.

'I know, but I can't resist teasing you.' At that point Mr Black said something in Dex's ear, and the amusement left his face.

'Sorry, Beth, I need to go to the office, but I'll show you the rest on the way. This is just for starters. The bar and restaurant are through there.' He gestured with his free hand as they reached the bottom of a grand staircase. 'Up here there are two more gaming rooms, where the stakes rise accordingly. Plus the offices,' he informed her as they ascended the stairs, his arm dropping from her waist.

Beth watched him as they walked up, and saw a stranger. Dex was suddenly all efficiency, no trace of humour left. Tall and aloof, he strode up the stairs and through to another room, taking deferential greetings from various people with a word, or a nod, and a smile that never reached his eyes.

His plain black dinner suit and conservative white

shirt could not conceal the powerful muscled body beneath, or a certain air of danger about him. The other people in the room faded into insignificance beside him. It was obvious to Beth, and everyone else, that this man was the master of all he surveyed, the hard-headed, powerful ruler of the lot; the Boss. It wasn't just his height or his build, but the intangible aura he carried with him, a dynamism that radiated from him, a supreme confidence in his own worth that made weaker mortals shrink back.

Beth shuddered; a ghost is walking over my grave, she thought, but dismissed the notion when Dex halted her with a large hand curving over her shoulder. The touch of his hand on her bare flesh was enough to make her forget every rational thought.

His dark head bent towards her, and in her heightened emotional state she imagined he was going to kiss her, but she was sadly disillusioned when he said starkly, 'This room is for the high rollers, where the real money changes hands. Black is getting you some chips so you can play.'

Play! She wouldn't know where to start. Curious, Beth looked around: no slot machines here, but a peculiar silence, punctuated by the occasional voice of a croupier. Around the large green baize tables were expensively dressed customers, some obviously from the Middle East, judging by their garb, and the few ladies present, mostly old, wearing enough jewellery to pay off the National Debt.

'Here, Beth.' Dex thrust a handful of round tokens at her. 'Enjoy yourself. I won't be long.'

'Can't I come with you?' she blurted, suddenly feeling completely out of her element. 'I'm not a gambler, and I don't think I want to be.'

His fingers caught her chin and he tilted her head up. 'You look stunningly beautiful, Beth, and I will get my business concluded much quicker without you to distract me. Understand?' His grey eyes roamed over her delicate features. 'You will be perfectly all right on your own; no one will bother you.' His glance slid down her body like a warm caress, and back to her face again. 'Everyone knows you're with me,' he ended with unconscious arrogance, and, letting his hand slide from her chin to her shoulder, he squeezed her gently in a casual reassuring gesture.

'Yes...w-well,' she stuttered. Her flesh burned beneath his fingers and her body was aware of him with every pore.

She tore her gaze from his and glanced distractedly around the room. Her green eyes widened in astonishment as she caught sight of someone she knew—Paul. Even in this crowd he stood out.

Tall, his blond hair turning here and there to white, his exquisitely tailored dinner suit fitting his slim, elegant body to perfection, he looked what he was: a man of distinction. The lines of character in his face reflected his fifty-three years, but in no way detracted from his handsome features.

Paul Morris... He looked across, his blue eyes surprised when they met Beth's. She watched as he made his way towards her, determination in every stride. But he was supposed to be in Italy. What was he doing back so soon? she wondered. Her lips curled in a slow smile. At least she wouldn't be alone.

She glanced back at Dex, whose hand hadn't left her shoulder. 'Okay,' she said. But he was not looking at her, instead he was watching Paul approach, with a dark frown on his face.

'No, you are right. You are coming with me,' Dex ordered curtly, his hand dropping to her waist and hauling her hard against him.

'Bethany, what on earth are you doing here?' Paul stopped a foot away, and, taking in the proprietary arm around her waist, he flashed a hard smile at Dex. 'Giordanni. I'd heard you were buying the place. Congratulations.' Then, turning worried blue eyes back to Beth, he continued, 'I didn't know you knew Mr Giordanni, Bethany.'

'And I thought you were in Italy,' she shot back. She had dined with him ten days ago and he had told her he was going to his estate in Italy.

'Oh, I was, and I will be again in another few hours.' Paul glanced at the gold Rolex on his wrist. 'This is just a flying visit—twenty-four hours. I had some business that couldn't wait. That's why I didn't call you. But enough about me. What are you doing here? You don't gamble,' he ended sternly.

Beth opened her mouth to answer but was forestalled by Dex.

'The lady is with me, Morris.' His fingers nipped her waist, demanding her compliance. 'And we have urgent business to attend to in private—haven't we, darling?' Dex's grey eyes captured hers and his head lowered, his firm mouth brushing her parted lips. It was a fleeting kiss, but it was enough to set her heart racing, and she stared back at him, too dumb to answer.

'I hope you know what you're doing, Beth.' Paul said, bringing her back into the conversation.

She looked at Paul and smiled a misty, bemused smile. 'Yes, Paul.'

Paul sighed, a wry smile of acceptance curving his

mouth. She was a grown woman; it had to happen some
time.

'You're a man of the world, Morris, I'm sure you
understand,' Dexter cut into the silence. 'Enjoy your
gambling and excuse us.' And with a deft twist Dexter
spun Beth round.

She only had time to call, 'See you, Paul,' over her
shoulder as, with almost indecent haste, Dex urged her
towards the back of the room and a large nondescript
door. The incongruous note was the man who guarded
it and opened it at their approach. He looked like a
heavyweight boxer with the nose to match.

She registered that they were in a dimly lit hallway,
and had opened her mouth to ask where the fire was—
she would have quite liked to talk to Paul—when she
registered the stark fury in Dex's steely eyes.

'Old man Morris a friend of yours, is he?'

'Yes, a very good—' She never got the chance to
finish the sentence.

Dex pushed her back against the wall, his dark head
swooping down, his mouth capturing hers in a kiss of
pure male dominance. Shocked by his sudden aggression, the fierce pressure of his mouth, the feel of his huge
body hard against her much smaller frame, she instinctively struggled to break free. But she was helpless
against his superior strength, and his mouth ground
against hers with a demanding arrogance that was as
exciting as it was alien to her.

Then, suddenly, something peculiar happened. One
second she was fighting him and the next she felt her
body melting against his as his lips gentled against her
mouth. His kiss softened, his tongue traced the outline
of her mouth, his teeth nibbled gently on her bottom lip
until, with a sigh of complete surrender, she opened her

mouth to him. She lifted her hands, her fingers tangling in the silky black thickness of his hair, and kissed Dex back without realising what she was doing.

His mouth burned against hers, his tongue toying with hers in an erotic, thrusting dance. Her hands slid to his broad shoulders. She felt his muscles tense beneath the smooth fabric of his jacket and trembled as his hand slid down her naked throat, his long fingers tracing the soft curve of her breast and palming its lush fullness in his hand, before sliding lower, tracing the indentation of her waist, the soft flare of her hips. It was only when she felt his hand stroke up her leg to her naked thigh she began to panic again. 'No.' Beth uttered a cry of protest and closed her hand around his strong wrist.

Dex finally raised his head, his breathing surprisingly unsteady. 'Stockings as well. What are you trying to do to me?' he groaned as he slid his hand from under the hem of her short dress and, drawing away from her, brushed his ruffled hair from his brow. They stared at each other, neither one capable of speech for a moment. But it was Dex who recovered first.

'I guessed you would be dynamite, but I admit even I am surprised at exactly how explosive we are together.' His grey eyes glittered down into hers. She stared back, her pulse thudding erratically, her green eyes wide and bemused. She was so stunned by her own violent reaction, she couldn't speak.

'I was right; I should have left you to the gaming tables. You are more than a distraction; you're a lethal weapon, lady.' He grinned, a self-deprecating smile, and, clasping her hand in his, he added, 'Come and I will show you the rest of my newly acquired toys, before we get into any more trouble.'

Beth was grateful for his matter-of-fact attitude; it

helped to calm her leaping responses. Then Mr Black appeared at the end of the hall and it was back to business for Dex. They left her sitting in a functional office and retired to an inner sanctum, Dex having explained that it was the manager's office and also the strongroom.

Beth spent the rest of their evening together in an emotional haze, trying to deal with her chaotic response to Dex. She was glad when, on returning to the outer office, he suggested taking her home. In the car he arranged to call for her the next morning at ten, and, on walking her to the door of her apartment, the light kiss he pressed on her lips was warm and somehow reassuring.

Tired, but happy, she crawled into bed, expecting to sleep. But she lay awake for hours, her mind reliving the events of the night. The intimate dinner with Dex, the sound of his deep, sexy voice, the touch of his hand. She tossed restlessly, her body unnaturally warm, her breasts hardening as she remembered the casino, and the sudden passionate interlude on the way to the office.

She turned over onto her stomach and buried her head in the pillow. Any more erotic memories, Beth told herself sternly, and she would never sleep. Closing her eyes, she tried to make her mind blank, but something niggled at her conscience until finally she remembered.

Dex had thrust the chips in her hand and told her to play. It had been odd… One minute he had been determined to leave her at the gaming tables, and yet he had changed his mind in a flash when she had spoken to Paul. Maybe Dex was jealous! Surely that proved he was as smitten with her as she was with him. On that happy notion, Beth drifted off to sleep.

CHAPTER THREE

BETH woke up to bright autumn sunshine blazing through the window, and she smiled to herself. It was an accurate reflection of how she felt inside, and all because Dexter Giordanni had entered her life... She said his name out loud as she jumped out of bed and headed for the shower, loving the sound of his name almost as much as she loved the man.

She froze, one foot in the shower stall; the enormity of what she had just admitted to herself hit her like a bolt from the blue. Slowly she stepped into the shower and turned on the water. The impossible had happened. She had fallen in love at first sight.

A worried frown creased her smooth brow. What was she thinking of? In love...she couldn't be. Beth had always prided herself on being sensible where men were concerned, and had never let a man get too close to her. The example of her mother, Leanora, had taught her from an early age that there was no such thing as true love. And watching her stepbrother's girlfriends come and go like yo-yos had confirmed Beth's cynicism where the L-word was concerned. Yet here she was, mooning like a love-sick calf over a man she had only just met.

Dex was an experienced man of the world. He probably knew exactly how he affected her. Who was she fooling? Not probably, positively! Beth blushed at the memory of being locked in his arms, his hand on her breast, her thigh. Abruptly she turned the water from hot to cold, and when she felt thoroughly numb she stepped out of the shower and rubbed herself down with a large towel with a lot more force than was strictly necessary— memories of her years in the convent school reminding her of the sins of the flesh.

Dried, and dressed in navy trousers, a white silk shirt and a buttercup-yellow wool cardigan, Beth ate her breakfast of cereal and toast. Lingering in the kitchen over her second cup of coffee, she told herself she must slow down where Dex was concerned. She had dressed conservatively, and she would act with reserve in his company today. She was frightened of how he could make her feel, and her innate common sense told her she hardly knew the man.

It was a much more subdued Beth who opened the door an hour later to the object of her turbulent thoughts.

'Don't I get a smile?' Dex demanded in a throaty drawl.

She had managed to stay calm long enough to say hello to him over the intercom and let him in to the building. But seeing him in the flesh knocked every sensible resolution out of her head. He was leaning with one arm propped against the doorframe, his large body almost blocking the light and angled towards Beth.

She couldn't help it. Her green eyes widened in fascinated appraisal of the man in front of her. 'Dark and dangerous' flashed through her mind. She had only seen him wearing a formal suit before, but this morning he was dressed in a black roll-neck sweater, and a black leather blouson jacket sloped off his broad shoulders. His faded blue jeans were verging on the indecent, slung low on his hips, with a leather belt threaded through the loops that Beth was sure was not necessary to hold them up. They fitted him like a second skin, hugging his long, long legs, with a tell-tale lighter patch in a more intimate place. Flushing furiously, she raised her eyes to his and went even redder.

His grey eyes gleamed with a mocking, sensuous delight. He knew exactly how his overt masculinity affected her. 'Are you going to ask me in, Beth, or am I supposed to stay here all day?'

'No, no...of course. Yes, yes, come in...' she prattled like a demented fool, stepping back and signalling with her hand for him to enter. His husky laugh simply added to her confusion.

He stood in the middle of her sitting room and slowly looked around. 'This is not at all what I expected,' he said, with a wry shake of his dark head.

It was her home, and immediately Beth was on the defensive. 'I've only lived here a couple of months, and it takes time and money to buy furniture and things.'

Beth looked around her living room, trying to see it through Dex's eyes. It was small—one corner was completely taken up with her computer and a large drawing board, another with the television and CD player. On the walls she had pinned a few of her favourite posters. Her one and only armchair, in battered black leather, stood next to an old wooden chest she had bought on the Portobello Road to use as a coffee table. The rest of the furniture consisted of three cheap and cheerful scarlet bean bags.

Dex stepped towards her, and, tilting her face up to his, with a finger under her chin, said, 'I did not mean to offend you. I love your decor. It is like you—bright and colourful.'

'Yes, well.' With his grey eyes smiling down into hers, she was almost lost for words.

'I was surprised by the drawing board; you really do

work as a graphic artist and obviously take your job seriously if you bring work home.'

'Not so much bring work home; I like to experiment with ideas on the computer and then transfer them to the bigger, more traditional board. I find I get a better view that way,' she replied, finally managing to string a reasonable sentence or two together.

'A better view.' Dex's hand fell from her chin and he glanced around the room again. 'That is a good idea; I must remember that,' he said enigmatically.

Beth watched him, an odd breathlessness afflicting her as his grey gaze captured hers. His dark head bent towards her, and for a second she had the impression he was going to kiss her. But, instead, he lifted his hand and brushed a stray wisp of her hair behind her ear.

'Unless you want to give me a guided tour of your bedroom, I suggest we leave.'

There was no mistaking the teasing gleam in his eyes, and Beth reciprocated in kind. 'I am quite sure you've never needed to be guided around any lady's bedroom in your life. Your type are born knowing the way.'

Dex chuckled, and then laughed out loud. 'You know me too well already. That makes you a dangerous lady,' he drawled in genuine amusement, and he was still grinning when they left the building and he helped her into the front passenger seat of a black BMW car.

The shared humour lasted. As he drove Dex regaled her with stories of some of the more colourful gamblers he had met at his casinos. She howled with laughter when he described an elderly lady tourist who had holidayed on one of his luxury liners cruising around the Mediterranean. Apparently, after visiting the island of Sicily, the lady, on returning to the ship, had been most indignant and insisted on complaining to the captain, because she had been told the volcano, Mount Etna was live, but it had not erupted while she was there.

Listening to him talk, Beth also realised he took his work very seriously. His head office was in Rome, where he spent most of the time, but he also made a point of trying to visit every hotel, cruise liner and casino he owned at least once a year. At present he was staying at his London hotel until his business in London was completed. He had an apartment in New York, but he preferred Italy, and Beth surmised his real home was Rome.

The information he freely offered about his lifestyle should have reassured her. But in fact it only underlined what she already knew. He was a sophisticated, dynamic business tycoon, and way out of the reach of a struggling graphic artist.

But, glancing sideways at him as the car sped out of the city and into the open countryside, Beth hoped she was wrong. She noted the slight frown lines between his eyes as he tried to read a signpost, and somehow he looked younger, not quite so self-assured. Maybe it was the casual clothes he wore, she mused. For a long moment she stared at him in pure feminine appreciation of his virile male form, the fast-becoming familiar feelings exploding inside her.

To get her mind off his sexy body, and under control, she asked, 'Where are we going? You never said.'

He flashed her a grin. 'All the way,' he drawled, and paused until he saw the colour flood her cheeks. 'Relax. To the New Forest, I hope.'

'You do know the way?' Beth queried.

'Don't worry, I have a picnic hamper in the back. We can eat in the car if we have to.'

But they did not have to. Dex soon parked along a forest trail at the edge of a clearing. Beth got out of the car and looked around in delight: a more perfect destination would be hard to find. The New Forest in October, with its deciduous trees a blaze of red, yellow and gold, in stark contrast to the deep dark green of the pines, was a feast for the eyes.

Roaming through the woods hand in hand, they spotted red squirrels, dozens of rabbits, and of course the wild ponies the forest was famous for, along with the unexpected pleasure of seeing a small deer. Returning to the car, Dex collected a hamper and blanket from the trunk. He spread the tartan rug on the ground beneath the branches of a massive oak tree and placed the hamper in the middle.

A hamper from the best department store in London, what else! Beth thought with a wry grin, but nothing could spoil her enjoyment of the afternoon and her companion. The unusual warmth of the autumn day saw them both shed their jackets and lounge on the blanket, the hamper between them. They investigated its contents and nibbled caviar and pâté, washed down with champagne. Then they dined on chicken and French bread, along with various cheeses, with fresh exotic fruits to finish. Finally, Beth collapsed flat on her back and fell asleep.

She stirred and turned her head; something was biting her ear, something else was crawling up her arm. Her eyes slowly opened. Not something but someone, she realised, with a leap of her heart.

'You look so irresistible when you sleep,' Dex's seductive voice rumbled in her ear.

Supporting himself on one elbow, his long body was hovering over her and his free hand was stroking gently up her arm while his mouth nuzzled her ear.

'Dex,' she murmured, 'where has the hamper gone?'

She had fallen asleep with the picnic basket acting as a barrier between them and had awakened to find herself almost joined with him from the hip down, the heat of his body burning through the fine fabric of her trousers.

'So practical and yet so perfect,' he opined softly, trailing a string of tiny kisses down from her ear to her mouth and gently back to the tip of her nose, his grey eyes smiling lazily down into hers.

Beth was totally captivated. She drank in the tangy masculine scent of his cologne, along with the exquisite frisson of excitement that tingled through her body as he moved his hard, muscular thigh restlessly against her, bringing a blush to her cheeks.

'I moved the damn thing because I thought you were never going to wake up, and I had a much more pressing appetite. I needed quite desperately to hold you, to kiss you.' And he did.

His mouth covered hers in a kiss of achingly tender passion, and Beth closed her eyes and gave herself up to the kaleidoscope of hitherto unknown sensations rioting within her.

'You drive me crazy, Beth.' He whispered the words against her throat, then, raising his head, he demanded huskily, 'Look at me, Beth. You will be mine?'

She opened her eyes, but his kiss had stolen her breath away and she could not speak. Instead, her body now shaken with unfamiliar feeling, she stared up at him, unconscious of the fact that her huge green eyes, under their thick lashes, and the soft, swollen fullness of her mouth combined with her aura of innocence were tantalising challenges to a man like Dex.

He smiled a soft, slow predatory grin. 'No answer, my sweet? Then let me persuade you.'

Shockingly, she knew she wanted him too. Heat

surged from the centre of her body to every part of her as she recognized the power he had over her.

'But—' They were lying on a blanket in broad daylight; anyone could walk past, she meant to say. The words caught in her throat as his hand slid slowly across her breast and his head descended. His tongue flicked teasingly around her mouth, enticing a response she was helpless to withhold—did not want to!

With devastating intent, Dex carried on kissing her, parting her swollen lips, his tongue delving deep, and any lingering inhibitions Beth might have felt were vanquished by his sexual expertise. She ardently returned his kisses, her small hand curving around his neck to hold his head down to hers.

'At last,' he growled against her parted lips, 'you want me.' And, lifting his head, his silver eyes staring down into hers, he added, 'And God knows I want you. I ache.'

Beth lay immobile, trapped by the long leg he had moved over hers, the hard, masculine length of him making her vitally aware of exactly how much he wanted her, while her pulse-rate shot off the Richter scale. She made no objection when, with a deftness that underlined his vast experience, his long fingers unbuttoned her blouse. But when he deliberately drew back she could not hold back the soft sigh of regret that escaped her.

'Ah, shame,' he teased her, 'today you're wearing a bra.' In a second the front fastening was flicked open and he had peeled back both shirt and bra. 'If that was meant to deter me, Beth, it didn't work,' he mocked softly, his glittering gaze studying her naked breasts with lazy pleasure. 'You are so beautiful, and so perfect.'

Beth felt her whole body blush, the blood rushing through her veins like quicksilver. Her green eyes roamed, helpless with longing, over his handsome face—noting the darkening flush across his high cheekbones, the sensuous twist to his full lips, and she shivered in anticipation as his dark head lowered slowly, not to her mouth, but to the rosy tip of her breast.

She had never allowed any other man such intimacy, but she was helpless where Dex was concerned. What she had feared was true: she could not deny him anything. Her hands tangled in the black silk curls of his head while her slender body arched involuntarily towards the source of its pleasure. He slowly sucked her taut nipple into his mouth, rolling his tongue around the rigid peak until she moaned out loud. When he moved to give the same treatment to her other breast, she thought she would faint with the pleasure.

She made no demur when his hard-muscled thigh gently nudged her trembling legs apart, or when he swiftly unzipped her trousers and eased one large hand down over her flat stomach. She felt an instant of loss when his mouth deserted her breast and he reared up. But his passion-darkened eyes, glittering with a ferocious need, told her he was not deserting her, and then, once more, his mouth sought hers in a possessive, hungry kiss.

Beth traced his broad shoulders with trembling hands, moving them down to slide them up beneath his sweater. The feel of his satin flesh was an aphrodisiac all on its own. She felt his great body shudder, and gloried in his hard-muscled flesh. Moist heat flooded her loins as a teasing finger eased beneath her scanty briefs and found the secret part of her. It was only when he rolled over her, covering her completely, and she could feel the rigid length of his masculine arousal hard against her, that she panicked like the frightened virgin she was.

Her eyes flew wide open. She saw the swaying branches of the tree and the blue sky above. What was she inviting? 'No! No, Dex.' She squirmed beneath him, her small hand closing over his strong wrist. 'I can't!' Though every nerve in her body was crying out with need, her fear of the unknown, ultimate intimacy was greater, and she began to struggle in earnest.

'No? You can't say no—not now, Beth.' His throaty voice grated on her taut nerves, his fingers flexing as though to throw off her hold on his wrist.

'Please stop.' For a long moment she thought Dex was going to ignore her plea. His full weight pinned her down and he buried his head in the blanket over her shoulder. She felt his long body shudder and heard him groan, and then suddenly he rolled off her to lie on his back.

'I'm sorry,' she whispered, her body still pulsing with aching desire. Though she wasn't exactly sure what she was apologising for.

'Not half as sorry as I am,' he snarled, jumping to his feet to tower over her. 'I despise women who play games.'

She gazed up at him in disbelief. The lover of a moment ago was gone, replaced by a furiously angry man. His grey eyes narrowed contemptuously on her half-naked, dishevelled form. 'Get dressed, before I forget I am a gentleman and take what you are so obviously begging for but haven't the guts to admit.'

The contempt in his tone, the ice in his eyes, cut her to the heart. She lowered her own eyes and was forcibly reminded of his aroused state, which he made no attempt to hide. Bending her head, she hastily fastened her clothes. He was right; she did want him. But not like

this, under a tree in the open where all could see, with
no commitment on his part other than a desire for sex.

With that thought uppermost in her mind, some of
Beth's pride and common sense surfaced. It was not all
her fault. Dex was just as guilty as she was; after all, it
was Dex who had started making love to her, not the
other way around. The frustration seething in her over-
heated body, and a strong sense of pique at his attitude,
gave her the determination to get to her feet, and, tilting
her head back, she looked him straight in the eye.

'If you were a gentleman you would not have tried to
seduce me in a public place anyway,' she said flatly.

'If—if...' he repeated furiously. 'God knows, I should
have learnt my lesson by now. You are just like my—'
He stopped, and as she watched a subtle change came
over his features. 'Forget it. I have,' Dex finished tightly,
and, swinging on his heel, he snatched up the hamper
that had been cast to one side and headed for the car.

But Beth was intrigued, as well as stubborn. 'You
can't just walk away, Dex.' But she was talking to his
back. Hurrying after him, she caught his arm. 'Who am
I like?' she demanded.

Dex turned, brushing her hand from his arm, and he
stared at down at her. For a long moment the silence
stretched between them, and Beth thought he was not
going to answer. Then, suddenly, he spoke.

'You are totally unique, Beth, and I am a frustrated
jerk. And I should have had more sense than to make
love out in the open like a callow youth.' He smiled
with a twist of his firm lips. 'You would probably prefer
an older man with more restraint than I possess, I think.'

She should have been satisfied. His earlier anger had
gone and he was actually smiling at her. But the smile
did not reach his eyes, and why the cynical crack about

an older man? For a fleeting moment Beth recalled the episode in the casino, and wondered again if he was jealous of Paul. No, Dex couldn't be; maybe it was just his possessive Latin nature. Or maybe, she realised suddenly, he was simply trying to change the subject. He hadn't answered her question, and Beth could not let it go.

'And I think you're avoiding my question. You said I was just like someone. Who?'

'Tenacious little thing, aren't you?' Moving closer, he linked his hands loosely around Beth's back in a non-threatening embrace. 'I was going to say my sister. You are exactly like her. Sweet, and certainly not the type to have sex with a man without some form of commitment, like a ring on your finger. I am right? No?' he queried.

His grey eyes caught and held Beth's, the intensity of his gaze leaving her in no doubt of his sincerity. He understood... She heaved a deep sigh of relief, a broad grin lighting up her lovely face.

'You know me so well,' she said, with a toss of her auburn curls.

'Not as well as I would like, though I have a very strong feeling that will be remedied eventually. But I promise not to rush you.'

But rush her he did, though surprisingly not in a sexual way. Which was why, five days later, Beth stood in front of the mirror in her bedroom eyeing her reflection and chewing nervously on her bottom lip. The exquisitely tailored cashmere coat in palest cream, was a perfect fit. Designed by a top Italian fashion house and purchased by Dex.

She had seen him every day since their picnic on Sunday. They had dined out every night. Dex had a talent for finding the most intimate little restaurants. They'd also driven out into the country and visited quaint pubs. They'd talked about their likes and dislikes. Beth loved Elton John and opera, and Dex—a typical Italian—loved opera too, knew every aria ever written by heart. But when he'd tried to sing, Beth had burst into fits of laughter. Surprisingly, he was totally tone deaf.

When Beth had tried to explain that, as a working girl, she needed to stay home some nights, he had overruled her objections, but had been considerate enough to make sure she was home by about eleven. They usually parted on the doorstep with a chaste goodnight kiss. In fact, Dex had behaved as a perfect gentleman: no sexual advances. But in every other respect he always got his own way, Beth ruefully admitted to herself.

The coat was a case in point. Dex had insisted on buying it for her when they had met for lunch the day before. At first he had wanted to buy her a mink coat, and when she had flatly refused he had compromised with the cashmere, overriding all her objections, by finally saying, 'You're a beautiful woman and you deserve beautiful clothes. I love England, but not even the English like the climate. You are my woman and I have no intention of letting you catch cold.'

His high-handed attitude rankled, but his 'my woman' had secretly thrilled her. So she had accepted the coat.

Later that evening, clinging to Dex's arm as they walked along the riverside towards the boat where they were to dine, she was glad of its warmth. But, once seated at a table for two, with the banks of the Thames passing by, the millions of city lights reflected in the dark waters, she had no need of its warmth. The romantic setting, the heat of Dex's gaze, his hand holding hers, the latent desire in his eyes lit a flame inside her that she knew would burn for ever.

It was over coffee that Dex dropped his bombshell.

'Have I told you tonight how lovely you are?' Reaching for her hand, he turned it over in his own, his thumb idly stroking the palm.

There was nothing idle about Beth's reaction; she could feel a tingling sensation right down to her toes. 'Yes, a dozen times,' she responded huskily, her starry eyes roaming over his chiselled features. He was so attractive, sometimes she had to pinch herself to make sure what was happening was real and not a fairy tale. She had seen the avid glances the other female diners cast in his direction. He was certainly the most dynamic virile man in this floating palace of a restaurant.

'You have that effect on me, Beth. I'm so besotted by you, I end up repeating myself like a parrot.'

'You! A parrot! Never,' she exclaimed. 'A hawk, now… That I could believe,' she teased, while hugging his words to her heart.

'Parrot, hawk—whatever. But this bird has to fly away tomorrow.'

'You're leaving?' Beth could not hide her consternation. 'But when? Why?'

'As it happens, I have promised my sister I will attend her birthday party in Italy tomorrow night. But, that aside, I have to be in New York on Monday. I do have a business to run, Beth. Usually I only visit London once or twice a year at most. Surely you must have realised I cannot stay here indefinitely.'

The more he talked, the more her heart sank. So much for her fairy tale romance. Dex was leaving. Withdrawing her hand from his, she picked up her coffee cup and drained it, then replacing it carefully on the table, she looked back at him.

'Yes, of course. I mean, who would want to spend their life living in one of the best hotels in London?' She tried to joke but her voice shook, and it took an almighty effort of will simply to hold his gaze. But Dex saw through her charade immediately.

'It is not the end of our relationship, Beth. In fact, it could be the beginning.' Grasping her hand once more, his eyes narrowed intently on her face. 'You can meet me in New York. I will arrange it, and I promise you will have a great time.'

Beth's heart lurched in her breast. The desire flaring in his eyes was a potent reminder of how it could be between them. If she let it... But common sense prevailed. How could she take off around the world with Dex? Just like that? There was her work, her friends, her apartment. And what exactly was Dex offering? She noted he had not asked her to his sister's birthday party; he was not about to introduce her to his family.

Obviously a brief fling at best was all he had in mind.

'No, sorry. I have to be at work on Monday,' she managed to say prosaically.

'Of course, foolish of me to ask.' Dropping her hand, he signalled for the waiter and ordered a brandy.

The boat docked some five minutes later; the diners were allowed to linger, but Dex suddenly seemed in a hurry to leave. He paid the bill, and, slipping the coat he had given her over her shoulders, urged her back on shore. The walk to the car and the drive back to her apartment were completed in silence.

Beth cast a few sidelong glances at her companion, but he appeared deep in thought and disturbingly remote. Had she blown her chances by refusing to go away with him? The thought hurt, but her sensible side told her it would hurt a whole lot more if she gave in to his demands and had a brief, lustful affair.

Finally, when Dex stopped the car outside her apartment, he turned in his seat and spoke. 'Would a ring make a difference, Beth?'

She shot him a startled glance, not sure she had heard correctly. 'A ring?' she queried. His features were shadowed in the dim light and she could not read his expression. But his husky chuckle was all too audible.

'Why the surprise, Beth? After last Sunday, I should have realised it is the obvious solution. I want you in my bed and in my life.'

God alone knew that was where Beth wanted to be, but she couldn't hide her amazement. Wide-eyed, she stared at Dex. Was he actually proposing?

'You mean an engagement ring?' She couldn't believe her ears.

'Of course. And, sliding his hand into the inside pocket of his jacket, he produced a small velvet ring box. 'I hope you like it, Beth, darling.'

She stared transfixed at the diamond solitaire ring nestling in the open box. 'You mean it? You really mean it?' It was all her wildest dreams come true. She turned moist luminous green eyes up to Dex, emotion overcoming her.

'You love me, you want to marry me,' she said, in a voice that shook with the enormity of the occasion.

'Of course.' And, lifting her left hand to his lips, he sucked gently on the third finger of her hand.

His lips felt like a ring of fire, and a million sensations flooded through Beth's slender frame.

Dex's silver eyes smiled into hers, and gently he slipped the diamond ring onto her wet finger. Then, folding her fingers in his huge hand, he murmured huskily, 'Consider yourself engaged, hmm?'

'Engaged?' Beth repeated.

'Heaven forbid. You have caught my parrot syndrome.' Dex chuckled again, a dark melodious sound, and with consummate ease slid her into his arms, kissing her with a thoroughness that left her a long time later staring bemused and breathless up into his darkly handsome face.

'Now that is settled, do I finally get to see your bedroom?' he demanded throatily. 'Say yes. You know you want to.'

'But it's so sudden, and I still can't go to New York,' Beth mumbled stupidly, so bowled over by the ring, his proposal, his kisses—simply by the man. She couldn't think clearly. 'I have to be at work on Monday.'

His eyes narrowed, moving slowly over her, and his mouth twisted. 'You're right, as usual,' he agreed. 'I did promise not to rush you.'

She shook her head 'Oh, no, Dex.' She lifted her hand to his face, her finger tracing the firm line of his mouth. 'I didn't mean...'

'Hush, Beth, you're tired and I am an insensitive fool.' And, opening the car door, Dex slid out, came around to the passenger's side and helped Beth out. He picked her up and carried her in his arms into her apartment building. He set her on her feet at the door of her apartment and kissed her once more, before taking the key from her purse and opening it.

With a large hand on her back, he urged her inside. 'The bedroom can wait, but remember you are mine. I will be back on Friday. Be good.' Then he was gone.

Beth was left standing looking at the closed door, her head spinning and her heart pounding. She was engaged.

Dex loved her. They were going to be married. She stumbled across the room and sank down on the only armchair. She twisted the ring around on her finger, watching the dancing lights in the heart of the diamond, studying it from every angle. It was a token of his love and commitment. A soft sigh parted her love-swollen lips. She had foolishly let Dex leave, thinking she was still not ready to share the ultimate act of love, when in reality her whole being was crying out for his possession.

Later, as she climbed into her lonely bed, she licked her lips, savouring the taste of his kisses. Dex loved her, and on Friday she vowed she would show him just exactly how much she loved him...

CHAPTER FOUR

BETH yawned widely and snuggled deeper into the soft bed. Dex was right. She was tired. But a tiny disquieting thought hovered on the edge of her mind. For a newly engaged man Dex had shown marked restraint! Friday could not come quick enough, was her last thought before sleep claimed her.

She woke up the next morning to the ringing of the telephone.

'Sorry to wake you, Beth.' Dex's deep, sexy voice brought a dreamy smile to her sleep-flushed face.

'Any time,' she murmured.

'I'm at the airport and I couldn't leave without hearing the sound of your voice. How is my fiancée this morning?'

'Wishing you hadn't left last night,' Beth said boldly, his 'my fiancée' giving her the confidence to reveal her innermost thoughts.

'Now you tell me,' Dex groaned. 'And I'm leaving in a few minutes. Hold that thought until next weekend. *Ciao.*'

On Monday morning Beth glowed with happiness as she walked into the office. Everything looked different; she was an engaged lady, she thought, and, bubbling over with the joy of life and her marvellous love, she proudly displayed the diamond ring on her finger.

Within minutes, everyone in the firm knew; the female

employees oohed and ahhed over the ring, and asked a million questions, until Beth's head was buzzing.

Linking arms with her friend, Mary, she stepped out into the pale autumn sunshine and the two girls headed for the local delicatessen-cum-diner, where they usually ate lunch.

'Come on, Beth. Who exactly is he? What does he do? I want the whole story from the beginning.' Mary was a couple of years older than Beth, tall and slim, with cropped fair hair and blue eyes that saw far too much. 'Are you going to stay at work when you marry, and when is the wedding?'

The last question gave Beth pause for thought. She had not heard from Dex since his brief call on Saturday morning. They had never discussed a wedding date, or her work, and suddenly she was prey to all sorts of doubts. When she thought about it, Dex's proposal in the car had not been particularly romantic. In fact, she could not remember his exact words, except, 'Of course'.

For some reason she did not understand herself, Beth answered all Mary's questions very circumspectly. She simply said his name was Dex, and that they had met through mutual friends. But she had fallen in love with him at first sight.

Mary was genuinely happy for her. 'All right, I'm convinced you love him. But marriage, Beth. Isn't it a bit quick? Whirlwind romances can be notoriously fragile.'

Beset by a host of conflicting emotions, by the time Beth got back home on Monday evening she was thoroughly despondent. After all, she hardly knew Dex. A few days was not a very long time in which to decide to spend one's life with a man, as Mary had reminded her as they'd left the office together.

But Dex's telephone call from America, half an hour after she got home, cured her blues in seconds. He was coming back early. His plane would arrive on Wednesday, at noon.

'That's marvellous news. I've missed you,' Beth said happily.

'Yes, well, I've missed you,' he returned flatly, without much enthusiasm. But as he continued Beth realised why.

Unfortunately, Dex explained, the purchase of the casino had not gone as smoothly as he had thought. The casino director, a married man in his fifties, had apparently been having an affair with his very clever young secretary, a devious young woman chasing after a much older man.

The thought crossed Beth's mind that Dex really had a thing about women who dated older men, but she didn't get a chance to speak as Dex continued.

Apparently, completely against company policy, the director had entrusted the girl with the combination of the safe. The secretary had not turned up today. When the director had made enquiries at her home he had discovered she had vanished at the weekend, and a great deal of money from the casino had gone with her. The police had been informed and the girl would not get away with it.

'I'm sorry you're having problems, Dex.' Beth finally managed to get a word in, and she was almost sorry for the thief. Dex would be an implacable enemy. Dismissing the thought, she added, 'But I'm glad you're coming back.'

'No, Beth, I'm sorry for boring you with business, but

don't worry, I'll have everything sorted out within a few hours of arriving in England.' His voice deepening throatily, he added, 'I'll call at your apartment no later than four. Be ready and waiting; we'll have an early dinner, and a long, long night together, hmm?'

Beth was glad he couldn't see her blush, but, at her mumbled assent, his sexy chuckle told her he knew exactly how she was feeling.

She looked around the small living room for the umpteenth time; not a thing was out of place. She had taken the day off work to prepare for Dex's arrival and the apartment was immaculate. The fridge was stocked with a selection of goodies, plus a bottle of champagne, she had washed and pampered her slim body with essential oils, her hair was styled in a mass of curls on the top of her head, and her make-up was as perfect as she could make it. There was nothing more to do but wait.

Glancing at her wristwatch, she sighed. It was no good; it was already five-thirty, and if she sat around her apartment another minute she would go mad. Without giving herself time to question if her action was advisable, Beth grabbed her purse, slipped on a tailored red wool jacket, the companion to her short straight skirt, cast one last look around her immaculate home and walked out of the door.

Signalling a cab, she climbed into the back and gave the address of the Seymour Club. She could hang about no longer. Dex had told her to wait for him but he obviously hadn't expected to be so long at the club, so why not give him a surprise and meet him there...?

She walked into the foyer and headed for the gaming rooms, then Mr Black appeared.

'You are a member, madam?' Not a flicker of recognition crossed his swarthy face.

Not an auspicious start, Beth thought, and for a moment she was hit by a sudden attack of nerves. She hesitated, then, remembering she was the fiancée of the owner, she said boldly, 'Mr Giordanni is expecting me, I am his fiancée.' Waving her engagement ring in front of his face, she added, 'If you remember, we met last week.' She was relieved to see the glimmer of a smile in the man's hard face.

'But, of course, Bethany Lawrence. Forgive me. Mr Giordanni is in the office. You know the way.'

'Thank you,' Beth said with a broad grin. Dex was here and in moments she would see him.

She pushed open the door of the outer office and walked in. Standing by the desk was a rather flustered-looking middle-aged woman, talking to someone on the telephone.

'I'm sorry, sir, but as a temporary worker I don't do overtime. I finish at six and I'm leaving now.'

As Beth watched, the woman's face turned scarlet.

'Don't worry, I won't be!' the woman yelled, and slammed down the phone. Catching sight of Beth, she said angrily, 'If you have come to see Mr Giordanni, he's in there.' She indicated the door with a wildly waving hand. 'With some other chauvinist pig like himself from America. Please yourself if you want to wait, but I'm out of here and I won't be back. The man is a tyrant.' Picking up her purse, she pressed a button on the telephone communication console and left.

Another bad omen, Beth thought glumly, as the other woman slammed the door behind her. So, now what? She eyed the closed door of the inner sanctum, and some of her courage deserted her. Dex was in, but apparently he had company. Should she just barge in, or wait?

She walked to the desk and sat down in the functional swivel seat. Perhaps if she rang through and told Dex she was here... She eyed the machine in front of her, not quite sure how the thing worked, then tentatively picked up the receiver and pressed a button. To her horror a voice spoke—not over the telephone, but from the intercom...

'As you've terrified the secretary into leaving, there's nothing more to do here. These notes will have to wait until the morning. So how about you and I have a night on the town.'

Beth, not recognising the voice, replaced the telephone receiver, but the speaker continued.

'Remember those two models last time? I have Deirdre's phone number. What do you say?'

Beth stared aghast at the buttons in front of her. Which one switched the damn thing off? She didn't like the way the conversation was going, and she wished she didn't have to listen to it.

'Sorry, Bob, but unfortunately I have a prior engagement.'

At the sound of Dex's voice Beth's heart jumped, though his 'unfortunately' was not what she wanted to hear. But what followed was even worse.

'Some other time, maybe. But we can have a drink together before I leave. This particular girl won't mind waiting.'

Beth's hand fell from the machine. She no longer had any wish to switch the thing off. There was something about Dexter's tone of voice, his confident assumption that she would wait for him when, by her reckoning, he was already two hours late, that made her back stiffen with outraged pride. It might be true, but he didn't have to tell his friend.

'Easy, is she?'

'Surprisingly, no. Beth is amazingly resistant to my charms, and clever with it,' Dexter said with a wry laugh. 'Which is one of the reasons I got engaged to her last week.'

The 'clever' part she didn't like. But Dex was defending her, and now he would tell his friend the other reason for their engagement was that he loved her, Beth thought, relaxing slightly. But she could not have been more wrong...

'My God, I don't believe it; one of the world's best-known misogynists and you're engaged to be married. Did you actually buy the woman a ring?'

'Yes, yes, I did.'

Dex sounded oddly defensive to Beth's ears, but at least he had confirmed they were engaged. The bark of laughter from the other man did nothing to reassure her.

'But I thought after the games your ex-wife, Caroline, played on you, the money she grabbed, you vowed never to marry again.'

Ex-wife... The words rang in Beth's head. Dex had never once mentioned he had been married before. Her lovely face went pale, and she pushed the chair back—she really must make her presence known. Eavesdropping on a private conversation was despicable, and it was not like her at all—even if it had been an accident. But she froze at Dex's next words.

'Who said anything about marriage? It might never come to that. Suffice it to say, the girl was going out with Paul Morris and I saw a chance to put a stop to that, and took it.'

'Ah, now I see. Your sister Anna is still nuts about Morris, is she?'

'Yes. Personally I can't fathom what she sees in the man, but she wants him, and you know me—I'll do anything to make sure Anna gets what she wants. Apparently, after a year together, Morris decided he was too old for Anna and told her she deserved someone younger, someone who could give her the family she craves... Which is ironic under the circumstances. But, anyway, they had an almighty row and he left Italy and returned to England.

'When I came over here on business last month, Anna came with me. She was determined to make it up with Morris. Unbeknown to me, she called his apartment and found out from his housekeeper where he was dining one night. Of course Anna persuaded me to take her out to dinner at the same restaurant. I never did get to eat that night. As soon as we arrived, Anna espied Morris with another woman, a younger woman than her. Knowing Anna's temper, you can guess what happened next. My first thought was to go after Morris, but Anna made me promise I wouldn't interfere, not so much as speak to the man.'

Beth's stomach churned. She felt sick; she had to get out. But she could not make herself move; the masculine-voiced conversation held her in masochistic fascination.

'So, how did you meet the girl if she was with Morris?' Bob asked.

'Pure coincidence—fate, if you like. You know Brice—we've done business with him before—he's after a new contract. A week or so after the restaurant fiasco, I had a meeting with him the same day his firm was throwing a party. A young couple arrived and did an impromptu dance—not very well, I might add—and the girl ended up flat on the floor.'

Beth heard the chuckles and the clink of glasses. They were drinking and laughing at her. What more evidence did she need of her own stupidity?

'At first I thought, Idiots! But when the girl gazed up at me, with great big green soulful eyes, I recognised her as Morris's dinner date. Beth is not the type I usually go for. She's young, and quite small, but there's something about her. I could see why Morris fancied her. And it gave me the perfect opportunity to help Anna without breaking my promise to her. The rest, as they say, is history. I decided to take her from Morris and give Anna a chance to get him back. It wasn't difficult; I let her know I was disgustingly rich, and, like all women, she was hooked.'

'But why on earth would you consider another gold-digger after Caroline? And, more importantly, why get engaged to the girl if you have no intention of marrying her?'

'I never actually said that, Bob. After all, I'm not getting any younger, and I would like a son and heir. I think Beth is young enough, and eager enough, to become quite an obedient wife.'

Beth had heard enough. More than enough. She stood up and swayed slightly. She put her hand down on the communication console to steady herself and ironically succeeded in doing what she should have done in the beginning: the voices stopped.

She closed her eyes, fighting back the tears. So, she was 'young enough, and eager enough, to be an obedient wife'. Now she knew what Dex really thought of her. A travesty of a smile contorted her lovely face. And it certainly had nothing to do with love! He had taken her out to stop her dating Paul Morris. But why? Why lie? Why go to such an extent for his sister?

She glanced down at her hand, still on the console. The diamond ring on her finger winked back. A token of love and commitment, she had thought; straightening, she wrenched the ring off her finger and stuffed it in her purse—she couldn't bear to look at it.

She needed to think, but not here, not now. Later she would feel the pain, the heartache, but her first priority was to get away without meeting Dex.

Silently she walked across the room, and, grasping the door handle, she hesitated and looked around the office. Streamlined, high-tech functional—a suitably sterile environment in which to lose one's dreams, her artistic mind thought bitterly. Opening the door, she left.

She ran down the stairs, oblivious to the casino's customers and out on to the street without being challenged. When she finally stopped running she collapsed against the railings of a smart townhouse, and with her arms wrapped around her waist she doubled over in pain.

'Are you all right, miss?' A voice broke into her anguished thoughts, and she looked up into the concerned face of a policeman.

'Yes, yes, I'm fine.' She forced herself to straighten up, and glanced around. A bus stop caught her eye.

'Are you sure?'

'Just out of breath. I was running for a bus,' she lied. But the policeman seemed to accept her statement.

Which was why, five minutes later, she was actually seated on a bus, staring vacantly out of the window as it chugged very slowly through the rush hour traffic. She had no idea where it was going and didn't care; she had simply shown the bus pass she used for work to the conductor and he had accepted it.

Wearily she laid her head against the window, the enormity of what had happened finally hitting her. Her so-called fiancé, the man of her dreams, didn't even like her, let alone love her. With her new-found knowledge of his real reason for taking her out, suddenly a lot of little things Dex had said and done made sense.

On their first date he had insisted on telling her how wealthy he was, something she had found uncomfortable. Now she knew why: he considered her, and apparently every other woman in the world, a gold-digger. Their first passionate kiss at the casino had simply been Dex's reaction to her talking to Paul Morris. Dex had been staking his claim, nothing more. His cynical comments about young women with old men suddenly made perfect sense. They had all been directed at Beth personally; it was how Dex actually saw her. She recalled the picnic, when he had said she was just like...and had stopped; he hadn't been comparing her to his sister, but to his ex-wife and the games she'd played.

He obviously considered his precious sister perfect. He would do anything for the woman—even get engaged to a girl he cared nothing about if he thought it would help his sister get her man.

Engaged. That was a laugh! The cost of a ring was nothing to a man of Dex's wealth. Mary had been right to warn Beth. Dex really was a bastard in every sense of the word. And Beth, fool that she was, had spent all day anticipating falling into his arms and into his bed tonight.

The tragedy of it all, Beth thought with a bone-deep anguish, was that it had all been so unnecessary. If Dex had just once been honest, had asked her a simple question, she would not now be sitting on a bus with a black void where her heart used to be... She could see it all so clearly now, could pinpoint the exact two days, when the farce that had led her to this point had begun. Gazing with sightless eyes at the darkness beyond the bus window, she relived the whole episode in her mind...

Beth looked around her with delight, then sent a beaming smile to her dinner companion. 'Paul, this is fabulous! I can't thank you enough.' Her green eyes sparkled in the small oval of her lovely face. 'Dining on Park Lane makes me feel quite deliciously decadent.'

'Unlike your mother, Beth, you couldn't be decadent if you tried.' Her strikingly handsome silver-haired companion responded with an indulgent smile.

He was so right, Beth mused. Her mother had married for the fifth time the year Beth turned eighteen. Beth hadn't seen her since, but she didn't care. She had long since given up any hope of a mother-daughter relationship.

But Paul Morris had been the one constant adult throughout her twenty-one years. He had been a friend of her father, and was her godfather. He had managed the small trust fund her father had settled on her for her education, and had supported her ambition to become a graphic artist, encouraging her to go to the local college in Torquay.

She'd quickly discovered, after graduating last July, that the scope for a budding graphic artist in her home county of Devon was limited. But Paul had stepped in and used his not inconsiderable clout to find her a job in the London advertising firm his own company used. He'd also helped her find a small apartment to rent in Docklands. She had been in London for over two months, and was so far loving every minute of it—and dining at one of the poshest restaurants in the city certainly helped!

Grinning back, she dismissed her musing and said jokingly, 'Oh, I don't know.' Eyeing the plate of exquisitely arranged noisettes of lamb, with accompanying vegetables, that the waiter was placing in front of her, she continued, 'I think I could very easily get used to this lifestyle.'

Paul raised his glass and Beth reciprocated. 'To you, Beth, and your future success as the greatest graphic artist ever. I might have pulled a few strings to get you in to Canary Characters, but according to Cecil, the art director, you're a natural—and nice with it. Which I always knew, anyway,'' he said with great satisfaction.

He was the father she had never really known, and probably the kindest person she had ever met. Emotion clogged her throat but, swallowing hard, she replied, 'To you, Paul; your help and understanding over the years have made me what I am today.'

They both sipped their champagne, a look of pure love and understanding passing between them. Then, all hell broke loose...

Out of the corner of her eye Beth saw a very attractive dark-haired woman approach the table. To her amazement, the woman picked up Paul's dinner plate and tipped his meal over his head.

'You bastard! You said *I* was too young...' With a vitriolic look in Beth's direction, the woman changed from English into a language that Beth recognised as Italian but which she did not understand—and that was maybe just as well, as she doubted the woman's words were complimentary.

Eyes like saucers, open-mouthed, Beth stared at Paul. Mint sauce was trickling down his forehead, a lamb noi-

sette sat on his head, another on his shoulder, the rest
of his food—small new potatoes and assorted vegetables—lay all over the table and in his lap. Stunned, she
looked down at the glass still in her hand and eyed the
single petit pois floating in it. Replacing the glass on the
table, she carefully picked the tiny pea out of her champagne.

She had read books where the hero got spaghetti
tipped over him by some irate woman, but somehow
lamb and potatoes did not have the same effect, Beth
thought inconsequentially, glancing back at Paul. He had
risen to his feet and was saying something low and hard
to the woman that obviously did not please her, if the
fury in her dark eyes was anything to go by.

Suddenly a man appeared and encircled the lady's
waist with a strong arm. He was tall, about six-two, and
built like a barn door—or a double door, Beth amended
in her mind. She couldn't see the man's face, only his
very broad back, black hair and long, long legs, but it
was enough to send a shiver of fear down her spine. She
didn't fancy Paul's chances with this burly hunk, obviously bristling with male aggression.

But she need not have worried. In a matter of seconds
the stranger was ushering the woman straight on, and
out of the restaurant.

Her face reflecting her astonishment, Beth glanced up
at Paul, and he, with the sophistication of the true gentleman, first asked Beth if she was all right and apologised
for the interruption, then calmly instructed the
maître d' to have the table reset and their order replaced.

Beth grabbed Paul's sleeve. 'Surely you don't want to
stay here now?' she whispered urgently, suddenly aware
of the amused looks of the rest of the diners, and blushing scarlet with embarrassment.

'Beth, darling,' he soothed, removing her hand from his sleeve and nonchalantly brushing himself down with his napkin before resuming his seat, 'remember the stiff upper lip and all that. The mark of a true Englishman is to remain cool, whatever the circumstances. Besides which, I'm hungry, and I have no intention of forgoing my meal for some over-excitable Latin female.'

'But who was she? And why did she—?'

Paul held up a hand. 'Forget her, Beth. I already have.'

'But she was furious...'

'I know—her type always are. I think it's one of nature's little tricks on the male of the species. While one prefers a fiery, passionate woman in bed, one avoids them like the plague out of it. Which is probably why I have never married,'

'You're incredible.' Beth grinned, with a rueful shake of her long auburn hair, the humour of the situation finally getting through to her. 'And you have sauce on your brow and cheek.'

Paul allowed the slightest trace of a smile to lighten his face before saying, 'Then will you excuse me a moment while I slip to the restroom?'

Of course Beth did, and when he returned, and their dinner was once again set before them, Beth said admiringly, 'You really are amazing, Paul. So suave. Most men would have died of embarrassment and rushed out of the restaurant after such an outrageous scene.'

'Put it down to years at prep school and Eton, and forget about it, Beth, darling. Enjoy your food before it gets cold.' Amazingly she did...

By the time Paul stopped his sleek black car outside the entrance to her apartment they were both in fits of laughter over the whole unfortunate episode. But later, curled up in bed, for an instant Beth wondered just exactly what kind of relationship Paul had with the unfortunate woman, and for a second felt a fleeting compassion for the lady.

Although Paul was like a father figure to her, she was woman enough to realise that he was a very attractive man. Tall, elegant and wealthy, he had inherited an estate in Devon and a vineyard in southern Italy from his parents, plus he didn't look his fifty-three years. In fact he was a very eligible bachelor, dividing his time between his two estates throughout the year, with frequent visits to his penthouse in London, behaving as a typical man about town. Perhaps he had been playing around with the woman... But, then again, she thought, just before sleep claimed her, the woman hadn't been alone at the restaurant. Beth had only seen the rear of her companion, but he had been quite a man...

At six o'clock the next afternoon, as Beth walked out of the elevator on the ground floor of the office block that housed Canary Characters, she looked up to see Paul walking in the door. They looked at each other and grinned.

'I won't mention last night if you don't,' Beth offered.

'That's what I love about you, Bethany Lawrence,' said Paul, giving her her full name. 'You have your mother's looks, but you definitely have your father's nature. Such a sensible girl. Now, how about coming out for an early dinner with me tonight? This time I can assure you it will be a totally uneventful evening.'

Of course she agreed, and after a quiet meal in a small bistro, Paul again drove her home.

Standing on the doorstep at the entrance to her apartment block, Beth turned to Paul. 'Would you like to come up for a coffee, or do you have a more pressing date?' she teased; it was only ten in the evening, and she knew his passion for the casinos when he was in town.

'For a young girl you are far too cynical and know me far too well.' Reaching out his hand, he stroked her cheek with the back of his knuckles. 'You're right, the tables await, and, as I intend spending the next few months stuck in the middle of the Italian countryside, I'd better be off. Look after yourself, and be good. You know how to get in touch if you need me.'

'Yes, and thank you again for everything, Paul.' Flinging her arms around him, she gave him a hug and pressed a soft kiss to his smooth cheek. 'And you be good as well.' Stepping back, she grinned. 'If you can, you old reprobate.' And with a last flashing smile she hurried inside.

Striding across the lobby with a spring in her step, Beth wondered when she would see Paul again. Sometimes there were months between their meetings, and, although she knew he was always there for her on the end of the telephone, she missed his company. But then he had his own life to lead, and she had hers. Her new job was going well; she had made friends with Mary, a new trainee like herself, and they often went for a meal or to the cinema, or simply gossiped over a drink. Life looked good... What more could a girl want?

Now Beth knew, and the knowledge caused her unimaginable pain. She had wanted Dex to love her, to marry her, but it had all been a game to him. Dex had taken her out to make sure she stayed away from Paul. That Dex actually thought she was the type of young girl who would date a man in his fifties simply because he was wealthy said it all. Dex had no respect for Beth as a person; he probably had no respect for any woman except his sister.

Thinking of Paul, and his comment about a stiff upper lip, she refused to cry, and swiftly brushed the tears from her eyes. Her full lips twisted in a bitter smile; coincidentally it was exactly three weeks tonight since her eventful dinner with Paul, and exactly thirteen days since she had fist met Dex. Unlucky thirteen was certainly true in her case...

'Hey, miss. Do you know where you're going?' The conductor's question broke into her bitter reverie.

'Sorry, where are we now?' she asked, stumbling to her feet.

'Corner of Leceister Square.'

'That's fine, thank you,' she murmured, brushing past him and stepping off the bus.

Beth looked around at the hordes of people, the flashing neon signs, and had never felt so alone in her life. She dearly wanted to cry, but she knew she couldn't. Not yet. She had nowhere to go except home, and if Dex wasn't waiting he would certainly call her. He was not the sort of man any woman stood up. She needed to have a plan, an excuse, some way to get rid of him without revealing what she knew. Pride alone would not let her behave any other way, and her pride was all she had left.

CHAPTER FIVE

STEPPING out of the tube station into the cool night air, Beth stiffened her shoulders and walked the short distance to her apartment building. She looked neither right nor left, her whole attention concentrated on the plan she had formed in her mind on the journey home. Her despair, after the destruction of all her hopes and dreams, had been replaced for the moment with an ice-cold fury.

No way was she going to tell Dex that Paul was her godfather; the swine and his sister could stew in hell for all she cared! They would find out eventually, no doubt, but certainly not from her.

'Where the hell have you been?' She was suddenly stopped in her tracks by a furiously angry Dex. His large hands grabbed her by the shoulders, and for a second she feared he was going to shake the life out of her. 'I have been sitting in the car for over four hours, waiting for you and being worried sick. Black told me you called at the club.'

She looked up into his darkly attractive face. The orange light of the street lamp cast flickering shadows over his chiselled features, and for an instant she actually thought she saw a shimmer of genuine worry in his steely eyes, but she was not fooled by it.

'Yes, I did, but what are you doing here? Didn't you get my note?' she managed to ask with a quizzical arch of one delicate brow, in an acting performance that would have done credit to a Hollywood movie star...

'Note? What note? What the hell are you talking about?'

he growled. 'And why am I having this conversation in the street?'

Beth was wondering the same; if she didn't sit down she would fall down, or worse, fall into his arms. His hands kneading her shoulders were playing havoc with her nerve-endings, and even though she knew he was a manipulative devil it didn't alter the fact that he was wickedly attractive.

'For God's sake, give me your key and let's get inside. This is not how I envisaged our reunion at all. I thought I told you to wait for me.'

His comment reminded her of his arrogant assumption to his friend—'This particular girl won't mind waiting'—and that was enough to stiffen her resolve.

'If you let go of me, I will,' she snapped. His hands fell from her shoulders, and she stepped back and silently withdrew the key from her purse and handed it to him.

He glanced down into her cool face. 'You look...' He stopped, his gaze piercingly intent. 'Never mind, it'll keep.' And he urged her inside the building and into her apartment without saying another word.

Beth could feel the tension simmering in the air between them, and when Dex's arm reached across her she shrank back, afraid he was going to grab her again.

Instead, with a sardonic arch of one dark brow, he drawled, 'Excuse me—unless you prefer the dark,' and switched on the light, slamming the door behind them.

Trying to behave naturally, when Beth's basic instinct was to turn on him like a howling banshee, took every ounce of self-control she possessed, but she succeeded. She walked into the centre of the room and, taking a deep breath, slowly turned to face him.

'Coffee, tea, something stronger?' she suggested, forcing a polite smile to her stiff lips. Dex was leaning against the closed door, his dark blue suit jacket hanging open, his tie pulled loose and the top few buttons of his silk shirt unbuttoned. He looked dishevelled and absolutely furious.

'I do not want a drink.' He straightened up and moved towards her, stopping only inches away. 'I want some answers, *cara*—my sweet fiancée.' He glared down at her and there was nothing in the least sweet about his expression.

'Well, I want a drink,' she said calmly, turning towards the kitchen door. 'Take a seat. I won't be long.'

'Oh, no, you don't!' A strong masculine hand encircled her upper arm, and suddenly she was spun back round to face him.

Her green eyes clashed with his, and something sinister flickered in the depths of his grey eyes that made her shiver with alarm. 'Please, let go of me,' she told him, trying to ignore the way her heart was thudding as he stood so close to her.

'I would never intentionally hurt you, Beth,' Dex declared silkily, and with slow deliberation he released her arm and slid his hands up to her shoulders, impelling her forward. 'Never,' he reiterated throatily.

His black head bent towards her and dumbly she watched, knowing he was going to kiss her, and unable to move. Then his mouth took hers in a forceful, demanding kiss. Beth clenched her teeth against his intended invasion. A silent moan of rejection rose and died in her throat beneath the relentless pressure of his mouth. His hands slid down her back and effortlessly brought her even closer against his masculine frame. Try as she might to remain cold and unresponsive in his arms, there was nothing she could do to prevent her wayward body melting against his hard length.

A soundless gasp escaped her lips, and, taking full advantage, his tongue sought the moist interior of her mouth with a coaxing, seductive sensuality that made her mind spin. Her eyes closed as he easily overcame her futile attempt to resist, and helplessly she kissed him back.

When Dex finally released her, she swayed and almost fell, but with a husky oath he curved a long arm around her waist and firm fingers lifted her chin.

'I should have kissed you first,' he opined, with a hint of arrogance in his smile, 'instead of shouting at you. I am sure you have a simple explanation. Forgive me.'

His grey-eyed gaze had changed from menacing anger to smug complacency at her submission, Beth noted bitterly. Forgive him! She wanted to kill him, and, swiftly lowering her lashes to hide the anger and humiliation she knew he would see in their depths, she began her well-rehearsed speech.

'No, Dex, it is you who has to forgive me.' Turning her head to dislodge his fingers, she twisted out of his arm, not at all sure her trembling legs would support her. She sat down in the one comfortable chair, her head bowed, her hands curled tensely over its arms, and added, 'I left a note with your secretary at the casino, telling you I had to visit a sick friend in hospital.'

Beth had thought it out carefully. Judging by the temporary secretary's outburst in Beth's hearing, it was highly unlikely the woman would ever return to work at the Seymour, so Beth felt reasonably safe with the lie. The timing was wrong, she had left long after the secretary, but no one had seen her leave, and she was banking on the great Dexter Giordanni not bothering to enquire. Why should he? He didn't give a damn about her.

For a long moment there was silence, and Beth could sense the force of his gaze upon her downbent head. It took all her self-control to lift her head and look at him.

'I didn't receive a note, but then I didn't see the secretary leave,' he said, his puzzled gaze holding hers.

'There you are, then…a simple mistake. Let's forget it.' And in an abrupt change of subject she went on, 'So tell me, did your sister have a nice birthday party? You never said.' Beth couldn't resist asking, hoping just once to dent his insufferable self-assurance. Cynically she watched as his grey gaze roamed over her and rested where her hands lay curled on the edges of the armchair.

'Yes, I don't see her very often, so it was a nice change.' He frowned and continued, 'A pity you could not come with me.'

Liar, she thought scathingly. He had never asked her. Probably too worried that Paul Morris would be there, and Beth would spoil his sister's chance with the man. His careful avoidance of her gaze only reaffirmed what she already knew.

But suddenly his head jerked back and his eyes narrowed intently on her face, a flash of some unidentifiable emotion flickering in their icy depths; then they became hard and implacable, his massive body unnaturally still.

'Forget the small-talk, Beth. You haven't visited any sick friend; you're lying, and I want the truth,' he warned inflexibly. 'And it had better be good. I am not known for my patience, and you are testing it to the limit.'

The temptation to tell him precisely what he could do with himself and his patience was almost impossible to ignore. But pride and common sense raised their logical heads just in time.

'Yes, I did. Mary from work,' she responded flatly, lying through her teeth and praying Mary would forgive her. 'Appendicitis,' she tacked on for good measure.

'Really?' Dex drawled, his tone telling her he didn't believe a word she said. 'Nice outfit. Chanel, isn't it? It suits you. Your friend must have been flattered.'

'Yes,' Beth said shortly, cursing her own foolishness yesterday, which had seen her spending her lunchbreak shopping in the designer section of London's most stylish fashion store. She had spent all her savings, and her next month's salary, on the elegant red suit and complementary camisole, plus ruinously expensive undergarments, all for Dexter's benefit.

'Surely a bit over the top for visiting a sick friend,' Dex commented derisively. 'Nor, to my knowledge, do hospitals extend their visiting hours until this time of night. What kind of fool do you take me for?'

She glanced up. His tanned, perfectly carved features were set in a cold mask, only the nerve twitching in the side of his face revealing his inner tension.

'I don't know what you mean,' she mumbled. Her courage had deserted her, and she couldn't control the nervous leaping of her pulse, or the shiver of fear that trickled down her spine as her eyes met his.

Suddenly, like a dam bursting, *'Basta!'* Dex roared. 'Enough of your lies!' His hands crashed down on her shoulders, the long fingers biting into her skin as he hauled her to her feet, fury evident in every line of his hard body.

'Now,' he snarled, 'you are going to tell me the truth.' His long fingers fell to her jacket and flicked it open, revealing the lace edged body-hugging camisole and the obvious absence of a bra.

She flushed scarlet. 'What do you think you're doing?' she snapped, but Dex ignored her, and in one lithe movement he slipped the jacket from her shoulders to drop it carelessly on the floor.

His glittering eyes raked over her, from her flushed face, then lower, to the soft fullness of her breasts. To her horror, she felt her nipples harden beneath his studied appraisal. With chilling slowness his glance lingered on her chest, her throat, and finally back on her face. He smiled and her blood ran cold.

'Very nice, but you are not the type to dress so for another woman.' His hand snaked around her slender wrist and hauled her hand up between their two bodies, holding it pressed tight against her breastbone.

'And I seem to remember giving you a diamond ring, *cara mia*. Lost it, have you?' His mouth twisted in a chilling, cynical smile. 'Or found someone wealthier? Someone who excites you more?'

Beth swallowed hard, remembering some of their more intimate moments together, and glanced bitterly up at him. Surely he knew? He was the only man who had ever aroused her to any great degree. How dared he insinuate she was a money-grubbing, flighty girl—she who had never known a man? For a moment Beth was too angry with him to form a reply. When she did open her mouth to speak, she discovered she had waited too long.

'Your silence is answer enough. Are you going to tell me who he is?' he demanded in a threatening voice. 'Or do I have to get it out of you?'

His other hand tightened imperceptibly in her hair, and she moved her head back and stared at him. But the fury in his eyes, she realised, was more bruised ego than

any genuine concern for her. He had jumped to the conclusion there was another man, whom he probably
thought was her godfather, so why not humour him?
Grasping the chance Dex had given her, she boldly held
his glittering gaze.

'All right, all right. I will tell you the truth.' She gritted her mouth tight with bitterness as she prepared to
compound her lie. To make Dex walk away from her. It
was what she wanted. But as Dex towered over her—
the heat of his body, the subtle scent of him enveloping
her—it was the hardest thing she had ever had to do in
her life.

'You're right, in a way. I'm sorry, Dex. I didn't know
how to tell you.' When it came down to it, she didn't
dare mention Paul Morris. For all she knew, Dex might
have seen him in Italy. Instead, she rattled on like a
steam train.

'I realised almost as soon as you left: you're not really
my type, we belong to two different worlds. I like living
in London, I love my work and I like going out with my
own circle of friends. Some more than others.' She
forced herself to smile into his eyes, subtly implying
there were other men in her life, without naming any
names. 'You and I had a brief fling. It was fun, but now
it's over.'

His face darkened. His mouth tightened into an angry
line and a dull flush spread over his high cheekbones.
His fingers tightened on her wrist and she lowered her
thick lashes to hide her lying eyes from his narrowed,
too intent gaze. Then suddenly she was released and fell
back into the armchair, all the breath expelled from her
lungs by the force of her fall. When she finally found
the courage to raise her head and look at Dex again, she
knew she had succeeded in her plan.

He had gone very pale. His silver eyes, burning with contemptuous fire, clashed with her wary green. He shook his dark head. 'You're just like all the rest, a lying, cheating, little bitch,' he drawled deliberately, watching her for a moment. Then, turning, he headed for the door.

How dared he call her names? How dared he pretend he was the one betrayed, when it was Beth who had been made a complete and utter fool of? He had even gone so far as to give her a ring. The ring! she thought, eyeing his broad back with impotent fury, and, grabbing her purse from the floor, she opened it. Her fingers finding the offending piece of jewellery, she stood up.

'Dex, wait!' He halted and turned. Beth stretched out her arm, 'Haven't you forgotten something?' she mocked with a cruel smile, giving him some of his own medicine. 'Your ring.'

Dex stood in the doorway, his features a hard mask of indifference. 'Keep it,' he said bitingly. 'A memento of a failed affair. Unless, of course, you want to pay for it in kind.' He smiled with a chilling twist of his hard mouth. 'Unlike the dozens before me, I still have not seen your bedroom.'

This mocking cynicism was the last straw for Beth's over-stretched nerves. Flinging the ring at him, she yelled, 'Get out. Go, go!' And the ring bounced off his cheek and fell to the floor.

His steel-grey eyes flashed with inimicable fury, and like a prowling panther he stalked back towards her. Beth knew she had gone too far. Her heart leapt in her throat as she backed warily away from him. A spot of blood stained his high cheekbone. Served him right, she told herself. Why should she have to put up with his contemptuous remarks, while Dex pretended his motives were pure as the driven snow?

'No one tells me to leave,' he stated softly, in a low tone.

'Until now,' she shot back, refusing to be intimidated but no longer feeling quite so brave as his advance had her backing closer into the hall that led to her bedroom.

'Never, ever,' he drawled quietly, and, catching her by the shoulders, he drew her close. 'And certainly not a devious little girl like you.'

Beth could not prevent the shiver that his large hands on her naked shoulder aroused, and he grinned, with a wolfish twist of his hard mouth.

'A little girl who doesn't know whether she wants to jilt me or jump me,' he mocked with biting sarcasm. 'I think we really need to know the answer, Bethany. Don't you?'

'No, no!' she cried, the implacable determination in his expression telling her exactly what he had in mind. She shuddered as his hands slid caressingly over her shoulders and closed firmly around her upper arms. She wanted to yell at him to stop, but the words stuck in her throat as, with slow deliberation, Dex lifted her up and buried his face in the valley between her breasts. He moved ever so slightly, his mouth covering the tip of her breast which was barely hidden from his view by the fine silk of the ridiculously brief camisole she was wearing.

She grasped his dark head to steady herself. 'Put me down,' she cried, her feet flailing wildly in mid-air, trying to kick him. But she was helpless against his superior height and strength, and, worse, against the exquisite sensations his warm mouth was creating as he continued to nuzzle her breasts.

'I will,' he said silkily, lowering her so they were face to face, 'as soon as I find the bedroom.'

'No!' she cried, disgusted at her own reaction.

But he carried her into the inner hall, deaf to her protest, and shouldered open the bedroom door.

'You can't do this. Put me down!'

'I can, and I will,' he grated, and suddenly Beth found herself sprawled on her back on her own bed, with all the breath knocked out of her. Stunned, she stared as, in a split second, Dex shed his jacket, tie and shrugged out of his shirt.

His muscular chest, tanned and with a light covering of black curling body hair, was a breathtaking sight. A dark line of hair arrowed tantalisingly down to his waist, where his long fingers snapped open the band of his trousers

Beth's green eyes widened to their fullest extent in a mixture of horror and fascination. Dear God, he was stripping! 'You can't do that!' He ignored her. 'Get out! I demand you leave!' He stepped out of his trousers. 'Put them on! Stop it!' she babbled, her voice shrill; he was naked except for a pair of white briefs that did little to hide his maleness. Swallowing hard, she scrambled to sit up. But she was too late.

'Oh, no!' Dex had joined her on the bed; what seemed like acres of naked chest leaned over her, and, raking his hand through her long hair, he lifted her head and his mouth covered hers.

Beth had expected harshness, but he confounded her with the soft pressure of his lips; his tongue traced the outline of her mouth while his other hand slid up over her breast and cupped its lush fullness. She groaned, and his tongue snatched the advantage to plunge between her parted lips.

It wasn't fair! she silently screamed, the echo fading in her mind as Dex continued to kiss her, his mouth exploring hers with sensual expertise. His hands began moving slowly over her breasts, slipping the thin straps of the camisole down over her slender shoulders. Her heartbeat quickened and she shook with the effort of trying to control the effect he was having.

His anger she could have resisted, but the caressing touch of his hands cupping her now naked breasts, and the feather-light brush of his fingers over the hardening peaks, sent sharp stabs of excitement shooting through her. Beth felt herself beginning to weaken. The reason for her fury with him seemed nothing in comparison to the sensual pleasure he was awakening in her.

He raised his head, his glittering eyes raking over her full breasts, their rigid nipples, and a slow, sensual smile curved his hard mouth as he deftly pushed the camisole and her skirt down over her slender hips.

'No,' she croaked, every nerve-ending in her body screaming with her effort to retain control of her drowning senses.

'Yes, Beth, yes. You want me. You know you do.' His dark head bent and his tongue licked teasingly over her breasts.

Beth groaned out loud and she arched against the hard heat of him as electric sensation spun from her breasts to her stomach. She grabbed his dark head and made a last futile attempt to push him away, then he drew one aching nipple into his mouth and she was lost. Instead of pushing him away, her fingers involuntarily tangled in the silky black hair of his head, caressing his scalp.

'That's it, Beth,' he rasped, moving slightly to give the same erotic concentration to her other breast. 'Let yourself go, sweetheart.'

Dex's strong, masculine hand traced the indentation of her waist, down over her stomach and across her thighs, taking her briefs with it. She shuddered as his long fingers stroked across her inner thigh and tangled in the dark red curls protecting the core of her femininity.

Beth's fingers clenched in his hair and then slowly they unfurled. Her slender arms moved tentatively around his broad back, her fingers tracing the line of his spine. The brush of his chest hair against her sensitised flesh was a sweet agony as his lips moved over her throat and found her parted lips once again.

His mouth closed over hers, his tongue fierce and seeking, and her response was immediate. Her body writhed helplessly beneath him; her hands slid down his back and curved around the tight male buttocks. When had he removed his briefs? She didn't know, and was past caring.

Dex nudged apart her legs and Beth shuddered, and shuddered again as his lips ground against hers in a hungry, rapacious kiss, while his fingers found those other secret lips and teased and tormented the delicate moist flesh again and again.

Never had she known such delicious sensations. His hard male body, the musky smell of sex, the tactile delight she found in touching him, and the incredible quivering in the pit of her belly. Still, a tiny lone voice of sanity told her she must say no. But, God help her, she didn't want to. Her body screamed out to know where his delicious assault would lead.

Beth looked up into his silver eyes, only inches from her own, and her heart stopped; the ferocious gleam of unbridled passion—more a glint of scarcely controlled rage—got through her drugged senses for a second, and she tensed.

Sensing her brief withdrawal, Dex growled, 'No, Beth, not now,' and deliberately rolled over between her thighs. His powerful body trapped her beneath him and his strong hand clasped her shoulders, pinning her to the bed. He reared back, his glance skimming over the length of her, her lush, full breasts. Sliding his hands from her shoulders to her chest, he rolled the turgid peaks between his fingers and thumbs. Then his hands roamed on at will over her burning flesh, the hard rigid length of his manhood pushing against her groin but no further.

Beth looked into his face, her eyes clouded with passion. She saw his sensuous lips quirk in a wickedly determined smile as he slowly lowered himself down upon her, but still he did not claim her. Instead he kissed her love-swollen lips long and hard, his hands still caressing that very secret part of her. Beth's arms curved around his back, her nails sinking into his broad shoulders in mute appeal. She wanted him now, filling her, anything to assuage the red-hot fire that burned through every vein and nerve in her trembling body.

Dex raised his head. 'Whoever you saw earlier certainly did nothing for you,' he grated, masculine triumph edging his tone. Reaching out to the bedside table, he picked up the protection he had placed there. 'I wonder how many other men have seen you like this, with your luscious body begging for them.'

She wanted to say, no one. To tell him the truth. But one hand stroked up deliberately to the engorged tip of her breast, and once more his mouth descended to it. His teeth bit gently, and she jerked helplessly; she was drowning in a sea of sensual delight and only Dex could save her. His mouth once more sought hers, his tongue thrusting, but this time his mighty body picked up the rhythm. He broke the kiss and raised his head, his grey eyes almost black with desire, fixed on her wildly flushed face.

'What do you want, Beth?' He surged against her again, his hard arousal sliding through the soft curls and between her trembling thighs, but still not giving her what her body craved.

'Say it, Beth…' A hard sheen of sweat glistened on his tanned skin. 'Say, I want you, Dex.' All the while his glittering eyes seared into hers.

Green eyes wide with wonder and want, she stared up into his face. He had betrayed her, but she loved him so much; she ached for him. Surely she deserved this one night of love. Was it so wrong? Instinctivley, she knew she would never again want a man as she did Dex. Then his hand slid between their two bodies and he touched her intimately again, parting her legs further, sending shock waves crashing though her.

'Please. I want you,' she confessed in a whisper, allowing her instincts to take over. She closed her eyes, her small hand stroking down his shoulder and over his chest, her fingers catching a male nipple, hard like a pebble and buried in lush black curling hair.

'Damn it! My name, Beth. Say my name.' His voice was a deep growl of masculine frustration.

'Dex,' she groaned, and pressed tiny hot kisses on his chest, her small hand stroking down the silky line of body hair to his flat belly.

Dex caught her hands and pulled them away from him, and, curving his large hands around her bottom, he drove into her with a fierce, thrusting, primeval power.

She felt a knife-like pain and cried out, but his mouth

covered hers and swallowed her cry with a voracious kiss. Then, for a moment, he was still.

His molten silver eyes burned into hers and he spoke in a torrent of Italian, not one word of which she understood. But the pain she had felt at his possession had subsided and her muscles tightened around him. This was no forced lovemaking. Dex was right; she had asked him to take her. Then, slowly, he withdrew.

'No, please!' He could not stop now. She moaned, and suddenly she was clinging to him as he moved in her once again, his huge body moving in a hard thrusting rhythm that sent her to the edge of some unknown cataclysmic state.

Then she was crying his name, and tipping over the edge into free-fall, her whole body shattering into a million atoms and, by some miracle, clenching over and over, and reforming again in a shattering climax. She felt Dex's great body shudder convulsively as he found his own release. He collapsed on top of her, his huge frame jerking spasmodically, the rasping note of their breathing the only sound in the stillness of the small bedroom.

Beth did not want to move ever again. Still joined to Dex, she lay and wondered at the miracle she had experienced. None of the books she had read, or any girl-talk, had prepared her for the absolute awesome glory of making love, and she did love Dex. She moved her arms around under his, stroking up his back and hugging him to her. His glorious weight, the heavy pounding of his heart—every move he made was a source of delight to her. For a long time she held him, glorying in her love, completely forgetting the reality of the situation, until suddenly Dex rolled over onto his back.

'I need the bathroom. Where is it?' he grunted.

With his familiar weight gone and his prosaic words, the cold reality of her situation hit her like a bucket of iced water.

'Mine is a tiny apartment. I'm sure a man of your intellect will find it with no trouble.'

'Sarcasm does not become you, Beth.' Dex sat up, his muscular thigh pressed lightly against her side, and her face flamed as he leant over her to drop a swift kiss on her swollen lips. 'Besides, my little innocent, these things are not reusable, and I have a feeling you and I are not finished yet.'

It was only then she realised he had used protection. Her face turned beetroot-red, as did the rest of her body, and, grabbing at the sheet, she pulled it haphazardly up over her naked body.

'Too late, Beth, I've seen it all,' Dex drawled with mocking amusement, and, completely uncaring of his nudity, he stood up.

Her fascinated gaze slid over his broad shoulders, his wide chest, still glistening with sweat, and lower, to where his manhood nestled in a dense black brush of hair, and down his long, long legs. He was a magnificent male animal, even if he did have the character of a pig. No—that was probably insulting the pig, Beth thought, but she couldn't tear her eyes away from his naked form.

'But you have a good look, Beth. To my surprise and delight, you have no experience of men at all.' And he laughed out loud as she turned even redder with embarrassment. Lowering her gaze, she burnt with anger and humiliation.

CHAPTER SIX

ANGER won.... A furious Beth picked up a pillow and threw it at Dex's retreating back, but it slid harmlessly down the door to the floor as he vanished into the tiny hall where the door to the bathroom was situated. The sound of his laughter echoing in the quiet of her room only infuriated her further.

She clenched her small hands together in impotent fury and glanced wildly around her bedroom. She looked down at her entwined hands and suddenly the enormity of what had happened hit her like a punch in the stomach. She was naked, the bed was a rumpled mess, and that hateful man was in her tiny bathroom and would be back any second.

Blind panic engulfed her. She leapt out of bed and dashed to the wardrobe, from where she dragged out a blue woollen dressing gown and scrambled into it. Tying the belt firmly around her waist, she stuck her feet into a pair of old slippers in the shape of two basset-hounds. Her eyes caught the glimpse of red on the floor, and viciously she kicked her skirt and camisole under the bed. She would never wear the outfit again, Beth vowed. Then, another emotion lending her wings, she was out of the room, across the small hall and into her living room in a trice.

She had to get rid of Dex. That was the only thought in her head as mechanically she walked into the kitchen and switched on the electric kettle. She needed a drink, a cup of coffee, to calm her shattered nerves. But she had an awful premonition that it would take a lot more than a few cups of coffee to make her forget Dex and the turbulent feelings he had awakened in her tonight.

The kettle boiled, and, opening the cupboard where she stored her crockery, Beth took down a porcelain mug and spooned a large dollop of coffee granules into it from the jar of instant coffee on the bench. She couldn't stop her hand from shaking as she added the water, spilling some on the worktop. Reaction was setting in. But she refused to give in to it and, gritting her teeth, willed her hands to stop shaking. She opened the fridge, took out the milk, poured some milk in the mug and then added two generous spoons of sugar; she needed the energy, she told herself, to face Dex.

Dex! Beth stifled a groan of pure anguish. A few hours ago she had been the happiest girl in the world, engaged to the man she loved and eagerly anticipating going to bed with him. Well, she was no longer engaged to Dex, but she had been to bed with him. And now she felt like the stupidest, dumbest girl in the world. She couldn't find words to describe her own self-loathing. Naive did not begin to cover it...

But, a wicked voice whispered in her head, she was no longer naive in some respects. She had succumbed to his lovemaking with a wild passion she had not known she was capable of. A vivid image of his huge naked body entwined with hers had Beth reaching desperately for the coffee mug.

She took a great gulp of the hot coffee. How could she face him? Before she could answer her own question, the door swung open and Dex appeared. She glanced across at him, her huge green eyes warily following him as in a few lithe strides he covered the space between them, filling her small kitchen with his towering presence. He was dressed again, after a fashion. His jacket hung open across his broad chest and the silk shirt beneath fell loosely over the outside of his trousers. He looked what he was: a man who had just slaked his sexual appetite with his lady. His black hair was a tangle of curls over his broad forehead.

Beth blinked and glanced down, but seeing her ridiculous doggy slippers did nothing for her confidence. 'Damn Dex to hell...' she muttered under her breath. He had no right to look so virile, so disgustingly smug, and what had taken him so long in the bathroom? The inconsequential thought popped in her mind.

Glancing back up, she stiffened. His slate-grey eyes sought and captured hers, and his sensuous lips parted over perfect white teeth in a knowing, roguish smile.

'I'll take a cup of coffee, Beth, as it appears, by your hasty exit from the bedroom, that nothing more is on offer.'

Beth slammed her coffee mug down on the bench, the sheer gall of the man taking her breath away. Any faint hope that had lingered in her subconscious mind that maybe she could forgive him and they could stay together vanished. What Dex had just said convinced her absolutely she was not in his league, and could never in a million years inhabit his sophisticated world. She stared at him with wide angry eyes, as though she was seeing him for the first time.

What she saw was a devastatingly attractive, one-hundred-per cent powerful male animal—'animal' being the operative word. He had the sensitivity of a rhinoceros. It didn't matter a jot to him that he had seduced her and taken her virginity. In fact, according to Dex, he could take her, or a cup of coffee...either would do!

'Beth, are you all right?'

All right! she would never be all right again, but what the hell did he care? Fury such as Beth had never known flooded her whole being.

'Fine. I'm fine,' she snapped. 'But as for you, you can get out of here now, this minute. I don't want to see your conceited, arrogant face again as long as I live.'

Dex moved closer. 'Don't,' she said, holding her hands up to ward him off. 'Don't you dare come near me. Haven't you done enough damage for one night?'

Dex's eyes burned into hers. 'You don't mean that, Beth,' he said thickly, and reached for her. 'You're upset, emotional; it affects some girls like that the first time.' His hands closed over her shoulders and he pulled her to him. 'But the next time will be better, I promise.'

Beth almost choked. 'There is not going to be a next time, you great oaf. I don't want anything to do with you. I told you that an hour ago, but did you listen? No. You forced yourself on me.'

'Forced you! You were with me all the way,' he exclaimed, catching her chin and tilting her head back. 'You were begging for it.'

'No.' She shook her head. 'You forced me into it.'

His fingers tightened on her chin, his grey eyes narrowing to angry slits on her flushed, furious face. 'Don't lie, Beth. You wanted me, you know you did, and I asked you every step of the way; you only had to say no.'

Tears stung her eyes, whether of anger or regret, she didn't know. She pushed his hand from her chin and closed her eyes for a second, breathing deeply to regain her self-control.

Beth didn't see the bitter anguish in his eyes as he looked at her downbent head and then stepped back.

She opened her eyes and raised her head. 'I tried,' she declared bluntly.

They stared at each other, the tension in the air electric. The anger in his eyes made Beth quake inwardly, but she refused to show her feelings. Then, abruptly, Dex straightened his broad shoulders; his lips narrowing in a tight line, his handsome face expressionless, he clasped her elbow in his strong hand.

'If you really think that, Beth, then we have to talk.'

'No.' She wrenched her arm free. 'I have nothing, absolutely nothing I want to say to you. Except, get out of my home and out of my life.'

Dex was silent for a long moment, watching her with narrowed eyes. 'I don't get it,' he said curtly. 'You break our engagement. Then you melt in my arms. Then you accuse me of forcing you into it and demand I leave?'

'So, go!' she cried, her throat closing up as his hard grey eyes came to rest on her swollen lips.

'Oh, no,' Dex drawled. 'Not until I have made you swallow your lies.'

Beth's eyes rounded as he suddenly drew her against him, one hand sliding around her tiny waist, the other cupping the back of her head.

'I don't lie,' she croaked, just as his mouth covered hers and his hand tightened on her waist. His thrusting tongue searched the moist cavern of her mouth with a sensual ease that overcame her pathetic attempt to resist him in an instant. Her tongue touched his and white-hot passion sent the blood pounding through her veins.

When his mouth finally lifted from hers, she moaned and stared helplessly up at him, her lips parted, red and pouting, her lower body pressing into his hard thighs with a desire she could not disguise.

Dex smiled, a devastatingly wicked twist of his mobile mouth. 'Force? I think not, my sweet Beth. You are mine for the taking,' he said in a dry voice.

Where she got the strength to push him away, she did not know. Maybe it was just one humiliation too much for her pride to take. But shove him away she did.

'So maybe "force" was too strong a word,' she said in a surprisingly calm voice, when her insides were shaking. 'But if you didn't force me, you certainly coerced me.'

'And you loved every minute. I have your claw-marks on my back to prove it,' he drawled silkily.

'Maybe so, but it was just sex, and I will probably have sex with a lot more men in the future. No big deal,' she said with a shrug of her shoulders.

She shot a quick glance at his face, and to her surprise she saw guilt and some other indefinable emotion on his harshly handsome features.

'Your prerogative, of course. You're a beautiful girl, and you obviously have a talent for sex. But—'

'Thank you,' she cut in sharply, with a voice dripping in sarcasm. He thought she had a talent for sex. Was that supposed to be a compliment? A red haze of rage blurred her vision. 'But I don't need your no doubt expert opinion. I simply need you to leave. What was it you said so crudely earlier? "I didn't know whether to jilt you or jump you." But it wasn't quite like that, was it, Mr High-and-Mighty-Giordanni? You jumped me, but I've been trying for the past two hours to jilt you, and for a sophisticated man you're being remarkably obtuse—you just will not get the message.'

'I got your message long ago, Beth. You're a gold-digging little tease.' He squared his massive shoulders, his silver eyes narrowed on her lovely face. 'Hanging on to your virginity as a bankable asset, hoping to sell yourself to the wealthiest bidder. But this time you tried it on with the wrong man.'

His last insult was too much for Beth's fragile self-control. Shaking with fury, she raised her arm and landed a cracking slap on his tanned cheek with the palm of her hand.

'Take that, you bastard, and get out,' she spat.

Dex lifted a large hand to rub the side of his face; with his other hand he clasped her wrist in an iron grip. The air crackled with undisguised animosity. She must have been insane to have ever felt she loved this man, she thought, as she furiously stared into his eyes.

'If you were a man I would kill you,' Dex offered, with a silky menace that made her blood run cold. 'But, in the circumstances, given your emotional state, I will allow you the one slap.'

Magnanimous swine... He would "allow" her... It was the final straw for Beth. Her head ached, her heart ached, her throat ached with the effort of holding back the tears. If Dex didn't leave in a minute, she would break down.

Her shoulders slumped, her head bent and she muttered desolately, 'Please get out.' Amazingly, when Beth lifted her head again, it was to see Dex walking to the front door, and with some spark of her pride rising in her exhausted brain, she yelled, 'Take your ring with you. It's around there somewhere.'

With a sense of *déjà vue* she watched as Dex once again turned around in the doorway. His eyes flicked briefly over her, his face a mask of total indifference. 'You keep it, Beth.' And with a flippant shrug of his broad shoulders, he added, 'You've earned it now.' With that parting shot, he walked out of her apartment and out of her life. Or so Beth thought...

* * *

Horrified, Beth looked at her reflection in the bathroom mirror. Oh, my God! I can't go to work looking like this. Her eyes were red-rimmed and sore, her lips still swollen from Dex's kisses. She looked an absolute mess. Hardly surprising, she thought bitterly, she hadn't slept a wink. After Dex had left, the tears she had held at bay for what had seemed like an eternity had started to fall.

Giving in to her grief, she had cried until she'd thought she had no tears left. Then she had taken a long, vigorous shower, determined to wash every trace of Dex from her flesh, and had tried to go to bed. But the sight of her rumpled bed, the scent of Dex lingering on the bed linen, had brought on a fresh bout of tears. Eventually she had curled up in her armchair and stared sightlessly into the dark living room, remembering every smile, every touch, every single second she had spent with Dex. Every lying word...

For once in her life Beth had been able to appreciate her wayward mother. If Leanora had suffered like this at every break-up, she must have the heart of a lion. Beth had never felt pain like it, had never realised mental pain could be so powerful... Her chest physically ached, her stomach churned, but, worse, her faith in herself as a woman, a valued human being, was almost destroyed. Dexter Giordanni had taken away her confidence, along with her virginity, by his deceit. She'd curled up in a small ball in the chair, hugging her knees, and wished she was dead.

The chiming of a clock in the distance had finally roused her from the well of self-pity and anguish. Six in the morning. Brushing the mass of hair from her eyes, she had got stiffly out of the chair and went to the bathroom.

Beth grimaced at her reflection once more, and headed

for the bedroom. Her heart squeezed at the sight of her bed, the covers a tangled mass, as she had left them last night. From somewhere she got the strength to rip off all the linen and shove it into the wicker basket in the bathroom. She refused to recognise the musky scent of their lovemaking, or the lingering trace of Dex's after-shave on the sheets. Five minutes later, she'd dressed in a plain black skirt and yellow sweater and was marching into the kitchen.

Hadn't she read somewhere that a slice of raw potato on one's eyes revitalised them? Quickly making a cup of coffee, she gulped it down, and then, finding a potato in the vegetable rack, she sliced it. Returning to the living room, she sank down into the armchair and plopped the two pieces of potato on her eyes. The tiniest hint of a smile twitched her full lips as she imagined what she must look like, and suddenly she realised that life must go on, and that it could be good again. She would laugh again. Maybe it would take a while—not maybe, certainly. But she was not about to let a man like Dexter Giordanni destroy her life.

Her determination was sorely tested when she walked into the building that housed the offices of Canary Characters. Every employer had to sign in as a security precaution, and as soon as Beth leaned over the reception desk to do just that, Lizzie, the receptionist, noticed Beth was not wearing her ring.

'Hi, Beth. Lost the rock already?' Lizzie asked jokingly.

Beth felt the colour rising in her face, but she forced herself to respond equally flippantly, 'The man, yes. The rock, no...'

'Oh, Beth!' Lizzie exclaimed. 'You mean, your engagement is off?'

'Yes. I'm free and single once again.' And, having signed her name, she straightened up and had to look at Lizzie, and the pity she saw in the girl's eyes made her cringe.

'Beth, I am so sorry.'

'Don't be. I'm not. I got to keep the ring—an investment for my old age.' She made herself grin before turning away, then crossed to the elevator that took her to the drawing office.

Lizzie's comment was not the first. By the end of the day, everyone from the director down knew Beth was no longer engaged. The comments varied from sympathy from most of the female members of the staff to jokes from a good proportion of the men. They ranged from 'The briefest engagement in the West', to an offer to 'ring the *Guinness Book of Records*, no pun intended, and register the shortest engagement in the world'.

Only Mary, her friend, didn't believe Beth's unconcerned attitude. Cornering her in the washroom, she asked, 'What really happened, Beth?'

Beth longed to lean on Mary's shoulder and confide the whole sordid business to her. Pride alone made her say, 'You were right, Mary. Whirlwind romances don't work. Dex and I shared a few kisses. He gave me a ring and I thought it was love. But yesterday, when I met him again after not seeing him for a few days, we both realised there was nothing there, no chemistry.'

God forgive her the lie, she thought. Remembering Dex's kisses was enough to make her ache all over.

'If you say so, but remember, if you need a shoulder to cry on, or someone to confide in, I'm here for you.'

Beth gave Mary a trembling smile. 'I know, but really, I'll be okay.'

*   *   *

Surprisingly, at the end of two weeks she almost *was* okay. Setting the small table in her kitchen for three people one evening, she actually found herself humming the latest hit tune. Mike was bringing his girlfriend, Elizabeth, over to meet Beth and have a meal, and later the three of them were going on to a Hallowe'en party. Beth was looking forward to it. Plus, she thanked her lucky stars she hadn't seen Mike since their cabaret act together, and consequently he knew nothing of her brief engagement. So there would be no awkward questions.

Her broken engagement had been barely a three-day wonder at the office. And by throwing herself into her work she'd had little time to think of Dex. Which was just as well, because she had heard not a word from the man. The ring he had given her she had found on the living room floor and stuck in the back of her dressing table drawer, unable to look at it.

It was the nights that were the problem. Alone in her apartment, her traitorous mind would relive the moments she had spent in Dex's embrace. She kept telling herself his every kiss had been a lie. But it didn't stop her body flooding with heat as she lay in her bed, remembering Dex sharing it with her.

Sleep, when it came, was restless... His face filled her dreams, and sometimes his whole body. On those nights she would wake up in the middle of the night, her body wet with sweat and aching with frustration.

But tonight, Beth promised herself, as she stood in front of the bathroom mirror, carefully applying thick black eye make-up, tonight would be different. She was going to start socialising again, having fun, even if it killed her. Knowing her stepbrother, if anyone could make her laugh, Mike could.

The doorbell rang and she hurried to answer it. Beth

opened the door and a smile of pure pleasure covered her face. Then she burst out laughing.

'Mike, that is you?' she asked, when she managed to stop chuckling. He was wearing a skeleton costume: black from neck to toe, with luminous ivory paint outlining the bone structure.

'Who else, sis? Allow me to introduce you to Elizabeth,' and Beth gasped again as Mike walked into the centre of the room with the most hideous-looking creature on his arm!

Beth immediately liked the girl. Any woman who had the nerve to meet her boyfriend's sister for the first time dressed in a witch's costume had to be a fun person.

'Delighted to meet you.' Beth grinned, and was struck by the laughing blue eyes that smiled back at her—even if they were set in a face that sported a huge crooked false nose, a mouth with half the teeth blacked out and a large wart on the chin.

'Hello, Beth, and let me say straight off this was Mike's idea.' The girl's eyes turned to Mike, and they smiled at each other.

The look of pure togetherness that passed between the couple made Beth's heart ache, and it hurt even more when Mike caught the girl's hand and held it out for Beth to admire.

'You're the first to know, Beth. Elizabeth and I got engaged last night.'

The ring was beautiful, a brilliant blue sapphire surrounded by diamonds, and Beth congratulated them both, brushing away a tear as she did so.

'And that's not all, Beth.' I was promoted on Monday to sales director, at almost double my present salary.'

'Ah, so I get back all the money I've lent you over the years,' Beth teased.

'Hey, hang on, sis! I haven't got the money yet, but my credit rating has soared.'

Elizabeth shook her head and gave Beth a wry smile, and they both burst out laughing.

The tone for the evening was set; amidst much laughter, the three of them ate the meal Beth had prepared of spaghetti *al guanciale* and crusty garlic bread. The party they were going to didn't start until ten, and as they were taking a taxi, the champagne Mike had brought with him was was soon finished, along with the bottle Beth had originally bought to share with Dex. With the bottle empty, Beth thought whimsically, she had finally closed the lid on the Dex episode.

Mike insisted on opening another bottle of wine, but Beth had had enough and made coffee, then served it in the living room.

Elizabeth and Mike shared her only armchair, and Beth curled up on a large red bean bag.

'So, Beth, you've heard all my news. How's life treating you?' Mike suddenly asked, and, not waiting for her reply, he grinned and added, 'You actually *look* like a cat curled up on that cushion. But don't you think it's time you bought some more furniture?'

Beth meowed very convincingly. 'My whiskers are in the bathroom.' Her cat costume consisted of a black bodysuit with a long tail, and a hood with two ears attached to cover her hair. 'I'll go and stick them on now,' she said, ignoring his questions and leaping to her feet. Beth knew Mike, and she knew before long he would get back to quizzing her about her private life, and she wasn't sure she could handle it.

Ten minutes later, Beth pranced back into the living room and did a pirouette. 'So, am I a cat? Or what?' she said with a smile. With the hood covering her bright hair, and long whiskers glued to her top lip, she looked every inch the black cat of myth.

'Cat? No.'

'No?' Beth looked at Mike, her smile vanishing. 'I thought the costume was good.'

'Kitten, maybe. You're so tiny,' Mike mocked, knowing just how to rile her.

'Fiend!' Beth cried, and made a leap for him, her hands outstretched like claws.

Elizabeth slid off the arm of the chair as Beth set about tickling Mike. She knew it was his pet hate, as her lack of height was hers, and in the ensuing uproar she didn't hear the intercom.

It was Elizabeth's voice that finally registered.

'I've told him to come up, Beth. Okay?'

Rolling onto the floor, Beth stood up straight. 'Told who? What?' She turned her puzzled gaze on Elizabeth, who was standing by the door.

'Dexter Giordanni. He said he was a friend of yours, and as Mike has mentioned doing business with the man, I guessed it was all right.'

'What?' Beth exclaimed in horror.

'Why, you sly dog, Beth. Or should that be cat?' Mike said, grinning from ear to ear. 'You're dating the great man himself.'

'No, I am not!' she snapped, just as the doorbell rang and Elizabeth went to open the front door.

Beth's green-eyed gaze shot to the man who stood in the living-room doorway. She couldn't move; she was frozen in shock. Dex was looking around in much the same state of shock.

'*Dio*, what is this? A mad house?' His startled gaze swept over the witch, the skeleton rising from the armchair, and finally settled on the cat.

Mike came to the rescue with his usual light-hearted manner. 'Come in, come in,' he told Dex, and then proudly introduced his fiancée, Elizabeth.

Elizabeth took one look at the tall, dark, handsome man, dressed in a formal black dinner suit and snowy white shirt, and turned on Mike.

'I knew I shouldn't have let you talk me into this costume. I look a sight.'

Beth wasn't surprised at Elizabeth's reaction. It was one thing to appear a freak to the man who loved you. But quite another to meet a very handsome stranger.

But Dex cut in. 'No, really, Elizabeth, you look absolutely stunning. I have never seen a better-looking witch.'

His deep velvet voice, threaded with amusement, grated along Beth's nerves. She watched him smile down into Elizabeth's face, her lips curling in distaste.

'Or a more lively skeleton.' He shared a grin with Mike. 'And as for the cat...' He turned his amused gaze on Beth as he walked towards her. 'I don't believe I have ever seen a more perfect feline.' His grey eyes raked her from head to toe, and she bristled, much like the animal she was pretending to be.

The smooth stretch-fur fabric moulded to every inch of her firm young body like a second skin, and Dex's blatant appraisal, the way his eyes lingered a shade too long on her high, full breasts, brought a furious flush to her small face. When he finally looked into her face, her green eyes flared back at him, shooting sparks of furious hostility.

'How dare you come here?' Beth breathed, keeping her voice low, so Mike and Elizabeth would not hear.

'The costume was made for you, Beth, darling. So appropriate,' Dex drawled, loud enough for the neighbours to hear, Beth thought bitterly, and then to her astonishment he caught her by the shoulders and lowered his dark head. She thought for a terrifying minute he was going to kiss her, but his lips grazed her cheek. 'And I still have the scratch-marks to prove it,' he whispered, for her ears only.

Beth blushed even redder. A vivid image of Dex's large naked body covering hers flashed in her mind's eye, and her own stupid reaction, her slender arms clinging to him as if her life depended on it. Angry with herself, and him, she pulled out of his hold.

Deliberately sidestepping Dex, and focusing her attention on her stepbrother, she said, 'Come on, Mike, we had better get going or we'll be late.' Safely in reach of the door, she dared to look at Dex again.

'Nice to see you again, Dex, but, as you can see, we're on our way out. Perhaps you can ring me the next time you're in town.'

'Yes, I will do that,' he said suavely, walking towards the door.

Beth opened the door for him with a polite smile on her face, tinged with a profound relief that he was leaving. She glanced at the keys in her hand, and realised she could hardly carry a bag.

'Give them to me, Beth,' Elizabeth suggested, seeing her dilemma. 'I'm the only one with pockets, as Mike so readily informed me when it came to paying the taxi fare on the way over.'

'That's Mike,' Beth said with a laugh, handing the keys over, and was complacently congratulating herself on her adult handling of the situation, even if her stomach felt as if a horde of butterflies had taken control of it, when Mike decided to get in on the act...

CHAPTER SEVEN

How it had happened, Beth did not know. One minute she was showing Dexter Giordanni out of her door, and half an hour later the same man was helping her out of his limousine while Mike and Elizabeth were already halfway down the steps to the open door of Mike's old college friend's restaurant in Holland Park. The restaurant was closed to the general public for the night in order to host the private Hallowe'en party.

Shrugging Dex's hand off her arm, she snarled, 'I don't need your help, thank you very much.'

Stuck in the back seat of the car, with Dex on one side and Mike on the other, it had been the journey from hell for Beth. Unable to complain at Mike's high-handed attitude in inviting Dex to accompany them to the party, she had silently fumed. The close proximity of Dex's large body had only infuriated her further. Much as she hated to admit it, his closeness, his warmth, the familiar scent of him, had set every nerve in her body on red alert.

'Temper, temper, Beth. There's no need to play the part of the spitting cat quite so enthusiastically,' he opined, grinning down at her.

'And there's no need for you to be here,' she shot back, wanting to knock the smile off his handsome face. 'You could easily have said no to Mike's invitation. You're not in fancy dress, and you'll stand out like a sore thumb. It's not your scene at all,' she ranted on.

But Dex silenced her by placing a long finger over her mouth.

'My scene or not, I could not desert you in your hour of need.'

Beth's eyes widened in puzzlement. 'My need?' What on earth was he talking about? She needed Dex like a hole in the head! She was still fighting to recover from their last disastrous encounter.

'I pride myself on being a gentleman, and it was obvious you did not have a date for the evening. You know what they say: Two's company, three's a crowd. I had to step in and save you any embarrassment.'

His mock concern raised her temperature another notch. 'Why, you patronising prig! If I had wanted an escort for the evening, I could have had one.'

'If you say so. But let us get inside; we are holding up the traffic.'

Only then did Beth notice the cars drawn up behind Dex's limousine, and about a dozen people approaching. Before she could think of a suitable retort, Dex slipped his arm around her waist and urged her down the steps and into the foyer. She knew he was winding her up deliberately, and belatedly she thought of an answer.

'I didn't have an escort because I didn't want one. I intend to play the field tonight,' she declared, with a casual sophistication she did not feel. At barely five feet two, and dressed as a cat with whiskers, sophisticated she was not... Anyway, it was a lie. Actually, all she really wanted to do was run home. But she refused to give Dex the satisfaction of knowing how much seeing him again had upset her.

'I am in the field,' Dex murmured, swinging her around in his arms and holding her close against his large body. 'Play with me,' he drawled huskily, his grey eyes narrowed intently on her face.

Beth swallowed hard. There was no mistaking the flare of desire in the depths of his eyes as one large hand slid down her back and pressed her hard against his muscular thighs.

Beth glanced wildly around. She tried to ease away, but it wasn't that simple. The small restaurant entrance was a mass of bodies, from ghosts to devils, druids—and drunks, by the look of it, as one particularly plump man, in what looked like a nightshirt, fell against her.

'Come on.' Dex's hand dropped from her waist and, curving a protective arm around her slender shoulders, hauling her hard into his side, he guided her through the crush of people into the large dining room where there was a lot more space.

Intensely aware of his thigh brushing against her hip, and his hand on her shoulder, it took all Beth's willpower to repress the shiver his touch ignited.

'I'm all right now,' she said curtly, slipping out from under his arm and glancing around.

Beth's green eyes widened incredulously at the scene before her. On a platform at one end of the room, a disc jockey dressed in a red Spandex suit, a cape and horns—the devil incarnate!—was doing his stuff. The music was loud, and multi-coloured flashing strobe lights cast weird and wonderful shadows over the centre of the room, where a couple of dozen people dressed as demons, witches and warlocks, and some very scantily clad women, gyrated in time to the beat... Around the sides, people lounged at tables, drinking and laughing. It reminded her of an oil painting she had seen in the Tate Gallery by a seventeenth-century Italian master, depicting hell.

The irony of it did not escape her. Hell was exactly how she felt. Acutely conscious of Dex's brooding presence beside her, she glanced up at him and had the terrible conviction that unless she escaped from this party pretty, damn quick, hell was where she was destined to stay!

'Your stepbrother certainly has some interesting friends,' Dex commented, one dark brow arching sardonically as he looked around the room.

Beth followed his superior gaze to where it rested on a particularly voluptuous woman, who appeared to be wearing three fig leaves and nothing else. What the brief costume had to do with Hallowe'en, Beth could not imagine. But, glancing back at Dex, she let her lips twist in a cynical smile. Obviously the girl in question knew why. Dex was drooling. How typical, Beth thought bitterly, and took the chance to edge away from him.

Catching sight of Mike and Elizabeth, she made her way towards them. Suddenly a sharp tug on the tail of her costume had her falling back against a rock-hard body. Fighting to retain her balance, she squirmed around and found herself staring at Dex's shirt-front. She put her hands flat against his broad chest and tried to push him away.

'Will you let go of my tail?' she snapped. Why, oh, why had she let herself be talked into wearing this ridiculous costume?

'But you have such a nice tail, Beth.' Her furious green eyes clashed with his and she saw the devilment lurking in their silver depths. She felt his hand twisting the offending appendage around his wrist until his palm settled firmly over her bottom, and she knew damn well it was not the tail of her costume he was talking about.

'In fact, I love your costume. Cats are my favourite

animal.' His other hand stroked slowly, very deliberately, down her spine, making her shudder. 'It is *purrfect* for you,' he teased huskily. Well aware of her involuntary reaction to his blatant caress, tossing back his head, he laughed out loud at the expression of frustrated fury twisting her delicate features.

His laughter, the flash of his brilliant white teeth, was too much for Beth.

'Add a pair of white fangs to your big mouth, and, hey presto! The perfect Count Dracula!' she spat back.

He pulled her closer, one hand easing up her back to clasp the back of her head, untangling the tail of her costume and settling his other arm more firmly around her, if such a thing was possible.

'Count Dracula. I like that, Beth.' His hand slid to the nape of her neck and she felt the pressure of his long fingers on her throat.

'Especially if you let me kiss your neck,' he declared outrageously, his eyes glittering with wickedly sensual intent on her flushed face.

The pulse in her neck leapt beneath his fingers; her body flooded with heat. She swallowed hard, the erotic image he had created swamping her mind. Her hands on his chest, supposedly to push him away, lingered against the soft silk of his shirt. She felt his hard thighs stirring against her, and was made shockingly aware of the man in the most primitive way possible. She opened her mouth to speak but no sound came out as his dark head bent and his mouth bit gently, then sucked, on the only bit of flesh exposed by her all-encompassing costume: her throat.

She went weak at the knees, a low moan escaping through her parted lips. Dex moved slightly, his long legs splayed, and he pulled her close between his thighs.

His hands tightened on her buttocks and back. What would have happened next? Beth did not dare contemplate it as Mike saved her from making a complete fool of herself.

'You two dancing, or what?' His cheerful voice echoed on the fringes of Beth's mind.

Dex lifted his dark head and grinned at Mike. 'Dancing—now—thanks to you.' Swirling Beth around, he deftly manoeuvred her into the crowd of dancers.

Mortified, her face burning, Beth stiffened in his arms, wishing with all her heart she was anywhere else but here. Not strictly true, a little voice echoed in her head. Being held close to Dex, his male warmth enfolding her, was as near to heaven as a woman could get.

Fool, she told herself. Dex didn't really want her. He had taken her out in the first place to keep her away from Paul Morris, the man his sister wanted. He had taken her to bed to prove he could, and she, weak-willed wimp that she was, had let him. How cold-blooded could a man get?

She sighed; the pressure of his hand on her back and the subtle movement of his body against hers was anything but cold, in fact it was the reverse. She frowned in concentration, worried that if she relaxed for a second she would find herself caving into him. She silently cursed her stupid costume yet again. A fine layer of stretch jersey was no protection against the powerful appeal of Dex's muscle-packed body. Her breasts hardened, the nipples rigid against the fine jersey. She didn't know whether to press herself against him to disguise her arousal or pull away from him and take the risk of revealing her vulnerable state.

'Don't worry, Beth. It will put premature lines on your beautiful face.'

His warm breath caressed her brow, and at the softly drawled words her head jerked back in surprise. The damn man could read her mind.

'So what? You won't be around to see them,' she said, shooting him a dismissive glance.

Dex grinned. 'I wouldn't be too sure, Beth.' His grey eyes gleamed with mocking amusement as he held her slightly away from him and added, 'Your delectable body tells a different story.'

'Don't flatter yourself,' she muttered, 'it's the heat. This catsuit is like a strait-jacket.'

Dex chuckled. '"Straight" is hardly how I would describe you.' His glance swept over her slender curves in frank masculine appreciation, and his chuckle changed to outright laughter.

Words failed her. He might find the situation highly amusing, but she was mortified. If he laughed at her once more she would hit him. But cold common sense told her that sparring with Dex was a losing game. Dancing was probably a whole lot safer than trying to argue with him in this crowd. Relaxing slightly against him, she felt his arms tighten around her. It felt so good, and, if she was honest, it was where she wanted to be. With a soft sigh she buried her head on his chest and gave herself up to the music.

Beth liked dancing, and for a large man Dex was amazingly light on his feet. They moved around the floor in perfect unison, not speaking, simply swaying to the sounds of the music. The seductive power of his body had Beth, against all her better intentions, melting against him.

The tempo of the music changed to a heavy jungle beat, and Dex bent low so that his breath brushed her cheek. 'Do you want to continue?'

'Yes.' Why not? she thought. It was a party and she deserved some fun, and, slipping out of his arms, she began to gyrate with the music. Her green eyes clashed with his. 'If you can,' she goaded him. And he could...

He danced the same way as he did everything—perfectly. She should have guessed. Beth had thought him the sexiest man on two legs before, but watching his long body move with sinuous grace to the heavy beat was a lesson in eroticism that made her respond in kind.

As if by some unspoken agreement for the next half-hour or more they danced, and laughed, and teased each other with their bodies in perfect harmony. When eventually the music returned to a slow beat and Dex pulled her into his arms, Beth went willingly.

'My little cat, my fantasy,' he murmured against the top of her head. His hands stroked up and down her arms, one hand finally settling at the base of her spine, holding her tightly against him, and his other hand curving around her chin and tilting her head back. 'Will you purr for me, Beth?' he asked, his dark eyes intent on her flushed face. 'Fulfil my fantasy?'

'My turn, I think.' Mike's voice cut in before Beth could answer.

'Okay...' Dex said, his hand falling from her chin and turning her deftly towards Mike. 'I'll go and find us all a drink.' He was in complete control in a second, while Beth was fighting for breath.

Beth didn't know whether to be grieved or relieved as Mike whirled her around the floor. 'Why the haste, brother dear?' she managed to get out when she had recovered enough to speak.

Stopping dead at the edge of the dance floor, Mike looked straight at her and demanded, 'What exactly is going on between you and Giordanni?'

'Nothing. Nothing at all.'

'This is Mike, your brother. I know you, and I remember the gooey-eyed look you had after you met the man at the boss's party. So what gives? Have you been dating him ever since?'

'Don't be silly. I went out with him a couple of times, and realised he wasn't my type. I haven't seen him for weeks.'

'So why is he almost devouring you on the dance floor? And why did he call at your apartment tonight?'

'Mike, you're beginning to sound like Big Brother with all your questions. I have no idea why Giordanni called at my apartment, and I don't really care.'

But she did care, and she couldn't believe her own oversight. She had spent the last hour with the man actually enjoying herself, if she was honest, and it had never occurred to her to ask Dex why he had called. She had to pull herself together. So far she had been reacting, not acting.

'Sorry. But according to Elizabeth you needed rescuing. Don't ask me why. "Women's intuition," she said, and, as her wish is my command, consider yourself rescued,' Mike informed her with a wry smile.

'You're a fool, but I love you.' She was touched by his protective attitude.

'As long as you're not a fool over Giordanni.' Mike's blue-eyed gaze was suddenly serious. 'He is a handsome devil, and I know he's a brilliant businessman, but his reputation with the ladies is the pits.'

'Who are you maligning now, fiancé mine?' Elizabeth arrived and tucked her arm through Mike's.

Beth glanced around the room, her eyes widening on the voluptuous lady, who was now exposing one breast, and shot quickly back at Elizabeth. 'The rather lively lady who has just lost a fig leaf,' she improvised, and immediately the attention of Mike and Elizabeth was diverted to the dance floor, much to Beth's relief. The disc jockey was yelling it was midnight, over the music, and the crowd was going wild.

'Oh, my God. Don't you dare look, Mike,' Elizabeth exclaimed, putting her hands over her fiancé's eyes, and laughing with Beth over his shoulder.

'Spoilsport!' Mike cried.

'Here, have a drink and cool down.' Dex's deep voice joined the conversation. Beth spun around to find him standing behind her, miraculously carrying four glasses of champagne in his large hands.

They all took a glass. Beth drank hers straight off; she needed it. She had been perilously close to forgetting why she had left Dex in the first place, and she hated her own weakness.

Suddenly she found the noise was deafening. Her head was beginning to ache, and the hood of her costume was feeling tighter by the minute. She glanced up at Dex. He was hovering over her like a vampire bat, she thought, her imagination running riot. If she didn't escape soon, she would faint. Elizabeth was saying something, Beth knew, but she could barely hear above the noise.

'What did you say?' Beth asked, as Elizabeth and Mike put their empty glasses on a convenient table and hand in hand turned to Beth.

'This party is turning rather wild,' Mike said, sharing a very male look over the top of her head with Dex. 'We're leaving.' And, grabbing Elizabeth's hand, he set off for the exit.

Dex took her glass from her nerveless fingers and set it on the table. 'So are we.'

Arrogant, domineering swine… 'No, the party's just

warming up,' she challenged, not because she had any desire to stay, but simply to thwart him. He was so damn superior.

'If it gets any warmer, it will be illegal,' Dex replied. Catching Beth's wrist in his large hand, he added, 'Mike and Elizabeth need a ride home. Come on.'

And, weaving through the crowd, he dragged Beth behind him.

Once out of the restaurant and in the fresh air, Dex stopped at the foot of the steps leading up to street level. 'Are you all right? You look a bit pale.' He slanted her a teasing grin. 'For a cat.'

'I'm fine.' Beth tore the hood from her head. She hated the catsuit. She ran her fingers through her hair and shook her head. The relief was unbelievable. With part of her costume gone, part of her common sense returned.

'But what about you? Why did you call at my apartment? Why did you come to this party? You could have easily said no. What exactly are you playing at?' she demanded, finally able to ask all the questions that had been preying her mind since Dex had walked back into her life.

'Questions, questions. You'd better watch it, Beth. Remember the saying. Curiosity killed the cat.' And he laughed again.

Sick to death of his stupid cat jokes, she turned on him. 'I wish I could kill *you*,' she said venomously, and, pushing past him, she ran up the steps to the street.

Mike and Elizabeth were standing on the pavement arm in arm, and Beth hastened to stand beside them. Dex appeared a second later. He gave Beth a hard-eyed stare but said not a word. A snap of his fingers and, by some miracle, the limousine drew up alongside the kerb.

'Where to first?' Dex addressed the question to Mike.

'My place.' He looked at Dex and smiled as he gave the address. 'My new fiancée and I have a lot to discuss.'

'Drop me off first,' Beth said quickly, and looked at Dex too. He stared down at her with narrowed eyes, his expression unreadable.

'Let's leave it to the driver.' He said coolly, his hand at Beth's elbow urging her into the back of the car. Nobody argued with him…

Mike and Elizabeth were in a world of their own, arms around each other, whispering sweet nothings, and it was Beth's sheer bad luck that Mike's apartment was a whole lot nearer the restaurant than hers.

'Here.' Elizabeth handed Dex Beth's door keys. 'Look after her.' After a hasty goodnight, the couple quickly headed towards Mike's door.

It was obvious what they had in mind, and who could blame them? They were young and in love. But, unfortunately for Beth, it left her alone in the back seat of the car with Dex. Plus, the man had her door key.

They sat side by side in tense silence as the chauffeur drove through the city. Beth slanted Dex a sidelong glance and quickly looked away. He was bitterly angry. She could sense it, see it in the rigid lines of his hard face. Her nerves were pulled as taut as a bowstring—if she didn't get out of the car in a moment, she would scream.

She felt the tension increase with every passing mile, and breathed a sigh of relief when the limousine cruised quietly to a halt outside her apartment building. The chauffeur got out and, after walking around the front of the car, held open the door. Dex slid out and stood on the pavement, waiting for her.

He was simply being polite, Beth told herself, and slid

out after him. 'Thank you for a nice evening,' she said stiffly, 'give me my key, please.' She held out her hand, hoping to get away with the social niceties. But she didn't.

Taking the hand she offered, Dex ordered, 'Inside,' and dragged her across the foyer and into the lift.

'There's no need for you to accompany me,' Beth said firmly, refusing to be intimidated by his high-handed attitude.

He pressed the elevator button, turning to her with an icy expression in his steely eyes. 'I decide what is needed,' he stated. Pulling her out of the elevator, then into her apartment, he added chillingly, 'Not you. Not any more.'

Beth looked up as he closed and locked the door behind him. 'Exactly what do you mean by that?' she demanded, but she couldn't help edging away from him. There was something in his expression, his cold, aloof stance, that sent shivers down her spine.

Ignore him, her common sense told her. Ignore him, walk away, and he'll leave.

'I'm going to get changed.' Beth turned her back to him. 'See yourself out.' And she headed for the door that led into her bedroom. She half expected him to follow, but amazingly he didn't. She closed her bedroom door behind her and wished it had a lock. Then she heard a door slam; she couldn't believe her luck. But she was taking no chances. Quickly she picked up an old green sweatsuit, and dashed into the bathroom. The bathroom *did* have a lock.

She listened for any sound from the living room, but everything was quiet. Slipping out of the embarrassing costume, she sighed with relief and stepped into the baggy pants. She slipped the sweater over her head and ran her fingers through her hair. Only then did she look in the mirror. A brief smile curved her full mouth, and she gave a grimace of pain as she pulled the whiskers from her face.

No wonder Dex had gone, she thought, still grinning. She looked an absolute sight. She thoroughly washed and dried her face, removing all the exaggerated eye make-up, and, picking up a hairbrush, briskly brought her unruly auburn hair into some sort of order. Sighing with relief, she saw she looked almost normal. She unlocked the bathroom door. A cup of cocoa, and then hopefully to bed and to sleep. She didn't want to think about the evening's events.

She walked into the living room and stopped dead. Dex was leaning against the small mantlepiece. He looked up as she walked in. A flick of his lashes sent his gaze skimming over her assessingly, noting the baggy green sweatsuit with a wry smile.

'Hardly haute couture, but all that can change,' he murmured, and she felt as though he was stripping her with his eyes.

'I thought you'd gone,' she exclaimed.

Dex shrugged his broad shoulders in a typical Latin gesture. 'No.'

'But I heard the door.' Beth was stunned, and it showed. She looked at the hall door, and back at Dex. He had loosened his tie and unfastened the first few buttons on his shirt. Thankfully he had not removed his jacket; it still fit perfectly over his broad shoulders. One hand was in his trouser pocket; the other was holding a glass of wine.

'It was the kitchen door; I raided your refrigerator. Drink?'

Then she saw the half-empty bottle of wine on the

mantlepiece and another glass. 'You—but…' Her mouth worked but she was too confused to get the words out.

'Sit down, Beth. Have a drink and listen. You asked me before why I called around here earlier. Before you decided you wished I was dead,' he reminded her cynically.

Looking down, she felt a brief flicker of shame, but it quickly expired as she watched him casually withdraw his hand from his pocket and pick up the other glass of wine from the mantlepiece. Stepping forward, he held it out towards her. 'Drink. You might need it.'

She was so surprised, she automatically reached out and took the glass. His long fingers brushed hers and she felt the contact right through to her shoulder.

'Why?' she muttered. She had suffered shock upon shock tonight, and her brain could not take it in.

'The simple answer is, I have a proposal for you.'

Taking a sip from her drink, she glanced over the rim of her glass. 'Go ahead,' she murmured. 'You will, anyway.' The cold determination in his grey eyes as they met hers was unmistakable.

'Usually I visit London twice a year at most, but since acquiring the casino—and more recently a trio of city centre hotels—I find I am going to have to spend a lot more time here. I'm a normal man, with normal needs, and I need a woman here. I want you to be that woman.'

Confused, she surveyed him. 'But I told you. I don't want to marry you.'

One dark brow arched quizzically, a ruthless smile curving his sensuous mouth. 'No more than I want to marry you. In fact, if you recall, I never actually asked you. I gave you a ring, a bauble. That was all.'

Embarrassment turned her face scarlet. Her only consolation was that at last he was speaking the truth. She had overheard him saying pretty much the same thing in the office that dreadful day. Forcing her turbulent thoughts into some kind of order, she tilted her head back and looked at him sharply.

Unease stirred inside her. There was something sinister in his austere features. 'I don't understand.' She shook her head. 'What do you mean?'

'Let me make it simple for you. I have bought an apartment in London and I want you to live in it. You can continue with your career—whatever. My only stipulation is, when I am in London you make yourself available at my convenience.'

Beth stared at him, her strained features reflecting her shock. Dex, the man she had thought she loved, was quite cold-bloodedly suggesting she live with him, albeit on a part-time basis. If she had not been so horrified, she would have been furious.

She searched Dex's harshly set features. He looked just as she imagined he would look when buying a casino or a company. His arrogance, his enormous conceit, took her breath away. But she was not in the market. Not for Dex. Not for any man.

Suddenly the black humour of the situation hit her. Of course she could see through his plan. Install Beth in his apartment and keep her away from Paul Morris. Obviously his sister was having some difficulty bringing Paul to heel.

'Why me?' she asked, wondering what kind of story he would come up with. She was sure it would not be the truth.

'I find after having had one bite of the cherry I have a burning desire to cultivate the rest of the tree,' he returned softly.

Beth had to repress a smile. He wasn't serious; he was simply trying it on. 'For a man whose first language isn't English, you have a great line in metaphors,' she quipped, letting the smile break through. Dex had wit, even if he was a devious devil.

But there was no corresponding smile from Dex. Instead he stepped towards her, a ruthless determination glinting in his narrowed eyes. 'So, is it a deal?'

It was unthinkable, but he actually was serious. Her body frozen with shock, Beth's eyes searched his face, looking for some indication that it was a joke. A Hallowe'en prank, maybe. But she could see nothing in his expression to allay her fear—fear for herself, because for a brief moment she had been tempted. The thought of once more experiencing the delights his magnificent body could give her had stirred an unwanted response inside her.

'No,' she said softly, whether denying herself or Dex, she wasn't sure. Then, as fury at his insulting proposition overcame her shock, she repeated forcefully, 'No! No, never in a million years!'

'So adamant, and so wrong.' His hand reached out and circled her throat, tilting her head up, and his eyes narrowed. 'I can feel the pulse beating madly in your throat. However much you try to hide it, you want me. You melt when I touch you. It is the same for me. Our relationship will be a mutually fulfilling affair.'

She opened her mouth to deny it and his dark head bent, his mouth taking hers. She shuddered beneath the hot, forceful passion of his kiss, desire and disgust battling inside her, and only dimly registered his words as he took his mouth from hers.

'You can't help yourself.' His silver eyes challenged her to deny him.

'Oh, but I can.' she shot back, and, shoving him hard in the chest, she continued, 'You can take yourself and your filthy proposition out of my apartment, and don't come back.' Swinging on her heel, she marched to the door.

'Wait, Beth. I have not finished.'

'Well, I have. In fact, I finished with you two weeks ago, and nothing has changed.'

'But situations do change, Beth.' He strolled towards where she stood at the door. 'Your stepbrother, for instance, he's gained a promotion, a much better salary and a fiancée, I believe, all in a couple of weeks.'

She stared up at him. Why had he changed the subject so quickly? Then, with a growing sense of dread, she listened to him.

'You see, Beth, the account I gave Brice Wine Merchants via Mike, the account that earned him his promotion, can just as easily be cancelled. Elizabeth is a lovely girl, but how will she feel when Mike's income is cut in half? Or he might even lose his job.'

'Are you threatening me?' she said, all the colour draining from her face, not wanting to believe what she was hearing.

'As if I would.' A ruthless smile curved his sensuous mouth. 'No, I am simply giving you a possible scenario... The rest is up to you. I will be at my usual hotel until ten tomorrow morning. I suggest you consider your options and give me a call before I leave.'

'That is blackmail, you bastard!' she cried, incensed that he would even try such a trick.

'Not at all. In the business world, that is a deal,' Dex

responded hardly, not in the least bothered by her outburst. 'Take it or leave it.' Withdrawing a pen from his inside pocket, he caught her hand in his.

Beth tried to pull her hand free, but with insulting ease he held it firm, palm up, and had the audacity to write on her soft flesh. Curling her fingers into a fist, he let her go.

'The number of my hotel and suite. Any time before ten in the morning, I will be available. You have until then to decide.'

'Why, you...' She couldn't think of a name foul enough, and swung out at him instead. But Dex caught her wrist in mid-air, and, grabbing her other hand with one large hand he encircled her slender wrists and pinned them back against the wall above her head. He stared down at her, rage contorting his features for a split second. Her heart jolted and she caught her breath.

Then he moved slowly, deliberately, his long body pressing her against the wall.

'I told you once before...' But he didn't finish. His steel-grey eyes raked down her body. His hand lifted and closed over her breast, kneading the firm flesh, his thumb finding the hardening nipple beneath the soft fabric, and she stifled a groan.

'All that fiery passion going to waste. How much more satisfying to channel it into the bedroom.' His hand slipped down and under her sweater, closing over her naked flesh. She knew he was doing it deliberately; he wanted to punish her. Still she groaned. She couldn't control or deny her surrender to the sweet torture of his touch.

'Remember this when you make your decision.' He watched her, his silver eyes burning through her.

Beth stared back, hopelessly disorientated. Then she recognised the glitter of masculine triumph in his eyes and burnt with shame and anger. 'Damn you!' she swore under her breath.

Dex abruptly let go of her hands and jerked back. 'Don't forget, before ten, Beth.' He opened the door and left.

CHAPTER EIGHT

MECHANICALLY Beth slipped the chain on the door and shot the dead bolt. *Dead bolt.* How appropriate. She felt half dead, and also like bolting.

Served her right, she thought guiltily. She had never celebrated Hallowe'en before, never really wanted to, probably because of her convent education. Look what happened the first time she did. Dexter Giordanni! The party had not really been her scene at all. Mike had talked her into it. But to give him his due even he had been quite shocked, and they had all left early.

Moving slowly, she made her way to the bedroom, switching off the lights as she went, though she didn't bother with the light in her bedroom. She slipped off her green sweatsuit, and climbed into bed, her mind spinning like a windmill. The magnitude of the night's events were too horrible to contemplate, but she had to...

It would be laughable if it wasn't so scary. Dex wanted her to be his—what? Girlfriend, mistress, lover? The awful truth was she was tempted to agree. Dex didn't love her, but that didn't stop her wanting him with every fibre of her being. She tried to tell herself it was just sex, but deep down she knew that for her it was much, much more. She wanted to take anything Dex had to offer—love or lust, she didn't care. She'd even agree to blackmail!

With a low groan Beth rolled over on the bed and buried her face in the pillow. She blushed with shame.

God help her. Had she no pride? No self-respect? Apparently not.

She had been fooling herself for the past two weeks, trying to pretend she didn't care. Telling herself she didn't love Dex, that it had been an indiscretion borne of inexperience, and thank God she'd found out the truth about him in time, before she'd got in too deep.

A bitter smile twisted her lovely mouth. Earlier this evening she had been congratulating herself on reviving her social life. Seeing Dex tonight had brought that idea to an abrupt end. When she had managed to swallow her anger she had enjoyed dancing with him, and the rest…his kisses, the feel of his strong hand on her flesh. Suddenly every pulse in her body responded at the memory, and, despising her own weakness she jumped out of bed.

She was too agitated to sleep anyway, and, slipping on her robe, she wandered back into the living room and clicked on the light. Her eye caught the ink on her hand. Staring at her palm, she traced the black numbers with the finger of her other hand. The man was seriously weird, she told herself as she paced the room back and forth, her mind in turmoil, too restless even to sit down.

Why? Why was Dex trying to force her into being his mistress? It didn't make sense. So, all right, he thought she was in competition for his sister's man. But surely a man of his intelligence must know enough about human relations to realise nothing would force Paul Morris into staying with his sister if he didn't want to. In fact Dex and Paul were very much alike: highly successful, wealthy, very eligible, and experienced enough to escape the clutches of any woman if they wanted to.

No. She was missing something. But what? The underlying bitterness, the anger she had sensed in Dex tonight was directed at her. Maybe it was simply a male ego thing. She had insulted Dex by jilting him two weeks ago, and compounded her folly by telling him tonight she would like to kill him. It was after that comment he had turned into a cold, hard-faced stranger. Then he had threatened Beth with her stepbrother's downfall unless she complied with Dex's demands. Somehow it didn't ring true.

She thought back to the first time they had met, at the Brice party. She had been bowled over from the minute she clapped eyes on Dex, but even then her feminine intuition had warned her to stay clear of him. But, uncannily like her mother, Beth had let her heart rule her head. For a few short days she had been gloriously happy, only to be plunged into the depths of despair when she'd discovered Dex, the man she loved, was using her for his own ends.

Jilting him had been the hardest thing she had ever done. Pride alone had seen her though the last two weeks, and if she gave in to Dex's disgraceful proposition now, she would lose even that.

But what of her stepbrother, Mike? What might he lose if she said no to Dex? Much as she adored Mike, she would not sleep with a man for him. Then it hit her—she could swallow her pride for Mike, and tell Dex the truth. If she'd done that two weeks ago she might not be in the mess she was in now.

The cold pale light of dawn was slanting through the window when Beth finally reached her decision. A wry smile tilted the corners of her mouth. It was so obvious she should have realised straight away.

Once she told Dex the real reason she had jilted him—she had overheard the conversation between Dex and his friend Bob—and admitted that Paul Morris was her godfather, he'd realize she was no threat to his sister. Any interest Dex had in her would vanish like a whistle in the wind, along with any need to harm Mike. Dex might even have the grace to feel ashamed of the way he had treated her. But she doubted it. He was ruthless in the pursuit of what he wanted, that much she had learnt from their brief relationship.

With her decision made, Beth went back to bed. She had time for a few hour's sleep before calling Dex at his hotel with the truth.

A long way off a bell was ringing. Beth stirred and half opened her eyes. The ringing stopped and she rolled over in bed and snuggled back down. She was so tired, and today was Saturday—no work, she thought contentedly.

Ringing! Her eyes flew wide open and she shot up in bed, the events of last night flashing through her mind. She turned her head, looked at the clock on the bedside table, and groaned. 'Oh, my God!' she exclaimed, and closed her eyes again for a second in disbelief.

She could not believe it. She had overslept. She opened her eyes again and looked once more at the clock. There was no mistake. Eleven in the morning. It could only happen to her! Still, she tried... Leaping out of bed and dashing into the kitchen, she picked up the telephone and studied the palm of her hand. Was that a three or an eight? The heat of her palm in her sleep had smudged the numbers.

Frantically Beth dialled what she hoped was the right number, and got a Mercedes car dealership! She tried again and heaved a sigh of relief when a female voice answered, announcing the name of Dex's hotel. Her relief quickly turned to horror when she was informed that Mr Giordanni had checked out not ten minutes ago and was on his way to Heathrow to catch the Concorde flight to New York.

Beth staggered into the living room, collapsed in the armchair and groaned. Well, fate had taken a hand. That was it. Dex had his answer by default. There was nothing she could do about it now. She tried to cheer herself up with the thought there was nothing Dex could do about Mike, at least not for the next two days. But Monday was a different matter.

Beth toyed with the idea of ringing Mike and telling him what had happened, then decided against it. There was no point in worrying her stepbrother unduly. It crossed her mind to try and get in touch with Dex, and then she realised he had never actually given her so much as his address or home telephone number. She didn't even know for certain where he lived. Rome or New York, he had said. She could ring the Seymour Club and ask how to get in touch with him, but did she really want to?

No... Swallowing her pride for her stepbrother had seemed a good idea last night. But Beth was a fatalist. Why bother? Mike was good at his job, and he was old enough and man enough to make it on his own. As for Elizabeth, Beth had no doubt the girl would stand by him whatever he did. It was real love she had seen between the pair of them last night. Not the shallow copy Dex had pretended to feel for Beth.

All those out-of-the-way intimate restaurants Dex had taken her to—she had thought they were romantic. With the clarity of hindsight she realised his reasons had been much more basic. He had never even once suggested she accompany him to his hotel. Dex had obviously not wanted their brief relationship or engagement made public. Because he had known from the start it was a fake.

Getting to her feet, Beth walked into the kitchen and made herself a cup of coffee. Sipping the reviving brew, she concluded it was probably as well it had ended this way. Dex could do his damnedest for all she cared. He no longer had any hold over her. He had broken her heart, but he would never know. She was young enough and strong enough to recover, she told herself. And if the thought echoed hollowly in the corner of her mind, there was no one to hear it but Beth.

She spent a miserable weekend, and could barely wait to get home on Monday evening and ring Mike. She quizzed him tactfully about work, but he was fine—his job was fine. Still Dex's threat preyed on her mind. As each day passed she found her nerves getting more and more strung out, waiting for the proverbial clog to drop...

Until she opened her mail on Friday evening. Curled up in the armchair, a glass of wine on the table in front of her, she read the letter again. It was a brief, cheerful note from her godfather, inviting her to stay with him at a villa on the Isle of Capri next weekend. He had already squared it with her boss, Cecil, and the air ticket was enclosed. She was to fly out the following Friday and stay until the Sunday. She was to bring her glad rags. He was getting married to 'the lady of the lamb noisettes,' he joked.

Beth dropped the letter and the ticket on the table, and, picking up the wine glass, took a large swallow. She needed it. Replacing the glass on the table, she grimaced. So that was it... Her worries were over.

Now she knew why Dex hadn't carried out his threat to ruin Mike. His sister had got her man. There was no need for Dex to pretend he wanted Beth. She was no

danger any more. And obviously by now he must know
Paul was her godfather.

À long drawn-out sigh escaped her. She supposed she
should be relieved, but instead she simply felt sad. Her
first thought was not to go to the wedding because she'd
see Dex. But she knew Paul would be deeply hurt if she
did not attend. Then, as she sat there sipping her wine,
mulling over the way Dex had used her, she got angry.
She was going to the wedding. It would be worth it just
to show Dexter Giordanni she could be as sophisticated
and blasé as he was, and if she embarrassed Dex by her
presence all the better...

With a sense of growing excitement, Beth boarded the
ferry boat that was taking her on the last part of her
journey to Capri. The flight had been uneventful; a taxi
driver with her name on a placard had met her at Naples
Airport and delivered her to the ferry boat. It was a beautiful autumn afternoon. The sun shone from a clear blue
sky and the temperature was a balmy sixty degrees. She
had never been to Italy before, never mind to Capri, and
she was really looking forward to it.

She stood at the prow of the boat, dressed in blue
jeans, a green sweater and a jacket, her auburn hair
blowing in the breeze. The island rose like a jewel from
the clear blue sea. It was more rugged than she had
imagined, but absolutely beautiful. Eagerly her eyes
scanned the dockside as the ferry tied up in the small
port, and, spying Paul's elegant figure standing on the
jetty, she waved frantically.

In minutes she was in his arms, and with the greetings
over he led her to a blue Mercedes car. Her glance darted
all over. There was a funicular railway that took passen-
gers up the sharply rising cliff, and the road Paul took

wound very steeply in a corkscrew up the hillside, the sea never far from view. She looked back down on the bustle of the port, and Paul pointed out where the famous Blue Grotto was. Finally managing to contain her excitement, she looked at Paul.

'So, you're getting married. Are you sure?' she asked. She loved him, but she knew just how volatile the members of the Giordanni family could be. Her godfather was a lovely man, but very British.

Paul glanced at her, his pale eyes serious. 'Yes, Beth. I have never been more sure of anything in my life.'

'I'm happy for you,' she said sincerely, and she was. Then the car was sweeping around a sharp corner and into the concealed entrance of a narrow road that dipped steeply down again. Beth gasped. It felt as though they were driving into the sea.

'Impressive, hmm?'

'That is an understatement,' Beth whispered as the car swept through large iron gates on to a wide drive, to stop in front of a magnificent whitewashed villa that faced straight out to sea.

Half an hour later, Beth stood beside a huge four-poster bed and looked around in awe. An elderly housekeeper had unpacked and hung up her few clothes, and left. The bedroom was exquisite, a symphony in white and gold, with just a touch of blue in the marble mosaic floor. She crossed to where another door opened off the room, and gasped at the sheer size and elegance of the *en suite* bathroom. Whoever owned this place certainly knew how to live. She was almost afraid to use the facilities, but she did. After quickly washing her face and hands, she kept her jeans on but changed her sweater for a white polo top. It was so much warmer here than in London; she could not believe it.

Making her way back down the grandly curving staircase, she felt almost like Vivien Leigh in *Gone with the Wind*. Her lips twitched. Except for her jeans and shirt. Catching sight of Paul waiting for her in the huge reception hall, she flashed him a full-blown smile. 'This is some villa.'

'Yes, it is nice,' he said in his understated way. 'But what can I get you, Beth? A drink? Something to eat?'

'Can we go outside while it's still light? I'd love to see the gardens.'

'I suppose so. Anna won't be here for a couple of hours yet; so we have time.' With an indulgent smile he took her hand in his and led her out of the door and across the wide drive to a band of immaculately manicured grass.

'Oh, can we go down the steps?' Beth cried in delight, pulling on his hand. An ornate balustrade encircled the whole villa, intercepted by massive semi-circular steps that led down to a wide terrace, with a swimming pool to one side.

'Sometimes I forget you're grown up,' Paul said, stopping for a moment and smiling down into her excited green eyes. 'You have the same enthusiasm for life as your father had.'

Freeing her hand from his, she reached up and cupped his face, and kissed him lightly. 'Thank you.' She stepped back just as a car screeched to a halt in the drive.

Beth glanced across, her eyes widening incredulously as she saw Dex leap out of the car, dressed in black. His face equally black with fury, he charged towards them.

'You bastard, Morris,' he snarled, his lips drawn back against his teeth in savage, primitive rage. His fist shot out and thudded against Paul's face, sending him sprawling flat on his back on the grass.

It had all happened so quickly Beth couldn't believe it. The air crackled with violent tension, and she stood frozen in shock.

'And you…' Dex turned on Beth, murder in his eyes. 'You—you…' His English temporarily failed him and he let go in a torrent of Italian as he grabbed her around the waist and dragged her towards the open door of the car. 'You're out of here.' His breathing ragged, he bundled her into the car, slid into the driver's seat and gunned the engine.

Beth grabbed the door handle, but it was locked. She glanced frantically out of the window, her horrified eyes catching sight of a dazed Paul trying to sit up. Then, in a death-defying turn, Dex spun the car around. Beth fell heavily against him, her hand grabbing his thigh. He jerked his leg away and shot her a vitriolic glance.

She struggled to sit up and fell back against the door of the passenger seat, as far away from him as she could get. She was terrified. She had never seen such speed before in her life. By the time she caught her breath Dex had the car off the drive and racing up the perilously narrow road.

'Slow down! You'll kill us!' she cried, her voice hoarse with fear.

'If it keeps you away from him,' he grated through clenched teeth, 'I will.' Dex glanced at her, his expression murderous.

'You're mad. Totally mad,' she cried as they hit what passed for the main road at what felt like the speed of light. The car skidded and Beth closed her eyes and prayed.

'You can open your eyes,' he spat. 'I am not going to kill myself for a whore like you.'

Beth felt the car slow down and she opened her eyes.

She shot a fearful look at Dex's granite-like profile. A muscle jerked in his cheek and his mouth was a tight line of rage. She could sense the violence radiating from him, and she hardly dared breathe. She dropped her eyes to where his long fingers curved around the steering wheel, his knuckles white with the pressure of his grip.

She didn't dare speak; she was too frightened he would drive them off the road. She tensed as a moment later he did drive off the road, swinging onto a cart track that led through a small copse of trees and stopping dead a few feet from the edge of a cliff. But it didn't make Beth feel any better.

Dex turned in his seat and watched her for a long moment. 'Nothing to say?' he demanded harshly. 'No whimpering feminine excuse?'

'Let me out of this car,' she whispered.

'The door is open.'

Grasping the handle, Beth opened the door and tumbled out of the car onto the ground. She crawled on her hand and knees, her breath coming in great gasps until she was well away from the car and its crazy driver. Then she sat down, drawing her knees up to her chest and resting her head on them.

She was trembling with shock. She bit her lip to stop herself crying and thanked the Lord for the hard ground beneath her. For a moment in the car she had really feared for her life.

'Tears won't wash away your sins, and they certainly have no effect on me.' Dex's harsh voice broke the silence, and reluctantly Beth lifted her head.

He was standing in front of her, dressed all in black— black jeans and a black sweater—his legs slightly apart and his hands clenching and unclenching at his sides. He looked like some dark avenging angel.

'I am not crying,' she managed to say, with a slight tremor in her voice. 'I am simply in shock. I have never been kidnapped by a madman before.' She was beginning to regain some self-control, and she was also beginning to get angry.

'You call me mad? *Dio*, woman, how could you? Have you no pride? No self-respect?' Dex demanded, his voice crackling with fury.

His words beat down on her like so many stones of wrath. She slid back and stood up, making sure she kept well away from him. She could feel the menace in him, and even as it frightened her it made her temper rise.

'You trek halfway across Europe after a man who is getting married tomorrow—a man who does not love you and is old enough to be your father!' he shouted, stepping towards her.

Fear made Beth step back, and she gasped, suddenly realising Dex didn't know the truth about her and Paul. 'He is my *god*father,' she emphasised, and shivered as his hard face convulsed with rage.

'Tell that to the marines,' he snarled. 'I know the Morrises of this world. They don't befriend innocent little virgins for nothing. And you thought I wasn't good enough for you. What a joke,' he drawled derisively.

Beth's face turned red, and then white with anger. 'I don't give a damn what you think.' Her green eyes blazed in the paleness of her face. 'Paul *is* my godfather and he *does* love me—always has, from the day I was born.' She registered the shock in Dex's grey eyes and relished in it. 'And I trekked "halfway across Europe", as you so nicely put it, because Paul asked me to be at his wedding. Now, what is your excuse,' she demanded furiously, 'for knocking out a perfectly innocent man?

You great bully!' She hurled the accusation at him, her green eyes, full of contempt, clashing with his.

Dex spun around, stalked back to the car and slammed the passenger door shut as if he wanted to knock it off its hinges. *Cristo*! He swore long and furiously in a vicious spate of Italian. Then, as Beth watched, he squared his shoulders, tension in every line of his long body, and turned back to face her.

His face a rigid mask, he stepped forward. 'If Morris is your godfather,' he grated in a chillingly quiet voice, 'then why did you not tell me?'

The great Dexter Giordanni had finally made a mistake, Beth realised, her anger subsiding. Finally the moment of truth. Revenge was sweet and she was going to enjoy every second of it.

'You never asked me.' She looked straight up into his dark face. 'In fact, if memory serves me right, we met Paul once in your casino and you never mentioned him again.' Get out of that one, you lying swine, she thought, but didn't say, and almost grinned at the host of conflicting emotions that warred in his steely grey eyes— not least confusion.

'Nothing to say, Dex?' she prompted. The phrase 'hoist by his own petard' sprang to mind.

Dex's head bent and he stared fixedly at the ground for a long moment. The silence stretched, fraught with simmering emotion. Then slowly Dex lifted his head again. He didn't look at her; his eyes avoided hers. His tanned face was a blank mask, but a muscle beating wildly in his cheek betrayed his agitation.

'You're right. I didn't ask you about Morris. I didn't ask because I was violently jealous.' His gaze flicked to hers and Beth was almost fooled by the glint of naked anguish in his eyes, 'Today when I saw you kissing

Morris I saw red. It was unforgivable of me to hit him, but you know how I feel about you. How much I want you. I am a jealous, possessive man. I can't help it where you're concerned.'

He took another step towards her, and Beth moved back.

'You're also a lying hound where I am concerned,' she said coldly. 'And have been from the moment we met. So save your play-acting for someone who might appreciate it.' She was disgusted. Even now Dex was not going to admit the truth, and she had had enough.

He watched her, his grey eyes narrowing intently on her small face, then he said curtly, 'I am not acting. Why do you think that?'

Beth looked past him to the edge of the cliff, the deep blue of the sea beyond, and on to the far horizon where the sun was sinking in a red blaze of glory. Her dream of love and happy-ever-after had sunk in very much the same way. Drowned in a red blaze of passion. She tilted her head back and looked up into Dex's face. And it was all his fault.

'Because, Dex, I know everything. I know why you took me out in the first place. You asked me out to keep me away from Paul, the man your sister wanted.'

'No...' he denied angrily, reaching out and grabbing her by the shoulders. 'It wasn't like that.'

'Don't bother to deny it, Dex, I heard you say it.' His hands tightened on her flesh, but she didn't care. Beth wasn't frightened any more; she simply wanted the whole sorry mess over and done with.

'When? Where?' he asked, his body rigid.

'The day you came back from New York. The day I called at the Seymour.'

'The day you jilted me,' he cut in, his dark brows drawn together in a frown, his grey eyes searching hers.

'Yes. I didn't leave a note. I didn't visit a sick friend. But I did sit in the outer office at the club. The intercom was on.' She wasn't going to tell him she had switched it on. 'And I heard you discuss in some detail your ex-wife—someone you conveniently forgot to mention to me—your so-called fiancée.'

His hands fell from her shoulders and he drew himself up to his full height. All the colour drained from his face, leaving him grey beneath his tan.

'You were laughing with your friend. Bob, I think?' She arched one delicate brow enquiringly.

'Bob.' He cursed under his breath, and Beth knew he was remembering.

'Yes, you were having a drink with him. You had plenty of time—the girl would wait. You told him you were engaged, but not necessarily getting married, and you also told him why. The girl was going out with your sister's man, and you saw a way to put a stop to it. Fate gave you the opportunity in the guise of Brice Wine Merchants party. Need I go on? Or can you put the rest together yourself?' she taunted him.

'I remember the conversation.' A dark red stain swept up his face. At least he had the grace to blush, Beth thought bitterly. 'And I know how it must have sounded, but—'

'Don't bother explaining.' Beth stopped him, raising her hand. 'I'm not a fool. Your only reason for seeing me was your sister. You recognised me as the girl dining with Paul when your sister threw his dinner over him. You used me, and you were still trying to use me two weeks ago. You even tried to blackmail me.' She laughed, a harsh sound in the silence. 'I spent a week worrying about Mike—until I got the wedding invitation and realised your problem was solved.'

He winced, but responded curtly, 'Not quite. No one told me about Morris. If you had been honest and told me the real reason for jilting me, the rest need never have happened.'

Lifting her chin, Beth stared straight into his eyes. 'Oh, so now it's my fault?' She shook her head, her auburn hair flowing around her face. 'If you had let me finish speaking when we met Paul at the club, instead of dashing us away and kissing me senseless...' Beth didn't want to remember their lovemaking and stopped. What was the use of arguing with Dex?

'You're incredible.' Beth shook her head sadly. 'You do exactly what you want, take exactly what you want, and never once question how anyone else feels. You disgust me.'

She had gone too far. Dex caught her wrist and twisted it around her back, bringing her flush against his hard body. 'Disgust you?' he said, with deadly coldness. 'It wasn't disgust but pure lust you felt in my arms in your bed. And I can prove it,' he grated harshly.

Beth stared at him, her anger dying fast as his grey gaze roamed insolently over her. She saw the hunger in his eyes as his dark head lowered. She raised a hand to ward him off, but he simply hauled her tighter to him, her hand pressed to his chest. Wildly she shook her head. 'Don't!' she gasped.

But Dex merely laughed. 'Why not? I have nothing to lose.' His other hand gently caught her long hair and wrapped it around his wrist. His mouth poised above hers, Dex watched her ruthlessly. 'You've made a fool of me and you're going to pay.'

Beth shivered, her tongue slipping out to moisten suddenly dry lips. He had her trapped. She moved her head back with a jerk as his mouth ground down on hers and he began kissing her with a savage, urgent passion. She tried to prevent her lips parting in response, her body from arching against his, but desire sharp as a knife flared up inside her, and helplessly she found herself responding.

Her lips moved under his as she kissed him back. She was beyond thinking sensibly any more. His hand stroked down to curve over her bottom and pull her hard against his thighs. A moan escaped her and she trembled at the evidence of his masculine arousal pressed against her soft female mound. She heard his swift intake of breath as her hips moved involuntarily against him, and rejoiced in the knowledge of how she affected him.

When he thrust her away from him she almost fell. A steadying hand on her shoulder kept her upright, but his touch was hard and impersonal.

'We have to go back—I to apologise to your godfather and you to gloat.'

She glanced up at his hard face and knew he was as disgusted with himself as she was.

CHAPTER NINE

DEX held open the car door and gestured for her to get in.

Beth hesitated. Dex was wrong. She had no desire to gloat. Instead she felt an overwhelming sadness for what she had lost.

He mistook her hesitation for fear. 'You have nothing to be afraid of, Beth. I wouldn't deliberately harm a hair of your head. Now get in. I promise I will not drive fast.'

The journey back to the villa was short and completed in absolute silence. Until Dex turned the car into the drive and saw another car parked in front of the entrance.

'*Dio*!' Dex groaned, and for a second rested his head on the steering wheel.

Beth glanced at him and for a moment felt some sympathy for him, but then she saw again Dex lashing out at the unsuspecting Paul, and she checked herself in time. He did not deserve her sympathy. Opening the door, she jumped out of the car and started towards the house.

Suddenly a woman came flying out, a woman Beth immediately recognised as Dex's sister, and she looked just as excitable as the only other time Beth had seen her. She shot past Beth and yelled at Dex.

Beth looked back in amazement as Dex stood granite-faced while his sister Anna bawled him out. She jumped when a hand fell on her shoulder. Turning around, she looked up into the familiar face of Paul.

'Are you all right, Bethany?' he asked quietly. The beginning of a magnificent black eye was marring his handsome features. 'In the excitement of the past few weeks, I forgot I saw you with Dexter at the casino until he dragged you off today. I was worried about you. Is there something going on between you two I don't know about?'

'No, of course not. I met him with Mike and he offered to show me his new casino—full stop.' Beth couldn't tell Paul the truth. 'And you have no need to worry, I'm fi—' That was as far as she got, before Paul cut across her.

'What the hell did you think you were playing at, Giordanni? Aiming a punch at me I can understand—maybe I deserved it—but dragging off my god-daughter...'

Beth spun around to find Dex standing stiffly behind her. One look at his dark face and she knew he had overheard her conversation with Paul. But he looked straight over the top of her head at Paul, his face a grim mask. Anna moved to link her arm through Paul's while smiling rather shamefacedly at Beth.

'Paul,' Dex said curtly, acknowledging the other man's outburst before continuing, 'I thought I was protecting my sister's honour. But nothing I say can possibly excuse my disgraceful actions. I apologise from the bottom of my heart. I should not have lashed out at you. I am deeply sorry and ashamed. I can only beg your forgiveness and hope in time you can forget my appalling behaviour. I have already apologised to my sister, and of course to Bethany.'

Beth slanted a glance at him from beneath her thick lashes. As apologies went it was a sizzler, and there was no mistaking the sincerity in Dex's dark eyes. But she did not remember him apologising to her, she thought mutinously. She was about to say so when Anna held out her hand towards her, and, nudging Paul, said, 'Please introduce me.'

The introductions made, Anna bent to kiss Beth's cheek. By the time the social niceties were completed, they were walking into the drawing room.

Beth hesitated, slightly overawed by the opulence of her surroundings. 'This is a wonderful house.' She turned to Paul. 'Have you rented it or what?' she asked, more for something to say than anything else. There was still tension in the air, undercurrents she did not understand.

'Good heavens, no.' Paul chuckled and led her to a cream silk-covered sofa, one of a pair, placed at either side of a massive marble fireplace. 'Dexter owns the villa, though according to Anna he's rarely here. Anna works and lives in Naples. That's where we met. Anna decided to get married from here because there's more room to accommodate the few close friends who are attending the wedding. At my age, and in the circumstances, a big wedding would be out of place.'

Dex really had been secretive with her, Beth thought. Not once had he mentioned a home in Capri. It only confirmed what she already knew: he didn't give a damn about her. But if she had known it was Dex's villa Paul had invited her to stay in, she would never have come—much as she loved her godfather. She didn't want to be beholden to Dex in any way whatsoever.

Dinner was served in a huge formal dining room, and was fraught to say the least! Beth ached to escape to her room. Revenge was not sweet, she realised, sitting at the table, eating the exquisitely prepared food and waited on by a houseboy wearing white gloves! She might not understand Italian, but it was pretty obvious Anna had not forgiven Dex for assaulting her fiancé.

Paul explained the arrangements for the simple wedding service the next day, but after that it was heavy going. Paul's eye had turned purple,and as far as Beth could gather Dex was being blamed for ruining tomorrow's wedding before it had even taken place.

As for Dex, he barely said a word. Beth found her attention drawn to him over and over again. He sat at the head of the great table, wearing a black formal evening suit and brilliant white shirt, his handsome features set in a hard mask of iron control. He looked even more dangerously formidable than usual. The few times he caught her glance, he stared at her so coldly she quickly looked away, afraid the others would notice.

She heaved a sigh of relief when the meal ended and coffee was served in the drawing room. She sat down on the sofa and gratefully took the cup of coffee the houseboy handed her.

'We did not meet in the best way,' Anna said, sitting down beside Beth. 'I am sorry, but Paul—we fight, I see you... I do not know...'

'I was his goddaughter.' Beth helped Anna out with her halting English. 'It's all right, we laughed about it afterwards, and I am very happy for you both.'

'Thank you. I wish to be friends.' They smiled a smile of mutual understanding. 'I also apologise for my brother. He thinks he protects my honour. He thinks Paul has betrayed me. He sees him kiss you and goes *pazzo*.'

Whatever *pazzo* meant, Beth was pretty sure she did not want to discuss it.

'Beth does not understand, Anna, and she looks tired.' Dex appeared at the side of the sofa, his narrowed gaze concentrated on his sister, and he said something quickly

in Italian before looking down on Beth. 'Come, I will
show you to your room.'

Her green eyes clashed angrily with cool grey. Cheeky
swine! she thought. More or less saying she looked a
wreck. And whose fault was that? 'I can find my own
way.' Beth jumped to her feet. Dex's height was intimi-
dating.

'After my disgraceful behaviour earlier, please allow
me to redeem myself by acting as a good host,' Dex
drawled smoothly.

She wanted to object, but he made it sound so reasonable. Was she the only one to recognise the cynicism
in his tone? She looked around for Paul but he had
joined Anna on the sofa, and unless she wanted to make
a scene in front of the happy couple there was nothing
to do but agree. She said her goodnights, and, not looking at Dex, walked out of the room.

Once in the hall Beth dashed for the stairs, but Dex,
with his long legs, was at her side in a second.

'You can drop the good host act,' Beth said tersely,
ascending the stairs, very aware of his long-limbed body
matching her step by step. 'I know the way, thank you
very much,' she told him, trying to ignore the way her
heart pounded too fast as he shadowed her so closely,
and vainly trying to convince herself it was the exertion
of climbing the stairs.

His hand gripped her shoulder as she reached the land-
ing and turned to go right. 'Not so fast, Beth, we need
to talk.'

Beth was wearing her one and only formal dress, the
slip of black and gold satin. She felt the searing imprint
of his fingers on her naked flesh, and trembled inside.
She shrugged, trying to shake him off. Looking up at
his harshly handsome face, she gave him a tight-lipped

smile, refusing to let him see how much he disturbed her.

'No, I think not,' she responded distantly. 'We are guests at a wedding, nothing more. Let's just leave it at that.' And, turning on her heel, she'd actually made it to her bedroom door when Dex's voice stopped her.

'Good, so you have no objection to my telling Paul the truth about the relationship between you and I? That is a relief,' he drawled sardonically.

Beth, in the act of opening the door, spun around. 'What?' she looked up, meeting his eyes with horror.

Dex was standing a foot away, his eyes narrowed speculatively on her flushed face. 'Lying even by omission can get a person into a heap of trouble, I always thought. Don't you agree?' he asked, in a voice laced with sarcasm.

Beth knew he was referring to her, and she had a feeling it would be a long time before he forgot she had lied to him. Nervously she backed into the bedroom. He followed her inside without waiting for an invitation, and closed the door firmly behind him. Switching on the light, he looked at Beth, and she almost stumbled under the sheer intensity of his gaze.

'I only want to talk,' Dex said, with the tilt of one dark brow. 'Not leap on you.'

'All right,' she breathed, but spun on her heel and crossed the room to the window. She needed the time to gather her wits, and, swallowing hard, she turned slowly around to face him.

He stared across the room at her. 'Is this bedroom all right for you?'

The mundane question came as a surprise. Beth glanced around the luxuriously appointed bedroom, her glance lingering on the lovely four-poster bed with the elegant floating drapes. 'It's fine,' she said. 'A vast improvement on mine at home.'

Seeing the direction of her gaze, Dex drawled, 'Oh, I don't know. I have very fond memories of your bed.'

Her head jerked back and she looked at him, a vivid image of his large naked body, limbs entwined with her own, flashing in her mind's eye. Her green eyes widened warily on his dark face. She didn't trust him an inch, and she was none too sure about herself. Suddenly the intimacy of the situation hit her. She shivered, and nervously smoothed the skirt of her dress down over her hips with damp palms.

Dex shook his black head and smiled grimly. 'Don't panic. I said talk, and that is what I meant.' He moved a few steps towards her and then stopped, and Beth had the weirdest notion that he was also nervous.

'So?' she prompted softly.

'I owe you an apology. You were right. I did ask you out because I thought you were going out with Paul Morris, and I did do it for my sister. Under the circumstances I would probably do it again.'

Beth finally had her apology, back-handed though it was. She should have been pleased. But knowing the truth and having it spelt out were two different things, she realised sadly. It was no surprise, she tried to console herself, but instead all she felt was simmering pain and anger. 'You really are despicable. I think I hate you,' she said flatly.

'Hate me as much as you like, but let me finish.' Dex raked a hand through his hair in a frustrated gesture, then hesitated for a moment. 'I overheard you telling Paul you and I dated once. End of story. I take it you do not want your godfather or my sister to know the truth?'

'You've got that right,' she muttered, wondering why

the abrupt change of subject but accepting it. 'For some
bizarre reason Paul thinks you were entitled to swing a
punch at him, so why disillusion him?' Her eyes met
his. 'And I'm sure it's what you want as well,' she gibed.
'I can still remember all the out-of-the-way places you
took me to. To avoid being seen with me,' she said,
bitterness making her voice harsh.

His grey eyes flared briefly, then the heavy lids narrowed, hiding his expression from her. 'Believe what
you like, Beth. I am not going to argue with you. I am
not trying to make excuses for my behaviour, it was
inexcusable, but I want to try and explain.

'I told you once I was illegitimate. In my mother's
circumstances it was considered the worst form of
shame. Anna is my older sister. I was born eighteen
months after my mother was widowed. Here in southern
Italy a young, innocent girl making a mistake might
eventually have been forgiven, but it wasn't very likely.
For a newly widowed lady to have had a child was
thought heinous. Even today, in the nineties, a lot of
older women still wear black for the rest of their lives
after the death of their husband.'

Beth's soft heart squeezed. 'You don't have—'

'I do. I want to,' Dex cut in. 'We lived in a little
cottage down at the port. Here on Capri everyone knew
of the circumstances of my birth. My mother braved it
out for years, until I had made enough money and moved
her to Naples.' Dex stared past her as if he was in a
world of his own, remembering. 'My mother died two
years ago a very bitter woman, still not forgiven by the
friends of her youth.'

'Why are you telling me all this?' Beth asked quietly.
Her eyes roamed over his darkly attractive face, the rumpled black wavy hair falling on his proud brow, and she

could easily imagine him as a young boy, an outcast and vulnerable.

Dex moved closer to her and watched her through narrow intent eyes. 'Because I want you to understand why I behaved as I did. I am breaking a confidence in telling you, but I think you need to know. The reason Paul expected me to hit him is quite simple. He is an honourable man. He understands our Latin code of honour. Anna is pregnant, but not yet married. As her brother, I am entitled to knock the man out,' he declared emphatically.

Beth heard the underlying thread of violence in his tone and winced, but as for the rest she was pleased as punch. 'Pregnant,' she murmured. 'That's marvellous.' She smiled, a beaming grin. 'Paul will make a wonderful father, I know.' She was genuinely delighted.

'Now, yes! But about three months ago Paul and Anna parted. I do not usually involve myself with my sister's affairs, but this time was different. She later came to London to see Paul. She called his housekeeper, who told her where he was eating, and she dragged me along with her.'

Beth knew he was telling her the truth, she had overheard him saying as much, but unthinkingly she confirmed his words. 'That's how I always contact Paul, via Mrs Bewick. She always knows where he is.'

'Yes, well, on this occasion perhaps it would have been better if she had not. I saw you in the restaurant long before Anna did. A beautiful young girl smiling so lovingly at a much older man is always worthy of note. So often money is the incentive,' he drawled derisively.

His natural cynicism surfaced for a moment, and Beth felt a stab of distaste. At least now she could understand his reasoning a bit better, but it did not excuse Dex using her for his own ends. Nothing he said or did could repair the damage he had done to Beth, both mentally and physically.

'The rest, as you say, is history. Anna went crazy, and I got her out of the restaurant. Later, when I saw you again, I thought, why not me instead of Morris? I know what it is to be a bastard, and anything I can do to make sure Anna's child does not suffer the same fate I will do willingly,' Dex declared bluntly, his gaze skimming over her, lingering on the proud thrust of her breasts against the soft fabric of her dress, then moving with a flick of his lashes back to her face.

'And you are a very beautiful woman, Beth. It was no hardship.'

No hardship! Her body froze as the full meaning of his words sank in. 'You swine.' She looked up sharply and was shocked at the sensual light in his eyes. 'You...you arrogant creep,' she spluttered. She had almost felt sorry for him, imagining him as a young boy, the other children calling him names. Vulnerable? He was about as vulnerable as a rattlesnake, and twice as deadly.

He smiled, and, reaching out, he ran one long finger down the side of her face.

'Now that is what I wanted to talk about, Beth. Your temper and your obvious aversion to me. We are agreed no one will know of our brief fling. We are casual acquaintances—no more. But if you continue to look daggers at me, as you did tonight at dinner, and flinch every time I come near you, Paul and Anna might get suspicious. So we need a truce between us for the next two days.'

'We need a continent between us,' she prompted bitterly. 'But until I get off this island on Sunday you can have your truce. I don't want to upset Paul and Anna's wedding any more than it already has been.'

Dex eyed her consideringly. 'You mean that, Beth? Friends for the duration, hmm?'

'Yes.' She tilted her head back and boldly faced him. It would kill her, but she would try for Paul.

His hand reached out, catching her wrist. 'Shake on it,' he murmured, looking down into her upturned face. Their eyes met and held. 'Or maybe kiss on it.'

Beth's heart skipped a beat at the look in his eyes, but common sense prevailed. 'Don't push your luck, buster... Leave.'

He chuckled under his breath and, lifting her hand to his mouth, pressed a kiss on her knuckles. 'Thank you. Tomorrow is going to be hell. Paul barely tolerates me, and Anna has told me several times I have ruined their wedding day. The wedding photograph they keep for their children and their children's children will always show the bridegroom with a black eye.'

'Serves you right,' Beth said bluntly. 'It might teach you not to manipulate everyone you meet.' Beth spoke with more force than she realised, but she could still feel the disturbing warmth of his lips on her hand, and she resented her own weakness.

Abruptly Dex dropped her hand. His face darkened. 'I realise I might seem that way, but let me remind you, Beth,' he prompted, an odd harshness in his voice, 'it didn't work with you. You never called.'

Beth stared at him dumbly. What was he talking about? 'Ah, Mike,' she exclaimed. 'You mean your little attempt at blackmail? Sorry, I overslept.' She told him the truth without thinking.

He chuckled mirthlessly. 'You overslept.' Shaking his head, he gave her a cool smile. 'No matter, Beth.

Tomorrow we will behave as friends. Goodnight.'
Spinning on his heel, he left, closing the door quietly
behind him.

Beth was tired and tormented, and all she wanted to
do was shower and crawl into bed. Ten minutes later,
her toilet completed and wearing a short white nightie,
she climbed into the four-poster bed. Drawing the drapes
around the frame, she snuggled down under the covers.
The rest of the world was shut out.

But it was not so easy to shut off her troubled
thoughts. She was dreading tomorrow—the whole weekend! To pretend she was just a friend of Dex without
putting her foot in it was well beyond her acting capa-
bilities, she feared. Her godfather Paul was an astute
man; he knew her better than anyone. Still, she thought
hopefully, Paul had a lot more to worry about than Beth.
His new bride—the ceremony—his black eye!

Beth groaned and buried her head in the pillow. In
her mind's eye she saw Dex's handsome face contorted
by rage, and poor Paul laid out on the ground. In a way
it was partly her fault. If she had refused the wedding
invitation it would never have happened. But then again
Dex was a very Latin male. He saw himself as the pro-
tector of the females in his family. Hadn't he just told
her quite emphatically he felt entitled to slug Paul to
uphold the honour of his sister? Whether he thought
Beth was a threat to his sister or not. The truth was
probably somewhere in between, and on that disturbing
thought she finally fell into a restless sleep.

The small church decked out in flowers and ribbons was
the perfect setting for a perfect wedding. Beth sighed,
her green eyes misty, and brushed a tear from her cheek.
Anna, looking stunningly beautiful in a cream silk suit

overlaid with lace, and wearing a matching wide-brimmed hat with a short veil over her eyes, made her responses clear and true, as did Paul.

Suddenly a large hand holding a white hanky appeared in front of Beth. She glanced sideways at Dex, and took the hanky. 'Thank you,' she murmured. He looked incredibly sleek and handsome in a silver-grey three-piece suit that exactly matched his eyes, and she hastily looked away and dabbed at her moist eyes.

'Emotional little thing, aren't you?' Dex murmured, while staring straight ahead.

'Better than being a heartless swine,' Beth murmured under her breath. Her head bent as she folded the hanky into a perfect square and thrust it back at him without comment.

Dex pressed his large hand over hers. 'Time to leave, I think.'

Sure enough, the bride and groom were halfway down the aisle on their way out, followed by the best man, to whom Paul had introduced Beth earlier as the manager of his Italian estate. Beth frowned, remembering the rest of the conversation. Paul had also informed her that Dex was to take care of Beth for the wedding ceremony and the rest of the weekend. Which was why she had ended up stuck next to Dex in the front pew of the church.

Dex stood up, still holding Beth's hand, urged her to her feet and escorted her down the aisle. But as soon as they got outside Beth dodged behind the main wedding party and tried to lose herself in the crowd. If this was a small Italian wedding, she thought ruefully, sidling along the side of the church, hoping to escape attention, then heaven knew what a large wedding was like. It seemed to her everyone on the island had turned out. Not to mention the shock she had received earlier.

She had awoken to a house full of caterers, managing to grab a bite to eat in the kitchen and a cup of coffee before making herself scarce by exploring the terraced gardens. To her surprise, the terraces led right down to the sea and a private mooring. There, a sleek yacht had been tying up, with a couple of dozen very elegant people on board. Not wanting to be seen, she had hidden behind a large bush and watched as Dex appeared, already dressed formally for the wedding, and greeted the guests. Beth had dashed back to the house and was frantically getting ready when Paul had walked into the room. She'd mentioned the boat to him. Apparently the guests had been accommodated in a luxury hotel in Sorrento for the night, prior to attending the wedding.

'Hello, lady in red.'

Lost in thought, Beth jumped and turned her head. A ginger-haired man of about forty, with an open freckled face, smiled down at her. She recognised his voice immediately; it was indelibly printed on her brain.

'I'm Bob, and red is my colour—as you can see. Put me out of my misery and tell me your name,' he demanded, his blue eyes lit with amusement and a very masculine interest.

Beth grinned. She couldn't help it; there was something boyishly appealing about him. 'Bethany.' She offered her small hand.

'No rings,' Bob murmured, turning her hand over and lifting it to his lips. 'Better and better. I missed the wedding, but I have a feeling I am really going to enjoy the reception.' Beth chuckled. He was the most outrageous flirt.

'Bob. Where the hell were you?' Dex's hard voice interrupted the harmless banter.

Beth's hand was dropped like a hot potato and Bob's

blue eyes flicked assessingly from Dex to Beth and back to Dex again. 'The flight from New York was delayed—everything backed up. Sorry I missed the wedding.'

'I'll see you later,' Dex said curtly, and, turning his back on Bob, let his steely gaze fall on Beth. 'Paul wants you in the family photograph,' he said, and, slipping a long arm over her shoulders, turned her back towards the wedding group.

'All right. You don't have to drag me,' Beth snapped, resenting his arm around her, and resenting even more the way it made her feel.

His fingers tightened on her shoulder and his dark head inclined towards hers. 'A word of warning.' His breath brushed against her cheek, and she tensed. 'Don't waste your feminine wiles on Bob. He is far too smart to get caught.'

Beth gritted her teeth, ignoring his deliberate insult. 'Truce, remember?' she said, looking up into his unsmiling face.

'I remember. And I remember the first time I saw you in that suit.' His grey eyes raked down over her body, bringing a blush to her cheeks. 'You wore it today deliberately to get at me. I am not a fool Beth, so don't take me for one,' he drawled hardily.

'Dexter, *caro*.' The bridesmaid, a tall, elegant dark-haired girl, a friend of Anna, called to him, and Beth was spared from replying as Dex let her go and walked over to the girl.

Beth drew a ragged breath and smoothed the short skirt of her red suit down over her hips. She had vowed not to wear it again after the first time, when Dex had stripped it off her. But she was a realist. She had spent a fortune on the suit a month ago, and she had nothing else remotely suitable for an autumn wedding, and no money to buy anything new. But having Dex remind her was more than she could bear, and she felt the prick of tears behind her eyes—tears of self-pity, she knew.

But then Paul reached out to her and pulled her to his side. 'Come on, Beth, I need you to detract from my black eye.'

Forcing a smile to her flushed face, Beth wished the happy couple good luck. Then quickly the official photographer arranged the group. The photographs were taken amidst what Beth surmised were a lot of ribald comments on how the groom had got his black eye.

She tried to slip back into the crowd when the photographer had finished, but again she was foiled.

'You're coming in the car with me,' Dex said, taking her elbow and urging her to the waiting line of cars.

It got no better when they reached the villa. Paul and Anna greeted all the guests in the grand hall, and an elegant major-domo led everyone to the tables set out in the magnificent dining room. Beth was at the head table.

The caterers had been busy since the crack of dawn, and it was a typical Italian meal that went on for hours and hours. The food was excellent, but Beth tasted very little of it. She felt as if she was on display, and with Dex once again seated next to her she was intensely aware of every move he made. The champagne flowed like water, the talk was loud and happy—not that Beth understood it—and Dex played his part to perfection. He included her in the conversation by offering instant translations, he smiled and was unfailingly polite. But only she could see the ice in his eyes when he spoke to her.

Finally the best man stood up to speak and Beth breathed an audible sigh of relief. It can't be much longer now, she thought.

Dex bent his dark head towards her. 'Your boredom is showing, Beth.' His grey eyes glinted mockingly into hers. 'Weddings not your scene?'

With a flash of insight she realised Dex was right. 'No, not really. After attending three of my mother's, they tend to lose their appeal,' she responded coolly.

'I'm sorry.' He smiled softly, and she saw a glint of something very like pity in his eyes.

'Don't be.' She didn't need his sympathy; she didn't need anything from Dex. 'I'm not. But I suppose it's different for you. This must remind you of your own wedding, no doubt. Bring back pleasant memories, does it?' she goaded. As a conversation-stopper it was perfect.

The slight smile vanished from his face to be replaced with a hard mask of indifference. 'No.' Dex picked up his wine glass from the table, drained it, and ignored Beth for the rest of the reception.

By ten in the evening Beth had had more than enough. There were people everywhere. A trio was playing dance music and the huge hall had become the dance floor. She had danced with a dozen different men, drunk a few classes of champagne and was feeling absolutely shattered. Paul and Anna had left hours ago, for a destination unknown.

Beth sighed. She was in a room full of people and had never felt so alone. Paul, the one constant in her life, was married, and very soon would have his own family—which was only right. But Beth couldn't help the tears that welled up in her throat. Things would never be the same again.

Beth was considering her chances of slipping off to bed when a voice in her ear whispered, 'Our tune—care to dance?'

'Bob.' She grinned as she realised the band was playing 'Lady in Red'. 'Very funny,' she said—at least he spoke her language. 'But, no, thanks. I'm too hot.' She didn't dare take her jacket off, knowing the brevity of the camisole underneath.

'Okay. I'm not much of a dancer anyway. So, how about a stroll outside?'

Why not? she thought, and, linking her arm through his, she followed him outside and down onto the lower terrace, where the floodlit swimming pool gleamed in the darkness.

'Fresh air at last,' she murmured, taking a few deep breaths of the cool night air.

'Here, sit down, Beth, and relax.' Bob indicated a small patio table surrounded by chairs and pulled one out for her. Beth gratefully sat down.

'This is much better,' she said as Bob sat down in the chair opposite.

'Some party.' Bob smiled. 'But Dex doesn't look too happy in there.'

'Maybe the food didn't agree with him,' she said lightly, and grinned back at Bob. He was a nice, uncomplicated man, and she needed someone to take her mind off how very alone in the world she felt.

'The food of love, maybe,' Bob said seriously. 'I know who you are, Beth, and I know you and Dex were engaged.'

Beth felt the colour rise in her cheeks. 'It was a mistake.'

'I don't think so. I've seen the way he looks at you; he has hardly taken his eyes off you all evening. That's not like Dex. I've known him for years and I have never seen him show the least interest in a woman.'

'Please, I don't want to talk about him.'

'Don't be too hard on him, Beth. His ex-wife did a

real number on him. He was just starting out when they married, and he worked like a slave while she spent like a queen! Eventually she took off with a very rich, very much older man.'

'Really, I'm not interested.' But in her heart of hearts she knew she was.

'Look, all I'm saying is Dex is my friend as well as my boss. In fact, I'm probably the only friend he has. He's a very hard man to get to know. But if you care anything for him you should make the effort, Beth. I don't know what went wrong between you weeks ago, but I do know he's been like a bear with a sore head ever since. He was always a workaholic, but lately he's driving himself to the edge.'

'That has nothing to do with me,' Beth muttered, getting to her feet. 'I'm going back.'

'If you say so.' Bob stood up and took her elbow. 'I don't usually interfere in other people's affairs, and if I've offended you, I'm sorry.'

Arm in arm, they walked back into the villa. The crowd was thinning out and Dex saw them immediately. He strolled over, his grey eyes narrowed on Beth. 'Where the devil have you been?' he snapped.

Beth shrank from the rage in his eyes, but before she could answer he added furiously, 'Not content to flirt with every man you danced with, you have to go outside with one!'

'I wasn't flirting,' she choked, feeling incredibly angry. He hadn't spoken to her all night, hadn't danced with her, and now he had the gall to insult her. 'And I went outside because I was hot.'

'Hot.' His lips twisted in a sneer. 'I can believe that.'

'Dex, come on. The girl was with me, and she was perfectly safe,' Bob intervened.

Dex turned to look at Bob. 'I hope so, for your sake.' Then, as if realising where he was, seeing the curious glances of the other guests, Dex straightened his shoulders, his dark face expressionless. 'The boat is leaving in five minutes, Bob. Be on it.' Looking back at Beth, he added bluntly, 'As Paul's representative, you stay by me until we've said goodnight to all the guests.'

Smarting at his angry comments, she raised defiant eyes to his. 'I am not a child to be ordered around.' Dex had virtually ignored her all day except to tell her what to do: 'Get in the car' 'Get in the photograph.' He hadn't even asked her to dance, she thought, burning with resentment.

'Then stop acting like one and do as you're told,' Dex drawled hardily.

'No, thank you. I'd rather leave now. I can get the boat—it won't take me a minute to pack.'

One hand snaked out and closed like a manacle around her wrist. 'You are not going anywhere. Paul left you in my charge and you will leave as arranged tomorrow. I will personally escort you off the island. Understand?'

Beth understood all too well. He couldn't wait to get rid of her. Her brave notion of accepting the wedding invitation and stunning Dex with her sophisticated attitude was just that—a notion.

'All right,' she snapped. 'You can let go of my hand.' And, sticking a smile on her face, she did as he had commanded.

She stood stiffly beside him and accepted the flowing tributes, the smiles and handshakes, with the best grace she could muster. All the time intensely conscious of the dark, brooding man standing beside her.

'Thank heavens for that,' she murmured under her

breath as the last guest departed. Glancing around the huge reception hall, it crossed her mind that perhaps she should help to clean up, but the caterers were buzzing around clearing everything with remarkable efficiency. She wasn't needed, and her bed beckoned.

'My sentiments exactly,' Dex drawled, and took her arm as she stepped forward. 'How about a nightcap?'

She glanced at him quickly over her shoulder. He had loosened his bow tie and unfastened the first few buttons of his shirt. He was so devilishly attractive; her heart lurched at the sight of him.

'I don't think so. I've had enough.' And she was not just talking about drink. It had suddenly hit her that once the caterers departed she would be virtually alone in the house with Dex, and it did nothing for her peace of mind.

CHAPTER TEN

DEX'S black head inclined towards her. 'As you wish. I will show you to your room.'

'No way,' she said bluntly, placing her hand on his chest to ward him off. She raised her eyes to his. 'I do not need a repeat of last night. Go have your drink.' The heavy pounding of his heart beneath her hand found an echo in her own body, and she trembled from head to toe.

'It is not a drink I need,' Dex said thickly, his eyes glittering down into hers. 'I need to once more strip that seductive suit from you.' With one long finger he traced a line from her collarbone down the vee of her jacket to slide along the soft curve of her breast. 'And lose myself in your body. Unlike you, I can never have enough,' he drawled, his deep, husky voice playing on her over-sensitive nerves.

Beth was struck dumb. She stared up at him, her fingers shaking on his chest, her nipples hardening against the fine fabric of her top in shameful arousal. She was mesmerised by the smouldering desire in his silver eyes. For a long moment she simply stared, torn between the desire to know once more the pleasure of his possession and the certain knowledge that she meant little or nothing to him.

Would it be so wrong? she asked herself. To have one more night in his arms? She loved him even though he didn't deserve her love, didn't want it.

A loud crash brought her back to her senses with a jolt. One of the caterers had dropped a tray of glasses. Beth quickly snatched her hand back from his chest and, spinning on her heel, dashed upstairs. She only paused for breath when she was safely in her bedroom with the door locked behind her.

Thank God for a clumsy waiter! Another second and she would have slid her arms around Dex and been his for the taking, Beth bleakly admitted to herself. Stripping off her clothes, she showered and slipped on her white cotton nightie. She was exhausted, but too agitated too sleep, her body aching with frustration. Disgusted with herself, she methodically set about packing her weekend case. She was leaving in the morning and it would save time. She left out her blue jeans, a cashmere sweater and her navy jacket.

Finally, with nothing left to do, she got into bed. But sleep was elusive. She relived the events of the past two days in her head.

Her harmless walk with Paul and Dex's violent re-action had been terrifying. But had it only been on behalf of his sister, or could he possibly have been a little bit jealous of Beth herself? The thought brought solace to her bruised heart. And then later, in this room, Dex had reminded her she hadn't called him when he'd tried to blackmail her. She suddenly realised Dex had still not known Paul was her godfather, so at any time in the past two weeks he could have got Mike fired from his job, and yet he had not done it. Which proved Dex was not all bad...

Today he had hardly spoken to her, and yet he had warned her off Bob quite emphatically. Dex no longer had any need to pretend he liked her, so why warn her about Bob? Unless he was jealous. She was clutching at straws, she knew. But then again, Bob was convinced Dex *did* like her. He had told her in the garden Dex was a hard man to know, and that if she cared anything at all for him it was up to her to make the effort.

Bob's revelation about Dex's ex-wife went a long way to explain Dex's paranoid reaction when he'd thought Beth was going out with Paul, his constant assumption that Beth wanted an older man. Even on their picnic in the New Forest he had hinted as much.

And tonight, when he had asked her to have a drink with him and then quite deliberately tried to... She felt the heat rise in her face and she turned to lie flat on her back. She heard again in her mind his deep velvet voice declare he could not get enough and swallowed hard. If only he knew... She was quite desperate for him. But the difference between them was that Dex wanted her, but she loved him.

What kind of love was it, though, she asked herself, if she didn't dare admit it? She had been quite prepared to swallow her pride for Mike, her stepbrother. Surely she could do at least as much for the man she loved. Dex had once said he liked her honesty. Tomorrow she would be honest and tell Dex how she felt. After all, what was the worst that could happen? He could laugh in her face and tell her to get lost. But after tomorrow she was unlikely to see him again anyway. She had nothing to lose...

A banging on the door woke Beth. She groaned and rolled over.

'Beth, open the door.'

She scrambled out of bed and shot across the room to

turn the key in the lock. The door swung open and she had to jump back as Dex marched in carrying a tray in one hand bearing a coffee pot and cup plus fresh bread rolls and various jams.

Mindful of her decision last night, Beth looked up at him, a tentative smile curving the corners of her wide mouth. This morning he was casually dressed, in well-worn blue jeans and a white sweater that contrasted starkly with his dark good looks. Tearing her eyes away from his powerful body, she looked at the tray he carried. 'For me? Thank you,' she said softly. 'But you needn't have bothered. I...' She'd been going to say she could have eaten downstairs, but didn't get the chance.

'Yes, I did. My housekeeper has already called you once and she is far too old to be running up and down stairs for the likes of you.' His grey eyes scrutinised her slender form with a contempt that made her feel she was naked, lingering on the thrust of her breasts and then down to where her nightie ended mid-thigh before he strolled over to the bedside table and slammed the tray down.

'I'm sorry. I didn't realise.' Beth was trying to stay calm, but his obvious black mood was not helping.

'So you should be.' Dex swung back and walked towards the door. 'You certainly have a penchant for over-sleeping. Obviously you're not bothered by a conscience.'

'Now wait a minute!' Beth exclaimed, her small chin jutting belligerently. She might have been prepared to swallow her pride last night, but she was fast going off the idea as she stared at Dex's frowning face.

'You don't have a minute. It is ten o'clock.'

Beth's eyes widened in horror. 'Oh, my God!' Her plane departed from Naples at twelve forty-five.

'Exactly. I want you out of here in twenty minutes.' And he slammed out of the room.

Beth paused for a moment, her head bowed and her long auburn hair falling like a curtain on either side of her face. So much for Bob's idea that Dex might care for her. He couldn't wait to get her out of his house and out of his country.

Her lips tightened in disgust with herself. What a fool she was. Brushing the hair from her face, she stalked over to the bed, poured herself a cup of coffee and drank it, and then determinedly set about getting ready. She would show the arrogant pig just how fast she could be!

In a matter of minutes she was washed and dressed in jeans, sweater and jacket, thanking the foresight that had made her pack her case last night. She scraped her hair back and tied it with a scarf, flung her shoulder bag over her shoulder picked up her case and walked downstairs. All in the space of ten minutes.

Dex appeared from the drawing room door. His steely eyes swept over her and his lips curved in a grimace. 'You're ready. Good. I'll go and collect your luggage. Wait here.'

'This *is* my luggage,' she said curtly, indicating her one small weekend case.

His dark brows rose in astonishment. 'Amazing—a woman who travels light.' Striding over to her, he took the case from her nerveless fingers and headed for the door. 'Come on, we have no time to waste.'

She followed him out of the house and stopped, looking along the drive. 'Where is the car?' Beth demanded.

The sunshine of the past two days had given way to

grey, overcast skies, with black clouds rumbling along the horizon. She shivered as a cold wind whistled along the headland, and she fastened her jacket.

Dex was halfway across the broad expanse of grass, heading towards the terrace. He gave her a backward glance over his shoulder. 'No car. We are going in my launch.'

'But I came on the ferry.'

Dex stopped and turned around to face her. 'I know. But if Anna had seen fit to inform me you were coming I would have arranged for the launch to collect you.'

'Big deal,' Beth muttered under her breath.

'Hurry up.'

Still muttering, Beth followed Dex down the row upon row of terraces until they reached the jetty. Then she stared. It was not the yacht of yesterday but a twenty-foot speed boat, with a small cabin and wheelhouse, tied up against the dock. The blue sea was almost black, the waves lashing the boat against the side of the wooden structure.

Dex had already jumped on board, but Beth eyed the boat and the sea with dismay. 'Are you sure you know what you're doing?' she demanded flatly.

Dex turned back and, reaching a long arm over the side of the boat, caught her hand in his. 'For heaven's sake, woman, get on the boat and let's go.' He was almost dragging her up the short gangplank.

'The sea looks a bit rough,' she ventured.

'It wasn't an hour ago,' Dex snapped.

Even the weather was her fault now, Beth thought, thoroughly fed up. Stepping into the bottom of the boat, she pulled her hand free from his. 'Well, it is now,' she snapped back, glaring up at him.

His dark brows drew together in a frown of irritation. 'For once in your life will you stop arguing and do as I tell you? I am going to go up and start the engine—' he gestured with his hand to the wheelhouse '—and when I cry ''cast off'' all you have to do is slip that rope off that cleat. Understand?' He pointed to where a rope from a capstan on the jetty stretched out to an iron thing on the boat.

'Yes, of course. I'm not a simpleton.' Beth gave him a nasty glance, then looked from Dex to the back of the boat and took a deep breath. What she knew about boats would not cover a postage stamp, but she wasn't going to tell him that. She glanced back and saw he was already at the wheel. Slipping her shoulder bag off her arm, she laid it on a box-like thing and staggered to the back of the boat.

She bent down and tried to get her fingers round the rope. She moved around slightly, to get a better grip.

Dex started the engine and yelled, 'Ready, Beth?'

At the sound of his voice she jerked up, taking the rope with her. The next thing she knew she was flying through the air. She screamed! The rope slipped from her grasp and she hit the water flat on her back.

I'll kill the bastard, was the first thought in her head, and then she swallowed what felt like half the Mediterranean and sank like a stone. Her next thought was survival, as the cold black water closed over her, pressing her down. Kicking out with her feet, she pushed for the surface, but her heavy clothes hampered her. Struggling to hold her breath, she tore at the buttons of her jacket and wriggled out of it. Her lungs felt as if they were bursting as she kicked out again. Finally her head broke the surface of the water, and she took a great gulp of air before a wave smashed down on her, pushing her under once more.

Fighting again for the surface, she managed to gasp a few more breaths of air. She could see the jetty some ten yards away, and a metal ladder which disappeared under the water. She might not know much about boats but she was a good swimmer, and, mentally gritting her teeth, she struck out for the ladder.

Suddenly an arm shot around her neck, knocking what little breath she had straight out of her body. Panicking, she struggled wildly, and then she felt a sharp blow, and nothing more.

Beth's eyelids fluttered, and then she coughed, and coughed again, water streaming from her mouth. She groaned and slowly opened her eyes. Her head was pressed against a broad shoulder and two strong arms supported her and carried her along. But she was soaked, and frozen to the bone.

'*Grazie a Dio*! You are alive...' Dex's deep voice echoed in her head. 'Don't try to speak, my love. I have you safe.'

Her eyes fluttered closed again. She was shaking so much she couldn't speak, her teeth would not stop chattering and great shudders racked her small frame. She was vaguely aware of being lowered to her feet, that gentle hands were stripping off her sweater. She opened her eyes again. Somehow she was back in her bathroom, and it was Dex who was supporting her, with one arm around her waist, while with his other hand he was peeling her sodden jeans off her legs.

She tried to lift her hands to resist, but another wave of shivers convulsed her. Then once more she was lifted from the floor and suddenly she was being held under a cascade of water. She flinched, bowing her head as the hot water stung her numb flesh, then gradually some of the numbness faded and the warmth of the water began to sink through to her frozen bones.

Also it began to sink into her shocked brain that she was being supported by two strong bare arms. 'What...?' was as much as she got out.

'Shh, shh, Beth.' And she was wrapped in a huge fluffy towel, and strong hands began to rub her all over. 'I will take care of you.'

Take care of her! Suddenly it all came back to Beth: the boat, the sea—everything. Somehow finding the strength, she slapped his hands away.

'What the hell do you think you're doing?' she cried hoarsely, her throat raw from the sea water. And, staggering back, she grabbed the towel, wrapped it toga-style under her arms and knotted it.

'You need to get warm. You've had a severe shock.'

She whipped the tangled mass of her wet hair out of her eyes and lifted her head, and got an even bigger shock. Dex was standing in front of her, water droplets dripping off his black hair onto his broad shoulders, trickling down his muscular chest, his flat belly. She gulped. Her eyes flew wide open and trailed down to the brush of black curls, protecting the beginning of his masculine sex, and lower, to his long, muscular legs. He was stark naked.

'You...you...get out,' she squeaked, still shivering with cold but intensely aware of his magnificent all-male body.

'This is no time for modesty, Beth. I have to get you warm. You might have hypothermia.'

She was more likely to hyperventilate if he didn't put

something on—and quickly, she thought distractedly, glancing wildly around the bathroom, anywhere but at the naked man towering over her. Her eye caught a towel on the rail. 'So might you,' Beth choked, and, reaching out, snagged the towel and shoved it at Dex. 'Here.'

His large hand covered hers and pulled her towards him. Taking the towel from her nerveless fingers, he casually slung it around his hips. 'Your concern is touching, Beth.' He chuckled deep in his throat. 'But seriously, you were in the water a lot longer than I.' Reaching out, he pulled her into the circle of his arms and held her pressed tightly against him. 'Humour, me, hmm?' he murmured when she tried to pull free, and he gently stroked her back and buttocks through the towel.

For a long moment Beth gave herself up to the unaccustomed comfort of being held in Dex's arms. Gradually her shivering stopped and a slow warmth spread through her body. Her jaw ached and she cushioned it gently against the hairs on his chest. There was nothing sexual about it. Maybe she just needed the sense of care and protection Dex was offering.

'Better now, sweetheart?' Dex asked, rubbing his chin on the top of her head. 'Come on, let me get you into bed.'

The mention of 'bed' broke through her dazed brain. My God! What was she doing? She was supposed to be on a plane to England. Instead she was standing almost naked in a bathroom…and it was all Dex's fault.

Beth looked up at him. 'You've got to be joking.' She couldn't control her anger. He was smiling down at her. Clad in only a towel, he looked wickedly attractive, and a swift stab of regret pierced her heart, but she quickly vanquished her wayward feelings. 'You bastard.'

The smile left his eyes and his hard face tautened arrogantly. 'Bastard, yes. But I only mentioned bed for you—for warmth. Not for me. I can't help it if you have a one-track mind,' he drawled mockingly, his arms falling away from her.

Free and furious, Beth registered his mocking insult and it was too much for her fragile emotions. 'Why...you...you...supercilious swine. You're crazy...stark, staring mad... First you punch out my godfather, and then you try to drown me. Not content with that, you almost strangle me, and then you knock me out.' The pain in her jaw, she realised, was from when Dex had grabbed her in the water. Rubbing her hand over the bruise, she glared defiantly at Dex. 'What happens next...a knife in the gut?'

She had no idea how incredibly lovely she looked, her green eyes flashing fire, nor how heartbreakingly young and vulnerable, with one of her hands clasping the precarious knot in the towel around her slender body.

Beth was not aware of the fierce tension tautening Dex's large frame, her eyes were suddenly filling with moisture. The after-effects of the traumatic shock she had suffered were catching up with her.

'No knife. But I will love you to death,' Dex said hoarsely. And, catching her by the shoulders, his fingers digging into her flesh, he added urgently, 'If you will only let me, Beth.'

She gazed up at him and saw such anguish, such need in the depths of his silver eyes her heart stopped. She blinked, unable to believe what she was seeing.

'I love you so much, Beth. Please say something, anything,' he demanded, his voice raw with emotion. 'I thought I could let you walk away, but I can't.'

She stared at him. The cold, remote mask he showed the world was gone, and she saw his heart in his eyes. 'You love me,' she murmured. 'You love me!' she exclaimed, her own eyes overflowing with tears of emotion. The impossible had happened.

'Please don't cry, Beth. Please, I never meant to make you cry,' he pleaded. 'As God is my witness, I didn't tip you out of the boat. I asked if you were ready, and you cast off instead. When I saw you in the water I jumped in to save you because I couldn't bear the thought of my life without you. If I was too clumsy, I'm sorry. But carrying you back to the house was the most horrendous walk of my life. I wouldn't hurt you for the world. You must believe that. I love you.'

She lifted her small hand to his face and stroked from his temple down to his jaw. 'I'm not crying because you hurt me.' A wide smile of pure joy lit her lovely face. 'I'm overwhelmed because you love me—as I love you.'

Dex looked deep into her huge green eyes. 'You love me? Since when?' he asked roughly.

'From the first moment I saw you.' Beth stared up at him, and what he saw in her eyes told him she was telling the truth.

He groaned and swept her into his arms, kissing her with a hard, hungry passion. Beth clung to him, her arms around his neck, returning his kiss with equal passion, as though between them they could erase the heartache of the past few weeks. The towels fell away, they were naked together, and Dex's hard, aroused body ground against hers. His hands slid down to cup her buttocks and lift her bodily off her feet.

Involuntarily Beth locked her legs around him, afraid to fall, then gasped as the hard length of him nudged against the delta of her thighs. His head bent to her breasts and he took one into his mouth and suckled fiercely. Beth whimpered, her arms tightening around his neck as he did the same to the other one.

He lifted his head and his fierce silver eyes caught and held hers. 'I have loved you from the first time I saw you, too,' he growled, deep in his throat, and thrust up into her. She cried out, her eyes widening the second he took possession of her.

It was a wild, savagely quick coupling. Dex's taut face became a dark blur, and Beth gave herself up to the wild ride until with a hoarse cry Dex shuddered violently, spilling his seed inside her, and she convulsed around him.

Dex held her for a long moment as shudder after shudder racked his great body. Beth felt the lingering spasms in every nerve-ending of her body. Finally Dex lowered her slowly to the floor, and if he had not been holding her she would have collapsed at his feet. Her legs were shaking, her whole body shook...

'Hell! What am I thinking of?' Dex swore hoarsely, staring down into her flushed face. 'I am an insensitive jerk.' And, swinging her up in his arms, he carried her through to the bedroom and placed her gently on the bed.

When he would have stood up, Beth curled her hand around the back of his neck. 'So long as you are *my* jerk,' she prompted, a questioning light in her green eyes. The last few minutes had left her dazed and awed by the wonder and power of her lover. But did it mean the miracle had happened and Dex really loved her?

'Always and for ever,' Dex vowed, lowering his long body over her. His hands palmed either side of her head and he kissed her slowly, gently, with aching tenderness. 'But now, my love…' He rolled to one side and curved his arm firmly around her, so they were lying side by side, and with his other hand pulled the coverlet over them. He leaned over her. 'Now you need to rest.' He gently pushed back a strand of damp hair from her brow and stared down at her, the banked-down passion in his silver eyes firmly controlled. 'You could catch cold, pneumonia, and now I have you I am taking no chances on losing you again.'

She wanted to believe him, but still a nagging doubt haunted her. 'You're not just saying that because you feel guilty about…about everything?' she asked, stammering over the words.

'Making love to you so desperately you mean?' He favoured her with an ironic look.

'I…' She blushed. 'I didn't know you could make love like that. Standing, I mean, and so hot and fast…'

'There is a lot you don't know about love, and I am going to spend my life teaching you,' he said, gently outlining her lips with his finger. 'Before, in the bathroom, I could not have stopped myself, and neither could you. No matter what the differences between us, there was never any doubt from the first time I kissed you that the chemistry between us was electric.'

'In the casino,' Beth said softly, remembering. 'You were angry because Paul was there and I spoke to him.'

Dex sighed. 'For that I do feel guilty.'

'You only took me out because of Paul and Anna,' Beth said reflectively. 'So when…?' She hesitated. 'When did you fall in love with me?' It was the one question she desperately wanted the answer to.

'With hindsight, probably from that night. I kissed you and went up in flames.'

'Don't lie to me, Dex,' Beth said quietly. 'We both know that isn't true.'

'True? What is truth?' Dex demanded, looking into her worried eyes. 'You want the truth—I will give it to you. You know I have been married before, that my wife left me for an older, richer man?'

'That must have been hard.'

'Not really. I had long since stopped loving her—if I ever did. She was the first woman I had sex with, so I married her. She then proceeded to dole out her favours—very occasionally, and only after I had presented her with a suitably expensive piece of jewellery. She was a mercenary, frigid bitch, but it took me five years to realise it.'

Beth could her the anger in his voice. 'I'm sorry. You don't have to talk about it…'

'Yes, I do, Beth, because she coloured my view of women for years. Until I met you I had never been out with the same woman more than a couple of times. I am not proud of how I have lived my life, I admit, but when I met you I had no intention of changing.' He tenderly smoothed her hair down the side of her head, and dropped a soft kiss on her brow.

'But with you I met my Waterloo, Beth, darling. I kept telling myself I was seeing you to keep you away from Paul for Anna's sake, but I think I knew deep down I loved you. I vowed after my divorce I would never give another woman a piece of jewellery, and yet I found myself quite happily standing in a jeweller's shop, picking out a ring for you. The day after we got engaged and I went to New York I finally admitted to myself I loved you. A week in your company and I missed you so badly I wanted to phone you a dozen times a day.'

'You didn't, though,' Beth said, remembering her own doubts at the time. 'You didn't even tell me where you lived, about this house... Did you share it with your wife?' She still had doubts, she realised.

'The villa was built after my divorce, and, no, I didn't phone you as I wanted to. And then I got back to England, and the conversation you overheard. Well, it was my last-ditch attempt to pretend I was not desperately in love with you. I made myself have a drink with Bob. Bob knows me well, and I think he guessed the truth when I told him I had given you an engagement ring. I said the things I did to him because I was on the defensive, but in my heart I knew I wanted you and I was going to marry you.' His grey eyes hardened. 'I made myself delay seeing you only to discover you were out. Then you kept me waiting for hours and gave me my marching orders.'

She could hear the underlying fury in his tone. 'Only because I thought you were using me,' she responded, and gently stroked her fingers through the crisp hair on his broad chest. He caught her hand in his and placed it around his waist, one long leg moving restlessly against her thigh.

'What price truth, then, Beth? You could have told me.'

'Pride,' Beth said sadly. 'Plain pride. I thought, why should I tell you about Paul and put you and your sister out of your misery? It was nothing to do with me. And later, well...you were so angry...'

'Later...' Dex sighed, a deep frown creasing his brow. 'I behaved like an animal. Afterwards I stood in that tiny bathroom of yours for ages, afraid to come out, afraid to face you. And then you said I'd forced you, and, heaven help me, I still wonder. Can you ever forgive me for that night, Beth?'

How could she have let him think that? Especially now she knew how his ex-wife had treated him. 'Oh, Dex!' She stroked her hand up his back. 'There was nothing to forgive. I'm ashamed to admit I only said that because I was shocked at how much I wanted you and how much I—well...' She looked away, still shy even though they had been as close as it was possible for two people to be.

'Well, what?' He caught her chin and turned her back to face him, his silver eyes boring into hers.

'How much I enjoyed—no, loved what you did to me. Then I felt shocked, ashamed at my own reaction, and I took it out on you.'

A slow smile of pure male pride curved his sensuous mouth. 'And I took it out on you, in a way. I resented the fact that I had fallen in love with you, but in my conceit I thought you would be forever grateful I was going to marry you. My pride was shattered when you had the nerve to jilt me.'

'But you came back,' Beth said breathlessly as his hand trailed down from her breast and settled low on her stomach. 'Hallowe'en night. And you tried to black-mail me.'

'Ah, yes, the party,' Dex drawled huskily, lowering his head and brushing her lips with his. 'Seeing you in that cat costume has caused me more erotic dreams than I dare think about.'

'You wouldn't really have cost Mike his job?' Beth asked, just as he was about to kiss her again.

'I can't blame you for asking, but, no, I would never do anything that would harm you. It was the last, desperate try of a man crazy with love but not prepared to admit it. When you didn't call the next morning, I rang you.'

'That's right,' Beth realised. 'The phone woke me up.' But there was still something she didn't understand. 'If you knew you loved me, why were you so furious with me on Friday night?'

'On Friday I had just flown in from New York. Anna had not seen fit to tell me anything about the wedding, simply the time and place, and I arrived to see you kissing Paul. I yelled at you because I was mad with jealousy, and then when you explained I felt a complete fool. I hoped to talk to you later that night, try and start afresh.'

'I did think you looked a bit nervous when you came into my bedroom. This room.' She smiled up at him.

'You are so innocent, Beth.' His hand slid from her stomach to stroke back up her body and settle softly over one breast. Not for much longer, if Dex has his way, Beth thought, as her nipple hardened beneath his palm and she moved her hips restlessly from side to side.

He chuckled, his thumb flicking the nub of her breast. 'I can laugh now. But have you any idea what it does to a man's ego to have the woman he loves tell him she overslept? I spent the whole night at my hotel unable to sleep, waiting to hear your answer. And you overslept!'

'The answer was no, anyway,' she murmured, and nestled closer to his hard frame, rubbing one of her shapely legs against his muscular hair-covered one.

'I guessed as much. You're not the type of woman to

be bullied into anything,' he opined with an ironic smile. 'And God knows, I've tried.'

'I noticed,' she teased, and then frowned. 'But yesterday you ignored me almost all day.'

'Ignored you!' Dex grinned, his silver eyes gleaming with wicked delight. 'My god, Beth, I didn't dare look at you. When I saw you in the red suit again, my body reacted much the same way as it is now.' He flung a long leg over her slim hips and made her vitally aware of his aroused state.

'I could barely walk straight all day. I wanted to kill Bob for talking to you, but I didn't dare stay beside you myself. And as for dancing with you, I couldn't trust myself not to have you on the dance floor.'

'Dex, that's terrible!' She laughed, finally believing this proud, handsome man did love her.

He rolled over her completely. 'Truthfully, Beth, I resented the way you made me feel. I don't like to be out of control. And this morning, when you slept in again, after I'd had another sleepless night, I was furious. I thought, why waste my time yearning for a girl who obviously cares so little she doesn't lose so much as a minute's sleep over me? But when I saw you in the sea... Pride, conditioning—nothing mattered but that I told you how I feel. I love you and I want you to marry me. And you still haven't answered.'

'Yes,' she murmured, and answered him in the most convincing way. She slipped one hand around his neck as her other hand traced down over his hip and around his thigh.

Dex groaned and covered her mouth with his. This time it was a long, slow loving, and at the end Beth opened her eyes and watched his dark face contort in rigid lines of ecstasy before she was swept along in a torrent of sensations, her eyes closing, and she cried out as they reached the ultimate release together.

'Are you all right?'

She heard his voice and slowly opened her eyes. She could feel his heart slamming against his chest where he lay on top of her, her own equally as erratic. 'I'm…I'm fine,' she whispered, and, lifting her hand, she pushed back the errant black curl from his damp brow.

His grey eyes were almost black as they held hers. 'The rare times I could sleep I used to dream of you like this,' he rasped. 'Your glorious hair spread across my pillow, your luscious body beneath mine. But my dreams came nowhere near the reality, Beth.' He gently rubbed his mouth against hers. 'I want you to know it has never been like this for me before…ever…'

Beth wrapped her arms around him and hugged him to her. 'I'm glad,' she sighed.

'You are the only woman in the world for me and I will cherish you to my dying day. Understand?' Dex said, almost fiercely.

So typical of Dex, Beth thought, rejoicing in his avowal of love. Even when he was at his most vulnerable, sated with love and laying his heart at her feet, the arrogant, powerful man still shone through. She smiled lazily up at him. 'I understand,' she said demurely, and kissed him.

Dex rolled over and pulled her gently into his arms. 'Are you warm enough?'

Beth laughed out loud. 'If I was any hotter the sheets would catch fire and your housekeeper…' She sat up. 'Oh, my God. It's the middle of the day—anyone could walk in.' Her eyes slid down over his naked body and she blushed.

'Don't panic. The housekeeper and her son always have Sunday afternoon off.' Dex chuckled, amused by her embarrassment at his nudity.

'I've missed my plane. I have to go to work tomorrow.' In the euphoria of discovering Dex loved her, Beth had forgotten the more mundane aspects of life.

'Forget it.' Dex caught her around the waist and pulled her down on top of him. 'You don't have to work any more; you're going to be my wife.'

'A lady of leisure?' Beth queried. 'I don't think I'd like that,' she told him seriously, resting her arms on his chest and staring down at him.

'Remember the first time I visited your apartment?'

'What has that got to do with anything?' Beth asked. He wasn't taking her desire to work seriously.

'You have a computer for your graphic art, but you also keep a drawing board. Maybe you are more like your father than you know. I could convert one of the rooms here into a studio for you. Think about it, Beth. Given a choice, which do you prefer? Hands-on art or sitting at a computer?'

'You're right…you know me so well.' She looked down into his eyes and he grinned, his hands sliding down over her bottom.

'And now I'm going to know you again,' he drawled throatily. And he did…

Eighteen months later, the priest and a group of people stood outside the little church on the Isle of Capri in the spring sunshine.

'If they're not here in the next five minutes it will be

too late. I have another baptism at ten-thirty,' the priest told Mr Morris—who was holding his own one-year-old boy in his arms—and Mrs Morris, the prospective godparents.

A white Mercedes drew up with a squeal of brakes. Dexter and Bethany Giordanni got out, Dex carrying a small infant in his arms. They raced up to the church door, Beth very red-faced, her husband suffering from no such embarrassment.

'What happened to you, Dexter? You're twenty minutes late for your child's christening,' Anna reprimanded her brother.

Dex turned, looking at Beth, his silver eyes brilliant with reminiscent pleasure. Beth blushed even redder and Dex, with a wicked wink, turned back to his sister and said, 'We overslept.' And, with his baby girl in one arm and his other arm around his wife, he swept past an open-mouthed Anna into the church...

SECOND-BEST WIFE

REBECCA WINTERS

CHAPTER ONE

"I'LL be with you in a moment, Giovanni!"

The rap on Gaby Holt's door was a prearranged signal she'd worked out with the polite, twenty-two-year-old Italian student who was employed at the ducal palace museum and spoke excellent English. They were the same age and had become good friends during her study-abroad program at the University of Urbino.

Lately he'd had a habit of coming by the *pensione* after her evening meal. They'd walk to the main piazza in the warm summer night, talk about Italian art and history, and eat *gelato*.

Gaby had fallen in love with Italian ice cream. She'd put on a few pounds since her arrival in Italy, which made her figure more voluptuous. In a few weeks, after she returned home to Las Vegas, Nevada, in the United States, she'd lose the extra weight naturally. With no more delicious Italian pasta, no cannelloni to eat, she'd probably starve to death.

Giovanni thought she was perfect just the way she was and told her to stop worrying. Gaby smiled. She'd fast learned that unlike American men, the Italian male loved women of all ages, shapes and sizes. Fortunately, Giovanni was the non-leering, well-mannered type. A sweet, entertaining companion

who made her laugh and was a big tease, there was
no sexual attraction between them to complicate their
friendship.

If she had a problem with Giovanni, it was that he
was only five feet nine inches, *her* exact height.
Though he was strong and fit, she felt too big for him.
To play down her appearance, she purposely wore flat
leather sandals and kept her long, dark red hair con-
fined in a braid.

One look at her reflection in the mirror and she
decided a brocade vest over her cream-colored cotton
top and matching slacks was needed to camouflage
her curves. After rummaging through the mess on her
bed, she found the desired garment and hurriedly put
it on before opening the door.

"*Ciao*, Gaby."

"*Buona sera*, Giovanni," she answered in her best
beginner's Italian. It was a beautiful language, but she
had only learned the rudiments. *Oh, to have the
money to stay here for a year or two and really learn
it!* But at least she'd received a good start with her
six-week language immersion program. Giovanni had
been helping her learn her verbs. When she got back
home, she'd take more Italian at the University of
Nevada.

As they walked down the hall she stole a glance at
him. Where did he get the suit he was wearing? He
had no money. "You're all dressed up. How come?"

His warm, smiling brown eyes were the same color
as his smooth cap of hair. "Since you will be leaving
Urbino day after tomorrow, I thought I'd take you

someplace special where they serve the best food in all Italy.''

It sounded like he was planning to pay. She couldn't let him do that when he worked so hard for every lira. ''I've already eaten, and I'm not dressed for anything special.''

''You look perfect, and I know for a fact that you can always eat dessert.''

She chuckled. ''You're right about that.''

''Then we will go. The *macchina* is parked behind the *pensione*.''

She blinked. A *macchina* was a car. ''I didn't know you had access to one.''

They had reached the main floor of the boarding house where he ushered her past other students milling about until they arrived at the back entrance.

''Only on very special occasions. Tonight I thought we'd save ourselves some time by driving.''

His reasoning made perfect sense. On this particular weekend, Urbino was swarming with tourists who'd come from all over Europe for a two-day Renaissance Fair. Held the last weekend of August, the beautiful mountain town in the Marches region, a two-hour drive north of Rome, had become a mecca for lovers of Renaissance history and tradition.

For Gaby, the fair represented the culmination of her studies in a country which had taken her heart by storm. The thought of going home to a boring desert of one hundred and five degree heat was killing her, but she had no choice. She'd run out of money and couldn't ask her parents for a loan when they were overextended financially as it was. Six children to feed and educate was no small task.

This had been her idea, her project. She'd earned the money for it. Meeting Giovanni had made the whole experience even more enriching, but it was fast coming to an end and she had to face up to her disappointment. Today her studies were completed. Tonight she determined to savor the activities and not think about leaving this paradise any sooner than she had to.

As they stepped out the back door, an elegant black sedan parked in the minuscule alley filled her vision. This was the first time Giovanni had ever provided them with any sort of transportation.

She turned to ask him what was going on when she saw motion out of the corner of her eye. Because of the angle of the auto, she hadn't realized that there was a chauffeur at the wheel.

In an economy of movement, the man in the driver's seat levered himself from the car. The moment passed in a flash, but it gave her enough time to sense that he was a powerful male, hard and lean, considerably taller than Giovanni.

The shadowy light prevented her from making out details, though she could tell he had black hair and was dressed in dark clothing.

"Gaby, allow me to present my elder brother, Luca Francesco della Provere, who is home from Rome for the festival."

His brother?

Gaby knew Giovanni had family, but she hadn't

paid much attention because they were always so busy talking about their studies and interests.

Closer now, she could see a slight resemblance through the bone structure. But where there was softness in the angles of Giovanni's countenance, lines of experience had hardened his brother's aquiline features, and there was none of Giovanni's innocence in that brooding regard.

Those black eyes continued to appraise her, but his expression conveyed nothing of what he might be thinking. For an unknown reason, she shivered.

"You have a last name, *signorina*?" His deep voice revealed a less-marked Italian accent than Giovanni's. If his perfect English was anything to go by, he, too, appeared to have received the best kind of education.

"I—it's Holt," she stammered like a foolish schoolgirl. "How do you do?"

She would have put out her hand, but she had the oddest premonition that he wouldn't have reciprocated, so it remained at her side.

Gaby's European tour director, Gina, had warned her that because she was an attractive American on her own, she was a target for those Latin males who prowled for women with grotto-blue eyes and flawless creamy skin like Gaby's.

According to Gina, no Italian man could be trusted because they possessed an appeal and cunning all their own and represented danger to any woman whether she be nine or ninety-nine. Since they were master seducers, Gaby was to avoid them like the plague.

Gina had a rule of thumb. Never look any of her countrymen in the eye, never listen to their tragic, ridiculous stories meant to entrap you, always walk with a purpose. In most cases, the blatantly obvious, hopeful suitors would do nothing more than stare in adoration and eventually leave you alone.

At the Trevi fountain in Rome, where the local male inhabitants assembled in droves to watch the female tourists taking pictures of the statuary and then follow them around, Gina's advice had worked like a charm.

Gaby had managed to elude the most ardent admirers, specifically her Neapolitan bus driver who, though married with two children, flirted with Gaby every chance he got.

Oddly enough, the Provere brothers weren't anything like the men Gina had been talking about. Giovanni had never once come across as a man with a secret agenda. Nor had he pressed for a physical relationship with her. Initially, that was the reason why she'd allowed herself to become friendly with him at all.

As for his brother, who looked closer to thirty and was probably married, he didn't resemble the thousands of hot-blooded, working class, southern European males who conducted the local tours and waited tables.

On the contrary, there was an aloofness about him, an aura of wealth and refinement. The kind bred into his bones, which put him in an entirely different strata of man.

She was aware of an indolent ease in his demeanor which had probably been learned from the cradle because he'd been born privileged and cherished. Gaby had only had occasional glimpses of such men during early morning rush-hour traffic in the bustling cities of Rome and Florence.

They would alight from their Lamborghinis or Maseratis to enter their places of business. At the end of the day, she'd watch them whiz away into the twilight and wonder which palazzo they called home.

She could easily imagine this man returning to his fabulous family villa in Rome or, like several she'd glimpsed, hugging the mountainsides in this region of Italy.

If she were being fanciful, she could be forgiven. As Giovanni helped her inside the back seat of the plush automobile, which felt more like a dignitary's limousine, she noticed the ornament on the hood of the car which represented a crest of some kind with a coat of arms.

She couldn't imagine what it all meant and wanted to ask Giovanni. To her dismay, his brother had taken his place behind the wheel and started up the motor, which purred like an expensive German-made car. There would be no privacy now.

In any case, Giovanni had struck up a conversation with his enigmatic brother who drove to the end of the alley bordered by the bricked walls of centuries' old buildings. With several honks of the horn, he forced the holidaymakers to clear a path so the car could proceed.

While the latter made an occasional response, Giovanni, with his natural enthusiasm, did most of the talking. Except for a word here and there, the Italian flowed too fast for her to follow.

Giovanni acted happier than Gaby had seen him before. If the same dynamics applied in his family as in hers, the younger brother hero-worshipped the oldest one.

"Where are we going, Giovanni?"

She'd known him for six weeks, but this was the first time she had an uneasy feeling being in his company.

Except that Giovanni wasn't the one contributing to her distress.

The man studying her features through the rearview mirror was responsible for the trembling of her body. She'd become unbearably aware of him as a man, a brand new feeling for her. She didn't know how to begin to deal with it.

"Home," Giovanni answered, oblivious to the tension-fraught atmosphere in the car. "I've wanted you to meet my family for a long time."

"I'd like to meet them," came the automatic response, but she could scarcely concentrate. After being around so many olive-skinned, dark-haired European men, what mortified Gaby was to be caught staring at Giovanni's brother like she'd never seen the male gender before. So much for her tour guide's warning.

This wholly feminine reaction took Gaby by surprise. She averted her eyes and moved next to the door, away from his brother's line of vision.

"Where is home?" she asked in a quiet voice, hoping the other man couldn't hear her words.

In a surprise move, Giovanni shifted closer. "You know where I work," he whispered near her ear.

"Yes, of course."

"That's my home." He gave her cheek a kiss, then he sat back as they slowly made their way through the streets swarming with tourists.

Giovanni's behavior was totally foreign to her. Alarm bells went off in her head. *The ducal palace*?

"Be serious, Giovanni."

"I'm being very serious. Luca—" he called to his brother, giving the other man's broad shoulder a friendly squeeze. "Tell Gaby where I live. She does not seem to believe me."

"Stop teasing, please."

"What do you wish to know, *signorina*?" Giovanni's brother didn't sound as if he particularly cared one way or the other. "His home is at the palace, just as he said."

She stared at Giovanni in exasperation. This was no longer funny. "My brother enjoys a good joke once in a while. Is that what this is all about? A Renaissance custom? Like being at a masked ball, only you've decided to throw away your mask?"

Giovanni looked wounded. "On occasion I have been known to tease. But Luca never jokes about anything, do you, *fratello*?"

The word meant brother. Giovanni appeared to enjoy ribbing his elder sibling. Theirs was a strange relationship. She felt undercurrents but didn't understand them. Until the car stopped, she had no choice but to go along with their charade.

Her *pensione* was situated on the outskirts of Urbino. Slowly the car made its way into the center. In the off-season, it would have taken five minutes at most to reach the walled, ancient inner city. But due to the crowds out for the celebration, fifteen minutes passed before Giovanni's brother was able to maneuver them from the more modern area to its Medieval heart.

Soon Gaby's attention fastened compulsively on the rounded towers which formed the perimeters of the ducal estate. The fading light of the hot summer evening glinted from its recessed windows and brought out the mellow pink rose color of its crenelated walls.

They didn't stop at a side entrance used by the tour buses to gain entrance to the part housing the museum. Gaby had known they wouldn't. The men were playing a game.

She started to tell Giovanni that she hadn't fallen for his trickery when the car unexpectedly turned and followed a mazelike path. It led to an inner courtyard of the castle and ultimately a covered archway, taking her back to a time in the fifteenth century when the awesome beauty of the Renaissance camouflaged secrets, intrigue and treachery.

"You are cold?" Their driver's low voice grated

on her nerves. He'd seen her body quiver in response to her surroundings and made no apology for watching the two of them through the mirror.

Giovanni lifted her hand and kissed it. "You don't feel cold to me," he murmured as they came to a stop before an entrance portico.

A great medallion motif hung above the brass door and the busts of Italian statesmen stood sheltered in the arched niches. But Gaby couldn't appreciate their splendor because Gina's rules about avoiding Italian men had come back to haunt her with a vengeance.

She could have sworn that Giovanni didn't have amorous feelings for her, so why was he acting this way now? Was he just having some fun in front of his brother? At times Giovanni could be a terrible tease, like a couple of her brothers.

Each day when her classes were over, they'd laugh their way through their walks to galleries and old churches, anything free. "Tell me the truth. Are you two the sons of the chauffeur or the gardener? Is that how you got a job in the museum, how your brother drives this expensive car?"

His brown eyes danced before they flashed to the taciturn man at the wheel. "You hear that, Luca? She wants the truth. I have an idea. While I run in and inform Mama that we have company, you be the host and reassure my lovely guest."

"Giovanni—" she cried, and hurried to get out of the car to stop him. By the time she was on her feet, he'd disappeared. To her chagrin she'd been left alone with his brother, whose forbidding nature didn't quite mask his devastating sexuality.

Compelled by an urge she was helpless to fight, her vagrant blue eyes wandered over this imposing man who was Italian from the hand-sewn leather loafers cushioning his feet to the small gold cross nestled in the dusting of black hair on his chest.

When he breathed, she could see it glint through the neck opening of the black silk shirt where his skin appeared to be as darkly tanned as the rest of his hard-muscled body clothed in black trousers.

Unlike the other Italian men she'd met, however, her presence seemed to irritate him in some way. She almost felt as if he disliked her.

Most men, Italian or American, found her attractive to the point that they became obsessive about it. At times their unsolicited advances made her defensive.

She'd dated a few nice boys in college, and she adored her father and brothers. But it was a fact of life that she'd been fending off older men and un-wanted admirers since she was fifteen years old. Giovanni's brother was proving the exception.

He made her feel that she'd trespassed on his pri-vate person. Otherwise his veiled black gaze wouldn't have returned the compliment by sweeping over her face and curves with a boldness she wasn't prepared for.

Gaby looked away, confused and shaken.

"Why pretend that you didn't know this was Giovanni's home, *signorina*?"

His question shocked her. Her gaze flew back to his. "You think I'm pretending?"

A long silence ensued. "My brother tells me you two met when you came to visit the palazzo museum."

"Yes, but he was a guide and—"

"He gave you a personal tour of the rooms housing the jewelry collection, did he not?" he broke in.

"Yes, but—"

"Then you know that the House of Provere has been in existence for over five hundred years."

Her arched brows drew into a delicate frown. Certain facts she'd been learning in her history class about Urbino came back to her. It was in this city that the Renaissance reached heights to rival Florence and Rome. During that period, there was a very important fourteenth-century pope who was of the lineage of Provere, endowing his family with riches beyond her comprehension.

A cry escaped her throat. "You don't mean that you and Giovanni descend from *that* Provere?"

He fingered his cross absently. "Your reaction almost convinces me that you know nothing of my little brother's responsibilities or his vast bank account."

"*What*?"

Confounded, her eyes searched the inky darkness of his for verification that he was telling the truth.

"You truly didn't know that he is the most important person in Urbino?"

Incredulous, she cried, "*Giovanni*?"

Her thoughts darted back to the pleasant, studious

young man with whom she'd been spending her free time. She'd assumed he was as poor as she was. He walked everywhere and never spent money except to buy them a drink. Often she insisted they go Dutch treat, and he went along with it.

Through new eyes she surveyed the castle walls, the grounds and enclosed garden filled with topiary trees and flowering bushes of every hue. She tried to picture Giovanni as master of this ambience, and couldn't.

The only person she could imagine fitting such a role was the disturbingly masculine figure trapping her between the car and the entryway.

Their gazes held until she could hardly breathe from the tension stretching between them.

"When our mother dies, he'll inherit the title of Duke."

A hand went to her throat. "Your mother is titled?"

Another troubling silence enveloped them. "Though titles aren't used today, our mother is the veritable Duchess of the House of Provere."

She shook her head. "I had no idea. He's only ever said that he had a family, but he's never talked about anyone in particular. I—I know nothing about you." Her voice throbbed.

A tiny nerve throbbed at the corner of his sensual mouth. Her oldest brother, Wayne, had a similar tick that only showed when his emotions were in upheaval.

"One day Giovanni's word will be virtual law.

He'll command the respect of everyone in the Marches province. So will his wife,'' he added in a grating tone.

"Why do you suppose Giovanni has been so secretive?'' Her voice pled with him.

His answer was a long time in coming. "Every man wants to believe that the woman he has chosen for his bride loves him for himself, and no other reason.''

"*His bride*?''

Luke's lean body tautened. "Surely by now you must have guessed that our mother is inside the palazzo waiting to be introduced to the *future* Duchess of Provere.''

When his words finally computed, she groaned aloud, unable to take it in. "Tell me you're not serious.''

His dark brows furrowed. "I assure you I would never lie about something as crucial as my brother's happiness.''

"But I'm not in love with Giovanni,'' she replied in complete honesty before she broke down and buried her face in her hands.

"He hasn't asked you to marry him? The truth now!'' came the sharp demand.

Her head flew back, revealing tear-stained cheeks. "No! The subject has never come up. He's a dear friend, but that's all.''

A grimace marred his dark features. "Then he must be the last person to know it. It appears you've captured his heart, something no other woman has been able to accomplish,'' he murmured in thick tones.

"Did Giovanni *tell* you we were getting married?''

His eyes wandered over her upturned face. "He has gone so far as to assemble the family to meet you, which is virtually the same thing. He phoned me in Rome, insistent that I come home for the occasion even though he knew that I had—'' He paused. "Well, let's just say I had other pressing commitments.''

Though the night breeze was warm, she shivered. "I can't imagine what he's thinking. Even if I were in love with him, I'm totally unsuitable and he must know it.''

Giovanni had been born into a royal house linked to the papacy, had been brought up in these incredible surroundings, enjoying luxuries most people couldn't even imagine.

Their family name was held in the highest repute, one of the greatest houses of Italy. Their family crest was emblazoned on the pages of the country's textbooks, not to mention their fleet of cars.

If she were in Luke's place, she'd be more than skeptical about his brother bringing home a foreigner to meet the family. No wonder she'd felt that hint of animosity.

She was from America, that upstart nation from across the Atlantic, as the Europeans viewed it. A penniless college student who was still having trouble pronouncing *Prego* correctly. The only girl among five brothers sadly lacking in the polish and education of a woman fit to be Giovanni's wife and chatelaine of such a dynasty.

Clasping her hands to keep them from shaking, she asked, "Do you think you could find Giovanni and tell him I have to talk to him right away?"

Before his eyes narrowed, she saw anguish in those black depths.

"I love Giovanni more than my own life, *signorina*. Under the circumstances, I'm going to insist that you allow him to keep his fantasy until after dinner when you are alone with him. I refuse to see him destroyed before the festivities begin."

"But that would be dishonest to everyone!"

"No more than he has been with you," came the retort.

She shook her head. "I couldn't do that to your mother. It wouldn't be fair."

"Our mother will survive. It's Giovanni I'm concerned about," he said in bleak tones.

"Luke?" she called to him without thinking. His head reared back as if she'd struck him. "*Signore*—" she amended, embarrassed for the faux pas, "I'm sor—"

"It is not necessary to apologize," he interjected on a terse note. "I'm not used to hearing my first name pronounced in that way. What were you going to ask me?"

For a moment Gaby couldn't think. Heavy perfume from the roses filled the night air, making her senses swim. Luke had been talking to her about his brother. Yet her mind couldn't concentrate on anything but the virile man standing in front of her. In his presence, new inexplicable yearnings were coming to life.

A soft breeze had sprung up, disturbing his luxuriant black hair. It overlapped his tanned forehead. There were stray tendrils at the base of his bronzed neck, as well. She wondered what they would feel like if she touched them, touched him...

"*Signorina*?" he prompted.

Gaby was thankful for the darkness. Otherwise he would have seen the blood rush to her face.

"It's possible you've misunderstood Giovanni's actions. Maybe he got tired of the responsibility, he decided to play the pauper and give the prince a rest."

When Luke didn't say anything she started talking faster. "I—I'm sure this was part of his plan for the Renaissance Fair— To spring a surprise on me by visiting the ruling family of the province, a family who just happens to be his own flesh and blood. With his sense of fun, it's the kind of thing Giovanni would do, don't you think?"

Still he said nothing, only watched her mouth with unnerving intensity.

"If he wanted me for his wife, I would have known about it long before now, and then none of this w—"

Luke's grim countenance choked off the rest of her words. "Giovanni wants my consent before he marries you. It's the only reason I came home. As it is, I must return to Rome in the morning."

"*You're leaving so soon*?" she blurted, her disappointment more acute than she would have believed.

Luke's chest heaved, revealing its definition through the thin silk material, making her more aware of him than ever. Her mouth had gone so dry it hurt to swallow.

"Poor Giovanni. He won't want you to go. I can tell he loves you very much. I have a feeling he always listens to you."

He stood closer to her now. She could feel the shudder that passed through his taut physique. "Yes," came the haunted reply.

"Then before it's too late, go inside and tell him you don't approve of me, which is only the truth. Please, Luke—" she appealed to him in an agonized whisper.

"*Per Dio.*" The muttered imprecation sounded torn out of him. "What you are asking of me is impossible. No, *signorina.* Giovanni has made his plans. I won't shatter his dreams and turn the occasion into a nightmare. *Neither will you,*" he warned in a voice of unquestioned authority. "It appears we are both doomed to play a part until he takes you home."

Much as she hated to admit it, Luke was right. She could never hurt Giovanni intentionally. But she didn't know how she was going to make it through this dinner, let alone confront him later.

"My brother is without guile," he murmured thickly. "That is why everyone loves him and would never want to cause him pain. When he phoned to tell me about the American girl I must meet, there was such joy in his voice, I couldn't bear to disillusion him until after I'd met you in person.''

Her instincts hadn't been wrong. "I knew you disliked me." How she hated the tremor in her voice. It couldn't help but let him know the depth of her hurt.

There was a sharp intake of breath. "Not you, *signorina*. The *idea* of you. I've never felt that any woman was good enough for my brother. Ironically, I now find that I must revise that opinion."

His admission was the last thing she would have expected to hear. It filled her with wonder.

"If this were several hundred years ago, I would ignore your feelings and force you to marry my brother to give him his ultimate happiness."

She raised startled blue eyes to him. "You mean, if you had been duke, your word would have been law. How is it that Giovanni is going to inherit the title when *you're* the firstborn son? I don't understand."

Even though night had fallen, she could see his expression close. With a new sense of loss she watched him retreat to that inner part of himself where he was impregnable. The intimacy they'd shared for those few, brief minutes was gone.

Devastated, she said, "I'm sorry. I didn't mean to pry."

"You wouldn't be human if you didn't ask. Unfortunately, now is not the time to discuss it. Giovanni will be looking for us and I haven't yet fulfilled my duties as host."

When he started toward the entry, she hung back.

He paused on the step, a magnificent figure in black. Perspiration broke out on her brow. "I'm frightened, Luke."

He raked through his hair. "Then you're not alone," came another of his shocking confessions. "I'll meet you inside."

CHAPTER TWO

SOMEWHERE in the huge palazzo Giovanni was talking to his family, but the enormous rooms swallowed sound. Like wandering into a church when no one was about, Gaby had that same isolated feeling now.

Luke had given her a moment alone to compose herself. He must have needed some time to himself, as well, but she wished he were here so she wouldn't feel like an intruder.

Her misgivings slowly changed to awe however as she found herself surveying the gallerylike foyer that had been part of Luke's home since birth. Above her head, the fantastic frescoes on the vaulted ceiling represented an allegory of the triumph of spiritual love. Gracing the walls were important scenes of the Provere family history.

Through one set of double doors she saw into another room devoted to the sun-god, Apollo. Over the head of the twenty-foot-high statue dominating its center, she grew dizzy studying the frescoes depicting one of the most famous legendary Greek myths.

Dazzled by the palazzo's priceless artwork and treasures, she moved to a sitting room containing trompe l'oeil panels with eighteenth-century Gobelin tapestries and Savonnerie rugs. Like a sleepwalker, she moved from room to room until she came to one which she claimed for her favorite.

Square in shape rather than rectangular, the floor gleamed of pure white marble. Every wall-covering, the richly hued draperies, the antique porcelain urns filled with fresh cut flowers, the Louis XV furniture and bracket clock, the frescoed ceiling with its depiction of heavenly angels surrounding God, all were a blend of red and white.

So exquisite was the harmony of design and color, so charming were the various appointments of the room, she had difficulty believing this was the work of human hands. If her eyes didn't deceive her, the central medallion over the doors was the work of one of the great Italian masters.

"Like you, my mother prefers this room to the others, *signorina*."

The deep, vibrant voice brought a surprised gasp to her throat. She whirled around to face the charismatic man responsible for the rhythmic change of her heart. *He'd been following her.*

Propped negligently against the door, his hands in his pockets, he murmured, "My father called her his *testarossa*. Perhaps there's a correlation."

"I don't know what that word means."

"She has red hair, too."

His hooded gaze took in her braid and everything else in between until it reached her sandals. Such a frank appraisal couldn't have been any different than the one she'd given him by the car. But now her palms grew moist and her body ached with inexplicable longings she'd never had to combat before.

"If I had known all this was Giovanni's heritage, I would have begged him to bring me here much sooner. I can't claim to have seen very many palaces, but this must be the most gracious, glorious home in Italy, if not Europe."

He gave a barely perceptible nod of his dark head. "Let's say it's one of the few."

"Am I right in thinking the medallion is Michelangelo's creation?" She must look such an anachronism against the bygone splendors of this room.

"You are," he murmured at last. Hearing his voice made her realize he was answering her last question rather than her own tortured thoughts.

"Cardinal Alessandro commissioned Francesco Salviati to create the gallery frescoes. Cardinal Odoardo employed the genius of the Carracci brothers who were responsible for the frescoes in the rest of the rooms.

"Many of the drawings are by Lagrenee, the statuary by Glycon. The palace architecture itself is the work of Sangallo, Giacomo della Porta, Vignola, and Michelangelo, not necessarily in that order."

Some of the most illustrious names in Italian art history. No wonder Giovanni was such a fountain of knowledge on the subject.

"Do you have any other questions?"

She wrung her hands. "Dozens, actually, but I can't think of one when I know I'm going to be meeting your mother in a few minutes. Is she happy for Giovanni?''

A mask slipped into place, wiping any expression from his arresting features. With negligent grace, he pulled away from the door. ''Giovanni is the child she almost lost in childbirth. The son she worships.''

What about you, Luke? Doesn't she worship you, too? The questions reverberated in her heart for no good reason.

''For the last six weeks our mother has known that she isn't the only woman in his life anymore. I'm afraid she's not ready to give him up without a struggle.''

Gaby rubbed her aching temples. ''But she isn't going to have to give him up! Before dinner starts you could take her aside and tell her everyth—''

''Brother Luca—'' Giovanni suddenly appeared in the doorway, effectively terminating a conversation which was tying her in knots. ''What terrible family secrets have you been telling Gaby to produce that look on her face? Come. Mama wants to meet you.''

Gaby's eyes implored Luke, but he remained an implacable figure. Her gaze flicked back to Giovanni. ''I wish you could have warned me what was going to happen tonight.''

He smiled, ignoring her distress when he knew full well that she was overwhelmed by everything that had transpired.

''Then you wouldn't have come. Admit it. We're not such an awful bunch as Luca has made us out to be. No poisonings have been reported for at least two years. Isn't that true, *fratello*?''

Normally she would have laughed at his remark. He could be very funny. But this was no laughing matter. She refused to look at him or his brother.

"If you wish, I will ask everyone to remove their rings before dinner.''

"Giovanni—'' she cried in exasperation. He had no idea how she was suffering inside. His was the sin of omission, but a sin all the same.

Praying he wouldn't announce something patently untrue which would rebound on all of them before she could escape the castle, she reluctantly accompanied him through the palatial rooms.

Luke might not be in her line of vision, but the prickling of hairs on the back of her neck let her know he wasn't far behind. She brushed one hand against her hip in a nervous gesture, wishing she hadn't worn pants. Though perfectly modest, they revealed too much of her figure to a man who made her feel her femininity to the very core of her being.

Breathless before they reached the grand salon with its walls of sage green damask, she counted twenty-six smartly dressed adults of all ages assembled. They sat in groupings near an antique piano at the end of the oblong room.

Beneath one of four magnificent chandeliers suspended from the painted ceiling, Gaby picked out Signora Provere. Small in stature like Giovanni, her short, stylishly cut Titian hair made her stand out from the others. For a woman in her sixties, she looked younger and perfectly lovely in a hyacinth-toned silk dress.

Gaby had difficulty believing this woman had given birth to Luke until she left off talking to one of the relatives and trained dark brown eyes on Gaby.

There was no question that her piercing regard hinting at an indomitable will, plus the possession of a daunting hauteur, had been passed on to her firstborn son.

Luke's father must have been responsible for the black hair and tall bone structure which had gone to create the most striking male she'd ever known or imagined. If there was a strong physical resemblance to his father, then Gaby had compassion for Signora Provere's loss because there was no man to compare to him anywhere.

"*Mama? Vorrei presentare la Signorina Holt.*"

The older woman lifted one hand to her younger son for him to kiss, the other for Gaby. "*Piacere, signorina.*"

Giovanni's mother used the word "delighted" in her response, but the cool, very brief handshake and lack of facial expression denoted not only extreme reserve, but distaste. If the situation had been different and Gaby had been hoping to become Giovanni's wife, she would have been crushed to tears by his mother's cold reception.

"*Piacere di fare la Sua conoscenza, signora,*" Gaby replied in her best Italian.

The older woman shook her head and gazed at Giovanni, perplexed. "*Mi dispiace, ma non capisco.*"

Gaby knew her Italian pronunciation wasn't perfect, but unless Giovanni's mother was hard of hearing, she couldn't have misunderstood her.

"I have no problem with her Italian, Mama." Giovanni championed Gaby, yet he showed no sign of irritation toward his mother. "With your permission, I will introduce her to the rest of the family."

Not waiting for a nod of approval from his parent, Giovanni began the lengthy process, which turned out to be an even greater ordeal than Gaby had expected.

Not because he'd said something he shouldn't. To her relief, and undoubtedly to Luke's, Giovanni explained that Gaby was a close personal friend and left it at that. Except for an aunt on his mother's side, and a pretty young woman close to Gaby's age who'd been presented as a goddaughter, the rest of Giovanni's relatives were enthusiastic in their greetings and made her feel welcome.

They seemed as sincere and cordial as any group of people might be when meeting a stranger. As for Luke, he remained in the background. A dark, unsmiling figure, he stood near a lighted candelabra which was as tall as he was.

Several times Gaby's gaze unexpectedly met his and she'd quickly look away again, wondering what he was thinking behind his relentless scrutiny. If he had a wife and family, a possibility which was becoming more and more insupportable to Gaby, then they weren't present, nor was there any mention of them.

While Giovanni related anecdotes that made everyone laugh, Gaby only went through the motions of responding. It was like being in a strange dream, with Luke her one reality.

"*Giovanni, mio figlio*," his mother called to him. "You will accompany me to the dining room. Luca will help Signorina Holt to her seat."

Giovanni chose that moment to take her hand and kiss it. "You're trembling," he whispered against her hot cheek. "Do not be afraid of my brother. I'd trust him with my life."

Gaby could understand Giovanni's devotion. Luke had a natural presence that inspired confidence as well as other more disturbing emotions she didn't dare admit to feeling. Giovanni must never learn of her attraction to his brother.

"Enjoy your dinner," he continued to murmur. "I asked the cook to change tonight's menu. He has prepared all your favorite dishes."

She felt like laughing hysterically. Giovanni's behavior left no doubt in anyone's mind that he was a young man in love. Worse, his reference to the dinner specially prepared in her honor was guaranteed to alienate his mother.

Gaby would choke on food right now. Luke must have sensed her traumatic state. Her heart thudded at his approach. "*La nostra madre* is waiting," he said in an aside to his brother.

For once, Giovanni's eyes did not smile at Luke. "Take good care of Gaby. She's a little fearful of all of us."

After he let go of her hand, he walked across the

salon to escort his mother to the dining room. Gaby had no choice but to wait for Luke who seemed disinclined to follow the others out of the room.

"A word of warning, *signorina*. The seating arrangements have been prearranged. You will be placed between me and Efresina Ceccarelli. Until you appeared on the scene disrupting our mother's carefully laid plans, Efresina had every hope of becoming the next duchess."

Gaby thought back to the pretty young woman with fine brown hair who had snubbed her during the introductions.

"Just so you know, Efresina has loved Giovanni from childhood, so be kind to her."

"As if I wouldn't—" Gaby's voice shook with pain and indignation. She started to turn away from him when a hand of steel closed around her wrist, holding her in place.

Her startled gaze flew to his dark, intelligent face. It was the first time he'd touched her. She wished he hadn't.

The sensation of skin on skin drove all coherent thought from her mind, leaving her body an aching mass of nerves, of wanting for things she shouldn't be entertaining under any circumstances.

She must have communicated something of what she was feeling because he suddenly let go of her arm, as if her skin had burned him alive.

"I only said that because you can afford to be gracious. You're the one Giovanni wants, and no other.

He made it undeniably clear when he asked me to
safeguard you a moment ago.''

But I don't want him, Gaby moaned inwardly.
She'd never truly known the meaning of the word
want. But just being in Luke's presence had awakened something in her which she sensed could burst
out of control given the opportunity.

Afraid he would devine her feelings, she tore her
eyes from his face. She couldn't just stand there, and
finally hurried past the piano to gain the next room.
But her footsteps came to a standstill when she realized she'd entered the dining room where everyone's
eyes registered surprise at her precipitous entry.

She could see two empty places at the end of the
banquet-size dining table and headed in that direction.
Giovanni and his mother sat at the opposite end.

Luke appeared at her side to pull out one of the
Queen Anne-styled chairs so she could be seated. The
grandeur of the room was illuminated by a groin-
vaulted ceiling frescoed in the *quadratura* style, but
Gaby couldn't appreciate it, or the lavish appointments of the dining table.

The ornate gold candelabras, crystal, silver and
hand-painted china, all displaying the family crest,
had little impact because her awareness of the disturbing male at her side had rendered her witless. It
was impossible to concentrate on anything else.

She turned in Efresina's direction to make an effort
at polite conversation, then gasped because she found
herself staring into a pair of familiar, piercing black
eyes beyond the other woman's shoulder.

They belonged to the tall, magnificent, white-robed figure depicted in the huge oil painting dominating the room. Without the mitre and other accoutrements of his holy office, the famous fourteenth-century pope of Provere lineage could be Luke incarnate.

His imposing stature, the strength in the jawline, the shape of the straight nose, the width of shoulder, the midnight hair, all his superb male attributes had been handed down through the genes to live five hundred years later in Giovanni's brother. Except for the fact that Luke wore black, the two could be twins. Incredible.

"Signorina Holt has already noted the strong resemblance between me and my illustrious ancestor." Luke spoke to the woman at Gaby's other side. "Since my mother insists on keeping the painting in here, rather than the museum, it would be impossible not to notice it, isn't that true, Effie?"

The woman warmed to his use of her nickname, but Gaby was still reacting to the uncanny likeness of the two men.

"Surely the public could never appreciate it the way we've done over the years, Luca."

After a small pause, she faced Gaby. "Do you have any idea of his importance in Urbino's history, *signorina*?" Her brittle question asked in excellent English warned Gaby to tread carefully.

"I've learned something about his prominence in my classes here at the university, Signorina Ceccarelli."

"Oh, yes. You're a foreign student. Why did you

come here to study? Le March is not well known abroad. Most Americans flock to Florence or Sienna.'' She said her words loud enough that she'd caught the attention of everyone at the table.

Silence reigned as Gaby lifted her wineglass and took a sip, hoping it would help fortify her for the onslaught ahead. Apparently Giovanni had not told his relatives anything about her.

''My great-grandmother used to say the same thing. She lived to be ninety-nine. Before she died, I had to promise her that when I grew up, I would go visit her birthplace.''

''Your great-grandmother was Italian?'' Efresina's shock seemed as profound as Signora Provere's.

''Yes. She was born Gabriella Trussardi, from Loretello. I was given her name because I inherited her red hair.''

Immediately there was an explosion of excitement around the table. His mother looked as if she'd gone into shock, but Giovanni smiled at Gaby across the expanse. He seemed to have a penchant for doing the unexpected and was enjoying the little bomb she'd dropped on his family.

''Your connection to Marchigiani blood, as well as your red hair, has taken our mother by complete surprise,'' Luke muttered in thick tones.

''But surely Giovanni told you.''

''My brother laughs and teases to cover up his emotions. The truth is, his innermost thoughts run very deep and no one is privy to them unless he chooses otherwise.''

As far as Gaby was concerned, Luke wasn't that different from his brother. Did anyone have access to his soul?

Just then another relative sat forward and addressed her. "What did your great-grandmother's people do, *signorina*?"

The man at her side was waiting, listening. It robbed her of breath. "From what I understand, they were poor farmers."

Another blow for Giovanni's mother to sustain, but he had placed Gaby in this untenable situation. She couldn't be rude and not answer their questions, even if the answers were unpalatable.

"Tell us more."

Gaby tortured the end of the napkin lying across her lap. "She fell in love and ran off with an impoverished artist from New York who would give away his paintings in exchange for board and room during his travels. They got married somewhere in Europe, living hand-to-mouth.

"Before World War Two broke out, my grandmother was born. At that point he decided to take his family back to the States, to the West where his artist's eye became enamored with the desert. They ended up in Nevada, my home."

As if coming to her relief, the uniformed servants began bringing food to the table, suspending conversation until everyone was served.

Through veiled eyes Gaby watched Giovanni's mother receive her second shock of the night. Instead of five courses, the entire meal had been put on one plate. All Gaby's favorite foods—buttered *taglia-telle*—noodles—veal cannelloni, a rich flatbread known as *crescia*, and peach *gelato* in a crystal dessert bowl. Hers had two large scoops, drawing everyone's attention.

While Gaby blushed, Signora Provere spoke in rapid Italian to her younger son, most likely telling him that nothing like this had ever been done before. His mother was being put through needless torture. Gaby groaned in pain. Food was anathema to her right now.

"Giovanni has risked our mother's displeasure by countermanding her orders to the cook. You can't refuse to eat when he has gone to so much trouble for you."

"I won't," she whispered, knowing what she must do without his prompting. Though she might have to run to the bathroom later, she would do justice to her meal.

Everyone did the polite thing and carried on with the dinner as if nothing untoward had happened, but Gaby noticed that the dainty Efresina only toyed with her food. Luke didn't bother to make a pretense of eating. But Giovanni wasn't watching him.

Being a taller woman with a fuller figure than the other females present, Gaby felt like a glutton eating everything including her last spoonful of ice cream.

"How did you like your dinner, Gaby?" Giovanni's voice spoke to her across the long expanse.

She took a deep breath. "It was wonderful. You

were right. This is the best food in all Italy. Thank you for being the perfect host, Giovanni.''

His face broke out in a broad smile. ''More *gelato*?'' He had done everything in his power to please her.

She was on the verge of being sick, but didn't want to disappoint him. Out of the corner of her eye she saw Luke's full plate and it prompted her to say, ''If I want more, I'll finish your brother's.''

The moment the words were out, Luke's hand tightened into a fist on his hard-muscled thigh.

Giovanni grinned, oblivious to the undercurrents. ''Normally Luca loves sweets, just like you. Since living in Rome he probably doesn't get them as often, and is a little out of the habit. Isn't that true, *fratello*?''

CHAPTER THREE

As IN the car on the drive to the castle, Giovanni enjoyed teasing Luke. She presumed it was because he missed his brother so much, this was his way of showing affection. But at the same time it created a strange kind of tension in Luke. She could tell it disturbed him on some elemental level not easily discernible to the others.

"Have you had an opportunity to visit Loretello yet, Signorina Holt?" one of Giovanni's uncles addressed her. His question didn't allow her to dwell long on Luke's private torment, whatever it might be.

"Yes. I went a few days after my arrival in Urbino. Before her death, my great-grandmother described it to me, but nothing I'd pictured in my mind prepared me for my first look at that tiny, fortified town."

He smiled. "You like Italy?"

"I love it so much that when I get back to Las Vegas, I know I'm going to be horribly 'homesick.' My family will wish I'd never gone away."

"Tell us about them," his uncle persisted in a kindly voice. Gaby could feel Luke's unsettling glance. He made it difficult for her to gather her thoughts.

"There are six children, five boys and myself."

Everyone expressed surprise over so many boys. "Are you the oldest?"

"No. I'm number four. Scott, my brother who is two years my senior, is the only one married so far."

"Are your parents living?"

"Yes. Mother teaches resource at a local junior high school."

"*Resource*?"

"Her mother helps students who have behavior problems, *Zio*," Giovanni explained.

"That must be difficult work."

"It is," Gaby agreed. "But very rewarding."

"And your father?"

"Daddy is a commercial artist who works in advertising."

"Are you an artist, too?" The older man appeared genuinely interested.

"Oh, no." She shook her head. "Daddy says I'm a dabbler. I have too many interests and will never master any of them."

"Don't be modest, *signorina*," a deep voice inserted. "There must be at least one subject you excel in."

"She excels at everything, *fratello*. I'm proud to announce that Gaby has received top grades in all her classes both here at the university and in Nevada. Like you, Luca, she thrives on learning."

Gaby flushed. "You love to exaggerate, and I am still struggling with Italian. It's such a beautiful language, but difficult. If I hadn't taken Latin in high school, I'd be lost. Thankfully, Giovanni has been helping me. If my Italian were half as good as the English you all speak, I'd be overjoyed.''

''They teach Latin in Las Vegas?''

The question came from Giovanni's mother, changing the tenor of the conversation. It was the first time since they'd sat down to dinner that she'd spoken directly to Gaby.

Giovanni chuckled. ''Of course they do, Mama.''

''I can understand why you'd ask that question, Signora Provere. Most people consider Las Vegas a den of iniquity because of the legalized gambling. Many of us who live there avoid that part of town as much as possible. My parents don't gamble. They don't believe in it.''

''It couldn't be a suitable place to raise children.''

Giovanni patted his mother's hand. ''That would all depend on the children, Mama. Gaby has grown up untouched by its influence.''

His mother looked less than convinced.

''There are many evil influences in the world today, Signora Provere. Is any place truly safe except inside the walls of our own homes?'' Gaby tried to reason with her.

Giovanni's uncle gave her a nod of approval. ''You make a strong point, *signorina*.''

Luke unexpectedly pushed himself away from the table and rose to his feet. ''If you will all excuse me. There are matters I've left unattended too long as it is. *Buona notte*.''

His parting salutation included everyone before he

strode toward the doors with the bearing of a Medieval prince and disappeared.

Gaby had to pretend not to be affected, but his abrupt departure stunned her. He couldn't go yet! After a whole evening in his company, she still didn't know anything about him personally or professionally. He'd be returning to Rome in the morning. Day after tomorrow she'd be leaving Italy.

What if she never saw him again? In a short account of time he'd become so important to her, she couldn't imagine not being in his company again.

Something had to be wrong with her to care this much about a man she'd only known a few hours. In one meeting, the kinds of feelings he engendered were tantamount to being in love....

She'd always scoffed at the idea of love at first sight. But tonight, through some unfathomable process, she was very much afraid she'd lost her heart to one Luca Provere.

"Gaby?" *Giovanni's voice.* "I know tomorrow is a big day for you, so if you are through, I'll run you back to your *pensione.*"

He must have picked up on her distress. Had her feelings for Luke been so transparent he could sense her interest in his mysterious brother?,

Mortified, she rose to her feet at the same time as Giovanni and turned to his mother. "Signora Provere, thank you for allowing me to be a guest in this magnificent palazzo. Of all my memories of Urbino, this evening will stand out as the highlight."

"*Prego*, Signorina Holt." She sounded less than enthusiastic, but it didn't seem to bother Giovanni.

Attempting to hide her desolation that Luke was no longer in the room, Gaby smiled at the other members of his family, even Efresina who'd said nothing for the last fifteen minutes and refused to look at Gaby. "It was a great pleasure meeting all of you."

For the most part they reciprocated in an affectionate fashion. Though gratified by their acceptance, Gaby could take little pleasure in anything when the man who'd brought her senses alive was nowhere to be found.

To her chagrin, she wasn't allowed to escape the room unscathed. The last thing she saw as she went out the doors were Luke's black eyes staring out of the massive portrait. They seemed to follow her through the maze of rooms to the front entrance of the castle.

"W-will your brother be driving us again?"

"Gaby—" He cocked his head. "You aren't still afraid of him, are you?"

"Of course not." She tried to keep the tremor out of her voice.

Giovanni eyed her speculatively. "Then you must be nervous about my driving. If you would feel safer with him behind the wheel, I will go to his apartments and ask him."

"*No*! Please don't!" she cried in panic. "I—I was only wondering, since he drove us here in the first place."

Seemingly satisfied with her explanation, Giovanni

led her down the steps to the waiting black sedan. Once they were both seated inside he confided, ''If Luca acts pensive and forbidding, it's because he has a great deal on his mind these days. After a year's absence, he's needed to come home and be surrounded by family.''

Luke has been away a whole year?

''He's concerned for your welfare, Giovanni.'' She might as well broach the subject which had been put off too long as it was.

''I know. That has always been his way. He makes everyone else's world right, but rarely does anything to please himself.''

''Obviously you two share a very special bond.''

''I idolize him.''

She bit her lip. ''In all these weeks that we've known each other, you've never talked about him. Why?''

''Because it's painful.''

By now they'd left the castle grounds and had entered the mainstream of heavy traffic.

Gaby didn't understand. ''In what way?''

''You saw the painting in the dining room.''

''Yes.'' She bowed her head. ''Except for the clothes, it could have been your brother.''

''Exactly. Almost from the day he was born, my parents thought the same thing. They saw our great progenitor in his face and body. Luke is a brilliant scholar with a keen mind and a grasp of the political and economic scene given to few men. It was a foregone conclusion that one day he would consecrate his life to God and rise to power like our illustrious fore-bearer.''

Gaby blinked. *What was he saying?*

The Luke she'd met tonight was a sensual man, the ultimate male, the antithesis of someone celibate. He had a way of bringing out her most primitive feelings.

Yet snatches of conversation came back to haunt her. Luke lived in Rome. He had his work there. Giovanni kept referring to him as *fratello*, that he trusted him with his life.

Dear God. The shock of his words immobilized her. She dreaded asking the next question, but her curiosity had reached its zenith.

''Are you telling me he's a *priest*?''

Giovanni nodded slowly. ''He's been training for the priesthood all his life, but father's death required that he put his church studies aside temporarily to run the estate.

''A year ago, when he felt I could handle things, he went to Rome to live and prepare himself. He'll be professed at the end of September on his twenty-ninth birthday.''

It was too late for Gaby to stifle her gasp. This man she'd been fantasizing about was on the verge of be-coming an ordained priest!

He'd be known as Father Luca. She'd never see him again. He'd be lost to her forever...

Gaby wanted to run somewhere and hide her feel-ings from Giovanni, but she couldn't. The car was stuck in traffic. More people than ever were out on the streets celebrating. This should have been her happiest night abroad, but Giovanni's news had robbed her of her joie de vivre.

"It's a miracle my brother was allowed to come to Urbino for twenty-four hours."

Not a miracle, she mused brokenheartedly. Luke left his life's work to check on the unsuitable American woman whom he believed would cast his brother aside when she'd gotten what she wanted out of him.

Now that Luke had met Gaby, he knew differently, and could return to Rome content that she wouldn't destroy Giovanni's life.

Had she made any impression at all on his older brother? Or was she reading something into those few precious moments when his smoldering looks melted her bones? Was it possible she would haunt his dreams as surely as he was going to haunt hers?

Gaby didn't think she could stand any more of this, especially when there was a vital issue that needed to be discussed with Giovanni.

Turning to him, she murmured, "Your brother loved you enough to make the effort to come home."

"Yes," came the solemn reply. "I should be grateful. One day Luca will wear scarlet robes. On rare occasions, I'll be lucky to be granted an audience to see him." There was deep pain in Giovanni's voice.

"You've missed him terribly, haven't you?"

He nodded.

Gaby could understand that. She already ached over Luke's absence. It was easy enough to picture him dressed in a cardinal's robes. He was a beautiful male specimen. Any clothes he wore would transform them.

But her heart couldn't imagine him living the life of a priest, let alone a cardinal or any other holy office. Since the first moment she'd laid eyes on him, she'd thought of him as a man who lived life to the fullest, who would crave the intimacy with his wife and rejoice in his children.

All this time she'd been afraid another woman had possession of his heart. Now to learn that long ago the church had laid claim to his body and soul—

"I feel the same way about my brother, Wayne. I adore him. But he works on a ranch in the Sierra Nevadas. I hardly ever see him."

"Is your brother happy working on a ranch?"

Gaby didn't have to think. "It's his life!"

"Then even if you miss him, it is easy for you to be happy for him."

"Yes, of course."

She pushed some stray tendrils off her forehead with a shaky hand. "What are you getting at? Are you saying that your brother isn't happy?" she asked with a heavy heart.

"I don't know. He isn't one to share anything that personal."

Her throat swelled with emotion. "He says you're a very private person, too." She looked at him, gearing up her courage. "Giovanni—I have to ask you a question. Please don't take it wrong. When you called him to come home, did you tell him you were going to marry me?" She had to know the truth.

"No."

The relief of hearing his admission was exquisite.

"But he and your mother are under that impression."

"That's because I love you. If I were to marry, I would ask you to be my wife, not Efresina, the woman my mother has picked out for me. Luca could sense this without my having to say anything. He's intuitive that way."

Gaby's nails bit into her palms. Luke had been right all along about his brother's feelings for her!

"Do not worry, Gaby. I know you don't care about me that way, but it was still important to me that my family meet you."

"I love you, too, Giovanni—as a dear friend." Her voice caught. How cruel that she couldn't have reciprocated by wanting to stay in Italy and marry him.

"I'm aware of that, and I'm hoping that when you get back to Las Vegas, you will remember the good times we had together. Perhaps by next summer, you will miss me enough to return to Urbino. Who knows what could happen by then."

There can't be anything between us but friendship, she mused. His brother had created a fever in her. Priest or no priest, while Gaby was feeling this way about Luke, she could never marry anyone.

"Giovanni—"

"Do not feel obliged to say anything," he broke in. "It was enough to have you in my home tonight. You were gracious and kind to my mother. She, on the other hand, behaved poorly. She's lost one son and is holding on to me for dear life. Please forgive her.''

''I do. She wants the best for you.''

Gaby's heart swelled with compassion for his mother, for him. Without Luke, she imagined a lot of joy had gone out of their lives.

''Your maturity and generosity are some of the many traits I find so appealing about you. Luke must have approved or he wouldn't have excused himself for the night without talking privately to me first. It makes me very happy to know that my two favorite people got along. You did like him, didn't you?''

He honked at a group of students blocking the street. They finally realized he wanted to get through and moved to the side.

''Yes, of course,'' she said in a tremulous voice.

''Luca has always been protective. Because I'm short, he championed me when I got into trouble with my friends, then took the blame from our parents even though I should have been the one to be punished.''

Everything he said made her heartache deepen. She smiled sadly. ''Somehow I can't picture you a troublemaker.''

''My father would tell you I had my moments, but a fatal stroke took him in my early teens. If it hadn't been for Luca, I would never have passed chemistry or understood philosophy. He had this wonderful mind, Gaby. He could do anything, be anything he wants.''

There it was again. A big question mark in

Giovanni's voice. As they turned into the alley at the back of the *pensione*, Gaby eyed her friend soberly.

"What is it you're saying, Giovanni? Don't you want him to serve the church?"

He pulled the car to a stop and turned off the motor. Still staring ahead he said, "More than anything on earth. But only if it's what he wants."

She was listening with her mind as well as her heart. That vital organ had given her no rest with its relentless pounding. "You don't think it's what he wants?"

"I don't know. Luca is a noble human being."

A long silence stretched between them. Gaby thought back on their conversation about his parents' lofty dreams for their firstborn son. No doubt Giovanni was thinking of them, too.

Taking a steadying breath, she said, "Your brother strikes me as a man who makes his own fires, who walks to the beat of his own drum, no one else's."

He turned his head in her direction and smiled. "You understand a great deal for having known him such a short time. And you're right about him. He's his own man and always will be. I don't know what got into me. I guess he and I are both in the habit of worrying too much about each other."

"My brothers and I do the same thing. You should have heard the lecture I got from Wayne before I left home."

Giovanni's eyes gleamed. "About Italian men?"

"About men, period. My brother, Scott, has already told the family that I'm just like our great-grandmother. That the Italian in my blood is going to make me fall for some foreign, godlike, down-and-out Lothario and I'll never come home again. Robbie phones me every week to make sure I'm still here.''

''I'm glad they care so much, Gaby.''

She nodded. ''I am, too.''

Giovanni was in a mood to talk. Normally she would have loved nothing better. But that was before Luke's advent into her life. Right now she needed to be by herself. The revelations about him had turned her world inside out. She felt like she'd just lived through an earthquake and was still experiencing aftershocks.

''Giovanni—thank you for a magical night. I'll never forget it.''

''That's good. Now, before I let you go, I have something to give you. I want you to wear it when we go to the masked ball at the university tomorrow night.''

He reached into the glove compartment and pulled out what looked like an antique porcelain jewelry box. When he opened it, her eyes widened in disbelief.

''That's the Renaissance hair piece! The one out of the collection at the museum!''

''The exact one.''

''I couldn't, Giovanni. It's a family treasure.''

His hands moved apart expressively. ''What are treasures for if they can't be worn once in a while? Your hair is perfect for it. Please do this for me? I've never asked a favor of you before.''

The night had brought many shocks which had left her drained and in pain. At such a low ebb, the hint of pleading in his tone was more than she could handle. Giovanni was determined to turn tomorrow night into another unforgettable highlight of her trip to Italy.

But she couldn't imagine finding any happiness knowing that Luke would be back in Rome. Though only two hours away by car, he might as well be on another planet as live at the Vatican. Not even his own family would have the right to visit him unless it was a matter of life and death.

Yet his leaving Urbino in the morning was creating a life and death situation for her. How would she ever get over him? She'd never met a man like him. She never would again. Tonight he'd left the table before she was prepared to let him go. If she could see him one more time, talk to him a little more...

"Giovanni," she murmured, "I'd be honored to wear this hair jewelry, but I don't have the faintest idea how to put it on. I'd need help, and don't trust anyone here."

"*Bene*. One of the maids, Luciana, often does my mother's hair when her own stylist isn't available. She will be delighted to assist you."

"It would have to be early in the morning because the rest of my day will be taken up with packing and getting ready to go home. The thing is, I realize y-your brother," she stammered, "is going back to Rome tomorrow and I would hate to intrude on your private family time."

Even as she said it, Gaby prayed to be forgiven for mentioning Luke, for still wanting him. He was on the brink of taking solemn vows which prohibited him from having a relationship with a woman. She was going to have to forget him, put him out of her mind. *But how*? her heart repeated the question over and over again.

"You couldn't intrude if you wanted to. I'll come for you at six-thirty. We'll go back to the palace and have breakfast together. Luca wants to be away by eight. Then Luciana can see to your hair."

Breakfast with Luke? A sudden rush of adrenaline made her want to jump out of her skin.

"I'll be ready," she said in a breathless voice. "Please keep the jewelry with you. It's far too valuable. I'd die if anything happened to it." She left the box on the seat.

He eyed her with a pensive expression. "No earthly treasure is worth dying for, Gaby. Now a sacred love, that's something else again."

She averted her eyes. Something told her Giovanni knew about her secret attraction to Luke. With those cryptic words, he intended to crush any thoughts she might be entertaining about his brother whose heart embraced a higher form of love.

She wondered if this had happened before— Giovanni bringing home a girl, only to have her fall in love with Luke. It was a horrifying thought. She felt so ashamed and so helpless.

"Good night, Giovanni."

"*Buona notte*, Gaby."

She slid from the car, shut the door and waved until he'd left the alley.

The happy girl who'd left earlier in the evening to enjoy the Renaissance Fair was not the same troubled woman who entered the back door of the *pensione*, wondering how life would ever hold the same meaning for her again.

She could return home to live in Nevada, surrounded by her loved ones. She could even find a way to move to this region of Italy, a part of her heritage. There was no more beautiful spot on earth. But either way she would be empty because of a man she'd only known three hours.

Whatever it was about Luke, meeting him had altered her life drastically. He was a man whose mere presence defined the role of woman in her as no one else had ever done or would do. A man to whom she felt bonded though his destiny lay in an entirely different direction.

Perhaps Scott was right and she had more of her great-grandmother in her than she had supposed. Gabriella Trussardi had lost her heart to a vagabond artist and had followed him literally to the ends of the earth.

Gaby Holt would do the same thing for the love of one Luca Provere. But where he went, she couldn't follow. Even if he weren't a priest, she had no right to love him. Not when his brother had met and loved her first.

Intense pain propelled her up the stairs to her room. Most of the students were still enjoying the fair. With sleep out of the question, she could get her house cleaning done for the next occupant without disturbing anyone.

After changing into a baggy T-shirt and cutoffs, she plunged in. The key was to keep busy until she dropped from exhaustion.

A half hour later, Gaby needed to escape the heat and went to the study-hall-cum-salon for an Orangina. There was no such a thing as ice, but at least it would be wet and quench her thirst.

To her surprise she found a roomful of students who lived at the *pensione*. They were huddled together in serious conversation, gesticulating back and forth. She heard smatterings of German and French.

Celeste motioned to Gaby the second she saw her. "You have heard the news, *oui*?"

She came to a standstill. "No."

"Aie... An accident down the street. You know? *Une auto, écrasée. Mon Dieu, c'est affreux.*"

Perhaps she was being paranoid, but Gaby found herself asking, "What color was the car?"

"*Noire*," Lise supplied. "Black. It came from *le palais*."

Not Giovanni... "That's my friend's car. Where did it happen?" Gaby cried in alarm.

After a discussion, the girls decided it would be easier to show her. Frantic, Gaby dashed from the room following the others to the front door of the *pensione*.

But once she gained the outside, her progress was blocked by a cobalt blue Maserati which had just pulled up to the entry. The bricked street was too narrow for cars to park, which meant she and her friends had to walk around it.

Gaby tried to dodge the person getting out of the driver's side and found herself face to face with the man who had transformed her life.

"*Luke*!"

Only the most tragic news would have brought him here. She felt the blood drain from her face. On cue, her legs started to give way.

With a fierce explanation he gripped her shoulders to prevent her from falling. "Gabriella," he said her name for the first time in the Italian way, giving her a little shake.

She tried to talk coherently. "The girls—they just told me about Giovanni— They were taking me to the scene of the accident."

His eyes penetrated the darkened blue of hers. "There would be no point. I've just come from the hospital. He's had a concussion, but he's going to be all right."

His words brought blessed relief. Gaby sagged against him. "Thank heaven his injuries weren't more serious," she cried softly, not realizing what she was saying or doing until her lips grazed the gold cross hanging around his neck.

The metal, warm from his hard body, scorched her. She sprang apart from him, guilt ridden and humiliated by her lack of control.

"I—I'm sorry. Please forgive me," she begged, her emotions in utter chaos. "I didn't mean—"

"There's nothing to forgive." His voice grated. "My brother has given us too many surprises for one night. Is there anything you need before I drive you to the hospital? Giovanni wants to see you."

Trying to think, she backed away from him, still unsteady. His gaze lowered to take in her attire. The blood returned to her cheeks with alarming swiftness.

She would never have worn this outfit in front of a man, let alone Luca Provere. Loose as it was, the thin cotton T-shirt revealed far too much of her figure. The cutoffs accentuated her long, elegant legs.

"I need to change," her voice trailed before she disappeared inside the *pensione*, only to face a barrage of questions from her friends. They followed her to her room.

While she put on the clothes she'd worn to dinner, they commiserated over Giovanni's accident. But what they really wanted to talk about was the gorgeous male specimen sitting outside in the Maserati.

The questions flew, but Gaby was too overwhelmed by Luke's appearance at the *pensione* to satisfy their curiosity. All she knew was that he made an unforgettable impact on anyone who met him.

She would never have wished for more time alone with him at the expense of Giovanni's physical well-being, but her heart didn't seem to know that. She couldn't remember her feet touching the ground as she made her way out the door to his car.

CHAPTER FOUR

GABY could hear the motor idling as she slid inside the luxury sports car. Luke had left the passenger door open and reached across her body to shut it once she was seated.

As he fastened the lap belt, his arm accidentally brushed against her midriff. The disturbing contact sent a prickle of expectancy through her system. Before directing his attention to the road, he slanted her a probing glance that left her dazed.

She linked her fingers together. "H-how did the accident happen?" Giovanni hadn't seemed upset when he'd left her, but now she knew differently. She'd been riddled with guilt since the moment the girls had told her about it.

"He had to swerve to avoid a group of students and crashed into a wall. I expect there'll be bruises, but on the whole, he was lucky to escape without getting himself killed."

"Your poor mother must be frantic."

He geared down to take a curve, controlling the powerful engine with practiced ease. "That's one way of putting it. Giovanni never was a good driver."

"Did—did you see the car?"

His jaw hardened. "If you mean what was left of

it, yes. We can thank God it happened after he brought you back to the *pensione*.''

The words he left out created a horrifying picture in her mind. Gaby shivered convulsively. ''I-it's my fault he's hurt,'' she said in a tortured whisper.

With a grimace, Luke maneuvered the car to the casualty parking area of the hospital and shut off the motor. ''So you did confront him.''

She bent her head. ''Yes.''

''Did he admit to wanting to marry you?'' Luke demanded in clipped tones.

Gaby wiped her eyes with the palms of her hands. ''H-he said that if he did marry, I was the woman he would choose, but he knew I didn't feel the same way about him. He's h-hoping I'll miss him and come back next summer.''

The man next to her stirred restlessly. ''And what was your response?''

''I told him I cared for him very much, but beyond that, I—I didn't know what to say.''

She heard a harsh intake of breath. ''He's still in the denial phase of your rejection.''

Her head jerked toward him. ''What do you mean?''

''He asked me to bring you to him. You're the only person he wants to see.''

''I don't understand.''

Luke flexed his hand. ''He refuses to talk to Mother or me.''

She was staggered by the revelation. ''This is a

nightmare. Luke, you have to believe I never meant to hurt him. He's a good friend. That's all!''

"You and I both know that," he rasped, "but love can change a man beyond recognition." The timbre of his voice revealed new layers of pain.

"If I'd had any idea—" she cried, shaking her head in disbelief.

She heard his muttered imprecation. "I thought I knew my brother, but I returned home to find a stranger inhabiting his body."

"I—I don't know what to do. The last thing I want is to make the situation worse. If I refuse to see h—"

"You won't refuse," he asserted the avowal. "His doctor says he mustn't be upset right now. Once more I'm going to have to ask you to play a part."

She let out a groan. "For how long?"

His dark eyes impaled her. "For as long as it takes," came the grating voice. He levered himself from the driver's seat.

She knew his hand at her elbow was an impersonal gesture to assist her from the car. Yet despite the precarious circumstances of Giovanni's accident, her body felt electrified by his touch. Somehow he must have sensed her reaction because he reeled away from her the second she was on her feet.

Following a few steps behind him, she entered the emergency room. The place swarmed with friends and relatives of victims brought in for treatment. She supposed the fair had produced an influx of casualties. When she thought of Giovanni's brush with death, another shudder attacked her.

"This way," he murmured. Together they proceeded past various cubicles to the end where a blue curtain had been drawn. With every step, the sounds and smells started to get to her and she felt sick.

"Wait—" She grabbed his forearm for support.

"*Mio Dio!*" he importuned before putting his arm around her shoulders. "You've gone white as alabaster."

"Just give me a moment," she whispered. For a time she was out of control of her actions. Until her ears stopped buzzing, she clung to him. Slowly the warmth and reassurance of his hard body seeped into hers. She became aware of other sensations which had no place at a time like this, let alone with a man like Luca Provere.

Beneath his black silk shirt, her cheek registered the strong pounding of his heart. Like a person under water, all her movements were slow as she reluctantly began drawing away from him. When her hands slid from his chest, she felt the tremor of his powerful body with a sense of wonder.

He stared at her balefully. "You're not up to this. I'm going to take you back to the *pensione*."

Out of self-preservation, she put some distance between them. "No— I—I'm all right. Giovanni is the one we have to think about right now." Without waiting to hear what his response would be, she moved to the edge of the curtain and pulled it aside.

"*Gaby!*"

"Oh, Giovanni. What have you done to yourself?" His forehead was wrapped to hold some gauzy pads over the spot where he must have hit the windshield. He couldn't have been wearing a seat belt. But other than the injury to his head, he looked in surprisingly good shape.

She rested her cheek tenderly against his for a brief moment, then raised back up. "You look younger dressed in that hospital gown. I can picture you the way you must have been as a boy."

He laughed. Thank heavens he still could. "I feel like a little boy with the staff waiting on me."

Tears stung her eyes. "I'm so grateful you're all right. When Lu—" She stopped, then started again. "When your brother came to find me and told me what happened, I was shocked. Are you in a lot of pain?"

"Not very much. Mostly I am ashamed to have wrecked the car. This is not my first accident."

"Compared to your life, a car means nothing. Giovanni—" She lowered her voice. "What's wrong? Your brother tells me you've refused to talk to him or your mother. Don't you know how much that hurts them?"

"Are they both here?"

"I haven't seen your mother, but Luke is right outside."

A sleepy smile broke out on his face. "Do you really call him Luke?"

She colored. "I—I didn't mean to, especially when I know he's about to become Father Luca. It just sort of slipped out. I'm afraid I'm very typical of my nationality. We don't often stand on formality."

"It's a refreshing change, Gaby. I'm sure he thinks so, too. Tell him to come in."

She blinked. "Now?"

"Yes."

Relieved for Luke, she murmured, "I'll get him." Patting his arm, she slipped outside the curtain. Luke stood a little ways off, his head bent in deep concentration. It gave her immense satisfaction just to look at him. What would it be like to feast her eyes on him forever, and have the right to do it?

"Luke?" she called his name softly. At the sound of her voice he turned. His eyes were dark and brooding on her face. "He wants to see you."

A stillness came over him as he continued to study her without giving away anything of what he was thinking. She grew uneasy before he indicated that he was coming. When she returned to Giovanni's bedside, Luke wasn't far behind. He walked around to the other side of the bed so he was facing her.

Giovanni stared at his brother with a look of such love, Gaby's heart swelled with emotion. "*Fratello*— You know Mama. She asks so many questions. Tonight I'm too tired to answer them. That is why I didn't want her here. At times like this, you are the only one who can help calm her down.

"As for Gaby, I thought if you brought her to the hospital, then I would only have to say things *once* to the both of you."

Luke's face was grim with concern. "Has the doctor found further injuries? Tell me!" His voice rang with love. Theirs was a rare, special bond between brothers.

"No. But he says I must stay in the hospital for observation at least two days. Gaby—" His heavy-lidded brown eyes slowly shifted to her. "I am sorry I won't be able to take you to the ball. I know how much you were counting on it."

Her hands spread apart emotively. "How can you even think about it at a time like this? I couldn't care less, Giovanni. All that matters is that you get well."

"What ball are you talking about?" Luke muttered in a low voice.

Gaby shook her head. "It's nothing. Forget it."

"The Renaissance ball held at the university," Giovanni persisted. "It's the culminating activity of Gaby's art history studies. Everything will be authentic. This is a once-in-a-lifetime opportunity for her. I wanted her to wear an authentic hair piece in honor of the event." Giovanni spoke to his brother as if she weren't in the room.

"It's over there in a bag the ambulance people brought in. The porcelain box was smashed at impact, but the jewelry wasn't damaged."

Like someone in slow motion, Luke found the bag sitting on a chair and lifted out the contents. When he examined the elaborate pearl headdress, she didn't think his eyes could go any darker, but they did.

Clearly shocked, his gaze flickered immediately to his brother, sending him an unspoken message she couldn't decipher. Giovanni didn't appear in the least affected by Luke's reaction.

"I planned to bring Gaby to the palace in the morning so Luciana could arrange it in her hair. It goes perfectly with the dress I'd picked out for her."

"*What dress?*" Gaby was nonplussed.

His eyes closed. Fatigue had taken hold of him. "It was going to be another surprise."

She hugged her arms to her body. "I think there have been enough of those for one day."

"If only you weren't going back to Rome in the morning, Luca, you could take Gaby in my place. Then I wouldn't have to disappoint her when she has been looking forward to tomorrow night since her arrival in Urbino."

"That's not true!" she cried, aghast at such a suggestion. "Do you honestly think I could enjoy myself knowing you are lying hurt in a hospital?"

"I am not on my death bed, Gaby. In two, three days, I will be up and around again. But you will never come back to Urbino. Deep down in my heart I know that now. That's why I want your last night here to be one you'll remember forever."

In the most gracious way possible, Giovanni had just told her in front of his brother that he'd accepted her rejection of him.

Luke's eyes captured hers, the throbbing nerve in his jaw clearly visible. "Tomorrow night is your last night?" he inquired in his deep voice.

"Yes. School is over. My tour bus leaves for Belgium day after tomorrow. I'll be flying from

Brussels to the States.'' I'll never see you again, Luca
Provere. *Why does that fact hurt me so much?* she
groaned inwardly.

Breaking eye contact with him, she leaned over
Giovanni and gave him a kiss on the cheek. ''I'll call
tomorrow to see how you are getting along. Since
your brother is leaving in the morning, I'm going to
go now so the two of you can enjoy the precious little
time you have left together.''

''I'll drive you, then come back,'' Luke announced
as if it were a foregone conclusion.

''No.'' She shook her head emphatically. ''I'm so
relieved Giovanni is all right, I feel like walking.''

Luke's features looked chiseled. He wasn't used to
being dictated to. ''It's getting late. You shouldn't be
out on the streets alone.'' He didn't let up in order to
emphasize the point.

She smiled bravely at him. The way she was feeling about him right now, there was much less danger
mixing with the crowd. ''Tonight everyone is out! My
pensione is only ten minutes from here. I need to walk
off that fabulous dinner and I'd like to stretch my
legs.''

Giovanni sighed. There were purple smudges beneath his closed lids. ''Do not argue with Gaby, my
dear Luca. She is an independent American woman
who knows her own mind and can protect herself.
When a scoundrel tried to pick her pocket two weeks
ago, she did a trick that made him double over, then
run off. Something her brothers taught her.''

Luke didn't appear impressed or convinced.

"Buona notte, Giovanni."

"Buona notte, Gaby."

She moved to the curtain, then paused. "It was a pleasure meeting you, Signore Provere." She fought to keep her voice steady. "Have a nice trip back to Rome. *Arriverderla*."

She hurried out of the cubicle and down the crowded hall to the doors, having no idea if he'd said goodbye or not. But she didn't dare stay to find out.

Once she reached the outside, she broke into a run. Thank heaven it was dark and the streets were starting to empty. She didn't want her glistening cheeks to attract any more attention than necessary.

All the way back to the *pensione* she turned over the night's earthshaking events in her mind. If she knew Giovanni, he'd send a car for her in the morning and follow through on all his good intentions. He'd probably dredge up one of his friends to take her to the ball.

This time she was one step ahead of him. Of course she wouldn't leave Urbino without saying goodbye. But she'd do that tomorrow night.

Tonight she would get all her packing done, then be up at daybreak. If she took the first bus leaving Urbino, she could spend the morning in Assisi and the afternoon in Loretello. By nightfall her bus would bring her back to town in time to check in on Giovanni. It would be hard to say goodbye for the last time. Under the circumstances, she felt it wise to keep her visit short.

The problem was, there was no way she could stay

in Urbino tomorrow knowing that Luke had gone to Rome. She needed to exorcize him from her heart. The best way to do that was to keep busy and fill her mind with new sights and experiences.

The trip to Belgium through Switzerland and France would help. When she got back to Las Vegas, she'd take a quarter off of school and ask Wayne if she could come and work for him on the ranch. No more Italian for her. She'd fulfilled her promise to her great-grandmother. That part of her education was finished.

When Gaby finally got back to the *pensione*, she met Celeste in the hall on the way to her room.

"Eh, Gaby. How is your friend?"

"He's going to be all right."

"*Grace à Dieu.*" She cocked her brunette head. "And the other one who is so *magnifique*?"

"He leaves for Rome in the morning."

Her brows frowned dramatically. "So you won't see him again?"

"No."

"*Quelle catastrophe!*"

"It doesn't matter, Celeste. I'll be leaving for home on Sunday."

"Do you want to come with us tomorrow? I don't know what we're planning, but we will amuse ourselves, *n'est-ce pas*?"

"Thanks. I appreciate the invitation, but I'm going to go away for the day."

"*Pourquoi*? The fair is still on! Where will you go?"

"I—I'm not sure yet," Gaby prevaricated. Celeste
was a nice girl, but if Giovanni had a car sent for
Gaby from the palace and the driver discovered she
wasn't at the *pensione*, he'd inquire as to her whereabouts. The always helpful Celeste would be the first
person to give information. Tomorrow was one time
when Gaby didn't want to be found.

"Good night. Thanks for caring."

"*Bien sur.* We are friends, *non*? I must find out
where you live before you leave. My parents are planning a trip to Los Angeles, Disneyland, next year.
You are close, *oui*?"

"Kind of." Gaby smiled sadly. "I'll be back tomorrow night. We'll exchange addresses then."

"*Tres bien. Bonne nuit, chérie.*"

The Medieval town of Assisi rested on an Umbrian
hilltop shrouded in early morning mist. Gaby's first
view of the ancient citadel was so lovely, so *Italian*,
it made her want to cry all over again.

She'd shed many tears on the two-hour drive from
Urbino. With every zigzagging kilometer, the rolling
landscape of green hills and valleys thrilled her heart.
Each knoll revealed oak and poplar-lined river banks,
walled towns, lush orchards. No matter where she
looked she saw well-ordered farms, crenelated castles,
chains of undulating pastoral countryside dotted with
vineyards.

Until she'd met Luke, Gaby couldn't understand
how her great-grandmother had left the charm and
color of a region so exquisite it looked like a

Renaissance painting come to life, for the love of a man.

To Gaby it was frightening to realize that such a powerful love could sweep you away so that nothing else mattered but to be with that one human being who colored your world for all time.

Luke had colored hers. She'd never be the same again and wondered if he thought of her at all. Last night there'd been certain charged moments when she'd felt a chemistry so strong, she'd grown sick with excitement. If he'd felt it, too, then how did he deal with his forbidden thoughts? How did he put them away? She'd like to know his secret.

By now he was back in Rome, swallowed up in a life she couldn't comprehend.

"*Signorina*?"

Startled, Gaby glanced at the driver. He was signaling that she should get off. Their bus had entered the parking lot below the town.

Embarrassed to have delayed him, she hurried down the aisle and stepped to the ground, congratulating herself on getting away from Urbino before anyone had seen her to ask questions she had no desire to answer.

A local hotel several blocks' distance from the *pensione* catered to tourists and started serving breakfast at six. Gaby had walked there and sipped cappuccino while she waited for the bus which had taken her to a town further south. From there she'd caught another bus for Assisi.

Other tourists had the same idea. The parking lot

had started to fill with the kind of tour buses she'd be taking to Belgium. This was her last day in Italy. Though her emotions were in chaos and her pain almost unendurable, she would give herself the gift of this day.

Inhaling the soft air sweetened by the fragrance from surrounding fruit farms, she set off to visit the holy abode of the legendary St. Francis of Assisi.

On the way up the many steps, she moved past groups of nuns and priests who'd come on pilgrimage to the sacred shrine. She tried to imagine Luke among them and couldn't, probably because she was in denial over his life's work.

Angry with herself for continuing to dwell on him, she went first to the dark, claustrophobic area under the church where St. Francis was purported to be buried. Then she ascended to the basilica to view the priceless frescoes.

Gregorian chant filled the nave. In the past, she enjoyed hearing priests sing their ancient music. But today the haunting sounds drove her from the church.

The mist had started to burn off, revealing a blue sky. Hoping it was a good omen, Gaby pushed forward, exploring the mazelike town with its cobblestoned pathways and hidden churches tucked away in mellowed-orange walls.

A ten minute walk from the main piazza, she came across many separate flights of stairs which she ascended. At the top, she spied the watch towers of a castle in the distance and was drawn to it.

Eventually she reached her destination and paid the

fee to enter the Rocca Maggiore. Free to wander around the outer bailey, she tried to imagine herself as a knight.

Unfortunately the only picture that came to mind was a vision of Luke, his dark head thrown back, his black eyes flashing as his man-at-arms helped to dress his incredible male body in battle armor.

Praying to rid his image from her heart, she moved through a dark corridor punctuated every so often by arrow slits. The staircase at the other end was pitch black. She'd have to feel her way if she wanted to go any further.

Determined to make it all the way, she started the climb. Round and round she went, half fearing she might bump into someone coming down. But she couldn't hear any sounds except her own footsteps. Finally she gained the top.

What she saw when she walked to the edge of the tower defied description. Ripple after ripple of meadow and farm delineated by hedges and tree rows stretched to the horizon. Every direction delighted the eye. She stood there for ages. This was a degree of beauty unmatched anywhere in the world.

"An anonymous poet once wrote that this region of Italy is the view from God's window. The soul of anyone trespassing here will go away enlarged."

Gaby had been standing with her hands on the ledge, her face raised to the sun. She'd been enjoying the slight breeze which wafted through her waist-long hair, lifting it from the sides of her damp neck. At the sound of the distinctive male voice coming from behind, she let out a small cry and her fingers dug into the stone parapet till one of them drew blood.

She had to be hallucinating and was afraid to turn around. Wanting Luke had become an obsession. Now her mind had conjured him up!

Knowing he was in Rome, Gaby worried that she might be on the brink of a nervous breakdown. In an effort to get control of herself, she remained in place, not trusting her senses.

"Giovanni told me you were a little frightened of me. I didn't take him seriously, but now I'm beginning to wonder." His wry tone caught her off guard.

Dear God. It *was* Luke. Shock made her breath come in pants. "W-what are you d-doing here?"

"You may well ask," he murmured cryptically. "You're as unpredictable as you are impulsive."

She whirled around. While her eyes were adjusting to the shaded area where he stood tall and dark in a charcoal shirt and trousers, she could feel his intent gaze roving over her face and body. She sensed he was making comparisons between her attire of last night and today.

In keeping with the hot summer weather, she'd worn a sensible pale blue cotton wraparound skirt and a white, short-sleeved top. Her Italian leather sandals had been everywhere and looked good with anything she wore. But when Luke looked at her, she felt exposed and warm, as if he had the ability to see what lay beneath the surface and ferret her womanly secrets.

Her breathing grew shallow. "W-why aren't you in Rome?"

"Giovanni had a bad night."

"How bad?" she asked in a tremulous voice.

"He's suffering dizziness, which in turn has upset his stomach. The doctor says this is to be expected with a head injury. It will pass. But our mother is taking it rather badly."

"I don't blame her. Dear Giovanni."

"Under the circumstances, I couldn't leave. Particularly not when Giovanni made me promise to call at the *pensione* and drive you to the palace to get your hair done for the ball."

She knew it. She just hadn't realized that it would be *Luke* who was the driver. Her body quivered. "That's very sweet of him, but I'm the last person he should be worrying about. I'm sorry you've been put to so much trouble to track me down."

His lips twitched. "It was no trouble. All I had to do was make a few phone calls in the right places and I knew exactly where to find the woman my informants refer to as the *squisita testarossa* from America."

Gaby blushed to the roots of her hair to hear herself described that way. What a fool she'd been to think she could elude the long reach of the Provere influence. Luke commanded the instant respect and cooperation of everyone in the Marches.

She cleared her throat. "Last night you heard me tell Giovanni that I had no intention of going out tonight. He carries his sense of duty way too far," she grumbled.

"That's his nature," he said in thick tones. "I'm afraid in this case, however, you don't have a choice. I made a promise to be your escort."

"*No!*" Her fearful cry rang in the air and she staggered back until she felt the rough ledge through the thin material of her blouse.

She couldn't possibly dance with him. To know his touch one more time, to feel his hands on her body when she knew he was a priest, was asking too much. It would be disastrous. *It would be wrong.*

His brows drew together in a forbidding black line. "After rejecting his love, do you care so little about him that you would deny him this last request before you leave the country? I wouldn't have thought you of all people would purposely hinder his recovery."

Luke's hands had gone to his hips, forcing her to be even more aware of his devastating masculine appeal. Angry because of her futile attraction to him—stung by his cruel insinuations—she cried, "How can you say that to me? I'd do anything to help him get better. But to go to—"

"*Bene.*" He prevented her from further remonstration. "Luciana will have an afternoon's work ahead of her confining all that hair in time for you to dress."

"No!" she cried again out of a sense of self-preservation.

He thrust her a long, unreadable glance.

She fiddled with the tie of her skirt nervously, unwittingly drawing his interest when she hadn't meant to. "I know what you promised Giovanni, a-and I certainly don't want to make his condition worse. But—" She paused to swallow. "I have no desire to attend a ball. That was always your brother's idea."

"He thought it would please you," came the wooden retort.

Guilt assailed her. "That's the problem. He tries too hard." Her voice quivered.

She felt his body tauten and knew she'd said the wrong thing, but now that she'd started this, she had to go on.

"T-there's something else I'd planned to do with my last few hours in Italy."

His sharp intake of breath warned her to tread carefully. "What would that be?"

"It's not your concern," she assured him in a meek tone, growing more uneasy by the minute. "The point is, he would never have to know about it. Not if we lied to him," she said in a small voice. "Just a little lie that would make us all happy."

"You're forgetting Luciana who will run to Giovanni if you don't show up. She adores him."

Gaby lifted pleading eyes to him. "You could explain to her that one of my friends at the *pensione* has insisted on helping me instead."

"He'll expect a full report after the ball."

"I realize that. Naturally I intended to say goodbye to him one last time. But you could put off your visit until tomorrow morning, couldn't you?"

"Our stories may not match," he persisted with maddening logic.

"Please—" she begged him.

The desperation in her voice must have reached him. He folded his arms, his eyes holding a strange glitter. "I might be willing to cooperate, provided you tell me what it is that's so important."

"After leaving here, I'd planned to go to Loretello one last time to see if I could find the farm that once belonged to my Trussardi relatives. I've had to budget my money, so I've only been out there once. But I never did find out any information. I speak a little Italian now, and hoped to talk to one of the old residents to see if they might remember something."

He ran a ringless hand through his black hair, signifying any number of emotions. "Why didn't you let Giovanni take you? He could have translated and been of enormous help."

She moistened her lips. "Because until last evening, I thought he was a poor, struggling student who didn't have enough money to buy me a *gelato*, let alone his own bus ticket," she added quietly when she saw the shadow that darkened Luke's face. "H-he was very resourceful and always found ways for us to enjoy ourselves without spending any lira at all."

"*Per Dio!*"

She winced from his anger. "I knew that if I told him about my frustration in not finding any information, he'd ask for time off from his work at the castle. That would mean he wouldn't earn as much take-home pay. Because he never talked about his family, I assumed they had few resources and that he was helping them out. Under the circumstances, I didn't want to place an unnecessary burden on him.''

Luke's smothered epithet left her trembling. ''I had no idea my brother could be this devious. He owes you an apology. So does my mother for treating you so abominably at dinner.''

''No. It's not important.'' She shook her head, overwhelmed to elicit this kind of response from Luke. ''We both know Giovanni meant no harm.''

''Do we?'' he asked in a voice she didn't recognize. ''I'm afraid my feelings aren't that generous.''

A troubling silence heightened her anxiety. ''Don't be upset with your brother,'' she appealed to him. ''He worships you. I honestly believe he'd throw himself off one of the palace towers if you suggested it. You know what a great tease Giovanni is. His pretense with me was nothing more than that. As you said yesterday, he has no guile.'

''I was wrong,'' Luke muttered with chilling ferocity. She hated being the cause of a rift between them and started to tell him so, but his next words stopped her.

''We'll drive to Loretello. By nightfall we ought to have located your relative's property. Come. I know a shortcut to the car.''

CHAPTER FIVE

DAZED by the knowledge that Luke hadn't gone to Rome, that instead, he had followed her to Assisi, Gaby couldn't think clearly. Too late, she remembered about the bus.

"Shouldn't I let the driver know I'm not riding with him?"

She turned her head in the direction of the parking area, inadvertently brushing the side of Luke's face and neck with the ends of her hair. Embarrassed because it hindered his vision, she pulled the strands away as fast as she could.

"I already took care of it," came the husky rejoinder. As the Maserati began eating the kilometers, she noted that his hands gripped the wheel tighter. Already there was tension in the car and they hadn't been in it five minutes.

Because of Giovanni, Luke's life had been thrown off balance and he had every right to be upset. But then, so had she.

This morning when she left Urbino, who would have dreamed that by lunchtime she'd be ensconced in a fabulous Italian-made car, whizzing through adorable towns in the Italian countryside with Luca Provere?

She'd fallen in love with a man whose life was dedicated to the church and it was killing her.

Gaby had never known anyone who had become a priest. Now would be her opportunity to ask questions and find out what spiritual forces had driven him to choose a vocation that denied him a life with a wife and family.

Had he never been in love? Didn't he wonder what it would be like to bring a son or daughter into the world?

Much as she wanted answers, she feared he would consider it an invasion of privacy. In fact, Giovanni had been so secretive with both her and Luke, it was possible Luke had no idea she knew he was about to take final vows.

Not that it would make any difference either way. But since Luke hadn't chosen to discuss anything of a personal nature with her, except where Giovanni was concerned, her instincts told her to say nothing.

"If you can wait another forty-five minutes, we'll come to a restaurant that serves a superb pasta dish called *vincisgrassi*, followed by fennel-stuffed rabbit that is out of this world."

"It sounds wonderful." Every minute she could spend alone with him was something to cherish.

"After we eat, we'll drive to Arcevia. That will be the spot where Loretello's civil and family group registries are located. We'll search the records and see if we can't come up with some information that will help you locate the plot of ground your great-grandparents once farmed."

"Why aren't the records kept in Loretello?"

"Like many Italian towns, it is too small to be what you Americans call the county seat."

"I had no idea." Her eyes fastened helplessly on his striking profile. "It sounds complicated and out of the way. I—I don't want to infringe on your time any more than I already have."

He darted her a shuttered glance. "I promised my brother to make your last day in Italy memorable. In my opinion, finding one's family roots takes precedence over attending a Renaissance ball, therefore I'm at your disposal."

"Thank you, Luke." Her voice caught. She looked away, afraid he'd see too much in her eyes. *This was her last day*. She couldn't bear to think of tomorrow without him.

"You don't need to thank me. To be honest, genealogical research has always intrigued me. You never know what kind of information will turn up."

"Well, it's certain there won't be a pope in *my* bloodline," she joked to cover her hectic emotions. "Probably just the opposite!"

His full-bodied laughter was the most thrilling sound she'd ever heard. She had the impression he hadn't let go and relaxed for a long, long time.

"With all that red hair, you could be right," he mocked dryly.

Heat swept through her body. "Maybe my great-grandmother didn't tell us the truth. Maybe she was trying to escape a bad home situation and ran off with the first person who could offer her freedom."

"Did she strike you as a woman with secrets?"

Gaby shook her head. "No. She seemed like a totally happy, fulfilled person, but then I was a child when she died."

"A child's instincts are rarely wrong."

"I don't know. Las Vegas is the antithesis of Loretello. I can't imagine her leaving this paradise unless she had to. You'd know what I meant if you'd ever traveled to Nevada."

"I've been there," he inserted quietly.

"*You?*"

Her astonishment produced another chuckle from him. "In my early twenties I traveled extensively in the United States which included an overnight stay in Las Vegas." Gaby would have been fourteen or fifteen, old enough to have developed a huge crush on him.

"I went on to school in California which gave me added time to explore. For someone from my country, the American desert has a beauty all its own."

She agreed with him, but the revelation that he'd once been that close to her made her blurt, "So *that's* why you speak English with hardly a trace of accent!"

"I'll take that as a compliment."

Gaby could scarcely credit they were talking to each other this way. She wanted the drive to last forever. "Did Giovanni accompany you? I don't recall him saying anything about it."

"No. He was too young. In any event, except for two months in England a few years ago when we went together at my instigation, he has never shown any inclination to stray far from home.'' Luke offered the information as if his brother's behavior continued to trouble him.

''I haven't known Giovanni long, but he seems very untouched by the world.''

A strange sound came out of the man sitting next to her. ''I thought so, too. That is, until he met you.'' His voice trailed off.

She didn't detect censure exactly. But there were undertones which filled her with trepidation. ''I—I'll be gone tomorrow, out of his life.''

''But not necessarily out of mind,'' he said rather intensely. ''Unlike his friends, he never dated girls in his teens. In fact, he's never had a romantic interest in women and treats Efresina like a sister. That's why his phone call about you came as a complete shock— in more ways than one,'' he added cryptically.

Oddly enough, the news that Giovanni had never been attracted to women didn't surprise her. ''From the beginning, your brother seemed to function on a different plane. That's the reason I enjoyed his company so much.''

''So you used Giovanni for protection.''

In an instant, the fragile rapport with him was gone. A tiny gasp escaped her throat. She jerked her head in his direction. ''What do you mean?''

''Exactly what you think I meant,'' he said in a deceptively silken tone. ''Let's not pretend you don't know the impact you make on the male population.''

Incensed, she cried, "You say that as if it's a sin to be a woman!"

"It should be, when she looks like you," he grated. "Not even my brother was immune. The minute I saw you, I understood why."

Stunned into silence by his frank remarks, she watched dazedly as he pulled off the main road and entered the parking area of a quaint inn.

At one time the Trattoria Alberto must have been a small villa. Intimate tables for two with checkered cloths and pots of flowers placed in every conceivable nook beckoned diners to its trellised patio.

But Gaby no longer found joy in the surroundings, let alone their outing. In fact she felt ill. Her companion must have noticed because he didn't immediately get out of the car.

"You are the only woman of my acquaintance who could twist an innocent observation and make it sound like an insult."

"*Innocent*?" Her eyes glazed an incandescent blue. "You accused me of using Giovanni."

"Then you misunderstood me." His black eyes impaled her. "Let me rephrase it. Knowing that Giovanni would always remain the gentleman, you instinctively clung to him out of a sense of self-preservation. What an amazing irony that he turned out to be as vulnerable as the next man."

His explanation should have soothed her, but somehow it didn't. Gaby had trouble catching her breath and averted her eyes.

"American women unwisely go where they want,

unchaperoned, never giving it a thought. But if I had been your elder brother,'' his voice dropped in timbre, ''I wouldn't have allowed you to step foot on Italian soil without proper supervision. Having said that, I suggest we go inside. I find that I am in need of sustenance.''

On legs as insubstantial as jelly, she entered the restaurant with him. Her ears picked up the background music of Rossini, the famous composer whose ancestral home of Pesaro was located in the Marches.

After they were seated, Luke helped her translate the menu. When their orders were taken, he excused himself. She decided to use the time to visit the powder room.

They met back at the table five minutes later. As if reading her mind he said, ''I made a phone call to Luciana who sounded disappointed she wouldn't be able to do your hair after all. No doubt she is on the line with Giovanni this minute, alerting him to the change in plans.''

Gaby's voice was hesitant. ''M-maybe we ought to call him and explain what we're doing.''

''The dye has been cast,'' he murmured, sounding vaguely impatient. ''Let's enjoy our meal.''

On that succinct note they put personal worries aside while she was treated to Italian cuisine at its finest. Along with the pasta and rabbit, they ate succulent melon wrapped in prosciutto, and a nutty whole-wheat bread with a *cru* poured over the top made from the olives of just one hillside of the region.

As if that weren't enough, Luke introduced her to

a lightly astringent white wine he preferred called *Verdicchio*. To please him, she drank some during the delicious meal, then allowed him to fill her glass again while she accompanied him and the voluble owner inside the villa.

The man was obviously honored by the presence of an illustrious member of the Provere family. He kept smiling at Gaby and insisted on showing her his private collection of an irreplaceable set of hand-painted *maiolica*, a china with the famous blue-and-yellow decoration made around Urbino during the late Renaissance.

The owner would have taken them on a tour of the entire villa if Luke hadn't indicated they were on a deadline and must be on their way. The man walked them to their car, his goodbyes effusive. Luke was probably used to a surfeit of that kind of preferential treatment, but it was a new experience for Gaby who was more or less floating by now.

Being with Luke felt too good, too natural. When he helped her into the car, she didn't pull away at the touch of his hand on her arm. In truth, she welcomed the burning sensation igniting her body. If he hadn't moved to shut the door, she would have rested against him.

Not used to drinking anything alcoholic, the wine had blurred the sharp edges of reality. She had wandered into a dangerous corridor of contentment, willing to follow wherever he led.

For a brief moment, she had the strongest conviction that if she'd turned in his arms just now and pressed her mouth to his, he wouldn't have found the strength to push her away.

Once on the road however, Luke seemed to have removed himself emotionally from her. Deep in his own thoughts, he concentrated on his driving, not bothering to make conversation.

Though she might be feeling the effects of too much wine, he didn't appear to be suffering from the same problem. Ashamed she felt so out of control and unable to suppress her overflowing emotions, she closed her eyes to blot him from her vision. But she hadn't counted on the rich food and lack of sleep the night before to conspire against her so completely.

Her lids grew heavy. She couldn't open them again and at some point oblivion took over. She didn't waken until she discovered them parked outside the small church in Loretello, a wheat-colored brick edifice which seemed to grow organically from the hillside. Earlier, Luke had stopped in Arcevia to make inquiries and she'd never even stirred.

"W-what did you learn?" she asked, smoothing the hair out of her face. Luke's silent scrutiny confused her, making it difficult to think. She was embarrassed to have slept so long.

One black brow dipped in concern. "Not a great deal, I'm afraid. Your great-grandmother's family did not own land in Loretello. They must have moved into the area, farmed someone else's plot of ground, then moved on. There are no Trussardis listed in the birth or death records."

Surprised at the depth of her disappointment, she

turned her head away. "It's possible my great-grandmother's memory was faulty and we've been led on a wild-goose chase. I—I appreciate all your help, Luke. You've gone out of your way for nothing."

"All is not lost," he reminded her in a voice of inherent authority. "We'll visit the church and consult the parish records. Sometimes a detail is overlooked when copies are made for the conservatory archives."

Gaby shook her head. "They won't turn up anything, and I don't want to put you to further trouble."

She heard a muttered imprecation which could have meant any number of things before he levered himself from the car. She scrambled out her door to accompany him, not wanting to incur any more of his displeasure when he'd been trying so hard to help her.

The Medieval facade gave way to an ornate interior and shrine. At the back pew she watched Luke cross himself, reminding her as nothing else could do, that in less than a month, the walls of a church would be his home for the duration of his life.

Her heart felt a sharp, stabbing pain as she, too, made the sign of the cross. Unaware of her turmoil, he asked her to wait while he searched for someone to assist them. Seemingly at home in this sanctuary, he disappeared through a side door.

In agony of spirit, Gaby closed her eyes and prayed for release from the invisible cords binding her to him. She begged for help in forgetting him once she left Italy, begged for peace to come into her heart.

Otherwise she'd continue to mourn him, and her whole life would be an utter waste.

"*Gabriella*?" She heard her name in a tortured whisper. She knew he was worried about Giovanni, but wondered if there wasn't something else burdening him, adding to his turmoil.

Brushing at the moisture on her dark lashes, she stood from a kneeling position, hoping he couldn't tell she'd been crying.

"I expected to talk to the local cure, but he's out visiting. Fortunately the caretaker is on hand. He's willing to let us scan the records in the office."

Only Luke's prominent name and vocation could have induced the groundskeeper to open up such valuable records to a stranger, a foreigner no less. Her debt to Giovanni's brother had grown beyond her ability to repay.

Keeping her head lowered, she turned and followed him to the small anteroom which served as an office with a desk, chairs and several floor-to-ceiling bookcases encased in glass.

She smiled at the wizened caretaker and thanked him in Italian for his kindness. He bowed politely and undid the lock on one of the bookcases. After putting a large tome on the tabletop, he left them alone and shut the door.

Luke indicated she should sit next to him and pushed the ancient-looking record in front of her. "According to what you've told me, your great-grandmother was born somewhere around 1883. Since the earliest she might have met her future husband would be at age fifteen, we can assume she was living here at the turn of the century.''

Trying to cover up the trembling his warmth and nearness evoked, she opened the cover.

Luke translated in a low, mellow voice. It resonated to her insides. ''This lists a church census covering some births, christenings and baptisms from the years 1834 to 1908. There's a note indicating that a fire in 1900 destroyed part of the record.''

''Just the year we're looking for,'' she lamented.

''Don't jump to conclusions. Let's start with 1885 and move forward.''

Throughout the book there were scorch marks, some too brown to read the names entered in ornate cursive handwriting. Gaby came to the portion Luke suggested and ran a nervous finger down the neat rows of names.

Dozens of the same appellation appeared because whole extended families had lived in the area. They turned page after stained-torn page. It became evident that there were no Trussardis listed anywhere.

The handwriting taught in the American public schools didn't resemble European penmanship dating back a century. Most of the time she couldn't tell the difference between a capital J, F, G, I or T.

But Luke, who studied each entry with absolute concentration, had no such problem. For him to spend this kind of time helping her research a name that meant nothing to him, made her love for him that much stronger and binding.

As the pendulum of the antique wall clock swung

back and forth marking the passage of time, she realized that she'd probably never know about her namesake's origins.

"Luke—" She touched his arm gently. His eyes swiveled to hers in puzzled query, and she removed her hand. "It's no use."

"Maybe," he murmured. "Maybe not. Will you hand me that large magnifying glass hanging on the peg next to the bookcase?"

"Yes. Of course." She got up and reached for it, then gave it to him. "Have you found something?"

"I'm not sure. There are about ten pages badly stained, but I can just make out some of the names." He stood up and went over to the window to take advantage of what little light it afforded.

For once Gaby had an excuse to feast her eyes on him. Right now she could easily imagine him in robes of an important holy office. There was a magnificence about his physical presence as well as a nobility of character that shone through. He would make his mark in the church.

Yet Gaby had glimpsed a sensuous side to his nature. Today there'd been brief moments of ecstasy when she'd caught sight of his rare smile and heard his full-bodied laughter. And there'd been other times when the hunger in his eyes had turned her body molten. She couldn't have imagined those looks, could she?

That's what was tormenting her now...the possibility that she'd wanted him so much, she'd fooled herself into believing her presence affected him in a similar fashion.

"*Santa Maria*!" she heard him mutter, jerking her from her inner torment. With her heart thudding, she rose to her feet.

"Luke—"

"The date at the top of the page is missing. But according to the ones I can read, we know it has to be sometime between 1882 and 1885. It appears that a Vittore Ridolfi and wife, Amalia, had an infant, Gabriella, christened."

His black eyes flashed with a strange light. "This is the only Gabriella I've come across in any of the records at Arcevia or here. How strange that there is no birth date on her when the Ridolfi name is quite prolific in this region." He sounded far away.

Gaby started to get chills of excitement. "What are you thinking?"

His gaze encompassed her flushed face. "There is no evidence that this couple had children born to them. It's possible they took someone else's daughter to raise."

Her thoughts raced. "You mean she might have been an unwanted pregnancy and was either abandoned by her real mother or given up for adoption."

A frown line etched his dark brow. "There could be many circumstances we're not aware of. Perhaps the natural parents were killed while in the area, leaving the child orphaned. Or the Ridolfis might have been so anxious to have a baby, it's possible they traveled further afield to find one needing a home. It wasn't uncommon for a family with too many mouths to feed to sell a daughter.''

A horrible reality Gaby hated to think about. "But if they raised her as their own, why didn't she take on their name instead of calling herself Trussardi?"

"Maybe one of the parents couldn't accept the child wholeheartedly and reminded her she wasn't their blood.''

"It might explain why she ran off with my great-grandfather at the first opportunity.''

Luke put the book and magnifying glass back on the table. "Whatever the explanation, we now have a name and something to go on. I want to talk to the caretaker. He must be in his seventies. If there are any present day Ridolfis living in Loretello, he'll know of them.''

Unbelievably, Luke seemed as caught up in the excitement of solving this mystery as she was. Before they left the church, the caretaker had given them directions to the farm of one Carlo Ridolfi.

Once they were in the car, however, guilt assailed her. "Luke, I'm more grateful for your help than you'll ever know. As far as I'm concerned, it's a miracle you came across a name that could have been my relative. It's enough to have learned this much, b-but we should be getting back to Urbino.'' Her voice caught.

When he didn't say anything, she bent her head. "I'm leaving early in the morning and still have things to do.'' Being in his company like this was tearing her apart.

At her words, an almost ominous stillness pervaded the atmosphere. ''You're not going anywhere until we find what we came for.''

Shaken, she murmured, ''But that might not be possible.''

''We'll see,'' was all he would concede, sending a thrill of alarm through her body.

CHAPTER SIX

By the time they found the Ridolfi farm on the outskirts of Loretello, the late afternoon sun had lost a little of its heat. Luke shut off the air conditioner and lowered the windows so they could breathe the luscious scent coming from the vineyards lining the road.

The tile-roofed farmhouse rested on a hillside surrounded by well-tended crops of vegetables planted in perfect lines. A middle-aged farmer working down one of the rows heard their car and waved.

After a brief exchange which she couldn't follow, Luke translated. Apparently the man named Lorenzo said they would find his father, Carlo, over the other side of the hill tying vines.

Once more the car followed the meandering lane until they arrived at another stretch of vineyard. Here they came upon the short, leather-faced family patriarch in dark beret and white shirt sleeves. He looked at least eighty years old, yet worked with the speed of his son.

Luke got out of the car and walked over to him. For the next ten minutes Gaby stayed put, watching and listening in rapt attention as the two men conversed back and forth, using their hands to demonstrate everything they were saying. A long time ago she decided that if you tied an Italian's hands, he wouldn't be able to talk at all.

When she saw Luke unexpectedly put a hand on the old man's shoulder and shake the other one in a firm grip, her heart rate accelerated because she had a feeling he'd learned something important.

Luke's black eyes held a triumphant gleam as the two men walked toward the car. The old farmer's mouth broke into a broad smile when Luke introduced her as Gabriella.

"What have you found out?" she cried, hardly able to contain her excitement.

"Carlo's great uncle once removed was Vittore Ridolfi. Apparently Vittore was the outcast of the Ridolfi clan who farmed a piece of family property in the next valley.

"The story goes that as a young man, he had a bit of a wild streak and went to Rome for a fortnight. When he returned, he brought back a young woman who'd already had a baby by another man."

"Amalia! Then that means my great-grandmother might have been born in or around Rome."

Luke nodded. "Yes. He insisted on marrying her, but the family refused to recognize the child. When the girl, Gabriella, grew up, she ran off with an American and was never seen again. It broke the mother's heart. They died childless."

"Oh—" Gaby's eyes smarted painfully. "How sad for them when my great-grandmother was so happy in her own marriage."

Luke expelled a breath. "Carlo says the girl was

known to have her mother's red hair. She was also reputed to be a great beauty, just like you.'' His voice sounded thick.

She knew he was only passing on the other man's compliment, but his tone made it so personal, her body trembled.

As if Carlo understood what was going on, he nodded and pointed to her hair. More Italian poured out of him. When he finished talking, a slow smile broke a corner of Luke's mouth, dazzling her with his masculine beauty.

''Carlo is delighted to learn that you are her great-granddaughter. One day soon he would like to gather the family for a picnic to meet you and hear all the details. There are twenty-five to thirty relatives still living in the environs.''

She swallowed hard. ''Tell him I would love that, but since I'm leaving in the morning, it's impossible.''

Lines slowly marred his handsome features before he began another translation. The old man listened with a frown.

''He says you must come back.''

She didn't dare meet the fierce intensity of Luke's gaze. ''Maybe one day.'' It was a struggle to keep her emotions contained. ''Would you ask him if I could see the place where she was raised?''

More conversation ensued. ''He says the original shell of the farmhouse is still standing, but nowadays the inside is used for storage by one of his cousins. He has given you permission to walk around and do whatever you like for as long as you like. I'll take you there now.''

With tears trickling from her eyes, Gaby thrust her hand out the window to shake Carlo's hand. To her surprise, he leaned forward, cupped her face and kissed both cheeks.

''*Squisita, signorina—*'' he murmured over and over again amid a volley of other words she didn't understand. When he finally let her go, she sat back in the seat, blushing outrageously from his spontaneous display of affection.

''You've made a real conquest,'' Luke inserted wryly under his breath as he started the engine and they drove off. ''He gave me his address. I told him you would keep in touch.''

''T-thank you,'' she whispered, overcome with such deep love for Luke, she couldn't find the words. To hide her feelings, she leaned her head out the window once more to wave at Carlo.

''*Arrivederci!*'' he called after her, using the familiar form of the word goodbye, a word reserved for family and close friends only. It warmed her heart. She shouted the same word back to him and kept waving until they descended the next hill and she couldn't see him anymore.

Settling back again, she let out a delighted cry to see another quaint farmhouse in the distance, sitting on a small knoll. Lush meadows interspersed with manicured cherry orchards spread to its foundation like the spokes of a wheel to its center.

She was looking at the playground of her great-grandmother. It was too perfect to be real.

"T-this is one of the most thrilling moments of my life." Her voice shook. "I owe it all to you." There were tears in her voice and eyes. "How will I ever be able to thank you properly?"

She heard his sharp intake of breath. "If you could see the look on your face, you'd know that you already have."

He pulled to the side of the road. When he suggested they go for a walk, she was already out of the car, running toward the farmhouse.

The slanting rays of the sun cast long shadows as she made her way through the orchard. She remembered her great-grandmother talking about climbing trees, playing with her doll in the top branches.

Gaby noted that cherry trees were absolutely wonderful for climbing. Shaped like U-joints, the branches which grew low on the trunk made it a simple matter to attain one level, then another.

Near the farmhouse she saw one large, sturdy tree whose cherries hadn't been picked on top. Perhaps it was a favorite of her great-grandmother's. Unable to resist, Gaby left her purse in the grass and started climbing. Three-quarters of the way up she found a bunch of dark red fruit and ate the cherries right off their stems. "Hmm... These taste like ambrosia."

Depositing the pips in her palm, then tossing them in the opposite direction, she plucked another spray. "Here—" she called to Luke, her mouth half full of sweet, ripe cherries. "These are for you."

She dangled the bunch so he'd be sure to spot it. An imp of mischief prompted her to taunt, "If you want them, you'll have to come and get them."

He wouldn't accept the challenge, of course, but she hadn't been able to resist throwing it out. Somewhere eight to ten feet below the leaves, he was standing there waiting for her to come down.

A particularly gorgeous bunch of cherries lured her another foot higher. As she grabbed for it, she disturbed an enormous black and yellow queen bee whose buzz sounded like a small motor. She screamed in fright and suddenly the entire tree shook as Luke made it up the trunk in record time.

"What's wrong?" he demanded, his dark head pushing through the leaves.

"A queen bee!" she screamed again as it tried to land on her hair. Ill with fright, she jerked to get out of harm's way and almost lost her footing.

"It's after you, all right," he muttered. "Stay perfectly still."

Trusting in him completely, she willed herself not to move, but the hideous whirring noise made her heart thud with sickening irregularity.

With a calm she could scarcely fathom, Luke broke off a good-size shoot of leaves and thrust the huge insect from her hair with all his force. A few strands were pulled from her scalp but she didn't feel them.

All she knew was an overwhelming sense of relief as she watched the bee sail through the air in a great arc, stunned by the whack Luke had given it. Her body shaking out of control, she hurtled herself into Luke's arms.

He crushed her against his chest. ''That bee won't be going anywhere for a while,'' he assured her in a low, soothing tone, his face buried in her hair.

''Thank God,'' she cried, burrowing into the warmth of his neck where she could feel a strong pulse beating frantically. ''I'm allergic to bee stings.''

He bit out a smothered epithet. ''Whatever possessed you to climb this tree?''

His hands moved over her back, sending tiny currents of electricity through her throbbing body. ''I don't know. I—I was so happy to have found her home I didn't stop to think, and the cherries looked so tempting.''

He lifted his head, his black eyes doing a lightning-fast appraisal of her red-stained mouth. ''There's cherry juice everywhere. No wonder the bee came after you.'' His voice sounded slurred.

Caught in a V of the tree, Gaby became conscious that her body was molded to the hard length of his. With no space separating them, she could feel the pounding of his heart, the tremors that shook his powerful frame.

''*Mio Dio!*'' he vented a violent imprecation. ''Talk about temptation…that heart-shaped mouth would drive a saint to commit the unforgivable.'' Groaning in self-denigration he closed his mouth over hers, cutting off any possibility of escape.

After aching so long for this intimacy, Gaby was

thankful to be trapped against his hard body with no place to go except to merge with him.

She knew this was a momentary aberration on his part. When he had satiated the desire which had temporarily flared out of control because they were wedged together, he'd let her go, regretting his weakness. They would return to Urbino and their separate lives, never to know this kind of exultation again.

But for Gaby, this was the supreme moment of her life. The man she wanted more than life itself was holding her, kissing her with breathtaking urgency. This moment would have to last her forever.

On a little moan of desperation she surrendered herself, denying him nothing, offering him everything in a kiss that blotted out time, space, conscience...

What she couldn't say in words, she said with her lips, her hands. She was starving for him and would gorge herself on his mouth for as long as he allowed this mindless ecstasy to continue.

Gaby had so little experience with men, she had no idea what she was doing. Right now she was driven by sheer, primitive, female instinct. The man she wanted was about to disappear from her life, never to be seen again. Until he thrust her away from him, she would show him just exactly what he meant to her.

''Gabriella—'' he groaned her name as if it had been ripped out of him, his hands possessive and exploring. When she felt his mouth against the pale, scented skin of her neck, coherent thought ceased. She yielded so completely to his demands, they moved as one living entity.

The black hair she'd longed to touch filled her hands. Intoxicated by his enticing male scent, her mouth followed where her fingers trailed, pressing feverish kisses to his throat, ears and eyes.

Blinded by passion, her lips memorized the lines and angles of his face, the sensuous curve of his compelling mouth. Wild with desire, she couldn't get enough of him.

In such a euphoric state, she suffered shock when he suddenly wrenched her forearms from around his neck, breaking their kiss so abruptly, she cried his name out of deprivation, her blue eyes hurt and uncomprehending.

"For the love of God, Gabriella—" She heard his tortured whisper before he started cursing savagely in his native tongue. "You will descend the tree first, *per favore*. Now!" he demanded when she hesitated.

Trembling from the force of her emotions, Gaby had to make herself do his bidding, but the going down was almost an impossibility. She was forced to cling to each branch for a minute while her body swayed, still giddy from reaction to his touch.

Here and there her skirt caught on a twig, lifting it thigh-high as her shapely leg searched for another foothold. When she realized that this was the reason Luke had insisted she go ahead of him, her face reddened in embarrassment.

By the time she'd reached the ground, total recall of the uninhibited way she'd responded to him in the treetop turned the upper half of her body scarlet.

Good heavens, what a trembling, love-crazed mess

she was! If either of the Ridolfis could see her now, they'd know exactly what she'd been doing. Her hair was a mop of dishevelment from Luke's questing hands and mouth. There were traces of lipstick and cherry stains on her white top.

To her consternation, her heart refused to resume its normal beat rate. She was breathing as if she'd just run a marathon, and her lips were swollen and tender from the explosion of passion Luke had unleashed.

Behind her she felt him jump to the ground. ''I'll meet you at the car,'' was all he deigned to say in a gravelly tone before leaving her on her own.

Startled, she turned to watch him, a dark, lean figure whose long, swift strides emphasized emotional as well as physical distancing from her.

She should have been ashamed of her wanton behavior. But how could she be when those moments in his arms had been so perfect? There was no denying he'd been an equal partner in the experience, that he'd been as witless as she during that fusion of mouths and bodies and souls.

At least *her* soul was involved, her heart cried in agony. According to Giovanni, Luke's soul had been reserved for God.

She wasn't so naive about men that she didn't know even a man of the cloth could be tempted to enjoy lovemaking in the purely physical sense without his emotions becoming involved. Given her out-of-control response, he'd succumbed to what she'd blatantly offered because Luke had his human side, too. Only the fact that they were in a tree prevented the inevitable from happening. But the experience hadn't changed his life out of all recognition. He'd been able to walk away from her without once looking back.

She, on the other hand, still ached from longings he'd aroused but would never assuage. What really terrified her was that she might remain in this untenable condition for the rest of her life.

For the moment her only resource was to take a little time to compose herself before she returned to the car. She had her pride and wouldn't allow him to see what he'd done to her.

Reaching for her purse, she tidied herself as best she could with her hairbrush and lipstick, then pulled out her instamatic camera. For the next few minutes she snapped various views of the farmhouse and orchard.

To her chagrin, she had a feeling every picture would be blurry because she was shaking so hard. Her family might be overjoyed with the visual evidence of her great-grandmother's home, but they'd want an explanation for her less than expert photographic prowess.

No one could ever know about this interlude with Luke. She would have to twist the truth and tell her family that a queen bee had been chasing her.

But that was the least of her worries. Right now she needed to deal with a much bigger problem. How was she going to face Luke who'd been sitting in the Maserati for a good fifteen minutes, no doubt regretting his momentary insanity and impatient to be gone.

It was late. Twilight had fast turned into evening. It stole over the colorful landscape, deepening the shadows, magnifying the serenity a hundredfold.

She should never have climbed that tree. While they'd been locked together, she'd lost cognizance of her world, ignoring the reality of the situation. Deep inside, Gaby had known there'd be a price to pay for tasting forbidden fruit. She just hadn't realized how excruciating the pain would be. It was like tearing her heart out to leave this paradise where she'd experienced rapture.

More time was lost as she fought to keep her tears at bay, then made her way through the fragrant orchard toward the car.

The low, purring sound of the motor told her how anxious Luke was to return to Urbino. With yet another reason to feel guilty, she climbed in the passenger side. The second she shut the door, a fluid motion of his hand put the car into gear and they were off.

On their way to the main road, she saw Carlo's lighted farmhouse out of the periphery. But she didn't dare look in that direction or she'd see Luke's forbidding countenance.

It didn't seem possible that she'd known a passion beyond belief in the arms of this remote, taciturn stranger piloting the car as if it had wings.

Obviously guilt was eating him alive. Gaby knew the feeling. They'd betrayed Giovanni, which was bad enough. But in Luke's own mind, he'd done something much worse this close to being professed. She couldn't let him take all the blame.

"L-Luke?" she whispered tentatively.

"If you don't mind, *signorina*, I prefer not to talk about what happened," came the wintry voice she dreaded. "You found the home of your namesake. Let that be the memory you take back to Nevada."

Intense anger intruded on her pain. His hurtful dismissal of something as earthshaking and intimate as what they had shared at the farm, blinded her to caution.

With eyes burning like hot blue coals, she flung her head around, causing the hair to swish against her hot cheek. "Is that the memory you plan to take back to the Vatican, Father Luca?" Her question rang throughout the tension-filled interior.

By the time she felt enough remorse to wish she could recall it, he'd pulled to the side of the road and shut off the engine.

With his right hand still on the wheel, he turned his head in her direction. His eyes were black slits of light. "How long have you known?" he demanded thickly.

She bit the inside of her lower lip. "Giovanni told me when he dropped me off at the *pensione* last night."

He muttered something terrifyingly unintelligible before ejecting himself from the car. The slam of the door gave eloquent testimony of his state of mind. She had the gut feeling few people, if any, had ever seen Luca Provere this out of control.

In other circumstances she might have congratulated herself, even rejoiced that she was the reason for his uncharacteristic behavior. But her conscience forbade her to feel anything but shame for the eagerness with which she'd played her part in that tree. Her feverish abandon had probably sent Luke into shock and he was still trying to recover.

When she thought she couldn't stand to be alone with her tortured thoughts any longer, the driver's door opened. Headlights of a passing car illuminated Luke's grimaced features before he climbed inside and shut it again. She held her breath until he spoke.

"We have to talk," his voice rasped, "but not on this road where someone will stop because they have the mistaken notion my car has broken down."

The powerful engine roared to life. She heard the tires squeal as he drove onto the pavement.

A nervous shiver invaded her body. "The alley behind the *pensione* is private. W-we could talk there," she stammered uncertainly.

The silence following her suggestion made Gaby realize she'd said the wrong thing. He probably thought she was hinting to be alone with him so they could continue what had gone on in the cherry tree.

"The traffic is heavier than usual tonight." He ignored her suggestion. "We won't reach Urbino in time to do anything but drive to the hospital. As it is, we'll probably have to waken Giovanni so you can say your goodbyes."

The bleakness of his tone caused her eyes to close tightly. She'd forgotten all about Giovanni.

"I can't go there looking like this!" She panicked.

"He'll know that we—that I—" Her voice caught. She couldn't finish what she was trying to say.

Luke raked an unsteady hand through his dark hair. "He'll know I couldn't keep my hands off you," he growled. "*Per Dio!*" came another soul-wrenching sound. "My little brother will see that I couldn't be trusted to do him the only favor he has ever asked of me." His voice shook with self-loathing.

She caught at the straps of her purse. "You're not to blame," she asserted forcefully. "I'm the one who is ashamed. I—I knew you were on the verge of taking holy vows, but it didn't stop me from—" All the air seemed to leave her lungs and she struggled for breath.

"The point is," she went on raggedly, "I'm as wretched as my great-grandmother. Her selfish desires for a man caused her to run away with him. She never stopped to consider the trail of broken hearts she left behind.

"The only difference here is—" Gaby paused to swallow. "We've done nothing so serious tha—"

"*Basta!*" He silenced her. "If we had made it as far as the inside of the farmhouse, we would still be in there and probably not venture outside again until someone disturbed us."

He was speaking the truth, which was why she couldn't say anything. The images his words conjured up sent delicious chills through her trembling body.

His black eyes bored into her. "Even in your naïveté, you realize that I almost made love to you."

"Yes." He dragged the word out of her.

"*Mio Dio*," he raged. "Do you think it makes me proud to admit that you reduced me to the level of an adolescent schoolboy hungry for his first experience with a woman? One look at those gorgeous legs disappearing up the trunk of that tree and every thought but one went out of my head."

She stared at her hands. "Please don't crucify yourself, Luke. I—I'm to blame for everything that has happened."

A strange sound escaped his throat. "What exactly does that mean?"

Girding up her courage, she said, "Giovanni told me you haven't been home for a whole year, that you've been closeted with other men of the priesthood. My father has always taught me that a woman has the power to tempt a man."

Bending her head, she murmured, "I should never have climbed that tree. I completely forgot I was wearing a skirt. It wasn't fair to you."

A bitterly angry laugh broke from him. "Your willingness to take my sin upon your head is nothing short of amazing. After your self-sacrificing speech, I hate to disillusion you, but the truth is, I've been lusting after you since the moment Giovanni introduced us."

CHAPTER SEVEN

LUKE'S bald admission was so unexpected, Gaby had no conception of where to go from here. Her instincts about him hadn't been wrong. Their desire for each other had been a mutual thing. But now reality had asserted itself.

She should be thanking God that they hadn't gone inside the farmhouse. To have known the joy of his possession and then watch him go back to Rome would have destroyed her completely. As it was, returning to Nevada meant facing a horrendous adjustment she didn't have the strength to contemplate.

Mired in his own black thoughts, the man at her side remained unbearably silent for the rest of the drive back to Urbino.

"W-what will we say to Giovanni?" she finally ventured when he pulled into the casualty parking lot an hour later.

He brought the car to a stop and turned off the motor. "We'll tell him you preferred doing genealogy to going to the ball."

"But—"

"It's eleven-fifteen," he cut in on her tersely. "There's no time for discussion. By now Giovanni will have been put in a private room. We'll get that information first. Come."

He didn't make a pretense of helping her from the car, but now she knew the reason why. He didn't trust himself alone with her. Under other circumstances she would have been elated at his astonishing confession.

But he was no ordinary man. He had a calling, a destiny. Since he'd been so honest with her, she had no business diverting him from his chosen path, no matter how unintentional her behavior.

As she followed him inside the emergency room, she made a promise to herself. Until they said goodbye, she'd do everything in her power to help them both forget what had transpired at Loretello.

She stood at the end of the main desk while he made inquiries, noting that only one cubicle was in use. Everything was much quieter tonight.

Try as she might not to look, her eyes seemed to have a will of their own and she found herself staring through veiled lashes at the man who'd kissed her into oblivion earlier in the day. He was in deep discussion with one of the nurses and appeared perplexed. Suddenly his jet black gaze found Gaby and he started toward her.

"Giovanni is no longer in the hospital." He ran a finger around the back of his collar in obvious puzzlement. "It seems he insisted on recovering at home, so his doctor released him. My mother sent a car."

"That's wonderful!" Gaby cried. The news that he was so much better brought her tremendous relief, particularly since she had no idea how she would have stood up to Giovanni's scrutiny. Very little passed by him unnoticed.

"Now you can leave for Rome in the morning with no worries," she said in a deceptively bright voice, determined to carry out her charade. "I hate to ask this last favor, but would you mind running me to the *pensione* on your way home?"

Luke's dark head reeled back as if she'd just struck him. His features looked chiseled. "You haven't said goodbye to him yet," came the solemn pronouncement.

She started to feel uneasy. "I—I realize that—but visiting him at the castle at this late hour is out of the question." She looked away from him. "Your mother would never approve, not when Giovanni and I aren't engaged to be married."

The truth of her words must have reached him because there was no swift retort. The tension was back, much worse than before. He was standing too close.

The male scent of his warm skin, the trace of fragrance from the soap he'd used that morning, combined to remind her of things she shouldn't be thinking about, like the taste and feel of his mouth, the way it had devoured hers, the incredible things it had done to her before he'd pushed her away.

A burning crept into her face and she gulped. "I—I have to be in front of the university at five forty-five in the morning to board my bus. I'll call him en route and say a final goodbye over the phone."

Unable to take any more of this, Gaby fled the emergency room and hurried out to the car ahead of him. Once ensconced in the Maserati, she rummaged in her purse for her camera while Luke took his place behind the wheel and started up the engine.

In the short time it took them to reach the outskirts of town, she wound the film and removed it from the camera, anything to keep her hands and thoughts occupied.

"Y-you can just let me off in front," she said jerkily when he turned onto the narrow street of the place she'd called home for the last six weeks.

The knuckles of his hand looked a pinched white as he wove between the parked cars to the entrance. For a moment she feared he would ignore her suggestion and drive around to the back alley.

The feelings running rampant inside her were too explosive for her to ever be alone with him again. Before he applied his brakes, she had the door open. A smothered epithet from his side of the car didn't discourage her from jumping out on the bricked street the second he slowed down.

Gaby heard her name called but she didn't pause. Instead, she shut the door behind her, then ran around the back of his car to the entrance of the *pensione*.

Ten fragile feet separated them. She refused to meet his scorching gaze.

"Thank you for all you did for me today." She fought for breath. "My family and I will forever be in your debt. Give my love to Giovanni. Tell him I'll be in touch with him soon." She clung to the handle of the door. "God bless you, Luke." Her voice cracked before she disappeared through the doors.

The minute she reached her room, she collapsed on

the bed in abject despair. Alone at last, she didn't have to hold back the tears. It was like a dam had burst.

Up to now, Gaby had led a very happy life. Like everyone else, she'd experienced moments of sadness and had shed tears. But she'd never known this kind of pain before. The mattress shook with her heart-wrenching sobs. Afraid the girls on either side of her room might hear, she attempted to stifle the sounds with her pillow.

The night seemed endless. Around four in the morning, she got up from the bed so puffy-eyed, no more tears could creep out her lids.

Quietly, she tiptoed down the hall to the bathroom for a shower. One look in the mirror while she was brushing her teeth and she recoiled from the ghostly looking apparition staring back at her. Anyone seeing her right now would think she was a witch.

After shampooing her hair, she stood under the tepid water, praying the rinse would wash away her memories of Luke along with the suds. But nothing could do that. Not even if she lived to be a hundred.

While her hair was still damp, she formed it into one long braid, then put on a clean pair of comfortable, well-worn Levi's and cotton blouse for the bus trip to Belgium. Twelve hours from now she'd be hundreds of miles from here. From Luke...

More tears started, burning her eyes. She refused to give in to them and marched out of the bathroom to her room. Within twenty minutes everything was packed in her two pieces of luggage.

The used linen she put in a laundry bag by the door for the maids. One short trip to Celeste's room where she slid a note with her address under the door, and she was ready to go.

Returning to her room, she looked around a last time, making sure she hadn't left anything behind.

Who would have dreamed that two days before her fabulous trip to Italy came to an end, all her joy would turn to debilitating pain?

It was so early, she assumed most of the girls were still asleep when she crept past the empty dining hall to the front door of the *pensione*. The thought of having to talk to anyone was anathema to her. So was food.

Normally she walked to the university every day. But with two heavy suitcases in hand, she'd never make it. This morning she planned to wait for the local bus which stopped at the end of her street and drove past the university as part of its scheduled run.

All the Americans attending Urbino university from around the U.S. would be boarding their tour bus within the hour. Arriving early at the meeting place in the piazza would ensure her a window seat up front, away from the gregarious party types.

If possible, she would try to save a couple of seats for her friends, Joan and Lorraine, who would be getting on in Florence. Their company would make the rest of her trip bearable.

After giving one last fond look around the interior of her bed and breakfast situation, she repressed the sob in her throat, stepped outside and quietly shut the door behind her.

"I'll help you with those." A low, familiar masculine voice broke the stillness, causing her to gasp.

Gaby whirled around, gaping at Luke incredulously as he reached for her cases and stowed them in the Maserati. In a slate blue silk shirt and dark trousers, he looked particularly stunning, robbing her of the little breath she had left.

"What are you doing here?" Her cry of alarm came out like an accusation, but she couldn't help it. Throughout the long night she'd fought an endless battle with pain. Now he was back, tearing her to shreds all over again.

His encompassing black glance swept over her, reducing her limbs to liquid. "Giovanni has disappeared," came the tight-lipped response.

"*Disappeared*?" She could never have anticipated such a turn of events.

In a state of absolute shock, she didn't remonstrate when Luke assisted her into the passenger seat. He shut the door and came around to start up the car. This close to him she noticed new worry lines etched on his striking features. He didn't look as if he'd had any sleep, either.

"Luke—" She called his name, suddenly remembering. "My bus! It's—"

"*Basta, Gabriella!*" he interrupted as if he couldn't take much more, then muttered something definitely unpleasant in Italian. She couldn't possibly translate the string of expletives, but it showed the depth of his turmoil.

"Right now we must deal with an emergency. Naturally I will make other arrangements for you to fly to Nevada. When we arrive at the palazzo, I will inform the tour company of your change in plans."

She moaned. Another delay. Another heartache. "W-when did you discover him missing?" By now they'd reached the end of the narrow street and had entered the mainstream of traffic.

"Luciana had instructions to keep an eye on him during the night. Sometime between three and four this morning, he left his room and hasn't been seen since. My mother is beside herself. She asked that I bring you to the palazzo."

His comments put new fear in her heart. "You mean you have no idea where he is?"

"None at all," came the grim rejoinder. "She was hoping that you might know something the rest of us do not." His clipped words underlined the stress he was dealing with.

She bowed her head. "I don't know any more than you do."

"You swear you're telling the truth?" he demanded like someone who'd reached the limit of his tolerance.

Hurt by his question, she turned on him. "Do you honestly think I would lie to you after—after—" She couldn't finish the rest and felt the shudder that passed through his body.

"No, I didn't think that." The words sounded

dragged out of him. "*Per Dio*, this is a complication I would never have imagined."

To her consternation, another car almost crashed into them. Only Luke's competence at the wheel prevented them from having an accident.

"When you returned to the palazzo last night, d-did you tell him we went to Loretello?" she ventured in a tremulous voice.

"I would have," he grated, "but when I entered his room, he was asleep. I preferred not to disturb him."

Another wave of guilt engulfed her. "Do you think he found out we didn't go to the ball, and he was upset about it?"

"I've been asking myself that same question, but it hardly matters now. He's nowhere to be found." His voice echoed her own growing panic over his disappearance.

"Does your mother know we were together most of yesterday and last night?"

"Yes," was all he condescended to say until they reached the covered archway at the rear of the ducal estate. A male servant appeared on the steps. Upon Luke's instructions, the older man retrieved her bags from the car and took them inside.

Gaby had never thought to see the palazzo again, let alone the inside of the red and white room. Yet that was where Luke's mother was waiting for them, her face a picture of anguish.

The second they stepped foot inside the paneled

doors, she got to her feet and rushed over to Gaby, reaching for her hands.

"Ah, Signorina Holt. Thank you for coming," she emoted softly, pulling Gaby down on the tapestry-covered love seat with her.

The older woman's reception was so different from the night of the dinner, Gaby could scarcely credit this was the same person.

Luke stood a few feet away from them, his hand rubbing the back of his bronzed neck in contemplation. Gaby couldn't forget what he'd told her, that his mother worshipped Giovanni. Evidently now that he was missing, even Gaby was welcome if she could help solve the mystery of his whereabouts.

"Tell me what has happened to *mio figlio, signorina*. He is still recovering from that horrible accident."

Gaby flashed Luke a signal of distress. His dark gaze swiveled from her to his mother. "I'm afraid Signorina Holt is as perplexed as we are, Mama."

"No—" She shook her head. "I do not believe that. My son intends to marry her, Luca. At the hospital, he refused to see me or talk to me. He has never behaved that way in his life. Only another woman could have that kind of power over him. That woman is *you, signorina*."

"Signora Provere," Gaby began, feeling as if she were drowning, and going under for the third time. "I'm afraid your son has led you to believe something that isn't true. The fact is, Giovanni never asked me to marry him because he knows I'm not in love with him." Her voice shook.

"What are you saying?" His mother's dark brown eyes flashed. "I do not understand. He loves you."

Gaby swallowed hard. "Nevertheless, Giovanni and I are not planning a wedding. We're simply good friends. He invited me here to—to—"

"Mama," Luke intervened. To Gaby's heartfelt relief, he broke into a spate of Italian, explaining the true circumstances of that night. His mother listened with downbent head, her expression changing from grief to shock.

"Is my son correct, *signorina*? You and my Giovanni do not have an understanding?"

"No, *signora*. As I have told you, we are close, more like brother and sister. I haven't seen or heard from him since the night of the accident. If I had any idea where he was, any idea at all, I would tell you."

Because it was the truth, her earnestness must have reached Giovanni's mother. The older woman slowly released Gaby's hands and stared into space through dimmed eyes, looking twenty years older.

Gaby could have wept for the pain Giovanni had caused his family. Why had he done this to them? He'd shrouded his actions in mystery, making it impossible for any of them to function normally.

As if she were in a trance, Signora Provere got up from the couch and looked straight at Gaby. "You've spent the last six weeks with him. Where do you *think* he might be, *signorina*?" she asked in a dull voice.

It was a searching question, requiring a response.

Luke's eyes were riveted to her, as well. He, too, was waiting for some kind of clue which would lead them to Giovanni.

Gaby clasped her hands, praying for inspiration. "If he has close friends, I never met any of them, nor did he ever mention their names to me. We spent hours going to museums and galleries, exploring the town. He knows everything about Renaissance art and history."

"That is all?" his mother rasped. "He didn't talk to you about what was going on inside of him?"

"Yes. He told me many things." Gaby stopped pacing. "As you both know, Giovanni's a very spiritual person. He's the kind of man who lives in the world, but isn't of the world, if I'm making sense."

Luke nodded gravely and put a supporting arm around his mother's fragile shoulders. "Go on," he urged, giving Gaby his consent to speak frankly.

"Well, for example, take the other evening when he drove me home from the palace. We had plans to go to the Renaissance ball the next night, so he brought me a jeweled hair piece to wear, and—"

"What hair piece are you talking about?" his mother interrupted, obviously at a loss to explain her son's abnormal behavior.

"Pollaiulo's elaborate pearl headdress masterpiece from our ancestor's private treasury," Luke supplied grimly.

Signora Provere's astonished cry rang throughout the room. She flung her hands in the air. "But that hair piece is priceless and now belongs to the church. It's valued at close to a million dollars.''

It was Gaby's turn to be stunned. ''I knew it was valuable, but I never dreamed—'' Her voice trailed. Now she understood the look Luke had sent Giovanni's way after opening the bag at the hospital.

''My son asked you to wear it?'' His mother's voice came out more like a squeak.

''Yes.'' Gaby hated to admit it, noting the other woman's complete shock. ''You see, Giovanni and I met in the museum while I was looking at it, trying to figure out how Pollaiuolo fashioned it to harmonize with the movement of braids. It was the most beautiful piece of Renaissance jewelry I have ever seen.''

When no one spoke, Gaby cleared her throat nervously. ''I often wear braids, but couldn't imagine how to arrange it. He got very excited and showed me a fourteenth-century painting of Simonetta Vespucci wearing the exact piece. That way I could see precisely how it should be worn.''

''If he did all that for you, then it appears my son was enamored by you from the moment you two met,'' Signora Provere murmured sadly, but there was no censure in her tone, for which Gaby was grateful.

This gave her the confidence to go on. ''H-he was very charming and so easy to talk to. He obviously remembered our conversation that first day in the museum, and insisted I wear the jewelry to the ball.

''But because I knew it was a family treasure, I told him I wouldn't be responsible for keeping it overnight. In fact, I remember telling him that I'd die if anything happened to it while it was in my possession.

"That's when he told me that no earthly treasure was worth dying for. But a sacred love, that was something else again..."

Signora Provere appeared dumbstruck while Luke's brooding gaze wandered over her, his thoughts inscrutable. "Did my brother often confide his innermost secrets to you?" he prodded with surprising tenacity.

"Some of them. I learned right away that his favorite place on earth is inside a church. When we first met, he made me promise to visit Assisi before I left Italy. He told me of a spiritual experience he had while visiting there as a teenager, but asked me not to tell anyone."

"*Mio Dio*—" The ragged oath coming out of Luke sounded agonized.

"I—I'm breaking his confidence by even mentioning it to you, but I'm too concerned about his disappearance to worry about that right now."

"I've never heard of any of this," his mother blurted in bewilderment. "Luca?" She turned to her son, laying her head against his chest. "What is she talking about? Has Giovanni told you of this experience?"

But Luke seemed miles away. His gaze held a strange glitter, exaggerating his pallor. That in turn frightened Gaby.

"Mama—" He unexpectedly put his mother aside. "Please take charge of our guest and offer her every comfort." His black eyes pierced Gaby. "Signorina Holt. You will stay here until my return." The edict fell from his taut lips.

"Luca—where are you going?" his mother asked the question in Gaby's mind, but his exit was so swift, he either didn't hear her, or he was in such a hurry, he chose not to answer. It was like a second death to see him go.

"Something very strange is going on with both my sons. *Santa Maria*! I don't know what to think. Please, my dear. Sit down. I'll ask Luciana to bring us coffee and we will talk. I need to ask your forgiveness for the way I treated you at dinner. As Luca pointed out, I was extremely rude to you and must make amends."

"Please, Signora Provere. There is nothing to forgive. Giovanni led you to believe something that wasn't true and it came as too great a shock."

"That's very charitable of you, *signorina*. I can understand why Giovanni adores you."

Gaby couldn't take much more of this and was growing more and more impatient to be gone.

"Much as I'd love to stay, *signora*, I don't have the time." Girding up her courage, she said, "I—I heard the clock chime on the half hour. My bus is leaving Urbino in a few minutes. If you could ask someone to bring my bags to the foyer and drive me to the university, I can just make it."

Her eyes were dark pinpoints of light. "You heard Luca. He expects you to be here when he gets back."

Gaby's instincts about Luke had been correct.

Though he might be forfeiting the title of duke because of his religious affiliation, he was the true heir and natural ruler of the House of Provere. Even his mother deferred to him, but this was one time when Gaby would have to go against his wishes.

"There is no reason for me to stay any longer, *signora.* I've told you everything I know, and I promise to keep in touch by phone. Naturally I'll want to know what has happened to Giovanni, but we've already said our goodbyes.

"A-as for Luke, he has his priesthood duties back in Rome." Maybe if Gaby said the words long enough, she'd start to believe them. "This is not the time for you to be entertaining a houseguest."

"So you know about my eldest son?" she asked too sharply. No doubt Luke's mother had been worried about them spending most of yesterday together.

If she ever found out—

"Y-yes. Giovanni has told me he will be professed in less than a month." Her voice caught.

"That is right." The older woman sounded relieved that Gaby understood the true situation. "He would have taken his final vows much sooner, but my husband's passing made that impossible." There was an uneasy pause. "Luca tells me he spent yesterday helping you trace your family roots."

Heat swamped Gaby's face. "Yes." They were trespassing on shaky ground now. Gaby didn't want to talk or think about Luke anymore. "H-he was able to clear up a mystery about my great-grandmother's true birthplace."

"Yes. He told me," the other woman murmured, eyeing Gaby with a familiar scrutiny that made her uncomfortable.

"I am very grateful to him, *signora*. You must be so proud to have two such remarkable sons." She purposely diverted the direction of the conversation away from Luke.

"I've been very blessed, but as you will understand, I'm devastated to think Giovanni would run away without explanation." Her brown eyes watered. "He's always been the perfect child, so open and obedient."

Gaby knew that wasn't completely true, but she kept silent.

"He and Luca are totally opposites, you know. Luca understands the world and runs his life by his own set of rules. If he went off without a word to me, I'd never question it. He can handle anything because of his brilliance. In time, he will surpass our noble ancestor in greatness and piety."

Gaby had heard of women who were ambitious for their children. But to dream such dreams for Luke seemed almost sacriligious, particularly after what she and Luke had shared in Loretello. The memories still had the power to shake the foundations out from under her.

"Surely the important thing for both your sons is that they be happy." Gaby voiced the opinion beneath her breath.

The older woman nodded. "That is why I am so

worried. Something is wrong with my Giovanni who has led a very contented, sheltered life up to now.''

"Sheltered or not, he's a remarkably strong individual who prefers to see the goodness of the world,'' Gaby observed forcefully. "I'm sure there's a rational explanation for what he's done.''

"I pray you're right. Poor Efresina loves him so.''

Gaby got to her feet, having forgotten all about the other woman Giovanni would never love.

"It's been a privilege to become acquainted with your family. I'm only sorry I can't stay in Urbino longer. The problem is, I've been given a roommate for the tour back to Belgium. If I don't show up, my friend, Joan, will have to be by herself and she doesn't like being alone at night. It would be very unfair to her.''

Everything she'd said was true except for the part about her friend hating to be by herself. But Gaby was desperate to get away from Luke. It was hard enough being in his home. But to hear his mother go on about Luke's destiny was only deepening an open wound. She had to get out of there as fast as she could.

"*Signora*—'' she implored the older woman who acted as if she still needed convincing to go against Luke's express wishes. "I have no doubts that Luke will eventually find Giovanni. Until then, I can do nothing to ameliorate the situation. I must go.''

"Very well,'' his mother finally conceded. "I will explain to Luke that you are a strong-minded

American woman who did not wish to be detained any longer.''

Gaby had the idea that deep down, Signora Provere couldn't get rid of her fast enough.

"Thank you. I've been away from my family for a long time and need to get home.''

The older woman rang a bell and almost immediately the servant Gaby had seen earlier appeared. "Please bring a car around for Signorina Holt who must be driven to the university at once. She will need her luggage, as well.''

"*Prego, signora.*''

"*Grazie*, Signora Provere.'' Gaby would have shaken her hand, but Luke's mother surprised her by kissing her on both cheeks instead. Her delight at Gaby's departure was obvious.

"Perhaps it's best that you are returning to the United States. Though you have broken Giovanni's heart, it will mend faster if you are not here. In time I have hopes he will marry Efresina. She's like a daughter to me you know. *Arrivederci, signorina.*''

CHAPTER EIGHT

"WE'RE coming to the border. Pretty soon we're going to go through the St. Gotthard tunnel."

"It's ten miles long, right through the mountains."

Gaby could hear excited conversation all around her and envied the noisy tour group their enthusiasm. Since morning, after barely making it to the university before the bus pulled out of Urbino, she'd tried to put up a brave front around the American friends she hadn't seen for six weeks.

But their arrival in Lake Lugano made her realize they'd be leaving Italy shortly. The pain was as real as if someone had driven a hard fist into her stomach.

"Gaby? What's wrong? You're as white as a sheet."

She avoided Joan's probing stare. "I—I think I ate something that didn't agree with me."

Joan sighed. "It's the atrocious heat. This bus is supposed to be air-conditioned, but I'm still hot."

Gaby hadn't really noticed the temperature. Her heartache was too acute to give thought to her creature comforts. Luke was slipping further and further away from her and there wasn't a thing she could do about it.

"Gina says it's cooler in Switzerland," Joan chat-

132

ted on. "Tonight we're going to an outdoor yodeling show."

A groan escaped Gaby's throat. After what she'd experienced with Luke, she wondered if she would ever find pleasure in anything again. It was terrifying to think one man could affect your life so completely, that without him there was no joy, no hope.

So far, Gaby hadn't been able to summon the courage to phone Signora Provere. Day after tomorrow, when they reached Brussels, she'd make the call.

Right now she was too afraid to find out what had happened to Giovanni. If he were still missing, then Luke probably hadn't gone back to Rome yet. To phone the palace and hear his voice would destroy her before she'd even begun to deal with her loss.

"Hey, Gina?" someone shouted in the back, drawing Gaby's attention. "How come we're stopping?"

"There's a whole bunch of policemen!" another person cried.

Their vivacious blond Italian tour guide stood up, lighting a cigarette. "I don't know." She exhaled with an Italian flare no foreigner could imitate—another reminder of everything Gaby was about to lose. "Probably they are searching for drugs. It happens. Do not get excited. I will go and find out."

As soon as she got off the bus, speculation intensified. Everyone had a theory about the presence of police who were backing up traffic for miles. Gaby had to admit she was surprised their bus had been stopped. Until now they'd traveled all through Europe without a hitch.

''This is kind of exciting.'' Joan strained to see what she could because Gaby had the window seat. Together they watched the rapid-fire exchange between Gina and one of the policemen. Her hands were flying.

''Whoa... Gina's upset about something.''

Gaby agreed with Joan. Their tour guide, who knew seven languages and could curse along with the best of them, was generally unflappable. But given the tight schedule, a delay would cost them time getting into Lucerne for the evening.

After another five minutes, Gina wheeled around and marched toward the bus, her features set. But instead of getting back on, she shouted something in Italian, and their driver, Mikaele, got off to talk to the police.

''Maybe *he's* in trouble,'' the girl in front of them theorized.

By now everyone was looking out the right side. To Gaby's astonishment, the police told him to open the panels where the luggage was kept. Mikaele didn't like the delay any more than Gina. He argued volubly, but had no choice except to unload everything.

A group of policemen surrounded him, blocking Gaby's view. Obviously they were checking each tag, searching for something. With thirty-eight students on board, each with two bags, the task was horrendous. Gaby didn't blame him for being upset. In fact, everyone was complaining. With the motor shut off, there was no air circulating at all.

It seemed like an eternity before Gina climbed on board. The din of noise faded as she started down the aisle followed by two policemen. "Gina's coming this way. She's looking at *you*," Joan whispered in a shaky voice. For no good reason, Gaby felt the hairs stand on the back of her neck.

A cigarette dangled from Gina's full Italian lips as she stopped at their seat. "Gaby, there is no easy way to say this, but you will have to get off the bus and accompany the police to their bureau."

"*What*?"

Gina shrugged her shoulders coolly. "I must admit I am shocked by what the police have discovered in your luggage. Whatever the outcome, you will require help from the American Consulate in Rome. Here is their number. I have written it on my card."

She handed it to Gaby who took it with trembling hands. "I don't understand," she cried.

Gina rolled her eyes. "You look as innocent as the Virgin herself. I, for one, would never have picked you to get into this kind of trouble. For now, I suggest you save any questions or explanations until you retain an advocate."

Panic welled inside her. "But I have to go home!"

"When you have straightened things out, call the main office in London. I will tell them what has happened, and you can proceed from there. The police want your passport."

Gaby couldn't believe this was happening. "It's tucked inside my money belt underneath my clothes," she whispered.

A trace of a smile curved Gina's lips before she turned to the policemen and translated. Both men stared at Gaby with icy contempt. She saw it in their eyes. On top of her crime she was an idiot American, which made her sin a thousand times worse.

"They say you can turn it over to them when they take you to the precinct. It's my opinion that what they found in your luggage was planted by a professional." Gina spoke out of the corner of her mouth, giving her encouragement. "Unfortunately, the burden of proof will rest on you."

Of necessity, Joan had to move so Gaby could get past her. Humiliated and red-faced, Gaby moved out into the aisle.

"If they let you, call me at the hotel in Lucerne tonight and tell me what happened," Joan murmured beneath her breath. "Otherwise, write me."

Gaby pressed her friend's hand before walking down the aisle with the police trailing her footsteps.

"Good luck, Gaby," both Gina and Mikaele called to her as she got off the bus.

An hour later, Gaby found herself at police headquarters in Lugano. She surrendered her passport and was booked and finger-printed. No one would tell her details about her arrest. She could make no phone calls. They informed her that the consulate in Rome would not be available until the next morning.

That's when she broke down and begged them to call the palace in Urbino, convinced that one word in her defense from the House of Provere would do more to exonerate her than all the red tape the American Consulate could accomplish.

But the police ignored her entreaty. To her horror, Gaby realized she would have to spend the night on a cot in a jail cell like a common criminal.

Only the knowledge that she knew she was innocent of any wrongdoing kept her from losing her sanity. That and the fact that as soon as she could do anything at all about her situation, she'd phone Signora Provere. Surely Luke was back home by now. With his power and influence, she'd be freed in an instant.

How ironic that this morning she couldn't get away from him fast enough. He'd ordered her to stay with his mother until his return. If she'd done his bidding, she wouldn't be locked up with no hope of being freed before morning.

A shudder racked her body. All the ifs in the world wouldn't change what had happened. She had run away from him, and tonight she was paying the price.

Dear God—what she'd give to see him standing outside the bars of her cell!

Defeated for the moment by her situation, she lay facedown on the cot in the dark, burying her face in the crook of her arm. Unfortunately other thoughts, all negative, began to creep into her psyche, paralyzing her with new fear.

It was possible Luke might not be available right away. If he were still looking for Giovanni, it could be several days before he even knew about her situation, let alone had the time to do something about it.

The more she considered what Signora Provere's reaction might be, the more she worried that Luke's mother wouldn't be willing to help her. She wanted Gaby out of Giovanni's life and wasn't the least bit happy that Luke had spent any time with her.

To make matters worse, Gaby was from Las Vegas, a place for the riffraff of American society in the older woman's mind. No doubt she would consider it more than a possibility that Gaby had stolen something not belonging to her. She would endorse any punishment the Italian authorities chose to mete out to her.

Exhausted from her ordeal, overwhelmed by all the emotions buffeting her body, she closed her eyes and gave in to the temptation to think forbidden thoughts about Luke.

"*Signorina*? Holt?"

Gaby thought she heard her name called and lifted her head, groggy because she must have fallen asleep for a while. A faint light at the end of the hall outlined two masculine silhouettes.

"Yes?" she answered tentatively and sat up, aware there were marks on her cheek where she'd been lying on her braid. One of the policemen unlocked her cell to allow the other man inside, then locked it again and walked away.

Gaby scrambled to her feet, suddenly frightened. "W-who are you?"

"Shh, Gaby. Talk softly so no one can hear you but me."

She blinked in the darkness. The voice sounded so familiar, but it couldn't be, could it? "*Giovanni?*" she whispered in shock.

"Yes. Sit down, Gaby, before you faint."

She half fell against the cot. "What are you doing here when you're supposed to be recovering from your accident? What's going on? Why have I been arrested? Please tell me. Why did you disappear? Your family is frantic."

"Be patient and I will answer all your questions. But we don't have much time. I must be gone from here before Luca comes."

Luke was coming? Her heart began to pound outrageously. "All right. I'm listening."

She couldn't imagine what Giovanni was about and wondered if she was in the middle of a strange dream.

"First, I have to ask you a question and you must answer it with total honesty because God is listening."

This was Giovanni talking to her, but he was being so mysterious. More than that, he sounded different, older, so solemn...

"W-what is the question?"

"You were with my brother all day yesterday, isn't that true?"

Gaby moaned in turmoil. This was the hardest thing she'd ever had to admit to in her life because she would never have hurt Giovanni intentionally. "Yes," she said with tears in her voice.

"Tell me everything that happened from the moment you saw him until you parted company last night.''

Obviously this was of vital concern to Giovanni or he wouldn't be vetting her like this in a jail cell. Perhaps Luke was in some kind of trouble with church authorities because of her. Gaby was beside herself with anxiety.

''He caught up with me in Assisi,'' she began breathlessly. ''He said that he'd p-promised you to escort me to the ball, and intended to take me back to Urbino so Luciana could do my hair.''

''That's very interesting, considering the fact that my brother informed me he could not carry out my wishes and had to be back in Rome without fail,'' Giovanni murmured as if to himself. ''Go on.''

By now Gaby was shaking, consumed by guilt. Giovanni was a very intuitive person. *He knew the truth about her and Luke*. But for some reason she didn't understand, he wouldn't let it go until he'd wrung every detail from her. This was a nightmare in a new dimension.

''I took the early bus out of town because I wanted to visit Assisi before I left Italy. H-he found me up on the ramparts of the castle and insisted that I return to the palace with him.''

''Which means he followed you there,'' Giovanni muttered.

Gaby hid her face in her hands. ''Yes.''

''Did you spend the whole day in Assisi?''

A little sob escaped her throat. ''No— We— We

drove to an inn for lunch.'' Every revelation damned them a little more in Giovanni's eyes.

"Tell me about it,'' he persisted in a calm voice.

"Why do you want to hear all this, Giovanni?'' she cried, knowing this had to be bringing him excruciating pain.

"Just humor me, please. Is that such a difficult thing to do for a brother? You told my mother that you loved me like one.''

"I do!'' She moaned the words once more. Hot tears trickled down her cheeks. *He'd already been in touch with Signora Provere.*

In the next breath Gaby told him everything she could remember about their meal. "Afterward, we drove to Loretello, but he stopped at Arcevia first.''

"Ah—to find your great-grandmother's farm.''

"Yes.''

There was a slight pause. "And did you find it, Gaby?''

She nodded, but no sound would come out.

"Something happened while you were there.''

"Yes.'' She moistened her lips anxiously. "Through the parish records, L-Luke found out that my relative was probably born somewhere in or near Rome. She was brought to Loretello to be raised by the Ridolfi family and remained there until she ran off with her future husband.''

"That is all very fascinating. But I'm talking about you and my brother.'' The ghastly silence almost destroyed her. "Did he kiss you?''

A groan came out of Gaby. She couldn't stop the convulsions of her body.

"All you have to do is tell me yes or no."

She sucked in her breath. "Yes." The blood was pounding in her ears.

"The way a man kisses a woman when he desires her?"

Gaby jumped off the cot, holding her arms to her chest. "Yes."

"Gaby—" he whispered in a shaken voice. "Did you kiss him back the same way? It's the last question I'll ask of you."

She wanted to die. "Yes."

He crossed himself.

"Oh, Giovanni." She broke down weeping. "Please forgive me. Forgive us. It just happened. Luke is as tormented as I am. I swear we never meant to hurt you."

"You haven't hurt me," he murmured in a strange tone of voice. "Thank you for telling me the truth. You've heard the wise-old adage that the truth shall make you free."

"Yes, but I also know that deep down it has shocked you and caused you pain, whatever you say to the contrary. What are you going to do now?" she cried in real concern for his welfare.

Instead of answering her, he leaned forward and kissed her forehead. "It won't be long before Luca effects your release. As a last favor to me, please don't tell him I was here and forced a confession from you. It would hurt him too much. He has always tried to protect me. Leave him that illusion, I beg of you, dearest Gaby.''

His earnestness confounded her. ''I promise,'' she vowed in a choked voice, wiping her eyes. ''But what if the guards tell him you were here?''

''They won't,'' was all he would say on the subject.

''Does he know you're all right?''

''I'm sure mother has told him. I know I can count on you to keep your word. Enjoy your trip home, Gaby.''

''Wait—'' she called as he turned and tapped on the bars of the cell. ''I want to know where you're going, what you're going to do. Don't shut me out!''

''There's no time,'' came the cryptic reply before the guard reappeared to open the gate. She clung to the bars long after Giovanni had gone, pressing her head against the metal in despair.

His niceness was terrifying because she knew it hid scalding pain. She would have done anything to prevent him from learning the truth. Now that he'd heard the words from her own lips, she would never be able to forgive herself.

But she'd made a promise not to tell Luke about his brother's visit. It was a promise she intended to keep for Giovanni's sake. There could be no point in wounding Luke who would always carry the pain of their betrayal of Giovanni in his heart.

At least he could return to Rome believing that his brother knew nothing about their romantic interlude.

All three of them would go on to pursue their separate lives. It was the way it had to be.

She went over everything in her mind, trying to put the pieces together. Whatever the reason for her arrest, the Provere family had known about it in time for Giovanni to come all the way to Lugano.

But he was leaving it to Luke to help her out of the mess she'd unwittingly gotten herself into. Now that he assumed they were lovers, Giovanni was too much of a gentleman to ever interfere.

Just the thought of Luke coming to the jail sent her heart tripping out of control. She felt like jumping out of her skin, but there was no place to go. After pacing back and forth waiting for the first sight of him, she finally gave up the vigil and flung herself on the cot.

It was probably close to midnight. Something had to be holding him up. Maybe he'd decided to wait until morning to do anything about her situation.

Heaving a forlorn sigh that resounded in the cell, she turned toward the wall, confused and broken. It was when her limbs started to grow heavy that the overhead light went on.

She heard her name cried out, followed by a burst of Italian invective delivered in a deep voice that sounded so fierce it couldn't possibly belong to anyone but Luke.

Gaby rolled over on her back in time to see the intimidated guard who had trouble undoing the lock. Then Luke came striding toward her like an avenging prince, his handsome features darkened by lines of fury.

"Per Dio!" he raged. In his anger he was truly magnificent. She caught a few words like barbaric and criminal, and there was something said about it not being the fourteenth century. Then he got down on his haunches and cupped her face in his hands.

"Are you all right, Gabriella?" His glittering black gaze seemed to devour her. She watched his sensual mouth twist into a white line of anger. "Have they given you anything to eat or drink?" All the while he was emoting, she could feel his thumbs following the delicate mold of her cheeks.

Gaby was so happy to see him, she couldn't talk or think. All she could do was shake her head. Another shocking epithet escaped his lips. It produced a guard who immediately brought her a glass of cold water.

Once Luke helped her to sit up, she needed no urging to drink thirstily. "Oh, that tasted good," she murmured after draining the contents.

A nerve throbbed along his jaw. "Have they allowed you to use the restroom?"

"No."

"Mio Dio!" he thundered once more. "No matter what they think you've done, they had no right to treat you in this despicable manner." His eyes narrowed. "Before I'm through, someone's going to pay heavily for this."

"I—I've heard about foreign jails. Maybe ours at home are just as bad. This is my first experience."

His chest heaved. "When I couldn't find Giovanni, I arrived home to discover many shocks. You'd not only disobeyed my instructions about leaving, but the police had contacted Mother to let them know you were in custody. You were falsely arrested, but I've straightened it out.''

Relieved, Gaby admitted, ''I begged them to call you.''

''Considering the way you've been treated, it's a miracle they followed through to reach me.''

''The police wouldn't tell me anything, but my tour guide, Gina, said something valuable was found in my luggage. She suspected it was planted there.''

Gaby heard his sharp intake of breath. ''Your guide was right.'' He was obviously trying to control himself and didn't realize his own strength. The hand on her shoulder tightened almost painfully, but heaven forgive her, she craved his touch, the warmth of his strong chest where her head rested. She'd stay in this condition forever if it meant being this close to him.

''Gina told me to call the American Consulate in Rome, but the police sergeant said they couldn't be reached until tomorrow.''

Perhaps he wasn't aware that one of his hands slid up and down her braid, bringing every cell in her body alive. ''They lied to you,'' he muttered in contempt. ''There is an emergency number for someone in your circumstances. But no matter now. If you're ready, we'll go to the office and gather up your things.''

Basking in Luke's strength and protection, Gaby had no desire to move. If she could spend the night on this cot with him, it would be all she ever asked of life. But of course that wasn't possible.

Because of the precariousness of her situation, they'd both let down their guard. She had to remember that if it hadn't been for the arrest, they would never have seen each other again. The thought produced a low moan he must have heard because he continued to steady her once she was on her feet.

"If you need food, I'll send one of the guards for something to eat."

"No, no. I'm fine. Honestly. I—it's just that I was asleep when you came in and I'm still trying to wake up."

His jaw hardened. "This airless room isn't healthy. Come." With his hand at the back of her waist, he ushered her out of the cell and down the hall to the main office where the balding police sergeant sat at his desk.

At Luke's approach, he stood up, his manner totally deferential. Luke fired several questions in Italian. A volley of comments followed. Then the other man undid a safe and handed him a large manila envelope which Gaby assumed contained the stolen item.

Luke didn't bother to unseal it. Instead, he escorted her to another room where she saw her two suitcases sitting on the floor. The contents were dumped on top of a rectangular wooden table. Other than three chairs, the room was as bare as the jail cell. The sergeant excused himself and shut the door.

Gaby was upset about the cavalier handling of her things, but she was more curious about the stolen property. Her eyes appealed to Luke. "A-aren't you going to open it?"

His dark gaze searched hers for endless moments. "I don't need to. The sergeant told me the tip-off about the jewelry came from the palace."

Gaby's brows formed a slight frown. "What jewelry?"

"The headdress Giovanni wanted you to wear to the ball."

Her rounded chin shot up. "Something worth almost a million dollars was in *my* luggage?"

"Let's take a look, shall we?"

With one fluid motion, he undid the top and pulled the pearl hair ornament out of the envelope.

A noise escaped her throat. "The last time I saw it, we were at the hospital visiting Giovanni. How on earth could it have gotten in my suitcase?"

A shadow crossed over Luke's face. "As your tour guide said, someone planted it to make it look as if you'd stolen it."

"But Giovanni was the last one to have it."

"No, *I* was," Luke corrected her. "After visiting Giovanni the next morning, I took it home with me and gave it to Luciana for safekeeping."

Silence stretched between them. Gaby was trying to figure it out. "You said Luciana adores Giovanni. Do you think she was angry with me because I stayed away instead of going to the ball as Giovanni wanted?"

"Angry enough to want to get you into this kind of trouble?" Luke questioned darkly. "I don't think so. Luciana has been with the family for years. For her to risk imprisonment makes absolutely no sense.''

Gaby's head lowered. ''It seems that someone in your household hated me enough to get me arrested—someone who knew where to find the jewelry and had access to my luggage this morning.''

Luke's features looked chiseled. ''Efresina doesn't live at the palace.''

''Your m-mother does…'' she said in a quiet voice.

His chest rose and fell harshly. ''No, Gabriella. She was very unkind to you at dinner, but she would never do anything to risk losing the love of her sons.''

''Luke, I'm sorry I said anything about your mother. Actually, she apologized to me this morning.''

''That's good,'' he almost growled. ''She should have done it before you left the palace the night of the dinner.''

Gaby rubbed her palms over her hips in an unconscious gesture of frustration, but Luke watched the movement with such intensity, she trembled.

''W-what about the servant who brought my bags in from the car?''

''Giuseppi?'' Just the way he said the man's name told Gaby that Luke cared deeply for him. In an aside he murmured, ''He's been with us longer than Luciana.''

She folded her arms. ''Then that leaves Giovanni, only he wasn't there.''

''*Wasn't he*?'' Luke rasped with an abruptness that caught her off guard.

She couldn't look at him right then, not when she knew that Giovanni had been in Lugano, that he'd sworn her to secrecy.

"A network of people were out looking for Giovanni all day," Luke muttered blackly, rubbing the back of his neck absently. "But it was as if he'd disappeared off the face of the earth."

At his words, a shiver chased across her skin. "Luke, I just remembered something he once told me." What she had to say wouldn't be disloyal to Giovanni.

"He said that during the Renaissance, secret rooms and passages were built in the palace for the family's protection. Because I thought he was a palace employee, I assumed that was part of the knowledge he had learned to inform the public."

"*Mio Dio!*" Luke cried, comprehension illuminating his puzzled countenance. "Why didn't I think of that sooner? Gabriella—you've just supplied me with the key to a very complicated riddle."

"What are you saying?"

He began pacing. "On the surface, Giovanni has always appeared very sweet and straightforward. But something has changed him out of all recognition. While I've been away, his behavior has undergone a drastic transformation. Like one of our more notorious Provere ancestors, Giovanni has become a cunning master of mind games and intrigue."

She shook her head. "I don't understand."

He sucked in his breath, straightening to his full height. "It began with the phone call to Rome." His voice grated. "With each convoluted step, he has managed to throw our lives into utter chaos."

A hand went to her throat. "You think he put the jewelry in my luggage?"

"I know he did, then he alerted the police. It's all part of a plan."

Deep down, Gaby believed that, too. There could be no other explanation for Giovanni's appearance at the jail, his ability to come and go as he pleased. It had to prove he'd been behind her incarceration. Right now she wished she hadn't made him any promises.

"You're right, Luke." Her voice shook. "He's been playing games from the moment I first met him at the museum."

Luke grimaced. "They're about to end. He's not a little boy anymore. As soon as I get you out of here, we're going back to Urbino. We'll find him in one of those labyrinths beneath the palace and we'll confront him together."

Much as she wanted to go with him, be with him as long as he wanted her, she knew it was impossible. Now was the time to be strong and back away from him, both mentally as well as physically.

"No, Luke. You two brothers need to solve this problem without an audience. I've said my goodbyes to Giovanni. My family is expecting me home." Her voice sounded ragged because she couldn't deal with the pain. "I have to go."

CHAPTER NINE

LUKE'S face looked wiped of expression, but the fact that he didn't argue with her felt like a second death.

He stood next to the table, a tall, rigid, powerful figure in black. She saw his gaze dart to her underwear, then a pair of canvas shoes, a Levi's skirt and three cotton tops like the pink one she was wearing, hose, drip-dry shorty pajamas, one pair of white shorts, and a dilapidated, one-piece faded black bathing suit.

Her toiletries and blow-dryer lay askew amid the absurd, cheap trinkets she'd picked up at various tourist traps since her arrival in Europe in June.

Because she was on a tight budget, she hadn't been able to buy anything expensive, but she refused to go home to her family and friends empty-handed. She had opted to buy a whole bunch of fun, joky gifts.

By the quirk of one raven-winged eyebrow, she could tell that the illustrious Luke Provere was unaccustomed to mingling with a common student and tourist like herself. He was probably appalled at the cluttered scene before him.

To her surprise he started poking around, as if to satisfy his curiosity. Unwillingly drawn by the play of muscles across his shoulders and back, she watched him pick up one item, then another for examination.

He held up a miniature iron maiden torture device

and a trace of a smile broke the corner of his mouth. "For someone with such an angelic face as yours, no one would guess at the Machiavellian mind lurking inside."

She smiled in spite of her pain. "My brother, Ted, plays Dungeons & Dragons. When he finds out what it was used for, he'll love it," she defended.

"No doubt," he muttered. "And this?" From his fingers dangled a leather strap with a Swiss cow bell on the end.

"That's for my brother, Wayne, who works on a ranch."

"It's too small for a cow."

Her smile broadened. "I was thinking of his dog, Grafton."

"Grafton?" His incredulity was more marked because of his accent. In other circumstances, she would have laughed.

Next, he pulled out a collapsible leaning Tower of Pisa. By depressing a button, it fell to one side.

"That's for my father. He's a fiddler."

Luke cast her a hooded glance over his shoulder. "He plays the violin?"

"Not exactly. He's the nervous type. Always touching things, pacing the floor. The tower will keep him busy."

"With a daughter like you, I'm beginning to understand."

Ignoring the blush that tinted her cheeks he pulled out an assortment of manufactured feudal weapons including a mace, a ball and chain, and crossbow purchased in Carcassonne. Another eyebrow quirked.

"My little brother Robbie loves knights and castles," she proclaimed before he could say anything.

Finally he came to an Eiffel Tower which she explained would serve as an outdoor thermometer for Scott's Jeep, and a pair of Egyptian *obélisque* earrings for her mom which she'd bought in Paris.

"Those snake rings from Morocco are for my friends," she commented when he'd come to the end of her treasures, fingering each one carefully.

After reflection, "No presents for yourself?"

"Except the ones I steal?" she joked, but it failed miserably. His hands had formed into fists. Her heartache intensified because Giovanni's spectre loomed too heavily over their lives. "A-actually I shipped my Italian texts and a few picture books home several days ago."

Evidently unable to help himself, Luke reached for one more paper-enveloped package which the police had left half opened.

Gaby had forgotten about that souvenir and moved quickly to intercept him, but it was too late. In a lightning gesture he'd already pulled out the simple inexpensive, eight-inch statuette of Jesus purchased in the Vatican city.

"Out of all the souvenirs you could have chosen to take home for a memory, you purchased *this* for yourself?" He sounded stunned.

"Yes," she defended. "I had to earn all my own money to come to Europe. As you can see, I've lived at the poverty level for some time now. I only had a hundred dollars to buy all my souvenirs."

His face closed up. "Once again you've misunderstood me. I wasn't referring to its monetary value."

Her face grew warm. Suitably chastened she said, "I'm sorry. I-it's just that we come from such vastly different backgrounds, even I can see how this must seem to you." Her voice wobbled.

"But even if it is cheap, the beautiful face on that little figure resembles my idea of what Jesus really looked like. I—I bought it when I first went to Rome and plan to keep it on my dresser at home."

They both stared at the graphic reminder of the tremendous gulf which was about to separate Luke from the rest of the world.

Damn. She could feel tears starting and tore her eyes away first. Quickly, before she lost it, she started packing her suitcases.

Luke put the souvenir back in the paper and handed it to her. "Are you an active churchgoer, Gabriella?" came the low-pitched question.

She shouldn't have been surprised by his query, not when Luke was the one doing the asking. It was just that they'd never discussed religion, or their views on theology.

"Yes," she murmured quietly, closing the last zipper. "I can't imagine what my life would be like without my faith to cling to."

With her packing done, she picked up both cases. "If you would be kind enough to help me get a taxi to the train station, I'll take the next one to Brussels and sleep on the way. My plane doesn't leave until the day after tomorrow so I'll arrive there with time to spare."

"You shouldn't be in a train station alone this late at night." That tone of command came so naturally to him, he probably wasn't aware of it. But Gaby

knew it was unwise to be in his company any longer.
It took all her strength of will not to beg him to take
her someplace private and make love to her.

To arm herself against his irresistible charisma she
retorted, ''That's nonsense. I've been doing everything on my own for a long time and can take care
of myself.''

''A few karate moves no matter how well taught
to you by your brothers won't protect you from a pack
of men intent on only one thing. You're coming with
me.''

''No, Luke!'' His declaration terrified her and she
backed away from him. But her reaction only seemed
to arouse his ire. In one swift movement, his hand
snaked out to grasp her wrist, making escape impossible.

Submitting her to a withering glance, he said, ''Until you leave my country, you will remain under my
protection whether you accompany me willingly or
not.'' His hold tightened.

''But you need to get back to the palace and find
Giovanni,'' she cried, frantically trying to think of
reasons to get away from him. ''Your mother must
be terribly upset with you gone.''

''She'll live.'' With the envelope under one arm,
he took the heaviest suitcase from her and started
pulling her toward the door. Gaby had to run to keep
up with him.

''W-where are we going?''

''To a hotel where we will get something to eat
and a good night's sleep. First thing in the morning
I'll put you on a plane to Brussels.''

The thought of being alone with him any place private set her heart racing out of rhythm. "Luke, you don't understand. I can't affor—"

"*Basta*! There are times when you drive me too far, Gabriella." Another savage oath silenced her. "My brother's machinations have put you in this situation. It goes without saying that I will make restitution for what he's done."

Before she knew it, they'd exited the police station and he deposited her and the luggage in a rental car. When Luke had heard she was in jail, he must have taken a plane to Lugano. Fresh guilt kept her silent as he drove through the quiet streets. She was afraid to say a word in case she unleashed another violent reaction in him.

Purposely keeping her head turned so she couldn't look at him, she noticed they were leaving the city proper. Before long they reached a road bordering the shimmering water. Every so often she glimpsed a fabulous villa through the foliage. This was a residential area. Only the very wealthy could afford to live along this section of the sophisticated lakeside resort.

"There aren't any hotels here," she blurted in trepidation, forgetting her vow not to talk.

"That's true."

"You lied to me!"

"Yes," he admitted with infuriating relish. "If I'd told you I was taking you to a property my family owns and uses on occasion, you would have refused to come and forced me to carry you bodily from the jail. It was better this way, don't you agree?" he questioned in a silky tone.

"How can you even ask me that?" Her whole body surged with exploding emotion. After their experience in Loretello, she didn't trust herself to go anywhere with him.

"I'm well known in my country, Gabriella." His deep voice grated. "I didn't tell you that to impress you. Only to remind you that for obvious reasons, I prefer to avoid scandal. If someone saw me taking a woman who looks like you to a hotel in the middle of the night, the paparazzi would get wind of it and your reputation would suffer along with mine."

He was right. It *would* look terrible. Luke couldn't afford that kind of talk this close to taking his vows.

She bowed her head, unable to argue with his logic. It was amazing that no matter the issue, he always found a way to reduce her concerns to so much trivia.

"I phoned the housekeeper from the jail and instructed her to prepare a light meal. It won't be the Trattoria Alberto, but we won't starve."

He shouldn't have reminded her of that halcyon day. The memories were too haunting and raw. "Thank you for being so thoughtful," she murmured in a subdued tone.

"It's the least I can do after the ordeal you've been put through today."

"I don't imagine this has been easy for you, either," she conceded. After a slight pause, "Did you have to get special permission to be away from Rome this long?"

She felt his body tauten. "Would it shock you if I told you I left without permission?"

Gaby shuddered involuntarily.

"I can see that I have," he observed dryly.

Fear for him made perspiration break out on her brow. "Are you in serious trouble then?"

"Yes. Nothing should take precedence over God."

Anger warred with anxiety. "Giovanni knew better than to phone you and place demands which could jeopardize your work."

Luke made a left turn onto a private road and they started a climb through the flowering shrubs. "My brother may have described you as a paragon without equal, but rest assured the decision to come home was entirely mine," he drawled. "If you must be upset, then blame my unorthodox curiosity which overcame duty."

Aghast, she cried, "What will you do?"

"I'll face the consequences as soon as I take care of unfinished business."

"You mean Giovanni." Her voice shook.

"*Sì, signorina.*"

Gaby had been so caught up in what he'd told her, she hadn't realized he'd stopped in front of a Ticino-styled villa with a deck on the upper story. The lights inside beckoned.

She looked behind her shoulder. "I'll need—"

"I'll bring them both," he cut in mildly, reminding her that he'd seen *everything* she owned and had watched her pack up her things without taking care what went where.

Prickly warmth sent her scurrying from the car, only to come to a complete standstill when she saw a sixtyish-looking Italian woman just inside the open door of the chalet-type domicile.

She greeted Luke like visiting royalty, her raisin eyes misting as she crossed herself and curtsied in front of him, kissing his hand.

A sharp stab of pain made Gaby turn away. The

woman's touching homage to the man she saw as a priest came as a tremendous shock to Gaby.

Giovanni's words flooded back, haunting her. Luke had been training for the religious role all his life. Her instantaneous adoration reflected that humbling truth.

Gaby had no business here, no business at all.

"Signorina Holt, this is Bianca," he said in the bland voice of the perfect host. "She speaks English very well. We'll follow her to the room she has prepared for you."

The plump housekeeper gave Gaby an incurious glance before she led them across tile floors and up the stairs to a charming bedroom facing the lake.

While Luke deposited her bags on the floor, Gaby stared at the quaint simplicity of the cozy villa which came as a surprise after the sumptuousness of the palace. Instead of gilt, statuary and tapestries, there was a comfortable-looking four-poster bed with hand-carved wooden furnishings. French doors opened out onto the veranda.

"I hope you'll be comfortable here. When you've refreshed yourself, come downstairs to the kitchen."

Gaby swung back around, not meeting his eyes. "I-if you don't mind, I'm not feeling very well and would like to go directly to bed."

Having said those words she got the distinct impression that she'd angered him. A ruddy flush dulled his cheeks. But she didn't have a choice. If they'd been alone, he would have argued with her until he'd broken her down and forced her to eat a meal with him.

Under no circumstances could she allow that to

happen. At Loretello, Gaby's unwise behavior had tempted Luke to show his human side. Tonight she was weakening where her own strength of will was concerned. All it would take was one smoldering glance from him and she'd lose the little self-control she had left.

Like a godsend, Bianca's presence acted as the perfect buffer. Gaby would cling to the housekeeper in order to distance herself from Luke until she could leave Italy altogether.

Ignoring his well-honed physique still poised near the doorway, she addressed the older woman. "I have a headache, *signora*. Do you keep any medicine here?"

"*Sì, signorina.*"

"Would you show me please?" she asked before Luke could offer his assistance.

The older woman nodded, indicating Gaby should follow her into the ensuite bathroom, the one place Luke couldn't accompany them.

Clearly not pleased, he watched her enter the spotless interior and disappear from his narrowed line of vision. To her relief, Bianca shut the door and pulled a bottle of pills from the cabinet.

Gaby turned on the shower taps so they couldn't be overheard. "Thank you, Bianca. If you'd be kind enough to bring my bags in here, I'll wash and get ready for bed."

"I'll bring up a tray in case you get hungry later."

"That's very thoughtful of you, but it's Father Luca who needs your help." In a confiding tone Gaby whispered, "I am a close friend of his brother Giovanni who was in a car accident."

The older woman looked shocked and crossed herself. "Is he all right?"

"He will be, but the poor Father has been worried about him and hasn't slept for several nights. Please do everything you can to make him comfortable. Force him to eat something. If you have a little *Verdicchio* wine, that might relax him. Then let him sleep in tomorrow morning. He must be well rested before he returns to Rome."

"Of course." The housekeeper nodded, obviously thrilled to be given such an important task. No doubt she loved fussing over the man she revered so much. "You can depend on me."

"I knew it." She pressed the other woman's hand, praying she'd won her confidence. "One more thing—" she murmured, eyeing the phone by the bed. "I'll be leaving before he awakens. Say nothing about that to him or he will insist on driving me to the airport. You know how good and kind he is. How he loves to take care of everyone else."

The woman's eyes brimmed over. "He is a saint."

A sad smile broke out on Gaby's face. "He's the most wonderful man I've ever known. But this is one time when we all need to watch over him. You understand what I'm saying?"

"*Sì, signorina*. I will do everything I can for him."

"God bless you, Bianca."

"And you, *signorina*." She crossed herself again.

Before the housekeeper left the bathroom, Gaby asked for the address of the villa so she could tell the taxi exactly where to come in the morning.

When she heard the door click, Gaby crossed her fingers and stepped beneath the spray. Since coming to Italy, she'd learned to conserve water by getting in and out of the shower as fast as possible. But because of her precarious circumstances, she remained inside for a long time and washed her hair. Anything to drag out the moment. Hopefully by the time she climbed into bed, Luke would have eaten and gone to his room for the night.

Finally, when she'd dried her hair enough to braid it, she crept into the bedroom, shut off the light and dove beneath the covers.

No sooner had she turned on her side than there was a tap on the door. It had to be Luke. Bianca would have walked in without permission. Gaby started to shake and couldn't stop.

"Gabriella?"

Though he only whispered her name, she could feel the deep intonation pierce her skin to the innermost core of her.

More than anything in the world she wanted to answer him. Instead, she got on her knees under the covers and prayed with all her might that he would go away.

He called her name again.

Gaby writhed in pain. If she encouraged him to come into the room, there was no telling what might happen. She couldn't live with that on her conscience and continued to beg for strength to resist him.

After a while, she had reason to believe he'd gone away. Her prayers were answered. For the rest of the night she sat propped up in bed with tears streaming down her face, watching the lights twinkle around the shoreline of the lake.

At dawn, she quietly slid from the bed and got

dressed, then phoned the operator to get the number of the taxi station. Within a few minutes, she'd called for her ride.

With that accomplished, she went out on the veranda where the spectacular view of Lake Lugano spread before her like a fairyland. But right now her main concern was escape.

There were steps leading up one side of the villa. If she climbed over the railing, it was just a small jump to freedom.

She went back inside for her suitcases, then lowered them noiselessly over the railing into the garden, one at a time. After shutting the sliding door, she went back out on the veranda and heaved herself down to the stairs.

Once her bags were in hand, she crept through the underbrush to the road where she hid beneath a flowering tree. Luke would never be able to see her from the villa windows.

The longest ten minutes of her life went by while she stood there terrified because Luke might discover her disappearance and come running outside to see where she'd gone.

But providence was with her, because she finally saw a taxi turn up the lane. Without waiting another moment, she ran toward it, hoping the driver wouldn't come abreast of the villa.

"Drive me to the train station, *per favore*," she cried in her best Italian, jumping in the back seat with her suitcases. "*Sono in ritardo*." She had told him she was late so that he'd hurry.

The middle-aged driver turned around and grinned

with typical male appreciation. "*Capisco, signorina.*"

All Italian cabdrivers were insane so it didn't take him long to reach their destination. Luckily the morning traffic had been light. There were fewer near-mishaps than usual.

She got out of the car dragging her suitcases, threw some lire at him and started running. It didn't matter which train was in the station. She'd take whichever one would get her out of town the fastest, even if it was going the wrong way. She could always get off at the next main station and regroup.

As fate would have it, a local commuter was heading south to Milan. Without blinking an eye she bought a one-way ticket and promptly dashed outside, looking for the right track. The train was just starting to pull out of the station.

She ran alongside it and literally tossed her suitcases into the passageway, then jumped on board. Out of breath, she stood on trembling limbs, clinging to the handrails on either side of the steps.

In the throes of agony, she felt her life pass before her as Lugano eventually disappeared from view and Luca Provere with it.

CHAPTER TEN

"GABY?"

At the sound of Wayne's voice, she paused in the act of washing the plates from lunch and looked over her shoulder at her brother who was putting on his heavy-duty gloves.

"I'm going out on the south range with Will for a couple of hours to do some fencing. When I get back, we'll take that ride up the saddle and camp out."

"Don't hurry on my account. I'm not in the mood to go anywhere, but thanks just the same."

He shoved a weathered cowboy hat on his blond head. "You know something, little sister? You haven't been in the mood since you got home from Italy. It's past time you told me about the man who has put you into such a severe depression."

"I'm not in a severe depression!" she snapped with uncharacteristic sharpness. White-faced, she resumed her task at the sink of the trailer home provided for his use as foreman of the Red Fork Ranch.

He chewed on a piece of straw, eyeing her shrewdly. "No? Dropping ten pounds, and not going to the university when you're two quarters away from graduating, is what I call pretty damn depressing. If that weren't enough, you're living up here with no salary to speak of, no girlfriends, and no hope in hell of finding an eligible male. All in all, you've changed so drastically, I'm beginning to think the folks are right.''

She blinked in alarm. ''What do you mean?''

''They want you to get professional help. I agree with them.''

''I don't need counselling.''

''Then you're going to have to prove it and talk to me when I get back later. Otherwise, I'm booting you out of here for your own good.''

''No, Wayne! Please!'' she cried in panic at her brother's defection. But he'd gone out the door and there was no calling him back. Once he dug in his heels, that was it.

Since her return, he'd given her her space, had made no demands. Wayne had always been her idol. She'd always been able to count on him. Or so she'd thought…

Gaby clung to the edge of the counter. The fact that Wayne agreed with her parents about her needing help disturbed her greatly because deep inside she was beginning to believe it herself.

Since her flight from Europe, each day had passed like a hundred years. There was a bleakness to her existence which had started to frighten her. Instead of time being the great healer, the opposite seemed to have occurred. Today was October fifth. Luke had been professed for a week now. Why couldn't she forget him? What was wrong with her?

In an effort to numb herself to the scalding pain of bittersweet memories, she finished the dishes and attacked her housekeeping chores with a vengeance.

By the time an hour had passed and there was nothing else to clean, she came to the conclusion that she'd better unload to her brother before she had a complete breakdown.

With hot tears gushing from her eyes, she flung herself facedown on the couch, wishing she could go to sleep and never wake up. Crying spells had become a habit she couldn't seem to break.

She knew she was pathetic and should pull herself together before Wayne got back. But drugged by her own inertia, she stayed curled up until she heard the sound of a motor.

Since there was no more dirt road beyond the trailer, most likely one of the hands was coming up to talk to Wayne about a problem. Then again, someone could be lost.

Mortified to be caught this way, Gaby jumped to her bare feet. But she didn't have time to check the mirror before she heard footsteps outside followed by a rap on the trailer door. No way could she open it in her condition.

"If you're looking for Wayne, he's gone to the south range and won't be back until supper." She'd been sobbing so hard, her voice sounded like a foghorn.

"I'm not looking for Wayne," came a low, masculine voice, distinctly unwestern.

Puzzled, she took a peek out the curtained window and saw an unfamiliar Buick Skylark parked next to Wayne's truck. Everyone who worked on the ranch drove pickups, which meant the man outside was a stranger.

For no good reason, a frisson of apprehension made her stiffen. Wayne had always warned her about keeping the trailer locked when he was gone. Thank heaven he'd locked it on his way out.

Struggling to sound calm, she said, "You must want Mr. Hayes, the owner of the Red Fork. If you'll go back down the road a half mile and turn left, you'll come to his ranch house." At this point she wasn't about to admit that Will wasn't home, either.

"I haven't flown ten thousand miles to see the owner. *Per Dio*, Gabriella. Open the door before I break it in."

Her heart gave a great thump.

It couldn't be... It just couldn't be!

When she'd first heard Luke's voice behind her on the castle ramparts in Assisi, she'd thought she was hallucinating.

But hearing that same voice on a hidden ranch in the Sierra Nevada mountains of North America meant she had really lost her mind. Slowly, Gaby backed away from the door.

"If there's someone inside with you, get rid of him. *Now*!"

She stood there paralyzed with shock, unable to make as much as a squeaking sound. Seconds later she heard the crack of splintering wood and suddenly Luke appeared inside the trailer, dwarfing it with his dark, powerful frame.

Her blue eyes widened in total disbelief to see the true Duke of Urbino standing in all his magnificence not two feet away from her. It didn't matter that he was dressed in Western jeans and a crewneck navy pullover. Nothing could disguise his striking aura, his sophistication.

Lines marred his unforgettable male features. With

undisguised intimacy, his devouring black gaze traveled over her face and figure.

She was wearing one of Wayne's Western shirts with the sleeves pushed up above her elbows. The hem hung lower than her cutoffs. It probably looked like she'd thrown it on in haste, and didn't have a stitch on underneath. With no lipstick, and her hair loose and disheveled, she could imagine what he might be thinking.

Judging by the way his hands worked into fists at his side, it was exactly what he was thinking. She felt fire lick through her veins.

He sucked in his breath. "If you've got someone in the bedroom, tell him to leave," he ordered in a deceptively quiet tone. "We have unfinished business."

He'd seen Wayne's pickup and had jumped to conclusions. "T-there's no one here b-but me," she stammered enough to be heard, but the trembling of her limbs had taken over her ability to function with any coherence.

"I don't believe you." His voice grated. The next thing she knew, he swept past her to explore the rest of the trailer. He moved about the claustrophobic interior as if it were his divine right. *Because he didn't know any other way.*

Gaby wouldn't want him any other way. There was only one Luca Provere, and he was here in this trailer instead of in Rome. She didn't know what it meant, but she thought she might die of joy.

Like shockwaves, the tension suffused her being as he reentered the tiny living-room-cum-kitchen. "Why didn't you open the door to me?'' His fierce demand caught her off guard.

Swallowing hard, she said, ''B-because I couldn't believe it was you. Seven days ago you took final vows.'' Her voice shook. ''I—I never expected to see you again. I thought maybe I was imagining you. You have to understand that I was afraid to open the door, for fear that y-you wouldn't be there after all,'' she admitted in a tremulous tone.

There was a brief pause while he studied her classic features, the passionate mold of her mouth. Then his questing eyes fell lower, over every line and curve of her quivering frame.

''Why did you run away from me in Lugano?''

She averted her eyes, twisting her hands together. ''You know why,'' she whispered.

''Tell me!'' he snapped.

''Because—'' she began, ''because I didn't trust myself to be around you.''

''Why?''

He wasn't about to give up. He'd keep digging away until he had answers.

''Because you were a priest and I had no right to think of you as a man.''

''If I hadn't been a priest, would you have opened your door to me that night?''

After a long silence she whispered, ''Yes,'' and heard another sharp intake of breath.

''Have you ever made love with a man before?''

Her cheeks burned. ''No.''

''Then why me?'' He was utterly relentless.

''Why are you torturing me like this?'' she blurted in agony, looking everywhere except at him.

"Because I want to hear the words." He moved closer. "You just told me you've never let another man touch you. So why would you have let *me* make love to you?"

"The reason doesn't matter." By now he'd backed her up against the edge of the kitchen counter. "Now I really don't know why you've come, but—"

"The truth, Gabriella!" He sounded like a man who couldn't take any more.

She couldn't, either.

"Because I fell in love with you," she began in a husky voice. "Because I'll always be in love with you, and it hurts so much, I'm dying over it. There!" Her moist eyes darkened in intensity as she finally looked up at him. "You have my confession. Are you satisfied now, *Father Luca*?"

He grasped her shoulders, his black gaze impaling her. "That's not my name, so never use it again."

"W-what do you mean?"

His fingers tightened on her flesh through the soft material of her shirt. "To take final vows meant losing myself to the will of a higher authority. It meant never looking back at what might have been."

His palms molded to her shoulders possessively. "I searched my soul and found I couldn't make those sacred promises wholeheartedly. To stay would have been a lie... So I left." His voice dropped several registers.

Gaby stood there in shock. "But you've planned for this your entire life!" She simply couldn't comprehend what he was telling her. "What happened to change everything, to change you?"

His eyes smouldered. "*You're* what happened to

me,'' he cried softly before his dark head descended, blotting out the light. ''Help me, *mia testarossa*. Give me what I've been hungering for,'' he murmured feverishly before his mouth closed over hers with a savagery that told of his deep need.

She wanted answers to so many questions, but couldn't think of one. After the deprivation of the past month, to be in his arms like this without the accompanying guilt of knowing he was a priest turned her startled gasp into a moan of surrender.

Like a tenacious vine, Gaby wound her arms around his neck and embraced him with primitive longing, feasting on his mouth which had the power to drive her to mindless ecstasy. One kiss melted into another. What had been ignited in that cherry tree caused their hands and bodies to become an extension of each other.

''You're so beautiful, so *squisita*.'' He muttered thrilling endearments in his native tongue against her mouth and throat, his breathing as ragged as hers.

Rapture transported her. She had no idea how they happened to end up on the couch. The need to become one flesh was fast turning into a reality as Luke's body followed hers down against the cushions.

''I want you so much, Gabriella, I don't think I can wait,'' he admitted. His eyes glazed with raw desire before he buried his face in her fragrant hair. His accent had become more pronounced, underlining the depth of his passion.

Gaby feared this might be a dream and held him tighter. ''Don't stop loving me, darling. Please— you're my whole life. Don't ever stop—'' she begged, once more finding his mouth with her own, allowing him no escape.

Consumed by mutual wants, both were driven to assuage; neither of them heard footsteps outside. Not until the fury in her brother's voice penetrated her brain, did a cognizance of her surroundings come back to Gaby, particularly the door dangling from the only twisted hinge left holding it.

"You've got one second to get off my sister before I blow your head to kingdom come, you *animal*!"

"*No, Wayne! Don't shoot!*" Gaby screamed when she saw the barrel of the shotgun pointed at Luke's back.

In a lightning move, Luke had gotten to his feet, but Gaby was faster and leaped in front of him, protecting him with her own trembling body.

The confusion on her brother's face before he lowered the gun would have been funny if the situation hadn't been so precarious.

"I know what this looks like, Wayne, but you'd be completely wrong in anything you're assuming. This is the man I love!" Her throbbing voice rang with the undeniable declaration.

"I'm Luca Provere," the man behind her spoke up boldly before she could officially introduce them. With possessive hands that caressed her waist in response to her unequivocal pronouncement, he pulled her against his hard chest, letting her know he wanted her right there, that she wasn't to move.

"It's a privilege to meet you, Wayne. I've heard about you and your brothers. Please accept my apology for the damage done to the door. Naturally I'll have it repaired. Gabriella didn't believe that I had come for her.''

He encircled her in his arms. ''Drastic measures were needed to convince her otherwise,'' he drawled, nestling his chin in her hair.

A distinct blush covered her neck and face, causing her brother's mouth to twitch. Gaby saw admiration and respect for Luke in her brother's eyes. Wayne's approval meant a great deal.

''She's been waiting for you, Luke. It's been hell around here. I was about to apply a few drastic measures myself. What took you so long?''

She heard Luke's satisfied chuckle. ''Gaby and I became acquainted in Italy, but because of extremely unusual and delicate circumstances, we parted on less than satisfactory terms. As soon as it was humanly possible, I came after her.''

''Thank the Lord,'' Wayne murmured. ''Under the circumstances, I apologize for interrupting. While you two finish getting reacquainted, I'll mosey down to the shed and get the tools I need to fix the door.''

His blue eyes—identical to Gaby's—glanced at the splinters on the floor, then he winked at her. ''Judging by the look of things, it'll take me a while to find everything I need.''

When he left the trailer, Luke spun her around. ''I like your brother very much,'' he whispered against her lips before devouring them all over again. ''He has the good sense to know we need our privacy.''

Gaby nodded wordlessly, too entranced by their physical proximity to think, let alone talk. She never wanted to be apart from him, not for one single second. Overflowing with the love she had to give him, she began raining kisses on his face, then captured his mouth.

But when he unexpectedly broke their kiss and put her firmly away from him, she groaned in agony, staring at him with wounded eyes.

His breathing grew shallow. "*Mio Dio*. Don't look at me like that," he grated. "You don't think I'm in as much pain as you are?" He raked his hands through his hair. "We have to talk, Gabriella, and talking is a physical impossibility when I feel your beautiful body melting into mine. It's best your brother broke in on us when he did."

With those words, the joy went out of her world. "Is that because you're going to leave me as soon as you tell me the reason for your unannounced visit? Are you trying to do the noble thing by saving me from myself?" Raw pain laced her questions. "If that's the case, I wish to heaven you'd never come!"

A spate of unintelligible Italian escaped his lips. "If I weren't in love with you, if I didn't place that love above duty, do you honestly believe I'd have broken down that door to get to you for any other reason?" His challenge resonated in the minuscule interior.

Her heart hammered unnaturally. "Y-you're in love with me?"

He expelled a tortured sigh. "*Sì, signorina*. The moment my little brother introduced us, my life was thrown into utter chaos, and that was something that has never happened to me before."

"Are you saying that you decided not to take your vows b-because of *me*?"

Lines darkened his face. "Sit down, Gabriella. This

is going to take some time to explain and I can't do that when you are standing this close, looking so desirable that all I can think about is crushing you in my arms.''

After hearing his admission, she was hardly able to breathe and did his bidding by subsiding on the couch where they'd lain so briefly. But she couldn't keep still.

"Please, before you tell me anything else, how is Giovanni? I care for him so much.''

Luke took a deep breath. "Giovanni is in Assisi. He has begun his training to be a priest.''

A priest. She mouthed the words.

They stared hard at each other for timeless moments while Gaby reflected on Giovanni whose spiritual makeup had separated him from the worldliness of men.

"I—I never expected to hear a revelation like that. Yet I can't honestly say I'm surprised.''

"Nor can I,'' Luke concurred.

"The night of the accident, he inferred that it would be noble to die for a sacred love. But I thought—I thought he was discreetly warning me not to fall in love with you!''

"He's happy for the first time in his life. To think he fooled everyone all these years, Gabriella. He never told the family of his spiritual leanings, or his soul-changing experience at Assisi. Only you were privy to that information.''

"But it makes perfect sense, Luke. He loved you so much, he didn't want to take anything away from you or your parents' dreams for you.''

She rose to her feet, unable to stay seated. "Everything's becoming clear to me. On our drive to the *pensione* after dinner, he kept telling me how worried he was about you. He said you were such a noble person, you always put everyone else's needs ahead of your own. I finally asked him if he was upset that you wanted to serve the church.''

Luke's black eyes pierced hers. ''What did he tell you?''

''He said he wanted that for you more than anything in the world, but only if it was going to make you happy.''

He rubbed the back of his neck. ''My brother knew me better than I knew myself.''

The mysterious tone of his voice prompted her to ask him what he meant.

''It's very simple. Giovanni knew I never had a vocation for the priesthood.''

''*Never*?'' she whispered. ''You mean you went through all those years of training to please your parents?''

''Nothing is that simple, Gabriella. I grew up knowing nothing else and went along with it. I'll always be grateful for the excellent education I received, the great minds who imparted their knowledge. There were men I loved, men who will one day rise to become great men. I'm not sorry for the years I spent learning about God. It was all to my good.

''But to answer your question, I never received the calling. That's the reason I left Rome to go home and help Giovanni run the estate after our father died. I knew the most important ingredient for my life as a priest was missing. I thought that if I went back to the family, maybe my life would be touched in some way to let me know I should take final vows.

"Unfortunately, I received no special witness. On the other hand, my life at home held no particular attraction for me, either. There were several women, but the relationships were brief and unsatisfying. I felt like I was caught between two dimensions. Nothing was clear."

Gaby's eyes began to prickle with tears. "How awful for you."

His expression grew bleak. "I won't lie to you. For a time, I floundered. But in the end, I chose to serve the church because I knew it would be a good life and make my mother happy."

"Giovanni was right about everything," she murmured emotionally.

Luke nodded. "Over the years my brother observed all of this while keeping his own burning desire a secret. And then he met *you*. That's when he conceived his cunning plan."

The way he said it sent a chill chasing across her skin. "What plan?"

He shifted his weight. "When you fled from me in Lugano, I concluded that it was best not to go after you until I'd confronted Giovanni. To my surprise, he was at the palace waiting to confront me.

"We said a lot of things to each other. Things that should have been said years ago. During the course of that conversation he confessed that he knew I was unhappy, that he'd been praying to find a way to help me find peace in my life.

"He said that from the moment he met you, he had the unmistakable conviction that you and I were meant for each other. All it would take was for us to meet and spend time together.''

She buried her face in her hands. ''I don't believe what I'm hearing.''

''Only Giovanni could have hatched such a plot, planning every move like he would a chess strategy. Even the accident was deliberate.''

At that revelation, Gaby's eyes widened in shock. ''But he could have been killed!''

''No, Gabriella. He staged everything to make it look that way. In reality, he influenced the doctor and staff to say he had a concussion so that you and I would be forced to stay together. Worse, he planted the jewelry, then arranged for the police to arrest you and lock you up so I'd have to come and bail you out. At that point, he knew I was so in love with you, I'd never return to Rome.''

Her throat constricted. ''He loved you enough to do all that?''

''He loves you, too,'' Luke said in a haunting whisper. ''All that's left to make his joy complete is to hear that you have agreed to become my wife.''

He moved swiftly, cupping her flushed face in his hands. ''You have to marry me, Gabriella.'' His voice shook. ''I knew I wanted you for myself long before the dinner at the palace concluded. That's why I left the table when I did, because I suddenly discovered that the missing ingredient in my life had been sitting at my side all evening, torturing me with invitation, and my hands were tied for more than one reason.''

Gaby moaned. ''I couldn't bear it when you got up and left so quickly. I was afraid I'd never see you again. It was one of the worst moments of my life.

Much as I hated to learn that Giovanni had been in an accident, I was overjoyed when you came to the *pensione* for me.''

Luke brushed her lips with his own. ''He didn't have to manufacture a reason for me to stay in Urbino. Nothing could have made me return to Rome. I was determined to spend the next day with you.''

Her eyes glowed a hot blue. ''It was a time I'll never forget. That's when I knew I'd fallen so deeply in love with you, I realized that if I couldn't be your wife, I'd probably remain single because no other man could ever compare to you.''

She slid her hands up his warm chest, feeling the heavy thud of his heart. ''I adore you, my darling Luca. There's nothing more I could ask of life than to be your wife, but I'm afraid your mother won't approve.''

Luke felt the contour of her lips with his thumb. ''Mother surprised both Giovanni and me by giving us her blessing. After the three of us sat down together, she, too, had some confessions to make. Among them, the fact that she'd sensed for some time that neither of us was truly happy.

''She insisted that it was her fault for thrusting something on me which should have been my choice. She also blames herself for not seeing Giovanni's pain. At this point, Mother is so overjoyed that one of us is going to get married and provide her with grandchildren, she's ready to give you a proper welcome. As for the rest of the family, you won them over at dinner.''

''Thank you for telling me that,'' was all Gaby could manage to say in her emotion-filled state.

His expression sobered. "I have yet to meet your parents. How are they going to feel about their only daughter living in Italy?"

"They won't be at all surprised. The whole family knows I fell painfully in love while I was abroad. Daddy half expected it because of my great-grandmother's history, but no one knows the details. I couldn't bring myself to talk about it, not when I thought you were lost to me forever."

The memory of so much unhappiness made her shudder and she clung to him all the harder.

"We'll leave for Las Vegas now. I want to marry you as soon as we can, surrounded by your family and friends. Later we'll renew our vows in Assisi with my family in attendance."

She smiled up at him, blinding him with its radiance. "I can't wait to be Signora Luca Francesco della Provere."

He lowered his head and smothered her with kisses. "I can't wait to give you one of your wedding presents."

"You already have presents for me?"

"Let's just say that this one has been sitting in Tivoli for years, waiting to be discovered."

Her mind began turning over all the possibilities. Tivoli was an ancient city outside Rome. "Does this have something to do with my great-grandmother?" she cried in pure delight.

A mysterious smile broke out on his handsome face. "You're going to have to wait for the truth until we've taken our vows *mia testarossa*."

She sucked in her breath. "I feel like I already made mine in that cherry tree."

"We both did," he murmured thickly. "But humor me once more, Gabriella." His black eyes burned with an intensity of feeling. "I need legal permission to love you so I can really start to live…"

EPILOGUE

LUKE'S mother, resplendent in tearose pink *peau de soie*, rang the small crystal bell, signaling that she wanted the attention of everyone in the wedding party.

Throughout the succulent feast served immediately after the five o'clock ceremony in the palace chapel, Gaby had been aware of Luke's possessive hand on her thigh beneath the dining room table.

A month ago he'd followed her to Nevada. She didn't know how they'd survived the marriage preparations this long without going to bed together. But they'd both agreed that waiting until their wedding night to make love for the first time would be their priceless gift to each other.

Too feverish to do anything more than toy with her food, she slid her hand over his, aware that in just a little while, her new husband would become her lifetime lover. Unable to do otherwise, she lifted adoring blue eyes to him. The devouring look in his thrilled her almost to the consuming of her flesh.

He lifted her hand and kissed the palm. "It's time we forgot the world and concentrated on each other."

"Darling—" she whispered breathlessly at the husky tone of his deep voice, "I still can't believe I'm your wife. The last time we sat at this table, yo—"

"Don't think about it, Gabriella. That is all in the past, when I was a different man."

She clung to his hand. "I—I hope your mother will come to accept me one day."

"Mama is making great strides. By the time we produce a new little Provere, she'll be calling you her treasured daughter." Gaby blushed. "If you'll notice, the portrait of my illustrious ancestor no longer dominates this room."

"I hadn't realized!" she blurted. Being with Luke caused the world around her to recede because *he* was her world. She loved him with a fierceness that almost frightened her.

"One day soon a painting of Giovanni will grace that wall."

Just then Giovanni's warm brown eyes captured her attention from across the table and they both smiled. His face glowed with an inner happiness he no longer had to hide.

"If I don't miss my guess," Luke murmured, "Efresina is going to make a full recovery. Have you noticed how she and Ted haven't spent one minute apart since they met?"

"*Ted*?"

Shocked by Luke's observation, she gazed down the long table at her family. Everyone loved Luke and had come for the wedding. But they were overwhelmed to discover the kind of family she'd married into and were still looking a little dazed.

Ted, the shiest of her brothers, was not only dazed but smitten with the lovely Efresina. Her dark eyes sparkled from all the attention he was giving her.

Gaby darted her husband an illuminating smile.

"Ted got his sandy-red hair from our great-grandmother. Something tells me we might be seeing a lot of him in the months to come."

His smile faded to be replaced by a look of such smoldering sensuality, her heart turned over. "As happy as I am for Efresina and your brother, I'm glad you said months, *mia testarossa*, because it's going to take that long before I'm willing to share you with anyone."

"Luca, we're all waiting to hear you say a few words," Giovanni prodded with an infectious grin.

In a swift movement, Luke rose to his feet and brought Gaby with him. Hugging her around the waist, he started toward the door. "I'm sorry, *fratello*," he called over his shoulder, "but Gabriella and I need to do some communicating of our own first."

With her heart thudding because she was finally going to get her heart's desire, Gaby honored American custom and threw her bouquet over her head so it practically landed in Efresina's lap.

While everyone in the room responded with cries of excitement and laughter, her husband exercised his age-old right as Duke of Urbino and carried off the most willing, besotted maiden in the Marches to the bridal chamber.

Modern Romance™
...seduction and
passion guaranteed

Tender Romance™
...love affairs that
last a lifetime

Sensual Romance™
...sassy, sexy and
seductive

Blaze
...sultry days and
steamy nights

Medical Romance™
...medical drama on
the pulse

Historical Romance™
...rich, vivid and
passionate

29 new titles every month.

*With all kinds of Romance for
every kind of mood...*

MILLS & BOON®

Makes any time special™

MAT4